Haunted Hearts

JOHN REYNOLDS

National Library of Canada Cataloguing in Publication

Reynolds, John Lawrence
Haunted hearts / John Lawrence Reynolds.

ISBN 0-7710-7400-X

I. Title.

PS8585.E94H39 2003 C813'.54 C2002-905927-5
PR9199.3.R459H39 2003

We acknowledge the financial support of the Government of Canada through the Book Publishing Industry Development Program for our publishing activities. We further acknowledge the support of the Canada Council for the Arts and the Ontario Arts Council for our publishing program.

Published simultaneously in the United States of America by McClelland & Stewart Ltd., P.O. Box 1030, Plattsburgh, New York 12901

Library of Congress Control Number: 2002116593

Designed by Cindy Reichle
Typeset in Janson by M&S, Toronto
Printed and bound in Canada

McClelland & Stewart Ltd.
The Canadian Publishers
481 University Avenue
Toronto, Ontario
M5G 2E9
www.mcclelland.com

1 2 3 4 5 07 06 05 04 03

To the memory of Dolly Gagnon

If we question deep enough
there comes a point where answers,
if answers could be given,
would kill.

– John Fowles

CHAPTER I

McGuire saw them first and he signaled to DeLisle, who sat back on the bench and spoke into the lapel of his leather jacket. Sleeman, who had been jogging towards the bandshell, did a slow U-turn when DeLisle's voice barked, "Okay, two up," through Sleeman's headphones, and he ran on the spot watching McGuire, who stood on the slight rise beneath the elm tree maybe a hundred feet away. Hetherington heard DeLisle's voice too, through the earphone hidden in her long, red hair, and she stopped pushing the baby carriage to lean forward and reach inside, as though adjusting the blanket.

They were in their teens, one white and gangly, the other black and grinning so everybody could see his gold incisor tooth.

The woman they approached was older, perhaps thirty. She wore tight designer jeans and a short suede coat, a little glitzy maybe, but with Newbury Street class. She sat on a bench below and to the left of McGuire. Her eyes closed, her chin raised, she was spending her lunch break trying to retain her tan in the September sun, a magazine on her lap.

The white guy stopped in front of her and spoke. Her eyes opened, first in anger then in fright, while the black kid grinned and sat next to her as though they were buddies.

Neither touched her, and neither spoke in a voice loud enough for others to hear. When the woman heard their words, her face creased and burned red. The white guy snatched the magazine from her, holding it open for his friend to see. Something on the page made them laugh in false hysterics. When the woman reached for it, the white guy skipped away and tossed it to his buddy, who jumped up and taunted her until the woman gave up and walked in quick, short steps towards Boylston.

"Leave her," DeLisle said into his lapel. Sleeman began jogging towards McGuire. Hetherington opened her purse, pulled out her compact, and checked her makeup.

The two young men tossed the magazine in a trash can, and the black youth, still grinning, looked up and saw McGuire standing there with the Nikon around his neck, wearing a Red Sox souvenir T-shirt. The hoodlum's expression told McGuire all he needed to know.

"I'll do the T-shirt, but forget Bermuda shorts," McGuire had told DeLisle.

DeLisle said okay, but McGuire would have to wear sunglasses and new sneakers too, and McGuire grunted and nodded. "And carry this with you," DeLisle added. He handed McGuire a worn Boston tourist guidebook.

"Let 'em see the camera," Sleeman told McGuire. "That's what they'll go after. Camera like that'll get 'em three, four hundred, easy."

McGuire aimed the camera at DeLisle and snapped a frame.

"Don't screw around, okay?" the detective said. He looked annoyed. "You promise me that? You won't screw around? You got a reputation for screwing around, you know."

So, McGuire became a tourist in his own city. He rode the Beantown Trolley, stared up at the Hancock Building, and ate greasy fries from a paper plate while watching the swan boats in the lagoon. Joseph P. McGuire, twice-decorated and once-disgraced cop, was now a hundred-dollar-a-day decoy, a cog in the machinery to cut Boston's wave of tourist muggings.

The black guy grunted at his buddy, and both of them looked at McGuire, who raised the Nikon to his eye and aimed it towards Beacon Hill.

The muggers separated. The white kid, straight black hair tied in a ponytail and wearing an oversized army jacket, torn jeans, and hiker boots, continued along the walk below McGuire's line of sight, scanning for cops, for anything suspicious. The other climbed the slope in a flanking move towards McGuire. He wore a gray, hooded sweatshirt over tight black jeans and high-cut black Nikes.

McGuire zoomed the lens out and sighted through the camera with one eye, using his other eye to watch the muggers approach. To McGuire, they weren't a threat, just two punks who needed their asses kicked, ten years too late.

They circled, approaching from either side. When the one with the ponytail was in position, he walked towards McGuire, hands deep in his jacket pockets. The other materialized from behind. They stood that way for a moment, two street hoods beside an ex-cop posing as an overweight tourist.

"Nice camera, man."

McGuire turned to see the black kid showing his tooth, smiling. McGuire said nothing. "Don't talk too much," DeLisle had warned him. "Tourists don't want to talk, they just want to save their butts."

McGuire turned away and sighted the Nikon across the Common again. The camera's auto-focus system made a soft purr.

"You see my man, next to you?" the black guy said after McGuire had taken a picture.

McGuire lowered the camera. What he saw in the black youth's face, the cockiness, the dedication to his task of intimidating people, tripped something in McGuire. He wondered what they had whispered to the woman. He forgot everything DeLisle had told him.

"Hey, man. Take a look at my buddy," the black kid said to McGuire again. He was still smiling. "You see him there?"

McGuire turned to his right. The white guy was smiling back at him, his thin lips closed, his small eyes squeezed almost shut. A large red pimple blossomed to one side of his nose.

"Ugly fucker, isn't he?" McGuire said, and he raised the Nikon to his eye again.

The white guy's smile faded, and he licked the corner of his mouth. "What'd you say?" he asked.

"Man's got a gun pointed at you," the black kid said, but his voice had lost its edge. Tourists don't call muggers ugly fuckers. Tourists start to shake and their eyes shift away, looking for cops to rescue them and their Japanese toys.

"What'd you call me?" the white kid said.

"How big?" McGuire asked. He released the shutter and shot a frame of DeLisle stretching his arms above his head, like a businessman who'd had enough relaxation for one day and was ready for a walk to the doughnut shop.

"What's how big?" the black kid said.

"He call me ugly?" the white guy asked, looking across McGuire to his buddy.

"How big's his gun?" McGuire said.

"Big enough to blow your head off," the white guy said, keeping his hand inside his jacket.

"Just gimme the camera, man, and we walk away," the black kid muttered. He looked around. This wasn't in the script, this wasn't the way the others had gone.

"What'd you say to that woman?"

"Give him the camera, man," the white guy growled.

"Let's go, Tard," said the black kid, and he began to back away, but McGuire's hand shot out to grip his arm.

"You like terrorizing women?" McGuire said. Below the rise, DeLisle broke into a trot towards him, Sleeman jogging behind. Hetherington parked the baby carriage and waved frantically at a uniformed cop posted near the tourist information booth on Boylston Street.

"Gimme the camera," Tard said, reaching for it.

The black guy twisted out of McGuire's grasp. He had lost his cocky expression. "He's a cop, man."

Tard's brain took a few milliseconds to process this unexpected information, which was enough time for McGuire to pull the hand holding the camera in a short arc across his body, then reverse its direction to swing it at Tard, the side of the zoom lens connecting with Tard's nose in the vicinity of the pimple.

"Jesus!" the kid said, and he twisted away. He dropped to one knee and pulled his hand from inside jacket pocket, and McGuire was looking into the muzzle of a nickel-plated .38 revolver shaking like it was alive. Blood drizzled from the kid's nose and down his narrow chin. He looked ten years younger now, not a street tough but a punished child torn between crying for help and lashing out, unsure of the choice to make.

"Drop it or you're dead!" DeLisle screamed from his crouched firing stance at the bottom of the rise, the gun in his hands not shaking but pointing at the white kid's chest, while Sleeman chased the black kid back towards Boylston.

The kid looked into DeLisle's Glock nine-millimeter, back at McGuire, then down at his feet. He dropped to his knees and released the revolver.

"Son of bitch," said McGuire. He walked away, shaking his head. "Didn't think he had a gun."

"I don't believe it."

Frank DeLisle crumpled the coffee cup into a ball and tossed it at the wastebasket. He missed.

McGuire shrugged. "Hey, I'm the one who should be pissed. You told me these kids never show a weapon. I could be lying on a slab right now, and you'd be standing over me, still bitching. Why didn't you tell me he was carrying?"

"Who knew?" said DeLisle. "Real tourists just give them their cameras and their wallets, and then they stand there with that nice warm feeling you get when you're peeing your pants. You're the only goof who ever asked to see the gun."

"What the hell'd you hit him for?" Sleeman stood scratching his leg under his jogging suit. "Frank told you, just hand over the camera, give us the sign, and we're on him."

McGuire stared back at Sleeman. "They upset that woman. She was sitting there minding her own business and they scared the hell out of her. They needed somebody to show them a little muscle. You convict them, they get six months, a year at the most, and they come out like graduates, knowing more tricks. That's all they'll get, you know that."

"McGuire, how long were you in homicide?" DeLisle said. He sounded weary, as though he were the one who had chased the black kid.

McGuire swept his hand through his hair. "Nearly twenty years."

"Some people think you and Schantz helped drive Kavander to an early grave, breaking all his rules . . ."

"Ollie and me? Break rules?" McGuire's grin widened. "Where'd you hear that stuff?"

Several years earlier, Boston Police Captain Jack Kavander had collapsed at his desk, victim of a massive heart attack. Rumors persisted that he died clutching a memo in his hand, the most recent report on McGuire's success at circumventing the directives of his overweight homicide captain. It was a fanciful idea, nothing more; at the time of Kavander's death, McGuire had already resigned from the force and was working as a part-time security guard at a Revere Beach warehouse.

Frank DeLisle sat in his torn swivel chair, swung his feet onto the corner of his desk, and bit his thumbnail. Well, he'd been warned about this.

"You're going to *what*?" Eddie Vance had said to DeLisle. The captain's head jerked up as though somebody had pulled a string in his neck. He used to be Fat Eddie Vance, but the erasure of thirty pounds from his girth, and a directive from the Commissioner that he would tolerate no nicknames representing race, gender, sexual preference, or "inappropriate physical descriptions," had abbreviated it to Eddie.

"Use McGuire as a decoy," DeLisle had answered. DeLisle thought it was a damn good idea. "I've got three people and a memo from Commissioner Gunn, says I gotta make enough arrests by the end of the month to get some ink in town and stories on the wire."

The summer had broken records for tourism in Boston. More visitors than ever had trekked Boston streets, slept in Boston hotel rooms, devoured meals in Boston restaurants, and left imprints of their credit cards in Boston retail shops.

But crimes against tourists had soared just as dramatically. An average five tourists daily were mugged during July and August. Three had been shot, four stabbed, and one perished under the wheels of a bus when he bolted from the Common across Boylston in panic, pursued by two young muggers.

"North Miami?" cried the headlines in the *Globe* one August Sunday, and police Commissioner George Gunn vowed to clear the city of predatory criminals.

"All we'll do is sweep 'em south so they go back to mugging poor people in Dorchester," muttered DeLisle when the Commissioner fingered him to lead Operation Safe Haven.

"Tourists bring more money into the city than Dorchester pays in taxes," Commissioner Gunn said.

"Can't do it with three guys. Not if I use one for a decoy. Most of these guys operate in pairs. Can't make a nab until they're away from the victim, and if they split . . ."

"You've got two plus you," the Commissioner cut him off. "That's it. Find a way to make it work."

"Have I got an operations budget? Can I get a freelance, something like that?"

"Whatever's approved for special operations, take the maximum."

"That's five hundred a week."

"Alexander Graham Bell invented the telephone with twenty dollars' worth of junk," Gunn smiled. He was wearing his police uniform, getting ready for a charity luncheon at the Four Seasons.

DeLisle stared back in disbelief, as though the Commissioner had just revealed he was actually a woman in drag.

"You really want McGuire?" Eddie Vance had asked yet again.

DeLisle had been thinking about it, what a good idea it seemed to be. He needed somebody who wouldn't panic, somebody who knew procedures and rules of evidence, somebody out-of-shape and middle-aged, who looked like a dentist from Des Moines, maybe. Somebody the creeps on the street wouldn't finger as a cop right away.

McGuire was perfect. Still a legend for being maybe the best homicide cop on the force, he'd been retired for over three years now, living with his former partner Ollie Schantz and Ronnie, Schantz's wife, up in Revere Beach. McGuire had put on a little weight, lost a little hair, didn't walk with that cockiness he used to have, but he knew procedures for evidence, knew how to avoid an entrapment plea.

"Why not?" DeLisle said. "Hundred dollars a day to walk around downtown, eating hot dogs, reading guidebooks. What can go wrong?"

Then Eddie Vance did a rare thing, something few people on Berkeley Street could recall, something DeLisle had never seen him do, had never pictured him doing.

Eddie Vance laughed. He laughed so hard he had to sit down, and when he couldn't stop laughing he stood up again and headed for the men's john.

"Eddie's in the can, laughing," Sleeman said when he came out a minute later. "I never seen that before."

That had been a week ago. Since then, using McGuire as a decoy, DeLisle's crew had collared two kids who tried to do a snatch-and-run with McGuire's camera, and a forty-five-year-old hooker known to Vice as Arlene the Anvil, who propositioned McGuire on the steps of the State House.

Now they had one kid with a nickel-plated .38 and a broken nose, telling his legal-aid lawyer he wanted to press charges of police brutality. His partner was last seen running hurdles down Boylston Street, pulling away from Sleeman like an Indy car passing a beer truck. Sleeman gave up chasing him after two blocks and was leaning against a telephone pole trying to get his wind back when DeLisle and McGuire found him. "We know him, the guy with the tooth," Sleeman said later. "Name's Hayward, Hayhurst, something like that. Got him for B and E couple years ago. Cocky little bastard."

Back in DeLisle's office, the senior detective finished completing his arrest report and tossed his pen aside. "This isn't working out, McGuire," DeLisle said.

McGuire grunted. "You want your T-shirt back?"

"Keep the shirt. Give me the camera. I'll send you a check next week. Looks like you're unemployed again."

McGuire shrugged. "Maybe I'll go work for the other side."

"Other side?" Sleeman said. "What other side?"

"Bunch of lawyers." McGuire stood up. "Called me a couple of weeks ago."

"Lawyers?" Sleeman snorted. "You're gonna work with ambulance chasers?"

"It's mostly civil law, corporate stuff, divorces."

"Sounds like a lousy way to make a living."

McGuire paused at the door. "What's the other kid's name, the white guy?"

"Eddie Sprague. We know him. Street name's Tard."

"Tard? Where's that come from?"

"As in retard." DeLisle bit at a hangnail. "Kid could hold a conversation with a tree stump and they'd both get something out of it."

McGuire met Hetherington at the top of the steps leading to Berkeley Street Police Headquarters. "Why'd you blow it?" she said. "Whatever those guys said to that woman, she'd probably heard it a thousand times before. So why'd you let it get to you?"

"They harassed her," McGuire said, "just because she's a woman. That's how they get their kicks."

Detective Cheryl Hetherington was maybe thirty-six years old, McGuire wasn't sure. He remembered her as a uniformed cop, ten years ago when McGuire and Ollie Schantz were at their peak. "Cute little rascal," Ollie had said after she'd briefed McGuire and Schantz on their arrival at a murder-suicide domestic scene. Hetherington had been married to the headwaiter at a restaurant on Newbury Street until she left him to marry another cop. Two years later the marriage ended, and she drifted through affairs with other officers, some single, some married, some in between. One of them had given her a son along the way, and when McGuire learned she was the third partner in DeLisle's Operation Safe Haven he wanted to talk to her, to ask how she'd managed to screw up one part of her life, the one that existed beyond Berkeley Street, while being so successful at the other part of her life, the one that earned her Officer of the Month three times in the last four years. Just to compare her errors with his own. Just to see if maybe they shared the same genetic flaws.

"Hormones," she'd shrugged when he asked her. "A weakness for men with curly hair and deep voices. And vodka martinis in dark bars." Nothing McGuire didn't already know.

"It's life in the city for a woman," Hetherington was saying to McGuire now. "She's probably forgotten about it already, and we missed a chance to nail a couple of stars for the department. You should've just played along and not said anything to those jerks, just because they upset her."

"Whatever happened to chivalry?" McGuire asked, half-joking.

"What?" Hetherington said.

She didn't know what the word meant, McGuire realized. She doesn't know what the hell it's all about.

"When's the last time you saw a woman in a gingham dress?"

Ollie Schantz was lying on the bed that was his world, grinning up at his ex-partner. It had been seven years since Ollie snapped the third vertebra in his neck on his second day of retirement. He had been bedridden since, would be bedridden until he died.

McGuire had finished describing the afternoon's events that ended his career as a decoy. The day was fading into evening.

"What's your point?" McGuire slouched in the chair next to Ollie's bed sipping tomato juice and vodka, no spice, no celery stirrer. Just vitamin C and Smirnoff.

"You know how old Doris Day is?"

"Doris Day? I don't know. Sixty maybe?"

"More like eighty. She's an old broad, McGuire. There ain't women like her any more. Never was, probably. That's what you've been chasing all your life, some squeaky Doris Day to wear gingham dresses and bake you cookies in a house with shutters . . ."

"Gloria wasn't like that." Meaning McGuire's first wife.

"You're right, Gloria wasn't like that. Gloria was young and pretty and a little wild, so you tried to *make* her like that, which helped screw things up, in case I never told ya before. But Sandi was like that when you married her. First time I met her she was wearing a gingham dress, hair in a ponytail . . ."

"She was a good-looking woman."

"They were all good-looking women, you squirrel. That's not what I'm talkin' about . . ."

"Hey." McGuire gestured with the hand holding his drink. "You married a woman who stayed home, baked you cookies, kept things sane for you . . ."

"The last of a vanishing breed, Joseph. She's the last of a breed. That's what I'm tryin' to tell you. Women have changed, they don't need protectin' from you any more."

"Sure they do."

"You wish. Half the women have lipsticks in their purse. The other half have Smith & Wessons."

"I like taking care of women."

"They like it too. Just don't need it. And they're sure as hell not going to thank you for it."

McGuire thought about that. Then: "Where is Ronnie, by the way?"

"At her painting class. You see that picture she did last week, the one of the old barn?" Ollie's voice swelled with pride. "The woman's got talent she hasn't even used yet. She's damn good, Joseph."

"You want to watch the game?" McGuire reached for the television remote on Ollie's bed.

"Who're we playin'?"

"Jays, I think." McGuire punched the power button and the screen came to life with an electronic hiccup.

"Dumb-ass team with no pitching?"

"I'm taking them." McGuire drained his drink.

"You want to lay two bucks a hit?"

"Three for doubles, four for triples, five for a dinger?"

"One for an RBI." The picture flickered to life.

"Let me get another vodka."

"Have one for me. Get a pencil and paper to keep track of your losses too. Look it this, we've got second and third with one out, and McCluskey's up. Open your wallet, Joseph."

During the seventh inning the front door opened and closed, and Ronnie Schantz's footsteps pattered down the hallway. She entered the room, shining behind her smile, her hair gathered on her head with loose strands escaping in curls across her forehead. She wore a moss-green topcoat over a gold high-neck sweater and pleated slacks.

"Hi guys," she said. She walked to Ollie's bed and bent to kiss him on the forehead. She held his good hand in hers and squeezed it. "You hungry?" she asked her husband.

"My stomach thinks my throat's been cut," Ollie said. "McGuire's been suckin' back Bloody Marys, leavin' me here to waste away."

"I offered you a sandwich," McGuire protested.

Ronnie kissed McGuire's cheek. "I'll get him something. Who's winning?"

"Joe's down three bucks and the Sox are leading eight to five." Ollie watched his wife shrug out of her coat, his smile beaming at her.

"I'll make coffee," McGuire said, standing. "Square up with you tomorrow."

He knew what Ronnie would have to do now. Change her husband's diaper. Rub ointment on his bedsores. Wash the man's body, care for him as though he were a helpless baby.

Fulfilling the duties she had performed every day, without let-up, for seven years.

"It's the best thing I've done in my life. The very best thing."

The baseball game had ended. Ollie was sleeping, aided by pills washed down with fruit juice. Ronnie smiled at McGuire over the rim of her coffee cup, holding it in two hands. Music drifted into the kitchen from the radio in the living room.

"It's as though something came alive in me, something I didn't even know was there." She set the cup down, smiling with excitement in a way McGuire had never seen before. "I always liked to draw pictures when I was a kid, and in art class at high school. Everybody did; it was more fun than math. Now I'm learning things, little secrets and techniques. I love it."

"What is it, a big class?" McGuire poured himself another coffee.

"Just seven of us, plus the instructor. Wow, is he good! His name's Carl Simoni. He's had shows all over the country." Her smile beamed even brighter. "One of his watercolors is hanging in the State House."

"Ollie's proud of you."

"I'm pretty proud of myself." Her eyes lingered on McGuire. "More than I've been for years." She rose from the table. "Wait'll you see what I bought today. It's really extravagant, but I thought I'd treat myself." He heard her walk down the hall, open the closet door, and return to the kitchen carrying what looked like a polished wooden briefcase. She set it on the table, slid the brass locks aside, and opened it.

Inside was an assortment of watercolor pads, brushes, cotton cloths, textured paper, and other materials McGuire couldn't identify. "Nice," he nodded.

"Isn't it beautiful? It's just like Carl's, only smaller. Made in Switzerland." She lowered her voice and said in a stage whisper that was almost a giggle, "It cost me nearly three hundred dollars! For God's sake, don't tell Ollie that."

McGuire promised he wouldn't.

An hour later, McGuire was in bed, in his room at the rear of the house, thinking of Ronnie's happiness, her new enthusiasm, and recalling that she had been wearing more makeup than he had seen on her in years. Eye shadow and lip liner, and something that accented her cheekbones. She had tinted her hair blond, and where the hell did she get that figure recently . . . ?

CHAPTER 2

"Gotta do something."

McGuire tossed the morning paper aside and stared out the window next to Ollie's bed, at the ocean visible beyond the shore road.

"Yeah, but lawyers?" Ollie was propped up in bed, the remote control in his hand. Two heads were conversing on the television screen.

"You go where the money is. My pension's barely covering food and my rent here, and don't give me that crap about not needing to pay my way. My car needs a transmission overhaul. Or maybe just a kick in the ass, if you knew where to kick a Chrysler." McGuire had purchased the ten-year-old hardtop when he was working as a part-time security guard. The job lasted less than a month. It ended the day McGuire suggested that his supervisor's brains were located immediately behind his testicles.

"You really wanta work with a bunch of lawyers? Can't Frankie DeLisle, Wally Sleeman, one of those guys, find something for you to do, help 'em clean up the city?"

"I can't work with DeLisle. Couldn't when I was at Berkeley and sure as hell can't now. Sleeman's a lot of fun, but he's not the brightest cop I ever met."

"Yeah, well." Ollie moved his head in the semblance of a nod. "Wally's the kinda guy, he's gotta get naked to count to twenty-one." His eyes swung to McGuire's, a smile playing on his face when he saw McGuire grinning. "But Christ, Joseph. How you gonna work with a bunch of ambulance chasers?"

"It's Zimmerman, Wheatley and Pratt. They're mostly corporate, civil law, divorce lawyers, family law . . ."

"Come on." Ollie managed to turn his head far enough to follow McGuire's gaze through the window. "You're tellin' me you're not gonna run with hounds, you're just gonna trot with dachshunds. Dogs are dogs."

"What am I supposed to do the rest of my life? Stay here as your gardener, mowing the lawn, taking out the trash, helping Ronnie with the groceries . . ."

"You're talkin' about stuff I used to do." Ollie said it without anger or self-pity. Ollie had a way of stating obvious facts in an obvious manner.

"Okay, so I'm making like a husband around here." McGuire realized what he had said, what he was implying.

Ollie's eyes remained on the water. "You doin' that too?"

"Aw, for Christ sakes, Ollie." McGuire stood up, his hands in his pockets.

"Listen, it can happen." Ollie's voice was free of rancor. "You don't think I know Ronnie's still a good-lookin' woman? Remember old Dave Sadowsky? He was always findin' reasons to drop by when I wasn't here, tellin' Ronnie what a honey she was, how she could do better'n me. Till I told him one day, he ever tried to lay a finger on her I'd make him do a pole vault on a friggin' twelve-gauge." Ollie grinned at the memory, but his eyes avoided McGuire's.

"I don't believe you can even *think* . . ."

"I hear you two out in the kitchen, late at night. I hear Ronnie laugh. You make her laugh, Joseph. One of the sexiest things a man can do for a woman is make her laugh. We spend all those years, us guys, tryin' to dress the right way, drink the right brand of Scotch, lift weights and do sit-ups, all that stuff, and most women are just lookin' for a guy with a sense of humor."

"Ollie, I am not sleeping with Ronnie . . ."

Ollie's head moved in an arc until his eyes locked on McGuire's. "I'd understand if you did," he said. "See, that's the point. I'd understand."

Zimmerman, Wheatley and Pratt occupied two floors of a downtown bank tower, the office a gaudy display of post-modern architectural hubris in cinnamon-colored marble. "An excess of good taste," was how one critic described the atrium lobby, with its brushed brass accents and crystal light fixtures.

Stepping from the elevator and walking to the law firm's fifteenth-floor reception desk, McGuire entered a world of Edwardian elegance. The walls were wainscoted in dark oak beneath flocked wall coverings in shades of deep reds and hunter greens. Next to the reception desk, a wide staircase spiraled down to the firm's fourteenth-floor library and the steno pools, accounting, records-keeping, all the engine-room mechanics that permitted the legal professionals to function on the floor above them.

McGuire was wearing a blue Oxford button-down shirt and blue cotton slacks, plus his trademark tweed sports jacket, custom-made for him by a Charlestown tailor who had owed him a favor. The tailor had done a superb job, adding leather trim on the buttonholes, Mandarin silk lining, and other details. McGuire had seen the same fabric on a jacket in a Brooks Brothers window. Without the custom tailoring and detailing, the Brooks Brothers version was priced at $800. The tailor had charged McGuire only for materials.

McGuire had done the tailor a very large favor.

McGuire owned three of the jackets, one brown, one blue, one gray. He wore them year-round with jeans or with tailored slacks, in rain and snow, on all but the hottest, most humid, summer days. He suspected he would be buried in one of them. They looked both expensive and defiantly unfashionable. They suited him even now, in the rarified climate of one of Boston's most prestigious law firms.

"Mr. Pinnington has been expecting you," the receptionist smiled when McGuire announced his name. A minute later Richard Pinnington, senior partner, was walking across the Axminster from somewhere beyond the reception area, his hand extended, and his patrician face beaming a smile at McGuire.

"It's a matter of having access to a special kind of talent."

Richard Pinnington leaned forward, his eyes on McGuire. They were seated in matching wing chairs covered in green leather with brass upholstery studs. The leather was soft and yielding, and the aroma of the tannery still rose from its buttery surface. Between them, a silver tea service and two ornate bone-china teacups rested on a low, glass-topped oak table. Pinnington's office, encompassing as much square footage as the entire ground floor of Ollie and Ronnie's house, stretched to a bank of windows overlooking the Atlantic.

Pinnington was in his early sixties and he carried his age, like his upper-class bearing, in a manner that members of a privileged class often do: with elegance and grace. His hair, thinning but still wavy, was pewter-gray, a color repeated throughout the man's wardrobe. His Egyptian cotton shirt sported a subtle gray stripe, his maroon tie was flecked in an amorphous gray pattern, and his blue suit had an undertone of gray.

McGuire suppressed a rare feeling of inadequacy in Pinnington's presence.

"You're not that involved in criminal law," McGuire said, settling back in the chair facing Pinnington. "Why call on a cop who spent his career on the street?"

"Well, you're absolutely right." Pinnington sat back, mimicking McGuire's posture. "We are not specifically a criminal-law firm. Just two criminal lawyers on staff. But things are becoming so complex for us that we need . . ." Pinnington looked for the phrase in the air beyond McGuire's shoulder. "We need a radar detector, a sonar device is maybe a good way of putting it, that can alert us to potential criminal activity."

"On the part of your clients?"

"Perhaps. More likely, of course, on the part of our adversaries. Also, we often make use of certain criminal investigative techniques in our civil cases."

"Such as?"

Pinnington shrugged. "People who can locate lost individuals for us. Assembly of evidence in perhaps a more effective manner than civil lawyers can muster. And there are borderline cases where civil and criminal law seem to be overlapping at a faster rate every day. Child-custody cases, for example.

That's become a big part in our practice. Abduction is a serious criminal offense. Assuming wide interpretations of custody laws is a civil matter. See my point?"

McGuire nodded.

"Business espionage is another concern. We can become involved in corporate civil law and discover the possibility of criminal activity by employees or officers."

"These are hardly my field."

"No, they're not. But we can use your perception, your instincts. I have a colleague who practices criminal law. Marv Rosen. I think you know him. Anyway, he's our criminal-law counsel."

McGuire knew Rosen, would never forget the ferret-faced lawyer. He had physically attacked Rosen in a courtroom years earlier, a foolish move that cost McGuire a demotion and two weeks' income. "He tried to charge me with assault once," McGuire said. "He dropped it in exchange for an apology, and told everybody I'd given him the best PR he'd ever received."

Pinnington smiled. "Marv still talks about it. It's his best dinner-party story. I've heard it over and over. Now, I'm not saying Marv would enjoy sharing a slow boat to China with you, but he has a keen respect for your intuitive abilities." Pinnington leaned back in his chair, his hands behind his head. "One of the many things you *don't* learn at law school is how to hone your intuition. But the more I practice law, the more I value that . . ." He hesitated, then found the word. ". . . skill. So I decided a few weeks ago I could either try to inject it into each of our partners and staff, or I could consider buying it on the open market, so to speak."

"Which is me."

"Which is you."

"What are you offering?"

"Five thousand dollars' monthly retainer, plus itemized expenses. It's flat, whether you work eighty hours a week or none. And your workload could vary that much. Let's assume a firm three-month contract to start. After that, we'll review your hours and make adjustments to the fee if necessary. Maybe reassess the whole arrangement. This is an experiment for us. For you as well, I suspect."

"How does it work?" Pinnington was offering an income equal to McGuire's best years as a homicide detective. Fix the Chrysler's transmission? Hell, he'd dump it for something a little flashier and a lot more reliable.

"Each lawyer has the right to draw upon your skills as he or she sees fit. Partners take precedence over non-partners. Senior partners have ultimate prerogative on your time. Any conflicts among staff regarding your availability will be resolved by me. You track your hours per case, and they're pro-rated against the docket by the lawyer who contracted your services. We'll make a small office available down on the fourteenth floor. It's not spectacular, but it gives you a telephone and a desk. As I said, after three months we review everything."

"Do I have to wear a tie, dress like a lawyer?"

"Not unless you want to. Wear a tie, I mean."

"Will I be testifying in court?"

"We will do our best to avoid that eventuality."

McGuire nodded. "Sounds okay."

Pinnington almost leaped to his feet, his pleasure mixed with impatience to move on to other things. "Sounds like we have a deal. When can you get started?"

"What time is it now?"

"Unspectacular" was hardly the appropriate word for a windowless space that, a few days earlier, had functioned as a combination document-storage area and passageway, and was now to serve as McGuire's office. He entered it through an unmarked door from the word-processing area, where several women sat at computers and printers, preparing long documents for the lawyers who occupied the offices above them. Another unmarked door exited to a hallway leading to the fourteenth-floor elevator foyer.

"It's so we can keep people apart," said Pinnington's secretary. Her name was Woodson. "Mrs. Woodson," was how Pinnington had introduced her to McGuire, never referring to her first name, which McGuire soon learned was Connie.

Pinnington had asked Connie Woodson to escort McGuire to his new office and introduce him to key staff members. She was warm and pleasant, and her eyes reflected a hidden humor, a sense that she found the world amusing in a manner that she was unable to share with others.

"We used to bring people through here while their adversaries, or anyone else we didn't want them to meet, waited in Reception upstairs," Connie Woodson explained. "But Mr. Pinnington has made other arrangements."

"It's perfect," McGuire said. And it was. He could come and go through the hall door without being seen. He had a small metal desk, a swivel chair, two metal side chairs, a telephone, a water cooler, and two filing cabinets set beneath a dusty black-and-white photograph of Cambridge that appeared to date back to the 1920s. An equally dusty coffeemaker sat atop one of the filing cabinets. "That work?" McGuire asked, and Connie Woodson nodded.

"Mr. Pinnington said I am to provide you with anything you need," she said. "If it's urgent or I can't look after it myself,

I'll get the message to him. I'm preparing a memo to the full staff about your presence and duties. Would you like to see it before it's distributed?"

"No," McGuire said, testing the swivel chair. "Whatever you and Pinnington want to say about things will be fine with me."

She beamed with relief. McGuire's attitude was clearly different from the lawyers, who believed that any document that had been drafted fewer than three times was likely libelous or erroneous. "The key to the hall door is hanging there, over your desk," she said. She led him out through the word-processing area. "Mr. Pinnington is very pleased that you have joined us."

She escorted McGuire through the offices, introducing him to partners and lawyers and various department heads, who handed him their business cards and greeted him with responses ranging from undisguised impatience to fawning praise. Two partners booked appointments with McGuire for later that day. One wanted to discuss a wrongful-dismissal suit in which the fired employee departed with a copy of the firm's long-term strategic marketing plan. The other told McGuire of an employee who may have suffered his back injury in a bar-room brawl instead of at his place of employment, as he claimed in a three-million-dollar lawsuit. A third lawyer, an unsmiling fair-haired man barely half his age, peppered McGuire with questions about his background and abilities until McGuire cut him off, suggesting he check with Pinnington about his credentials. The younger man, stunned for a moment by McGuire's impertinence, said he would.

One lawyer studied McGuire intently and posed questions to him about his experience in tracing criminals on the run and dealing with dangerous individuals face to face, while

Connie Woodson stood nearby, smiling and shifting her weight impatiently, anxious to continue escorting McGuire through the partners' area.

The lawyer's name was Orin Flanigan, and McGuire judged him to be between fifty and sixty. His head was bald, save for a fringe of fading red hair, the color of sandblasted brick houses. He dressed like the other partners in well-fitted suits in subdued colors, and his body shape confessed to years of rich meals and expensive wine, but instead of shrewdness, his eyes reflected distant but still-remembered pain. "I would like to chat with you some time," the lawyer said.

"What about?" McGuire said.

McGuire's words appeared to surprise Flanigan, as though he were unprepared to be questioned by anyone. "Nothing in particular," Flanigan said.

"What does he do?" McGuire asked Connie Woodson as she led him along the corridor towards the next introduction.

"He's in family law. He specializes in child-custody cases. Mr. Pinnington believes he is the best in his profession."

McGuire's instincts told him that Orin Flanigan would be calling on him for some service, probably something furtive and risky. So he wasn't surprised when the lawyer made a pretense of stopping by McGuire's office the following morning, inviting McGuire to join him for lunch at The Four Seasons.

They walked the three blocks together, Flanigan asking questions about McGuire's background, where he was born, where he went to school, what hobbies McGuire had. "Hobbies," McGuire said, "are things people do when the stuff they're being paid to do isn't what they want to do. When I was a cop, I was doing what I wanted to do. So I didn't need any hobbies."

"That's some people's definition of success, you know," Flanigan said. They had reached Boylston Street. The Four Seasons was a block away. "Doing what you want to do."

Inside the hotel dining room, Flanigan was greeted with exaggerated pleasure by the maître d', who led the lawyer and McGuire to a corner table. "I always sit here whenever I come for lunch," Flanigan said when they were settled. "Always order the same thing, too. A glass of California Merlot, whatever the soup of the day is, and a rare roast-beef sandwich on rye bread, black coffee to follow. What do you think of a man who is so set in his ways?"

"That's he's probably satisfied with himself," McGuire said.

"You're being diplomatic."

"Maybe I'm being a little envious, too." McGuire looked up from the menu, and around the paneled dining room.

"Of course, you can be doing what you want to do and perhaps not feel successful after all." Flanigan was calling the maître d' over. "The New York strip steak is very good, I understand," he said to McGuire.

McGuire ordered it, and a Heineken.

"You didn't say if you have any children," Flanigan said when the waiter left.

"I don't."

"Do you regret that?"

"Sometimes."

Flanigan watched him, as though waiting for more. "The things that happen to children," he said after the waiter had brought their drinks, "are the most egregious of all the sins of a society. Any society."

"You make your living correcting them."

"I make my living dealing with them. Correcting them is often out of the question." He sampled his wine and set the glass aside. "They can haunt you, you know. You can say you're just dealing with the legal aspects of things, and I try. But after thirty-odd years, some stuff still haunts you."

McGuire asked the lawyer if he had any children.

"Not any more," the lawyer said.

To someone else, McGuire might have pressed the issue. What did that mean, "not any more"? That the children were grown? They were estranged? The expression on Flanigan's face said the issue was painful. McGuire found himself liking this man, who appeared embarrassed by his own success, yet locked within its trappings.

"You ever been to England?" Flanigan said, and McGuire said he hadn't. "My wife and I go every summer for our vacation," Flanigan said, and for the rest of the lunch Flanigan described public footpaths across the Cotswolds, tiny stone churches on high hills overlooking the sea, and thatch-roofed pubs in Devon and Cornwall.

After lunch, outside the hotel, the lawyer checked his watch and said he was meeting someone down by Quincy Market. He asked if McGuire would excuse him, and they shook hands there in the sunshine on Boylston Street. Flanigan's handshake was firm and he looked McGuire in the eye and smiled, as though McGuire had provided him with some important information, as though it had been McGuire who had hosted the lunch and picked up the check and played the benefactor, instead of Flanigan.

Later, when Orin Flanigan's body was undergoing an autopsy, McGuire would tell himself that he had expected it, had known that any man who openly expressed such deep human concern and empathy could not help but face the consequences.

CHAPTER 3

"They're all gray suits and country-club drinkers," McGuire said to Ollie Schantz two nights later. He was seated next to Ollie's bed, balancing some warmed-up left-overs on a tray.

"What've they got you doin'?" Ollie asked. He was staring out the window next to his bed, the one with the view of the ocean. It was a soft evening, warm and humid, unusual for a New England autumn. Ollie Schantz had been looking at this same scene from his same semi-reclining position for years. It was his only alternative to the television set suspended on the wall at the end of his bed.

"Biggest thing is possible fraud," McGuire said. "Guy in a warehouse says he was handling a shipment that was loaded the wrong way. It fell on him and wrenched his back. He's looking for a pile of money from the insurance company, who's our client." He sampled some macaroni and cheese. "Where's Ronnie?"

"Out doing her Picasso thing," Ollie said. "She's working on a surprise for me, a picture of something or other. Gonna hang it right over there on the wall, so I can look at it."

"You're gonna stare at a picture all day, it damn well better be good."

"It will, it will," Ollie said. "There a ball game on tonight?" he asked, and McGuire reached for the remote control.

An hour later, when McGuire saw that Ollie was sleeping, he turned off the television, dimmed the light, and climbed the stairs alone.

The man with the injured back was demanding three million dollars in damages, plus full wages for five years, claiming he had been struck by a falling crate. The company's insurer had retained Zimmerman, Wheatley and Pratt to fight the claim. Two doctors who examined the employee suggested the man, who was also sporting a broken nose, could not have injured himself the way he described. In front of a jury, however, the employee just might prove his case.

"Can you get us any evidence on what really happened?" the lawyer handling the case asked McGuire. He was hefty and pink-cheeked, and he carried himself with the casual assurance of someone who possessed a nimble mind inside an awkward body. On the law firm's list of partners he was shown as Fred Russell, but everyone called him Pee-Wee.

"You play clarinet as a kid?" McGuire asked.

"Dixieland," Pee-Wee nodded. "You heard of Pee-Wee Russell?"

"Hell of a clarinet player."

"I'm trying to have as much fun and make a damn sight more money than he did. How long will it take you to blow this guy's story out of the water?"

"You know where he lives?"

"We even know where he drinks."

"In that case," McGuire grinned, "I'll have it for you in a day."

McGuire returned to Revere Beach and changed into worn jeans and a denim shirt. Then he bought a copy of the *Boston Globe* and drove to the South Boston tavern named in the warehouse worker's file. He sat at the bar, ordered a fried-egg sandwich and a beer, and, after chatting with the bartender about the weather, about the Red Sox, and about the most recent political scandal at City Hall, began turning the newspaper pages, claiming he was looking for a story on a bar-room brawl he had witnessed the previous night.

"I wouldn't have your job," McGuire told the bartender. "Never know when some nut's ready to bonk you with a bottle these days, right?"

The bartender said McGuire was sure as hell right, and when McGuire asked if the bartender ever got himself caught in the middle of one, the bartender told McGuire about some guy, a few weeks ago, who got into an argument with a truck driver over Ronald Reagan. "Reagan himself can't remember what he did when he was down there, in the White House, right?" the bartender said, "and these two guys are goin' to war over him. That's his brother, the truck driver's brother, over there in the corner." The bartender raised his voice. "Tell him, tell this guy, about what your brother did to Sammy what's his name, works over at the warehouse in Cambridge."

The truck driver's brother described the argument that spilled into the street, and the punch that sent the warehouse worker sprawled across the hood of a Mazda and then onto the road, where the man screamed in pain, clutching his lower back and ignoring the blood flowing from his nose.

McGuire asked the truck driver's brother if they knew each other, he looked familiar. The brother said No, he didn't think they had met before, and they traded names. "Maybe it's your brother I know," McGuire said, and the truck driver said That could be, people were sometimes getting him and Harry mixed up, because there was only a year between them, Harry being the younger. The brother said he lived three blocks over, same street as Harry the truck driver, they grew up in this neighborhood and never moved out, not like the guys who hauled their ass to Braintree or some place near the Cape as soon as they got some money together.

McGuire agreed. Who the hell would want to live any place else but Southie? Then he left the bar and sat in his car, writing notes, recording names and descriptions. Nobody in the bar would have talked so openly to an insurance investigator, or anybody who smacked of downtown. They talked to McGuire as though he were just another potato-eater, and Zimmerman, Wheatley and Pratt would subpoena the truck driver if necessary to make sure he repeated his story in court.

Funny the way things turn out, McGuire thought as he drove away. If this had happened a few years earlier and the warehouse worker had hit the ground the wrong way, the truck driver might have found himself on the end of a second-degree murder charge, manslaughter at least, with McGuire reading him his rights. Then it would have been McGuire showing up in court, and the truck driver facing ten years in prison.

"Hi there."

McGuire looked up from writing his report for Pee-Wee Russell. Orin Flanigan was leaning through the door from the word-processing area. He entered, closed the door behind him, and offered McGuire a pink, fleshy hand. "Mind if I sit down?" and he was seated before McGuire could reply.

"What's up?" McGuire asked.

"I've been doing some thinking about our lunch the other day, what we talked about." Flanigan seemed to have acquired a number of nervous mannerisms: stroking an eyebrow, scratching his nose, clicking the nails of a thumb and forefinger together, adjusting his glasses, so that a part of him was always in motion as he spoke.

"We talked mostly about England," McGuire said.

"Yes, well . . ." Flanigan looked away, then back again. "You busy?"

"Wrapping up a personal injury claim for Russell . . ."

"Pee-Wee? He's a good guy, got some good clients." Flanigan scratched his wrist, adjusted his glasses, and pulled on his shirtsleeve to expose more cuff. "What else you got?"

"You sound like you have something yourself. For me to do, I mean."

Flanigan's smiled widened. "Oh, well, it's not a big deal, not a big thing, one of those little bits and pieces of a case that you can spend a week on and never use in court, never even mention in discovery."

The lawyer stood up and brushed imaginary crumbs from his trousers. Standing erect and looking down at McGuire, he grew more impressive and intimidating, suited to his reputation as a lawyer who worked in the heated arena of child custody and family law. "It occurred to me that you might be able to come up with something without incurring a great deal of expense," Flanigan said. His voice failed to match his posture. It remained uncertain and tentative.

"What's it involve?" McGuire sat back in his chair and studied Flanigan with new interest.

"It's a matter of finding somebody. Part of a custody case. Not a direct participant, but if we knew where he was, in case we need him, it would be an extra nail in the door, so to speak." Flanigan bent from the waist and looked McGuire in the eye. "Is that part of your job description? Finding people who have dropped from sight?"

"Part of it."

"Confidentially?"

"Everything's confidential."

"Doesn't go beyond you and me?"

"Not if you say so."

"I'll send a note down this afternoon. And a docket number." He relaxed, stood erect again, and smiled, then hid the smile. "You know the hardest, the most difficult part of what I do?"

McGuire shook his head.

"It's knowing that people, people on the other side, think that I don't have any feelings about their situation. It's all adversarial, that's the system, that's how it works. But it's not always true. You can win and still feel something for the loser, for the other side. Not everybody here feels that way, of course. I might be the only one who does. But the older I get, the more it eats away at me, sometimes seeing the other people, when they lose, become very emotional. I feel for them, some of them. There's no right and wrong in law sometimes, only winners and losers."

"Is this one of those cases?"

"Yes." Flanigan paused at the door. He smiled back at McGuire. It was a smile of embarrassment. "That's something else I'd appreciate if you didn't share. What I said just now."

A note arrived that afternoon in a sealed brown envelope carried to McGuire by Flanigan's secretary, a woman in her forties with large dark eyes and a mass of dense, curly black hair. McGuire remembered her from his tour of the office, when she had made a point of introducing herself and smiling at him.

McGuire could not recall her name.

"Lorna Robbins," she said. "Mr. Flanigan's secretary." Her voice was high-pitched, with a singsong quality. She wore a flowered silk blouse whose buttons strained to contain her bosom, and she seemed in no hurry to leave. "How are you making out? Is there anything you need?"

McGuire assured her there was nothing.

"Well . . ." She straightened the bottom of her blouse where it disappeared in the waist of her skirt, and walked to the door. "I guess we'll be seeing more of each other. If you're working on whatever Orin gave you there."

McGuire turned the envelope over. The flap was sealed with heavy tape. "You don't know what's in here?" he asked, holding the envelope up.

"No idea. Mr. Flanigan drafted it himself on his own computer."

"He does that often?"

"Not while I've been here."

"How long's that?"

"Eight years next month. The last two with Mr. Flanigan." She leaned against the door.

"Is he a nervous guy?"

"Mr. Flanigan's a wonderful man, and a good lawyer. One of the best."

"He's not nervous?"

"Why are you asking me this?"

"Maybe he's intense."

"A little, I suppose."

McGuire grunted.

"We all are. We carry a big workload upstairs, and some of our cases, Mr. Flanigan's especially, they can get heartbreaking.

The people, I mean. Mr. Flanigan, he gets wrapped up in his cases sometimes. I've seen him. It hurts him, some of these cases . . ."

"I wasn't prying . . ."

". . . and it's hard on him sometimes . . ."

"Trust me, Laura . . ."

"Lorna. It's Lorna."

"Lorna, I hear what you're saying. I made a mistake, bringing it up."

"Okay . . . A lot of us, you know, executive assistants and secretaries, we're a little nervous about having a police officer among us . . ."

"I'm not on the police force any more."

". . . because, you know, it's almost as though we've done something wrong."

She had a ripe sensuality that middle-aged women often acquired, one that McGuire was finding attractive. "Would you like to talk about what my job is, sometime?" McGuire smiled his warmest smile and tilted his head.

Lorna Robbins bit her lower lip and nodded. "Over coffee maybe?"

"I was thinking lunch."

She nodded again, this time more vigorously. "There's a little place that just opened on Harbor Street . . ."

"I'll look forward to it."

McGuire waited several moments after the door closed before opening the envelope and removing a single sheet of plain bond paper. A five-digit number had been written in ink at the top. The rest of the correspondence was spaced with the degree of clarity and neatness only a word processor and desktop laser printer can produce.

Due to the special nature of this case, it is imperative that you and I make direct contact at the outset. Charge your time and reasonable expenses, up to $1,000, to the docket number listed above. By the way, this is not a high priority. Work on it when you can.

I want you to locate a man for me named Ross Randolph Myers, age about 45. His last known address is 387 Gloucester Street, apartment 3B, but he hasn't lived there for two years. Mr. Myers once operated the Back Bay School of Business on Columbus Avenue, but it was placed in receivership about the time Mr. Myers vacated his condominium. Mr. Myers is about six feet tall, heavyset, has gray-blond hair, and no visible scars or blemishes. He is known as a heavy gambler, an activity that resulted, in part, in the collapse of his business and the seizure of his personal property. He served six months for tax evasion in 1999 and was released without restriction.

I am interested solely in Mr. Myers's current place of residence, which, if you determine it, I would appreciate hearing from you verbally. Please do not commit any of your information to paper.

Cordially,
O. Flanigan

"That all you got?" Ollie asked that evening, between spoonfuls of casserole fed to him by Ronnie. "Some guy skippin' out on child support?"

McGuire told Ollie about the warehouse worker, and his visit to the South Boston bar.

"Hell, any rookie whistle who's lost his cherry in this town could've done the same thing," Ollie said. "Lawyers, they don't think about getting their asses dirty, sitting on a bar stool and listening to somebody who doesn't say "whereas" and never wore a sheepskin on their shoulders."

"Some of them don't seem so sure of themselves," McGuire said. "One of them, anyway," and he told Ollie about Orin Flanigan's visit that afternoon.

"Doesn't sound like anything he needs to keep so secret," Ollie said.

"I get a feeling it's unofficial. Like he doesn't want his partners to know about it."

"He's a partner?" When McGuire nodded, Ollie said: "What's he got to be worried about, then? Unless he's breaking some kind of lawyer ethics. Whatever the hell they are." He waved away another spoonful of food and Ronnie began gathering the utensils together. "So, you gonna ask Wally Sleeman to help you, get you some dirt on this guy you're lookin' for?"

McGuire nodded. "Probably cost me some Scotch. Which reminds me. Remember that skip tracer from years ago? Woman lived over on Huntington?"

"Libby." Ollie grinned. "Old Libby Waxman. Christ, what a character. Haven't thought about her in years. Talked to her, lemme see, lemme see . . ." His eyes scanned the ceiling. Ronnie stood up, the plates and utensils in her hands, and left without a word. "It was when those two guys, couple of hustlers, took off more'n a year before . . . remember that guy they found down near the fens, head caved in . . .?"

McGuire was half-listening. He was concerned about Ronnie, the look on her face when she left the room.

CHAPTER 4

"Still call him Fat Eddie, and I catch hell for it."

Wally Sleeman leaned back and scanned the other lunch-hour diners at Hutch's, his small eyes flitting from one to another, pausing long enough to determine if the face was familiar, female, or threatening. Familiar faces warranted a lifting of Sleeman's heavy hand – the one not clutching the bottle of Moosehead – in greeting. Unattached women received a brisk up-and-down sweep of Sleeman's gaze and, if they stirred something in Sleeman's hormones, a lifting of his eyebrows.

Anyone who represented a threat, based on a recollection from a mug sheet or an arrest Sleeman made years earlier, earned a swivel of Sleeman's massive body, a motion that reminded McGuire of a freighter in Boston Harbor being positioned for berthing. Sleeman's eyes would fix on his target until he would nod and mutter, "Robbery with assault" or "B and E, theft over five" or simply, "scum-sucking lowlife." No one Sleeman observed in Hutch's this day appeared to be threatening. He rested two thigh-sized forearms on the table and expelled a long, reluctant sigh.

"Eddie's lost that much weight?" McGuire asked. He felt good, hanging around a tough old cop, maybe two years from retirement, to whom the term "political correctness" meant wiping your feet before entering the White House.

"Not that much. He's lost some, but the son of a bitch ain't never gonna be anorexic." Sleeman smiled over McGuire's shoulder at the blowzy waitress approaching with crab cakes and fries for Sleeman, mussels and salad for McGuire. "Now here's a vision of loveliness," Sleeman said when the woman arrived at their table. She had hair the color of carrots, a smallish turned-up nose that gave her a perpetually adolescent look, and a mouth that was too wide but slid into a smile with ease.

"You talkin' about me or the crab cakes?" she said. She was close enough to forty to behave as though she were younger, and far enough beyond it to accept the fact.

"Crab cakes I can get anywhere," Sleeman said, his eyes moving over her body. "Somebody nice as you, I'd have to go to Vegas for."

"They keep him tied up at night?" she asked McGuire.

McGuire smiled. The mussels looked good, the shells set in a garlicky tomato sauce, but he eyed Sleeman's french fries with envy.

"Hey, you into that stuff, sweetie?" Sleeman grinned at the waitress. "You wanta tie me up, say the word. Hell, I got some perversions you never thought of yet."

She struck a pose, one hand on a hip, and tilted her head. "Honey," she said, "trust me. You're a perversion I ain't thought of yet."

Sleeman laughed and seized his fork as though it were a sword, his body rocking with laughter. "Jesus, I love women," he said, and began spearing his fries.

"Wally Sleeman, right?"

McGuire and Sleeman looked up at a tall, slender man with oversized glasses and a heavy chin standing next to their table.

"Yeah," Sleeman said. He turned back to his lunch. "That's me. Who're you?"

"Name's Morgan. Rick Morgan." He extended a hand towards Sleeman, who glanced sideways at it before slicing his crab cakes.

"I remember, you played for the Bruins back in the sixties," Morgan said. He withdrew the rejected hand. "Right? Am I right?"

"You're right." Sleeman lowered his fork and lifted his dinner napkin to his mouth, wiping his lips as he spoke. "You remember that far back, do ya?" he said.

"Hey, I remember you knocking Bobby Hull on his butt one night at the Gardens," Morgan said, his face creasing into a smile. He looked over at McGuire. "Right on his butt. Bobby Hull himself. When he tries to go around Sleeman, Sleeman gives him a hip check and Hull's sliding into the boards."

McGuire smiled and opened a mussel.

Sleeman reached for the Moosehead. "Yeah, and ten minutes later, when the ref's not looking, Hull gets me in a corner and rams the end of his stick into the back of my head like a sledgehammer." Sleeman grinned at the memory and lifted the bottle to his lips.

"You were my favorite player back then, next to Bobby Orr," Morgan said, leaning on the table.

Sleeman lowered the bottle and stared off in the distance, his eyes narrowing. Anyone else might have thought he had spotted a face from a wanted poster, but when McGuire heard Morgan's words and saw the look on Sleeman's face, he knew better.

"Next to Bobby Orr himself," Morgan babbled on. "I mean, nobody's been better than Orr, right? As a player, I mean. Am I right? Am I right?"

"He was okay," Sleeman said. His mood had grown black.

"Okay?" Morgan grinned in disbelief. "Just 'Okay'? I never saw anybody skate like that. But I guess you should know, playing with him and all, right? Am I right?"

"I never played with him," Sleeman said. He returned to attacking the crab cakes as though they were predators that would leap from his plate if he didn't dissect them first.

"Really?" Morgan looked around, his mouth hanging open in disbelief. "Is that right? You never played with Orr? You sure about that? You never played with Bobby Orr?"

Sleeman dropped his fork to his plate and stared briefly across at McGuire, who watched the man's heavy forearms grow tense. "I'll tell you what, *Dick*," he said, turning his head to Morgan. "I play with myself every day in the shower more than I ever played with Orr, okay? Okay?"

Morgan looked from Sleeman to McGuire and back again. "Sorry if I disturbed you," he said. "Just trying to be friendly."

He pulled himself up to his full height, took a deep breath, and walked back to the table he was sharing with three other men near the front of the restaurant.

"Asshole," Sleeman said.

Mention Bobby Orr in the presence of older Boston hockey fans and you got a quiet nodding of the head, a smile maybe, and the launch of a dozen stories from people who saw Orr glide across the ice as though he had Roman candles on his skate blades. There were other stories from people who never saw him play in the flesh but wanted to believe they did. But not from Wally Sleeman.

Sleeman would duck his head and roll his sloping shoulders, the ones that once bulldozed their way against an opposition center coming across the blue line a dozen times a game, but now just continued their slope down to a heavy chest and a heavier belly. Then he'd look away, across the bar, maybe, and mutter, "Not bad, but over-rated."

If the conversation took place on Berkeley Street in Robbery Division, a rookie suit who was a whistle a few months ago would laugh and say, "What, you kiddin'?" and recall how Orr was probably the greatest defenseman in the history of the game, scored more goals than any other player in his position, we'll never see another guy like him, not in our lifetime.

"Guess who got bumped off the team to make way for Orr when he came up from the juniors in sixty-five?" people who knew Wally Sleeman's story would say, when Sleeman was out of hearing range. "Guess who was supposed to get his break the next year, set to go like gangbusters, the year Orr comes up and this guy, this poor unlucky bastard, gets crowded out and traded to Toronto where he dies, the poor bastard dies? Guess who that was?"

That's what happened to Wally Sleeman, getting his big break the same year Orr arrived to tear up the NHL. Sleeman was an eighteen-year-old with lots of promise, that's what he had been told all his life since he was a kid in Providence. Then he's the extra defenseman who shows up in camp the same year Orr does. Sleeman spent a year in Toronto, a year of throwing his elbows around like they were scythes and he was ass-deep in hay. Sleeman picked up so many penalties that the Leafs sent him down to the minors. One morning he woke up in a motel in Medicine Hat, Alberta, with his nose broken and his eye closed from a fight in the previous night's game, and said "The hell with it." He turned in his equipment and went back to New England, where he had grown up dreaming of playing for the Bruins. Now he was just some guy who once came this close to an NHL career, and that's when Wally Sleeman got himself a job on the police force.

"So anyway, ya can't call him Fat Eddie any more, right? Even if he was the same old lardass."

After the interruption by Morgan, Sleeman had resumed carving his way through the crab cakes with his fork, his elbows sticking out like a bird's wings, the same way he would set them going into a corner, chasing a hockey puck. His pink scalp shone through the few remaining hairs on his head. "I mean, these days you can't say somebody's fat, you can't say somebody's crippled, even if they got no legs and they're pushin' themselves across the street on a skateboard, right? So we can't call him Fat Eddie any more." He filled his mouth with a slab of crab cake the size of a playing card.

McGuire pried open another mussel, avoiding the sight of the half-chewed crab cake in Sleeman's mouth. "So now he's just Eddie?"

"Naw." Sleeman leaned back in his chair and looked around the room again, this time as though searching for something he had never seen before, or something he saw once and never wanted to encounter again. "See, him and Donovan are buddies now."

"Phil Donovan and Eddie?"

"Yeah." Sleeman's hand seized the bottle of beer and brought it to his mouth. "Eddie's always bitchin' about how things ain't bein' run tight enough, and Donovan's always agreein' with him, kissin' Eddie's ass before turnin' around and kickin' everybody else's. The two of 'em are a pair." He inhaled a mouthful of Moosehead. "We call 'em Snit and Snot."

"How're you getting on with DeLisle?"

Frank DeLisle was a straight-up cop, who bolstered his street experience with academic credentials, and indicated with a silent glare or a cautious word that he expected everyone to act as if they harbored ambitions to become Police Commissioner. DeLisle avoided profanity; he added new photographs of his family to the wall behind his desk on Berkeley Street each month; and he refused to accept any excuse for deviating from the Police Procedural Manual.

"DeLisle's ass is so tight," Ollie Schantz observed to McGuire one day, "the guy could eat coal and shit diamonds."

"Frank's okay I guess, when he's not preachin'," Sleeman said. He finished the last crab cake. "He's always tellin' me to dress better, eat better. Even said I should either take out a better class of women or try to get back with my wife. So I say to him, 'Make up your mind, Frank. You want me to mix with a better class of women, or you want me to get back with the wife?'" He drained his beer and scanned the restaurant again. From their table in the corner, Richard Morgan and his friends were gesturing towards Sleeman, their faces expressing disapproval. Sleeman smiled and waved one hand, its middle finger extended vertically. "You hear about that black kid, the one who came at you on the Common?"

"What about him?"

"Workin' solo now. Got himself a gun, sounds like a Beretta."

"He's been ID'd?"

Sleeman nodded. "The gold tooth. He's back hittin' tourists down around the market. Don't want cameras, just cash these days. Feedin' a habit, probably. Little bastard's getting cockier than ever. Herded some couple from Jersey into an alley behind the clam house down there last night. He's copping a feel from the woman with his free hand while her husband's digging for his cash and traveler's checks." Sleeman shook his head. "If I get him alone without the Beretta, I'll turn his ass pink with my boot, I'm tellin' ya." His mood changed. His face brightened as though power had been restored somewhere behind his eyes. "So you're still shuckin' for those lawyers, are ya?"

"Only been a week," McGuire said.

"Which is a week longer'n I figured you'd last." Sleeman leaned back in his chair. "You don't have a reputation for playing kissy-face with too many mouthpieces, you know."

"Always helps to see the other side. Anyway, they're not into criminal very much. The closest most of them get to a courtroom is for child custody or a civil suit."

Sleeman leaned forward, his eyes on McGuire. "Don't you get bored? Don't you wish, just once, you were out on the street lookin' for a nab, or you had some snivelin' piece of crap in the IR, feedin' you all the stuff you've been lookin' for on his buddies?"

McGuire shook his head. He probed the bowl of tomato sauce with his fork, searching for errant mussels.

"I know what it is." Sleeman's face creased into a grin. "It's the broads, right? Big lawyers like them guys, they got women stacked in the office like cordwood, right? So how many've you banged so far?"

"None." McGuire lowered the fork and raised his beer glass. "Not a one."

"Bullshit."

"It's true."

"What, you becomin' a monk?"

"Truth is . . ." McGuire drained his beer glass. "The truth is, I miss being married."

Sleeman blinked and looked through McGuire, as though the other man had vanished. "Oh, yeah," he said. He nodded his head and sat back in his chair. "I can see that. I miss it too. I also miss root-canal work and feeding my balls to a pack of rottweilers. What, you nuts? Miss bein' married? Hell, you've been single for how many years? What's to miss?"

McGuire shrugged. I've always missed it, he wanted to say. The best times of being married were better than the best times of being single. Instead, he said: "I need some information on a guy."

"Got a record?"

McGuire passed a sheet of paper across the table. In point form, he had written as much about Ross Myers as Flanigan had communicated to him.

"Whaddaya need?" Sleeman asked.

"Whatever you've got."

"Nothin' on paper, right? I get caught handin' you paper, my ass is in a sling."

"Could use a mug shot."

"C'mon, Joe. I just told you. Nothin' on paper."

"Just read me whatever's on file then."

Sleeman grinned and tucked the paper into his hip pocket. "You're gonna owe me."

"How does two bottles of Glenfiddich sound?"

"Sounds good. Probably taste better." Sleeman drained his glass.

The waitress returned and removed the plates from in front of McGuire and Sleeman. "How're you boys doin'?" she said. "Anything else you need?"

Sleeman's eyes traced the line of her body from her bosom down to the hem of her skirt and up again. "Well," he said, licking his lips, "tell you the truth, I could use a little pussy."

She leaned towards him. "So could I, sugar," she said. "Mine's as big as your hat." And Sleeman threw back his head and roared with laughter. The waitress gave McGuire a wink and swivel-hipped away, while McGuire smiled and reminded himself he never had this much fun working with lawyers, never would.

CHAPTER 5

"You don't want a fax or nothin', do ya?"

It was barely an hour later, long enough for McGuire to return to his office, make a pot of coffee, and find a reason to stroll upstairs past Lorna Robbins's desk and smile at her. His telephone was ringing when he returned. Sleeman began speaking, keeping his voice low so that McGuire had to press the telephone receiver tightly against his ear to catch his words. "Only if you got a photo," McGuire said. He grabbed a pencil and sat with it poised above a yellow lined notepad.

"No photos, Joe, like I told ya. Gotta sign mug shots out now, you hear about that? Anyway, this guy Myers is some kind of dancer. Got more moves than Fred Astaire. Found himself charged with a bunch of stuff three years ago. Fraud, embezzlement, minor assault, tax evasion. They nailed him on one reduced charge, bit of a deal they cut with him."

"What'd he get?"

"Six months. Served the whole time."

"He give an address?"

Sleeman snorted. "Yeah. The Seaview Motel in Fall River. Bit of a come-down from Marlborough Street, right? Anyway, Myers likes to live well. He was drivin' a Caddie Seville back in '99, belonged to a bunch of clubs in Miami, had a condo there, owned a couple of racehorses."

"Liked to play them, I hear."

"That's what brought him down."

"Married?"

"Divorced."

"Kids?"

"None shown. That's gonna take a fair bit of diggin', you want stuff like that."

"Probably two more bottles of Glenfiddich, too."

"Funny you should mention it."

"You still drop into Zoot's the odd night after work?"

"The odd night."

"Herbie Stone still tending bar in there?"

"Never misses a beat."

"Maybe Herbie'll have a little gift for you, you drop in tonight."

"Yeah? Now won't that be nice of old Herbie."

McGuire hung up and was refilling the coffeemaker when Richard Pinnington tapped lightly on the door and entered. "You want some good news?" he asked, his tanned face split with a wide grin.

"Long as it doesn't cost me."

Pinnington's grin vanished and he gestured at the coffeemaker. "You know, you could get one of the girls to do that for you."

McGuire poured the water into the top of the machine. "I like to do things myself." He turned on the machine and looked at Pinnington. "What's the good news?"

"I just had lunch with Russell. He left on the shuttle to New York, but he wanted me to tell you about the material you gathered on that back-injury case."

"Guy who hurt himself in a brawl?"

"Pee-Wee had an after-hours chat with counsel from the other side, a kind of off-the-record pre-discovery session. Let him see your report and gave him the name of the other guy in the brawl and his brother. Counsel for the plaintiff made noises about backing off, once he looked into things. He's probably advising their client that he doesn't have a case, and that he might even risk charges of attempted fraud. Meanwhile, our client's impressed all to hell by our efficiency. Your efficiency, I mean. Congratulations."

McGuire nodded.

"You know, you might have earned your entire month's income with that one project. Our client was facing a three-million-dollar settlement without it."

"Three million dollars to a guy who gets beat up in a bar fight and tries to do a con job on some insurance company." McGuire shook his head.

"Well, you struck a blow for ethics." Pinnington folded his arms and leaned against the doorframe. "So. Are you working on anything else, or do you plan to take the rest of the month off?"

McGuire gestured at a scattering of file folders on his desk. "Too busy. I'm looking at some guy who disappeared with a business plan, tracking a missing person for Orin Flanigan . . ."

"Orin gets into some heartbreakers, doesn't he? Abused kids, all the trash left over from divorces. But he's damn good. Sometimes, though, I get the feeling that he finds it hard to separate himself from the cases." Pinnington pushed himself from the door and checked his watch. "You want to get together for lunch some time? Maybe a drink in my office after hours, a little parachute to let you down easy at the end of the day?"

McGuire said Sure.

McGuire wasted the rest of the afternoon, leaving at four to purchase the Scotch for Sleeman and driving down Boylston to Zoot's, where he left the brown-paper sack with Herbie Stone. Stone had been a prison guard at Worcester until he and three other guards were taken hostage in a riot six years earlier. Neither Herbie nor the other guards were harmed, but for two nights and a day they watched as the inmates tortured and killed three prisoners, two of them child molesters and the third a suspected informer. The rioters used a blowtorch, screwdrivers, and their bare hands, and the screams of the victims etched themselves into Herbie Stone's memory, leaving scars he would never lose. Now he managed Zoot's, a dimly lit hangout for cops, with a sound system that played quiet jazz. There, the major drama of the day wasn't hearing someone scream as his testicles were burned to carbon, but running out of Triple Sec for frozen margaritas that Herbie claimed were the best north of the Rio Grande.

McGuire had a beer in Zoot's, nodding to the few cops whose faces he recognized. Then he walked down Boylston to a restaurant and devoured bacon and eggs, because he felt like eating bacon and eggs. As he ate he watched the other patrons, especially women his age or younger. He thought about Lorna Robbins and her little-girl smile, her giggles, her full bosom. He wondered if he would enjoy an evening with her, perhaps dinner, perhaps more. He knew she would accept his invitation for the same reason he would offer it. Out of loneliness. Out of a need to escape the feeling of waste, of irretrievable loss, for at least one night of their lives.

He read the paper, paid his bill, walked back to Zoot's to discover Wally Sleeman had already picked up his Scotch, then drove to Revere Beach.

He parked the car and strode up the walk to the front door, finding the interior of the house darkened and quiet. Behind him he heard another car arrive, and he turned to see Ronnie close the car door.

She watched the vehicle leave before she headed up the walk and discovered McGuire. "Hi," she said, trying to hide her surprise at his presence. "I've got something to show you," and he stood aside as she entered the house, carrying a large flat package under her arm. She set it on the kitchen table. "Look what I did today!"

Her fingers tore at the brown paper wrapping, and she withdrew a watercolor landscape set in a simple pine frame. Executed with simple, strong brushstrokes, the painting showed a farm field in spring, the bare ground seen through receding snow in brown furrows, and the sun shining, weak but with promise.

McGuire was impressed.

"I never tried this before, leaving white for snow like that, and just putting a blush of blue on it. See the blue? It's so faint, yet it's so strong like that, giving shadows and all." She held the picture in her hands at arm's length, her eyes glowing with pride. "Carl was so pleased with it, he insisted on taking it to his gallery and framing it himself. That's why I'm late."

"Carl?"

"My teacher. I told you about him. *God*, he has talent! I painted it from a picture he took in Vermont last year."

She set the painting on a kitchen chair and stepped back to study it as though never having seen it before. "Do you like it?" she asked. "I know I'm fishing for compliments. But I never thought I could *do* anything this good." She turned to McGuire. "Do you like it? Really?"

McGuire said he did.

She shrugged out of her coat and glanced at the clock. "I'd better tend to Ollie." She turned and began walking down the hall. At the mirror she paused to study her reflection and tuck an errant lock of hair into place.

McGuire watched her, glanced at the picture, looked up to see Ronnie entering Ollie's room, and turned back to the picture again.

CHAPTER 6

McGuire never knew how they did it, how they located people who could elude FBI computers, Internal Revenue bloodhounds, and neighborhood police precincts. But the handful of skip tracers working in any big city have their means, and most share a contempt for police procedures and computers.

He remembered Shoelace O'Sullivan, a gaunt Irishman who operated out of a former barbershop in Chelsea, and who traded tips with the cops in return for access to data, the same kind of information McGuire obtained from Sleeman. McGuire and Ollie Schantz visited O'Sullivan in his office one morning more than ten years ago. The Irishman looked twenty years older than his age and reclined in an old barber's chair, making notes on scraps of paper and nodding while they spoke. When the previous tenant died, O'Sullivan had taken over the lease on the barbershop, and the landlord assumed O'Sullivan was a barber himself. O'Sullivan set up an office without removing any of the previous tenant's implements. He arranged his library of ancient telephone books, city directories, and other sources in stacks on the floor and on glass shelves that once held clippers and shaving equipment, everywhere at hand. He changed nothing except the window glass, which he painted in opaque white. O'Sullivan even left the bottles of hair tonic, colored red and green like fruit drinks, on the shelves beneath the mirrors, and the Swedish straight razors in the drawers.

"I'll be callin' you on the weekend if I'm findin' anythin'," O'Sullivan told McGuire and Schantz when they requested information on a drug dealer who had dropped from sight three years earlier, and whose wife's skeletal remains had been located in a woods near Braintree.

The telephone rang that Friday afternoon.

"You'll be lookin' at twenty-three hundred Beverly Boulevard in Braintree," O'Sullivan told Schantz. "Row M, room nineteen." Then he hung up. Shoelace never said a word more than necessary, and seemed to enjoy adding an element of mystery to his comments. McGuire called it Gaelic poetics. Ollie dismissed it as Irish bullshit.

"What is it, an institution?" McGuire asked as he and Schantz drove to Braintree.

It was a cemetery. Row M, plot 19 held the remains of the man Schantz and McGuire had been searching for, buried by his family beneath a stone with his actual name carved into the granite, not the pseudonym he had used as a drug dealer in Boston.

"How the hell'd he do that?" McGuire wondered after they obtained positive identification. "How's O'Sullivan find this stuff out?"

But Shoelace O'Sullivan performed his magic for the wrong client somewhere along the way. A year later he was discovered slumped in his barber's chair, his throat slit from ear to ear with one of the straight razors he acquired with the business along with the barber's chair, mirrors, and hair tonic.

Which left Libby Waxman among the few remaining of her profession, living among Boston's most densely populated gay community.

McGuire climbed the stairs to Libby's apartment above Darling Decadence, a store specializing in old examples of nostalgic bad taste sold at outrageous prices.

The peephole cover in Libby's door swung aside when McGuire knocked, and one world-weary eye looked back at him for a moment before its owner gave a long bronchial sigh, the peephole closed, and he heard three deadlocks being slid aside.

Libby was already walking down the hall back to her parlor when McGuire entered. He followed her through an aroma of stale cigarette smoke, garlic, and grease to a small dark room, where she was lighting a fresh Marlboro and coaxing an overweight gray Persian out of her Barcalounger.

"Didn't think you'd remember me," McGuire said. He stood looking for a place to sit among the stacks of telephone books, magazines, newspapers, and three-ring binders.

"Hell, McGuire." Libby's voice had the coarseness of a dry transmission trying to shift into reverse while moving forward. "Just 'cause you don't come see me for years doesn't mean you're forgotten."

Legend had it that Libby had been Boston's last brothel madam, operating an elegant house down near Cherry Street during the fifties. It was while keeping tabs on the patrons of her business, politicians and outlaws alike, that she foresaw a career, a new line of work she would need when the cycle turned and the city's moralists cast a cold eye on bawdy houses. Which is precisely what happened. A week after City Hall vowed to wipe out Boston's brothels, so the story went, Libby called the Commissioner's office and told him she was willing to turn over her diary to him, a book that contained the names of over a thousand clients, including his own, if he would help her launch a new business venture.

The Commissioner invited her downtown for a chat.

In his office, she told him her new business would be as a skip tracer, tracking missing people down paths that no law-enforcement official could follow.

"It's a legit business," Libby pointed out.

"It certainly is," the Commissioner agreed. Libby's diary sat on the desk between them.

"Of course, I'll have a better chance of making good if I get some unofficial co-operation from you guys when I need it," Libby said.

"You certainly will," the Commissioner said.

The story was true.

"How long's he been gone?" Libby asked McGuire. She was settled in the chair recently vacated by the cat. A tattered apricot-colored chenille robe was wrapped around her shoulders. Her hair, the shade of a brass spittoon, had been freshly combed and styled. Folds of skin framed her eyes, and the lobes of her ears were oversized and waxy, like the drippings of well-used candles.

"About two years." McGuire handed her a slip of paper with all the information he had on Ross Randolph Myers. He looked around. "You use computers?"

Libby made a sound like a warm beer being opened and shook her head. "Says he likes to gamble. Horses maybe?"

"Could be. He plays the horses, or used to. Owned one, I understand. You plan to start with bookies?"

"Don't know. Maybe." She was staring at the paper as though committing it to memory. "This could take a couple days. Two hundred a day, which is my basic rate. Doesn't help he's a border-jumper. Then again, I might get lucky." Her face said she was already planning ways to obtain the information.

"Give me four hundred worth." A grin flashed across McGuire's face. "Didn't you and Silky Pete have a thing going, ten years ago, maybe?"

"Silky Pete's dead."

"I know. I investigated his murder."

"It was an accident."

"Yeah, a Buick accidentally hit him while he was hanging around the docks at three in the morning. Silky took bets, did some loan sharking, right?"

"Silky was just like me, doin' whatever it takes to keep the wolf from the door." She looked up at McGuire with a watery eye. "What're you up to these days? Freelancin'?"

McGuire stood and handed her his business card. "For a bunch of lawyers."

Libby sniffed the air, then brought the business card close to her nose and nodded. "Figured it was either that or the litter box needed changin'."

Barely an hour later, McGuire was back in his office draining his second cup of coffee when the telephone rang, and Libby began talking almost before McGuire finished saying his name. "You got a pencil?"

McGuire told her he did.

"Ross Randolph Myers is in Annapolis."

"He likes the navy?"

"He likes horses, like you said. They got more brains'n him. Every time this guy looks at a nag he sees a jockey on its back and money on its nose. Annapolis is close to Pimlico."

"Address?"

"Don't know. He hangs out at a place called the Academy Bar and Grill."

"How'd you get all this so soon?"

"What, you crazy?"

"I'm not goin' into competition with you. Just curious."

"Who keeps tabs on people better'n an ex-wife owed alimony?"

"A bookie."

"A bookie who knows a guy that's smart enough to tap an endless supply of scratch and dumb enough to bet the favorite to win all the time."

"Thanks for this, Libby."

"I don't do it for thanks. You owe me a couple hundred, McGuire."

When he hung up, McGuire called Flanigan's extension, and Lorna Robbins answered.

"He has a busy day, but I'll ask if he'll see you," she said. "How's yours?"

"How's my what?" McGuire said.

She giggled. "Your day. I heard Mr. Pinnington raving about you to a couple of partners this morning. He thinks you're some kind of genius. For what it's worth."

"By the way," McGuire said. "I haven't forgotten about lunch."

"Neither have I. Just a minute." McGuire listened to thirty seconds of silence from the receiver before she returned. "Can you be here at ten minutes to twelve?" she said. "He can see you then. And how about today? For lunch, I mean. He'll be finished with you at noon. That is, if you're still interested."

McGuire said he was.

At ten minutes to twelve he arrived at Lorna's desk. She looked up at him, smiled, and bit her lip. "You keep your promises," she said.

"I try to."

"What a guy." Lorna lifted her telephone receiver, entered a number, and tried to avoid looking at McGuire while she twirled locks of her hair between her fingers. "Mister McGuire's here," she said formally. "He's waiting for you," she said to McGuire, replacing the receiver. She placed her arms on the edge of her desk and leaned against them, watching McGuire as he entered Flanigan's office.

Orin Flanigan fingered his tie with one hand, his eyes never wavering from McGuire's. On the walnut credenza behind him sat a framed photograph of an attractive middle-aged woman with vaguely Slavic features, her dark hair frosted with gray, her smile poised for the photographer. Next to it he saw a portrait of a younger woman whose face echoed the same features. Wife and daughter, McGuire assumed.

"How did you do that?" Flanigan asked.

"Do what?" McGuire was slumped in a leather chair facing Flanigan's desk. Through tinted windows, he could see aircraft lined up over the ocean, waiting to descend into Logan Airport.

"Locate someone with such little information."

"He's a gambler. Gamblers leave tracks."

"How do you know it's really him?"

"I don't. But I'm sure it is."

"How sure?"

McGuire took his eyes from the aircraft and stared at the lawyer. "What are you getting at?"

Flanigan stopped fingering his tie and removed his glasses. "Can you go down there and positively identify him?"

"Are you asking me to?"

"I'd like to know it's him. I'd like to know where he lives, and I'd like to know where he's employed. If anywhere. Charge your expenses to the docket number I gave you."

"I could use a picture of him."

"There are no pictures of him. None that I have."

"If he's got a record, there'll be one on file."

"You might try that, with your connections. You have a description of him. When could you leave?"

McGuire shrugged. "Tomorrow." He stood up. "Do you want to tell me why you're so interested in this guy?"

"I don't think it's necessary."

"Is he considered dangerous?"

"Not to you." Flanigan looked at his watch. "Let me know if there's a problem."

McGuire nodded and crossed the carpet to the office door, closing it behind him. In the anteroom outside Flanigan's office, Lorna Robbins was stapling some legal documents together. Across from her, seated on the oversized leather sofa, a slender woman with streaked blond hair began to rise when the door opened, then sat back again when she saw it was McGuire, but McGuire was struck by the expression he saw in the instant before she turned away, as though the woman had been prepared to launch herself towards him before settling back on the sofa. A curious expression, as though she were about to be rescued. And a familiar appearance, around the eyes.

McGuire raised his eyebrows at Lorna, who glanced at him before turning away. He walked to her desk and bent to speak just as the door behind him opened. McGuire turned to see Flanigan gesturing to the woman on the couch, and she rose and entered Flanigan's office in several brisk, short steps. The lawyer avoided McGuire's eyes and quickly closed the door behind them.

Lorna Robbins leaned towards McGuire. "You know, staff members aren't supposed to date each other. It's against policy."

"It's not a date," McGuire said. "It's lunch."

Lorna smiled. "Darn, I'd rather it was a date. I can always get another job."

"Meet you downstairs in five minutes," McGuire said, and Lorna bit her lip and nodded.

Looks like I'm going to Annapolis, McGuire told himself as he descended the stairs. He wondered if the slender woman with the streaked blond hair and the strange manner had something to do with it all. He remembered her eyes, the look of hope and pleading he saw there.

Lorna met him at the elevator, watching the other employees and saying very little to McGuire. As they left the building, he held the door for her and she glanced at him in mild surprise.

The restaurant was narrow, crowded, and dark. Seated at a table far to the rear, Lorna relaxed. She ordered pasta and salad, then looked directly at McGuire for the first time since leaving the office building. McGuire told the waiter he would have the same.

"Are you nervous about being seen with me?" he asked her. "Do they take the rule about not dating staff that seriously?"

"No." She continued staring at him, one hand toying with her hair.

"Then why so tense?"

She sat back in her chair and crossed her arms. "A little frightened, I suppose."

"Of what?"

She shrugged. "Are you seeing anybody?" she asked. "I mean, are you involved with anyone right now?"

"No," McGuire said. "You?"

She shook her head. "I had a bad experience with a man last year. We were supposed to get married, move to Cape Ann, and open a bed and breakfast. We told my friends, my kids, I almost handed in my notice at the firm, and then . . ."

"He got cold feet."

She smiled, without humor. "I don't think his feet had anything to do with it. I think the only thing cold about him was in his chest."

"He told some lies?"

"Not some. A lot." Her hand went back to her hair and she teased it with her fingers.

"Hey." McGuire reached across and touched her hand. "It's only lunch."

"I know. But I've been careful since then, you know?"

"It's a good idea," McGuire said. "Being careful."

Their meal arrived and they busied themselves with the food, McGuire ordering a glass of wine for each of them. Lorna mentioned a book she had been reading that she thought McGuire might enjoy, an insider's view of the life of a big-city detective. "I'll bring it tomorrow," she said.

"I won't be in tomorrow," McGuire said. "I'm going to Annapolis for Orin Flanigan."

"You are?" She paused with her wine glass halfway to her lips. "He never said anything to me about it."

"He made the decision in his office just as I was leaving. Probably fill you in when we get back."

"Orin tells me everything," she said, setting the glass down again and frowning at it. "Orin's the most predictable person I've ever met."

"Well, nobody could predict that the man he wanted me to find would be in Annapolis."

"What man?"

"Somebody named Ross Myers. He's a gambler. You know him?"

"Never heard of him."

"Get Orin to fill you in when we get back."

She seemed distracted through the rest of the meal, but by the time coffee arrived she had grown more open, almost mellow. McGuire made her laugh with stories from his police career. He enjoyed hearing her laughter. He always enjoyed making women laugh. It was an assurance that they were pleased with his company, the only one he trusted, and he told her other stories as they walked together back to the office, some of them a little racy, taking care to avoid offensive language and descriptions. He mentioned Fat Eddie Vance, who wasn't fat any more but was probably the same ineffectual man, lost beyond the confines of police procedural manuals.

"I've known people like that," she said. "They're not just cops, you know."

"Yeah, well," McGuire said. "My buddy Ollie had a saying that nailed Eddie perfectly."

"What was that?"

"It was a little crude."

"Hey, I'm a big girl. Is it funny?"

McGuire nodded.

"I can take crude, if it's funny." They were at the entrance to the office building. She leaned towards him. "Tell me," she said. "Come on."

"Ollie used to say," McGuire said, "that Eddie Vance couldn't get laid in a woman's prison with a fistful of pardons."

Lorna laughed so loudly that she covered her mouth and leaned against the building wall, hiding her face from McGuire and passersby. "You have so many stories," she said. "Have I heard them all?"

"I've got dozens more."

"Promise to tell them to me?"

"The cleaner ones."

"I want to hear them all."

They walked through the revolving door and into the lower lobby. McGuire would be leaving the next day, a Friday. "Guess I'll see you Monday." she said.

"How about Saturday night," he said. "Should I call you for dinner?"

"Is that a promise?"

He told her it was.

"Just a minute." She stopped near the elevator and used a mascara pencil to scribble a telephone number on a slip of paper. "You don't have to, you know," she said, handing him the paper. "I won't be disappointed if you don't." When he put it in his pocket she looked around and leaned towards him to whisper, "Yes I will," and kissed his cheek.

"No can do."

Sleeman's words over the telephone meant he'd done enough for McGuire. Four bottles of good Scotch could only go so far.

Behind Sleeman's voice, McGuire could hear the murmur of conversation and a telephone endlessly ringing. "He's got a record, there's a picture on file," McGuire said.

"Told ya," Sleeman said. He dropped his voice. "Verbals I'll help you with, Joe. Copies are another thing. DeLisle's on one of his moral housecleaning trips again. And everybody's uptight over changes around here. Guys gettin' transferred in and out, moved up and down. I mean, you gotta be careful. The toe you step on today might be attached to the ass you have to kiss tomorrow."

"So go get the mug shot and tell me what he looks like."

"What, you want me to buff and cuff him too? Jesus, McGuire, we're all up to our asses here trying to find that Hayhurst lowlife."

"Who's that?"

"The gold-tooth kid, the one with the Beretta, who tried to shake you down. I told you about him. He's working solo now, and he's wired all the time, probably doing crack by the bucketload. He's one for the books. Been a bad-ass since grade school. He took two shots at a couple of old ladies, schoolteachers from Indiana, last night. He was so wired up he missed them both. One thing nobody around here wants is a couple of schoolteachers from little towns in Indiana getting their scrawny butts shot off by a hopped-up street hood, right? So now we got a task force and I'm heading it. DeLisle wants Hayhurst and his Beretta off the street, with or without his gold tooth, and I'm the guy supposed to do it."

"Tell me what you know about Myers," McGuire said. He leaned back in his chair, his feet on a corner of the desk.

"Married twice, no kids," Sleeman answered. "Charged with assaulting one of his ex-wives, roughed up another guy who owed him money. Thinks he's got muscle to use, I guess. Got himself probation on a weapons charge, too. Then he beat some heavy-duty embezzling charges that his partner took a three-year government vacation for, and did six months for income tax that the IRS said he didn't pay, on money the court said he didn't embezzle. Usual crock of shit."

"So you're not making a copy of his mug shot."

"Sorry. Maybe your buddy Rosen's got a picture of him. Myers and Rosen, they probably threw a big party when he beat the embezzlement charge, for which he was facing five to ten."

"Rosen?" McGuire sat up in his chair.

"He was Myers's lawyer." Sleeman gave a dry laugh. "Hell, McGuire, you can always threaten to introduce your knuckles to his beak again, he doesn't come through for you."

McGuire muttered a goodbye to Sleeman and sat staring at the telephone. Then, as though his thoughts had flipped some switch within the instrument, it rang.

"I just wanted to thank you for lunch again," Lorna said. McGuire could feel the closeness of her lips against the receiver and he pictured her a floor above him, maybe toying with her hair.

"Not necessary," he said. "I enjoyed it."

"Please don't lose that telephone number."

"I won't." He thought about Saturday night, about all the Saturday nights over the past several months he had spent in the house on Revere Beach, watching television with Ollie and Ronnie, and thinking of sand flowing in massive quantities through a narrow opening into darkness. "Look," he said, hearing himself speak, almost eavesdropping on his own thoughts. "Why don't we make it a sure thing? Is there some place you'd like to go for dinner? Somewhere you haven't been in years?"

He heard a sharp intake of breath. "You know where I haven't been in *years* and I'd love to go but it's a little expensive?"

"Where?" McGuire asked. Where's she want to go? he thought. The Four Seasons? That French restaurant in the Hilton? He tried to remember if he had paid his Visa bill that month.

"The Parker House restaurant," she said. "You know it?"

McGuire knew it. Not his choice, perhaps, but more affordable than the others.

They agreed on dinner at eight. McGuire would pick her up at her apartment on Park Drive at seven-thirty. After hanging up, he booked a flight to Baltimore the following morning and reserved a car from Hertz. He made dinner reservations for Saturday night and read a stack of memos on his desk before leaving at three-thirty. He spent two hours in Zoot's, listening to stories from off-duty cops while working his way through a cheeseburger and a couple of beers. He walked for several blocks through the mild autumn evening, strolling to Newbury Street and down to the Public Garden, then back again to a restaurant near Zoot's where he stopped for coffee, wasting his time, measuring out his life in strolls and memories.

Ollie Schantz was watching a documentary on the erosion of America's ocean beaches. "You're a bird dog, are you?" he said when McGuire told him about his trip to Annapolis the following day.

"Guy's cut most of his ties. The lawyer wants confirmation, that's all."

"What's this lawyer do? Not criminal law?"

"Mostly child custody, child support, divorce stuff."

"He won't tell you what this is about?"

"Don't need to know."

"But you'd sure as hell like to."

McGuire nodded.

The television screen showed another section of Virginia sliding into the sea. "What's buzzin' in your head about this?" Ollie said.

"The guy's got a record, he's a gambler, he likes to live high." McGuire turned away, dredging up speculation that he hadn't articulated until now. "Flanigan, he's the lawyer, he's got something else in mind."

"This guy, the gambler." Ollie's eyes shifted from the television screen for the first time. "He have a record for rough stuff? May not appreciate you popping up between him and the tote board."

"Couple of assaults, one on a wife. And got caught on a weapons charge."

"Now you're showing up, asking questions he won't wanta answer. Better be careful."

"I've been there before,"

"Yeah, but you ain't been fifty before."

"What the hell's that mean?"

"Just be careful, Joseph. Just be careful. You wanta send Ronnie in? I think I got a diaper needs changing."

McGuire rose and met Ronnie coming from the kitchen, an uncharacteristic furrow between her eyes, drying her hands on a towel. "I heard him, I heard him," she said, sweeping past McGuire.

On the kitchen table, the remnants of a lone ice cube floated in a half-finished glass of gin and orange juice. McGuire brought the glass to his nose. A very strong gin and orange juice.

CHAPTER 7

McGuire's flight out of Logan was at eight in the morning. On the way to the airport from Revere Beach his car coasted to a stop while the engine raced wildly. He pulled to the curb, shifted into neutral, then dropped the lever into drive. A faint, high-pitched sound leaked from somewhere near his right foot, like a kitten calling for its mother. It ended with a thump from the transmission, and the car began moving forward again.

"Clunk," McGuire mimicked the noise the transmission had just made. "Well, now I know your name, anyway." He left the car in the airport parking garage without looking back at it, hoping someone would be foolish enough to steal it in his absence.

At Baltimore Washington airport he picked up the keys to a new Ford, and set out for Annapolis. He was feeling more positive about his life than he had for months. The day was warm, and the air carried sea-smells from Chesapeake Bay. McGuire had passed through Annapolis several years earlier, and he recalled the old town's colonial homes and busy harbor. In spite of the tourists and the dominating presence of the Naval Academy, the town remained in his mind as a tempting retreat, an enclave of taste and refinement. He remembered a basement jazz club at the Maryland Inn, and promised himself a dinner of crab cakes and beer and an hour or two of live jazz before returning to Boston.

He found a parking meter on State House Circle and walked to Maryland Avenue, where a white wooden signboard with black lettering announced the Academy Bar and Grill.

The door was locked. A menu displayed in a glass case told him the bar's hours were 11:30 a.m. to 1:00 a.m. McGuire checked his watch; it was just past 10:30. He leaned to squint through the leaded window in the door, shielding his eyes with his hand. He could see several small tables, each with four captain's chairs, set in a dark-paneled room. A long bar lined the left side of the room.

He walked along Maryland Avenue to a side street, turned right, and found a service lane running behind the shops. A Budweiser truck was parked at the rear door of the bar, and McGuire passed a beer deliveryman leaving the rear of the building, wheeling an empty pushcart. The man nodded at McGuire, who smiled tightly and entered a storage area, where cases of beer were stacked almost to the ceiling. Another door led to a small food-storage and washing area. From there, McGuire could look into the kitchen on one side and the bar interior on the other. He waited for the deliveryman to drive away, then entered the darkened bar.

A man's nylon jacket was tossed over one of the high bar stools. Near it on the bar was a woman's purse, made of cracked vinyl with peeling brass hinges. Two stemmed wine glasses, one empty, the other half-filled with tomato juice, sat further down the bar.

On the floor, at the end of the bar nearest the street, he saw a woman's shoe, a black high-heeled slingback. McGuire walked to the shoe and was looking down at it when he heard the sound.

His first instinct was to seize a weapon, perhaps one of the bar stools. But instead he held his breath and tilted his head to one side, knowing the sound was familiar in one sense, foreign in another.

He walked softly through the archway separating the bar from the dining room. At the back of the dining room, an open counter area fronted an empty cloakroom with bare wire hangers suspended from a worn metal pipe. The sounds came from the cloakroom, steady, rhythmic but unsynchronized, two voices and flesh speaking to themselves and each other.

McGuire approached the counter and looked down at the floor. He saw the man's bare back and legs, the trousers pulled down to his ankles, and the woman's legs elevated and shaking like flames in the air. The woman's eyes were squeezed tightly shut. The man's mouth was groping for an exposed breast.

McGuire turned and walked away, this time without any pretense of silence. He left the dining area, approached the bar, stood staring at his reflection in the mirror before thinking What the hell, and walked over to unlock the front door. Then, with a sweep of his hand, he tossed one of the wine glasses to the floor.

The sounds from the cloakroom ceased, and he heard the rustle of frantic whispers.

He knocked the other glass to the floor and sat on a bar stool, watching the mirror.

It took perhaps a minute for the man to appear. He was taller and heavier than McGuire. His head was shaved and he wore a black goatee that looked dyed, a red golf shirt over gray cotton trousers, and leather deck shoes. A heavy gold chain sparkled around his neck, just beneath the swell of a slight double chin.

"Hey, we're not open yet, pal." He was looking at McGuire in the mirror, his expression wary. One hand moved to his zipper to confirm his fly was closed.

"Front door's unlocked," McGuire said. He glanced at the remains of the glasses. "Sorry about that. I get clumsy when I need a beer."

The other man walked to the front door, pulled it opened, cursed, slammed it shut, and set the lock again. He returned to the bar and sat in front of the woman's purse, two stools from McGuire. He opened the purse, removed a pack of cigarettes and a lighter, offered a cigarette to McGuire, who shook his head, lit one for himself, and inhaled a long breath of smoke before looking at McGuire again.

"Three best things in the world, right?" he said, grinning. "A drink before and a cigarette after." He took another puff on the cigarette. "So, you really want a beer?"

"No." McGuire swiveled in his chair, but before he could speak, a woman's voice shouted from the rear of the dining room.

"You mind bringing me my shoe?"

The man with the cigarette hunched his shoulders and gave a small laugh. "Just a minute, we got company."

"Well, damn it . . ."

"In a minute!" the man barked. He looked at McGuire. "Give 'em a little love, they think you're their goddamn slave, right?"

"I'm looking for somebody," McGuire said.

"Man or woman?"

"Man. Named Myers. Ross Randolph Myers."

The other man's eyebrows moved up his forehead. "He owes you money, right?" He picked up the receipt left by the beer deliveryman and scanned it, then folded and placed it behind the cash register.

"Could be."

"Son of a gun's always got people after him for money."

"I was told he hangs out here."

"Not any more. Like I said, he owes money."

"Know where I can find him?"

The man placed the cigarette in his lips, tilted his head back, squinted his eyes, and looked at McGuire. "You a cop?"

"No. You?"

He stared at McGuire as though considering a reply, then turned away to face the mirror. "I can call somebody, might know where he is."

"That'd sure as hell be nice of you."

The man turned to look at McGuire as though he were surprised. "I'm a nice guy." He extended a hand. "Name's Wade, Rollie Wade. Yours?"

McGuire ignored the hand. "Joe McGuire," he said. "Just came down from Boston."

Wade nodded as though confirming a fact he already knew. "Wait here," he said. He walked to the bar, picked up the telephone, and dialed a number. He began speaking in a low voice.

McGuire strolled around the bar, examining the wooden frames on the booths, imagining it filled with students and professors each evening.

"Got something for you." Wade had hung up the telephone. "Sounds like he got himself a job over at Bay Ridge Yachts. You know where that is?"

"No idea."

"You go through town, past the Marriott, across the lift bridge, and turn left. There's a bunch of yacht brokerages in there, must be a dozen of 'em. He works for Bay Ridge. Now that's the last I heard, okay? No guarantees. Sure you don't want that beer?"

McGuire thanked Wade, shook his head, and entered the dining room, moving towards the front door. From the corner of his eye he saw the woman duck behind the counter of the cloakroom, her wide eyes watching McGuire, one hand holding the side of her hair back, the other clutching a comb.

After a few false turns, McGuire found the harbor, and the brown and boxy Marriott hotel. The harbor and slips were crowded with pleasure craft, most of them sailing vessels. Some of the boats were manned by tanned, fair-haired crewmembers wearing colorful shorts and tops. They were coiling lines, polishing hardware, or just doing their best to be seen aboard boats that cost more than the average American home.

McGuire speculated briefly on the amount of money invested in the teak, fiberglass, aluminum, and canvas toys that moved through the harbor or floated in the hundreds of slips on its perimeter. Tens of thousands of dollars a year to stand or sit on a boat going nowhere. Like watching golf televized and elective celibacy, it was one of those activities some people chose that McGuire could never understand.

He drove across the lift bridge and turned left to skirt the shoreline, scanning the brightly colored wooden buildings.

Bay Ridge Yacht Brokers was the seventh he counted, a large gray structure fronting the harbor, with a low brick office area along one side. McGuire parked his car next to a Volvo station wagon and entered.

The walls of the brokerage were hung with framed color photographs of yachts cutting their way through water of every shade of blue. A reception desk sat on a small carpeted area just inside the door. Three wooden desks, each with two upholstered chairs facing it, were located in the open office area. The office was empty except for a slim, dark-haired woman sitting at one of the desks, writing. She looked at him with eyes so shadowy they appeared black, set in a face with high cheekbones and a small, full-lipped mouth. "Yes?" she said. "Can I help you?" Her tone was cool, her smile careful and correct.

"I'm looking for a man named Myers," McGuire said, approaching her desk. "Ross Randolph Myers. I was told I could find him here."

"You could have yesterday," the woman said. She resumed writing. "Mr. Myers is on his way to South Carolina, delivering a boat to a client."

"When will he be back?"

"In about three days, maybe."

"Why maybe?"

She stared at him like a parent deciding how to respond to an insolent child. "Because," she spoke very slowly, measuring each syllable, "he may continue on to Fort Lauderdale to look at some boats for sale down there."

"And if he does?"

"I wouldn't expect him back for at least a week." She continued staring at him, and McGuire noticed she was slightly cross-eyed. Her manner remained somewhere between aloof and irritated. "Who should I tell him called?"

"Where does he live?"

"I'm sorry." Her voice belied her words. "We cannot release personal information about our staff without their permission."

"But he lives around here? Somewhere in this vicinity?"

"He works here. He shows up here every day when he's not on a buying or selling trip. So I guess you can assume he lives in the area."

Lifting his eyes to the windows behind her, where several dozen boats were anchored, McGuire said: "What's one of these toys cost?"

She smiled without amusement. "Are you in the market?"

"No, I'm just curious."

"If you have to ask . . ."

"It means I just want to know," McGuire interrupted. "That's all."

"The cheapest thing out there is twenty thousand dollars," she said. "I wouldn't trust it in water deeper than a bathtub. If you want a real boat, you'll have to spend at least fifty."

McGuire nodded. "And they're all used."

She handed McGuire a sheet of paper. "Here are our most recent listings. If you see anything that interests you, perhaps I could have Mr. Myers call you. When he gets back."

"Do you have one of his business cards?" McGuire asked.

"No, they're on order. But you can have one of mine." She handed him a card bearing her name in gilt lettering suspended over a color photograph of a sailboat silhouetted against a setting sun. Mrs. Christine Diamond, Sales Administration.

McGuire studied the list of boats for sale. The terms and descriptions meant nothing to him. The prices, most in six figures, were astonishing. He set the list back on her desk and pocketed the business card. "Thanks," he said. "Maybe I'll just stick to bungee jumping."

Outside, he started the car and glanced up to see the woman standing at the window watching him, her arms folded across her chest. McGuire smiled, waved in an exaggerated manner, and pulled away.

He found three R. Myerses listed in the telephone book, and called them all. He reached two answering machines. One message was a woman's voice; the other included the voices of two young children welcoming callers to the Myers Machine. The third call was answered by a human voice, an elderly woman who asked McGuire to repeat everything he said and told him she had never heard of anyone named Ross Randolph Myers.

McGuire drove to the Annapolis police station. "I'm looking for someone named Ross Randolph Myers," he told the duty officer. "Is that name known to you people? I hear he has a criminal record, and I thought he might be on your watch list."

The young officer grinned at him. "Watch list? Are you a police officer?"

"Used to be," McGuire smiled. "Doing a little private investigation. Just wondered if it rang a bell around here."

The cop leaned into a corridor and spoke to someone out of sight. "Don't have anything on him," he said when he turned back. "If he's here, he's keeping his nose clean."

McGuire nodded and left.

He sat in the sun at a dockside café, watching yachts enter and leave the harbor. The weather in Annapolis was warm and the air was soft, summerlike. He pictured himself living aboard a yacht, and chose the one that might suit him best. It was a child's game, like pressing your nose against a bicycle shop when you are six years old and you know that all the chrome and rubber and color inside will never be yours, not while you are young enough to be intoxicated by the sheer joy of owning it, but you look nevertheless, and you dream. He dreamed his way through two long beers.

A Holiday Inn on the edge of town provided a room for the night, and after checking in, he drove to the jazz club in the basement of the Maryland Inn, where the crab cakes were bland but the trio, led by a middle-aged jazz guitarist, was hot. McGuire sat through two sets and three more bottles of beer.

When he left the Maryland Inn he walked along State House Circle and entered the Academy Bar. Patrons were standing three deep along the bar area, and others, most of them St. John's College students, were seated at every table. McGuire was standing in the doorway, letting his eyes grow accustomed to the light, when a waitress with shoulder-length brown hair scurried by, a tray of sandwiches on her shoulder. Their eyes locked for an instant, long enough for each to recognize the other, and the woman became so flustered she almost dropped the tray.

McGuire was embarrassed at his voyeurism, his curiosity to see the woman as someone other than the pornographic actress she appeared to be a few hours ago, on the floor beneath the man with the shaved head. He edged his way through the crowd until he reached the cash register, where a man stood, alternately making change for the three waitresses and scanning the faces of the students, prepared to demand identification.

"You run this place?" McGuire shouted at him above the talk, laughter, and atrocious music.

"What?" The man tilted his head towards McGuire and looked at the floor, his mouth open.

"I said, do you run this place?"

The man straightened up. "Try to."

"You know a guy named Ross Myers?"

"What about him?"

"Know where he is?"

"In jail, I hope. I ran the son of a bitch out of here."

"Was he a problem?"

"Just your average class-A jerk. You're not a buddy of his, are you?"

"Not a chance. I hear he got himself a job selling yachts."

The man snorted. "Stealing them probably."

"How about a guy named Rollie Wade?"

"How do you know Rollie?"

"Met him here this morning. Know where I can find him?"

"Rollie? I dunno. At home, I guess, or maybe out on the water somewhere."

"Rollie's a good guy?"

"Sure. Known Rollie for years." The man looked at McGuire and frowned. "Who the hell are you?"

"Just a guy looking for Myers. I went to the yacht brokerage where he's supposed to be working, but I was told he's on his way to South Carolina, maybe Florida."

The man took a credit card from a waitress and began processing it. "Yeah, well if he's smart he'll stay there. He comes back here, I'll have his ass kicked into the bay."

"What'd he do to you?"

"Same thing he's done to everybody else he meets. Scams, lies. The guy's scum."

McGuire watched the man in silence for another moment, then thanked him and drove back to the motel room in the fading light.

There was a flight to Boston in the morning. He planned to be on it.

Ronnie was shopping when McGuire arrived in Revere Beach before noon on Saturday. Ollie was too drowsy from the medication he took for his kidney infection to talk, so McGuire read a book, walked on the beach, had a cheeseburger and beer in a sports bar, and returned home to find Ronnie watching an old movie she had rented. A gin and orange juice was gripped in one hand. She nodded to him and returned her attention to the screen, where Cary Grant and Audrey Hepburn were having dinner aboard a tour boat cruising the Seine.

"*Charade*," McGuire said after watching the screen for a moment. "Audrey Hepburn's rich husband was murdered and a bunch of people are trying to get their hands on his money, right?"

"Yes," Ronnie said.

"Cary Grant, James Coburn, George Kennedy . . . and Walter Matthau."

"Yes."

"Good movie."

Ronnie said nothing. Henry Mancini's music played in the background. Audrey Hepburn's face was bathed in candlelight.

McGuire looked down to see tears on Ronnie's cheeks. "A bad time?" he asked.

"Yes."

He knelt next to her. "Do you want to talk?"

She shook her head. He touched her on the shoulder, then climbed the stairs to his room.

He took a bath, read some of his book, changed his clothes, and came downstairs just after seven. "You ready for that talk?" he asked as he helped Ronnie put away clean dishes.

She gave him one of her shining smiles. "What talk?" she asked. Then she stepped towards him and kissed him on the cheek. "You're sweet. But I don't need a talk now. Thanks anyway."

"I'm having dinner tonight," he said. "And not with Wally Sleeman."

"Lucky you," she said.

In the car he looked back at the house to see Ronnie silhouetted in the window, waiting for him to leave.

CHAPTER 8

Lorna's apartment on Park Drive was near a Mexican restaurant McGuire recalled visiting with his first wife. The city was like that: scattered with monuments to McGuire's past lives, a cemetery of memories.

She greeted him dressed in a crimson silk blouse beneath a dark jacket and skirt. Her makeup was heavier than before, and her hair was swept back dramatically from her face. She reached to kiss him on the cheek before he helped put her coat on.

In the car she asked how his trip had been and McGuire said it was disappointing, the man he had been sent to find was somewhere on the ocean, sailing a yacht to South Carolina. Lorna spoke of the weather, and of the difficulty of finding good shoes at a reasonable price. McGuire tried to remain interested and to avoid wondering how many times Ronnie had been drinking alone and seething with bitterness. He couldn't remember her drinking alone before. He had difficulty remembering her bitter.

Seated in the dining room, Lorna toyed with an oversized earring and looked up at the vaulted ceiling. "It hasn't changed a bit." She dropped her hand from her ear and smiled at McGuire. "Thank you for bringing me here," she said. "It's perfect."

To McGuire's surprise he grew relaxed and began to enjoy himself. When she reached to touch his hand, he smiled at her and she tightened her grip.

In recent years, McGuire had found himself performing small gestures and making provocative comments to women, gauging their impact in advance and surprised at their success, like a musician who grows astonished at his own abilities in the middle of a concert performance. He told himself it was not manipulative but simply a new awareness of a talent he had developed through his adult life, and now used with greater skill than before.

"You are a woman's man trying to be a man's man," a former lover once told him. He recalled three dinners with her and two nights in her bed, and she had described him that way on their second evening together. She did not know it would be their final evening together. Nor, McGuire honestly believed, did he. He remembered her as a pleasant, insightful, and realistic woman who regarded their sexual adventures as little more than a passage in their private lives, and he was grateful when she accepted its ending – more abrupt and perhaps colder than McGuire intended – with grace and resignation. "You know how to do everything a woman likes," she told him on that last night together. "And I don't mean in bed. You listen. You try to understand. You seem to feel what a woman tells you. Do you know how few men can do that?"

When he was alone, McGuire missed the company of a woman as a companion, someone to provide strength where he was weak. Yet often he felt disappointed and guilty when he admitted to himself, usually very early in the relationship, that his attraction to some new woman would not grow into the permanent comfort he knew he was seeking, and had been seeking since he was a young man, that it was simply a diversion from some destination he was not certain he would ever reach.

He could no longer identify the destination. As the years passed, he recognized that the only deep-seated and sustained fear he had ever experienced was the fear of growing old alone.

Lorna ordered Dover sole and salad. McGuire chose scallops and rice. They shared a bottle of Portuguese wine, at Lorna's suggestion. "It's the only nice memory I have of a trip I took there," she said. "I love to travel." She lifted the glass to her lips, her eyes fixed on his. "You?"

McGuire told her he enjoyed traveling, but as he got older he lost his enthusiasm for traveling alone.

"I know," she said. "I hate it too. And traveling with girlfriends just isn't the same."

McGuire asked why she had bad memories of Portugal.

She smiled and shrugged. "I went there with a man I was supposed to marry. The one who was going to run a bed and breakfast with me in Cape Ann." She sipped her wine and looked around the room as though she had just entered it. "I've given up hope of getting married again," she said. "I mean, there are so few men who are worth marrying."

McGuire had heard this observation before, from almost every woman he had dated in the past few years. "It's a candy store out there," Wally Sleeman had told him over a beer at Zoot's one day. Sleeman and his wife of twenty-three years had separated six months earlier and Sleeman had shown no regret, no despondency at all. "Women our age these days, they're gettin' desperate. Things start hangin' funny on 'em and they figure the next boink they get could be their last. So you treat 'em like a lady and they think you're Prince Charles, for Christ's sake. Buy 'em a good dinner, don't stare too much at their tits, open the car door for 'em, and next thing you know they're draggin' you by the dick to the bedroom. What the hell's a guy our age in this town wanta get married for? It'd be like buyin' a cow when you're livin' in a dairy."

In the car on the way back to her apartment, Lorna laughed at his comments on Boston traffic. He listened to her tales of office politics, and how difficult they were for her to handle. She invited him upstairs for a coffee. In the small, brass elevator, when their hands touched, she seized his and held on.

Inside her small apartment he helped her off with her coat, and after she hung it in the closet she took his, then turned to him and said, "Thank you for a wonderful dinner and a splendid evening." She stood on her toes to kiss him, and when the kiss continued he began to probe with his tongue until he felt her lips part and he told himself, Yes, here we go, and No, I'll be damned if I'll feel anything but good tonight and tomorrow.

"I don't know if I want to," she said when she pulled away, studying his face. "I mean, I *want* to but . . ."

"You need to know if I would see you again," McGuire said.

"Something like that. See me, you know, as a person, as somebody to have dinner and spend time with. Not just as . . ."

"I'm not like that," McGuire said.

She smiled. "I know you're not. I could tell. But some men are . . ."

"I'm not some men."

"You want a drink?" she asked. She looked up at him from the crook of his arm, where her head rested. It was an hour later.

McGuire said No.

"You gonna stay the night? You can if you want. I'll make us an early breakfast. What do you like?"

"Orange juice. Coffee. Toast."

"That's easy."

"Scrambled eggs. Crisp bacon. Home fries."

"Okay."

"Smoked salmon. Eggs Benedict. Honeydew melon."

"Hey!" She began to laugh.

"Chicken à la king. Hot croissants . . ."

"Stop it!" Laughing, she pushed against him and raised herself above him, smiling before lowering herself again.

"Is this a permanent job at Zimmerman?" she asked.

McGuire listened to a pendulum clock strike midnight somewhere in the apartment. Beyond the bedroom window a tree branch waved across a streetlight, flashes of white shimmering on the wall. McGuire sank lower into the bed, enjoying the snugness, familiarizing himself with new surroundings, new views, new intimacies. He wondered if women knew the extent of the gift they offered by inviting a man into their bed. "I don't know," he replied to her question. "Why?"

"Because Orin said you were kind of like a hired gun, and nobody was sure how long you'd be sticking around."

McGuire shifted his hips towards her. "I don't know how long I'll stay. As long as Pinnington wants me, I guess. How's Orin to work with?"

She snuggled against him. "Like I said, Orin's a nice man. He can get a bit weird at times, but that's only because he's so old-fashioned and straight. Actually it's kind of refreshing."

McGuire looked down at her. She was tracing circles on his chest with one finger. "How old-fashioned is he?"

"Well, he'd be shocked to hear about us. You and me in bed together, I mean." She laughed, her finger still drawing circles. "I'm kind of surprised myself, tell the truth. Anyway, Orin and Nancy, that's his wife, they've been married thirty-five years. I know because Nancy came to meet him one night after work, couple of months ago, and they went out for dinner on their anniversary. Nancy is so sweet, a lovely woman. He calls her every day. He worries about her, she worries about him. She'll call and ask me if he's been working too hard, if he's had lunch, stuff like that. Maybe it's because of what happened to their daughter."

"What was that?"

"I don't know all the details, but apparently she was in college, Boston University, doing well, until she dropped out to marry some truck-driver or something. Broke Orin's heart. He and Nancy, they couldn't believe it, this guy could hardly put two words together and she drops out of college to marry him. She ruined her life, living with this guy out on Dorchester, and then one day, they were only married a few months but he'd already beat her up some, and he ups and kills her. Beat her so badly that she went into a coma and didn't come out of it. That was nearly fifteen years ago. Orin and Nancy, they never got over it. Connie Woodson, Mister Pinnington's secretary, she told me about it. You meet her?" She looked up at him.

McGuire nodded.

"Anyway, Connie said their daughter, Orin and Nancy's, was their only child. Thing like that happens, it either wrecks the marriage or makes it stronger. Guess it made Orin's stronger. And it's kind of ironic, you know, because Orin's specialty is custody stuff, making sure kids get to be with good parents, so it's really bizarre that no matter how hard he and his wife tried, they couldn't save their own kid, you know? Isn't that ironic?"

McGuire agreed it was.

"You got any kids?"

McGuire said No.

"I tell you about mine?"

"You said you had two." The clock still ticked, the shadows of the branches still moved across the wall.

"Boy and a girl. My son lives in Nevada, deals blackjack in a casino. Not Las Vegas, a small town in the north, you probably never heard of it. My daughter's out on the Cape, works in a restaurant there. I wanted both of them to go to college and get a degree, something I never had a chance to get. They had their chance and they blew it. But I still love them. You can't stop loving your flesh and blood just because they disappoint you, right?"

"What makes you sure Flanigan's so faithful to his wife?" McGuire said.

"I told you. He loves her. You can see it when the two of them are together. But you know, all lawyers are a little weird, I think."

"Even Orin?"

"Oh, sure."

"He sounds like such a straight arrow to me. What makes him weird?"

"Well." She studied the ceiling as though looking for her next words. "I don't need to know what you were doing down there in Annapolis. First thing you learn in a law firm is not to ask questions. But remember the woman waiting to see Orin when you and I went for lunch the other day?"

McGuire remembered her. The delicate features. The wide eyes. The slender figure. "Yes," he said.

"I think she has something to do with your going there."

McGuire was not surprised. "She's a client?"

"I don't know what she is. But she's definitely some kind of strange. Orin gets different when she's around. Kind of nervous. He rushes her in and out, never tells me anything about her. Doesn't even have a file or a docket on her, not one that I know about anyway. All I know is her name's Susan something. Schaeffer, Susan Schaeffer. She started showing up about a month ago. Comes in practically every noon hour to see him, except when he's in court."

"She only shows up at noon?"

"Uh-huh. Sometimes she brings lunch for her and Orin, in a paper bag." Lorna tilted her head to look up at him. "Do you think she's attractive?"

"Never thought about it," McGuire lied.

"Well she is, but she's just about the saddest person you'll ever meet."

"Orin seemed glad to see her the other day."

"Yeah, like I say, it's strange." Lorna was concentrating on McGuire's chest again, twirling the hairs with her finger. "One day last week, I came into his office, I didn't even know they were in there, and the two of them were hugging each other and crying like babies."

"But you don't think Orin's fooling around."

"No, but maybe he wants to. Or maybe not. He told me once that she reminds him of his daughter, so maybe that's all it is. Who knows?" She sat up and stretched her arms above her head. "Sure you don't want that drink now?"

He reached to touch her back, stroking the skin with his fingertips, and she lowered her arms and turned to face him, cupping her breasts in her hands again as though lifting them to where they had been twenty years earlier, and the gesture both excited and saddened him.

He woke in the morning to see her watching him. She was seated on the edge of the bed, wrapped in a cheap robe embroidered with oriental scenes: Mount Fuji, a golden pagoda, and thin men pulling laughing women in rickshaws. He had been dreaming of something. The aroma of coffee had been in his dreams, and now it was in his nostrils. He turned his head to see coffee steaming from two porcelain cups on a silver tray, flanked by glasses of orange juice and a plate of toast.

"We're all out of eggs Benedict," she said.

An hour later he kissed her at the door before walking through the gray morning to his car, waving at her as she stood at the apartment window, where she promised she would be watching him, and waving again as he drove past. He felt good about himself, and he looked forward to seeing her again, to feeling himself enclosed in her body.

Ronnie was seated at the kitchen table, the Sunday paper opened in front of her, one hand wrapped around a mug of coffee. But instead of reading the newspaper, she was staring straight ahead, through the window that faced north, her focus somewhere beyond Maine.

"Hey," McGuire said. He bent from the waist to smile into her eyes. "You okay?"

She smiled and nodded. "Sure. And I can tell you are."

McGuire shrugged.

"What's she like?"

"Who?" But he knew.

"Your new girlfriend."

"She's nice." He wished he had a photograph.

"She wear you out?" There was no humor in the question, no sense of teasing, nor even interest. It was designed to needle, to hurt perhaps.

"What kind of question is that?" McGuire's smile faded and he remembered the strong gin and orange juice, the surprise at her unaccustomed anger, and her tears that flowed because of scenes from a forty-year-old romantic movie.

"Just wondering." She folded her hands in front of her and he felt her relax, felt her genuine concern for him. "I'm happy for you," she said. "Honest. You want some breakfast?"

"Already ate." He glanced at the clock. "Ollie awake?"

"Not yet." She stood and carried her coffee mug to the sink.

"Told him I'd watch the football game with him this afternoon. Want to give me a shout when he's ready?"

"Sure." She stood at the sink, staring down into it. "I'll shout my lungs out."

McGuire walked to her and rested his hands on her shoulders. "I guess sometimes it gets to be too much."

She nodded.

"Anything I can do?"

She turned her head. Her face was wet and her eyes were swollen. "I wish," she said. "I wish there was."

"Tell me."

"Okay." She wiped her eyes with the back of her hands. "I'm a woman who is turning fifty this year, with a husband who can move his head and one hand, and a dead baby who's been lying in his grave for thirty years." She held her chin up, in defiance or perhaps just to keep the tears from flowing. McGuire didn't know which. "Fix it," she said.

"I can't," McGuire said.

"I know." She turned away. "Go upstairs and get some sleep. You look like you can use it."

CHAPTER 9

For all of his confidence and independence, McGuire was as subject as anyone to the flattery of knowing he was needed by someone he needed in turn, however shallow the need might be. Had he been younger, or the same age but less cynical, he might have told himself it was love. McGuire did not tell himself it was love, because he knew it wasn't. But it was pleasurable nevertheless.

On Monday morning he dressed in a sweater, slacks, and jacket, and slipped into a pair of moccasin-styled loafers. He poured himself a cup of coffee and carried it to Ollie's room, where Ronnie was feeding her husband.

"Hear you took my advice," Ollie said between spoonfuls of something that looked to McGuire like gruel. "Got yourself a warm squeeze."

"Promise to watch your language, I might bring her around and introduce you," McGuire said.

"That'd be nice, Joseph." Ollie made a slight motion of his head. "That'd be real nice of you."

"Catch you later," McGuire said. He walked to the door. "Don't count on me for dinner."

Ronnie raised the spoon and moved it towards Ollie's mouth, never acknowledging McGuire's presence.

Lorna Robbins smiled up at McGuire, twirling a yellow pencil in one hand. McGuire had called Flanigan's number as soon as he arrived, and Lorna told him to come straight up. "He's on the phone now. Told me to send you up as soon as you called." She beckoned him towards her.

McGuire leaned over her desk, absorbing her perfume.

"I thought about you all night," she said in a stage whisper. "And all the way to work this morning."

McGuire reached for her hand just as the door behind her opened. Orin Flanigan stood smiling at McGuire, one hand fingering the bottom of his tie. McGuire squeezed Lorna's hand before releasing it. He strode into Flanigan's office and chose the same leather chair he had sat in before, while Flanigan closed the door.

"Coffee?" Flanigan said. He paused halfway across his office to his desk. "I can ask Lorna to make us some . . ."

"You're a busy guy," McGuire said. "What I've got will only take a couple of minutes. So maybe we'd better skip the coffee."

Flanigan settled himself behind his desk, and made a tent with his hands. "What did you find out?" he asked. He spoke in a low voice, as though there were someone in the room, eavesdropping.

"Myers apparently works as a salesman at a place called Bay Ridge Yacht Brokers in Annapolis," McGuire said. He handed Flanigan the business card given him by the woman at the yacht brokerage. "There's the address. I'm guessing he hasn't been employed long. They're still waiting for his business cards."

Flanigan studied the card and frowned. "Who's Christine Diamond?"

"Another salesperson. She told me Myers was delivering a yacht to South Carolina and might go on to Florida from there. He could be gone a week or more."

Flanigan's eyes shot up to meet McGuire's. "You never met him?"

"Wouldn't matter much if I had. Your description was pretty broad, and I couldn't get Berkeley Street to give me a mug shot. But I got a pretty positive ID from a guy named Wade who seems to be a buddy of the owner of the Academy Bar. Myers has a bad rep all over town, from what I understand. They won't let him in the bar any more."

"Find out where he lives?"

"Hard to say. The police have nothing on him. I checked the listings for an R. Myers in the telephone book. There were three. None of them sounded like him, but I can do a more thorough investigation if you want."

"What would that involve?"

McGuire shrugged. "Staking out the addresses. Talking to neighbors. Figure on two or three days down there. And if that's the case, you're probably better off hiring a local private investigator. They'll do a better job than me, and for less money."

Flanigan gave the idea some thought. "Did you learn anything about him?"

"He seems to be doing the same thing down there he did here. Both guys at the Academy Bar confirmed he's got a reputation for living high, not paying his bills."

"Was he alone on the boat? The one he was sailing to South Carolina?"

"No idea. Would that be important?"

"It might." The lawyer's mind was in a distant place. "What did this woman look like, this Mrs. Diamond?"

"Dark. Attractive."

"Married?"

"It says she is on the card."

Flanigan looked at the card again.

"Would it help if I knew what this was all about?" McGuire asked.

"Not really." Flanigan opened a desk drawer and placed the business card inside, then closed and locked it. "Thank you," he said. "Thank you for this. You really are good at what you do. Very good. What's Annapolis like, by the way? Haven't been there in years."

"Nice town, if you like boats and seafood."

Flanigan nodded without listening. "And this Diamond woman again? What was your impression of her?"

"Bit of a snob. Or maybe just protective of Myers."

"Wealthy?"

"Couldn't tell."

"Fashionably dressed?"

"I suppose so."

McGuire anticipated more questions. "Short dark hair, brown eyes, slim, maybe five-foot-six. Bit of an attitude, like I said." He waited while Flanigan absorbed the description. "I thought you wanted me to look for Myers."

"I did, I did." Flanigan appeared to come out of some sort of reverie. "Thank you again. Send Lorna in to see me when you leave, will you?"

McGuire spent the rest of the morning reading documents being circulated through the law office, interoffice memos on topics he knew nothing about. Lorna called mid-morning to say she wouldn't be going out for lunch, she was busy with some details that Flanigan needed settling. "Can you come for dinner tonight?" she asked. "I want to show off my cooking talents."

McGuire said he'd be there with a bottle of wine.

At lunch he wandered through Quincy Market, ate a sandwich at a deli, scanned a newspaper, and returned to the lobby, where he waited for an elevator. He was asking himself why he should stay around for the rest of the day with nothing to do, thinking he would rather sit at the bar at Zoot's and absorb the patter of hustlers and off-duty cops who gathered in the neutral zone of the bar to rib each other and tell lies and trade stories. The elevator doors opened and McGuire, his head down and his mind still in Zoot's, stepped forward and collided with something warm, soft, and sweet-smelling.

"I'm sorry," the woman said before McGuire could respond. "Are you all right?"

She seemed concerned that she might have injured him, even though McGuire was almost a head taller. Her hair was the color of pulled taffy and sunshine and high clouds, and her eyes were green. She does look a little like the picture on Flanigan's credenza, McGuire realized. Around the eyes. "It's okay," McGuire said. "I'm fine."

"I'm sorry," the woman repeated. She looked at him again and something changed in her expression. Then she turned and walked away and across the lobby, clenching her purse in both hands, her shoes making a click-click sound on the marble.

Flanigan's noon-hour friend, McGuire realized as he stepped into the elevator. Flanigan's very attractive, very nervous noon-hour friend.

"Where the hell's Ronnie?" McGuire asked when he discovered Ollie alone in the house on Revere Beach late that afternoon.

"At her painting class." Ollie was watching the early television news, another mélange of disasters and imminent crises.

"Again?" McGuire tossed his jacket on a side chair.

"It's some sort of extra session, working with real models or something in natural light, I don't know. Besides, she loves it. And she's good at it. Leastwise, I think she is. What a mess in India, eh?"

"How do you feel about it?"

"I figure that's what happens when you pay more attention to cows than people."

"Not India, doorknob. I mean about Ronnie being away so much."

Ollie fastened his eyes to McGuire's. "Hey, she earned it. You've only been living here a few months but that woman's been building her life around me for years. So if she wants to play Picasso for a while, that's okay with me."

"I'm having dinner at Lorna's place," McGuire said. "You want me to fix you something before I go?"

"Naw," Ollie said, returning his attention to the television screen. "Ronnie'll feed me later. Lorna, huh? She's the woman put a knot in your drawers?"

"I'm going up to change," McGuire said. "I may not be home tonight."

"Whoa, we got ourselves a live one this time, have we?" Ollie said to McGuire's back.

Instead of climbing the stairs, McGuire walked to the hall closet. Open it and you're a jerk, he told himself. He opened the closet door.

Inside, on the floor, were two pairs of Ronnie's winter boots, a dust pan, an umbrella with the tip of its handle carved into a dog's head that McGuire had given Ronnie as a Christmas present last year, and Ronnie's wooden paint case.

Lorna greeted him at her door wearing her patterned crimson robe. Something bubbled on the kitchen stove, and aromas of garlic, butter, and onions flooded the apartment.

"How hungry are you?" she asked after kissing him and closing the door, her back pressed against it.

"A little," he said. "Why?"

"Cause dinner'll wait. But I can't." She opened the robe, revealing a black lace bra, narrow-cut panties, and black net stockings held in place with a garter belt.

They ate an hour later, spinach linguini in garlic butter sauce and a green salad, Lorna watching him over every morsel of food.

On the sofa, Lorna snuggled against him, and as they shared the last of the wine McGuire had brought, he asked about Orin Flanigan.

"He's going somewhere. He didn't have much scheduled for the next couple of days, and he starts a big court case next week. So he told me he wouldn't be in tomorrow or the next day. 'There's something I want to do,' is all he said. 'Better to do it sooner rather than later,' he told me. I don't know what's up, but it has to do with that trip you took."

"Was Susan Schaeffer in to see him at noon?"

"Yeah. Everything was on hold until then. I mean, he didn't make any decisions until she left. That's when he said he wouldn't be in tomorrow or the next day either."

"Where's he going?"

"He didn't say. I asked where I could reach him, and he told me it wasn't important. If something came up I could always call Nancy. His wife." She twisted in his arms to look up at him. "Let's go back to bed."

He didn't bother returning to Revere Beach the following morning because, he told himself, it wasn't necessary, even while admitting the real reason: because he didn't want to confront Ronnie. Not today. Not yet. He drove Lorna to State Street, where she left the car after blowing him a kiss. Then he parked three blocks away and walked back to the office alone.

McGuire still didn't fully understand the difference between staff lawyers and full partners, except that full partners seemed to earn more money and occupy larger offices. Nor did he care, when he entered his office to discover a handwritten note on his desk from a staff lawyer named Barry Cassidy.

During McGuire's introductory tour of the law firm's offices, it had been Cassidy who fired questions at him as though cross-examining a hostile witness, asking about McGuire's trial experience, investigative procedures, and educational background. Before cutting him off with a suggestion that the lawyer check with Pinnington, McGuire had replied with broad answers and an amused and tolerant expression. At the time, he considered Cassidy to be just another tight-assed ambitious young man, whose cocky, formal manner indicated he was blessed with more ambition than talent, and was more afraid of failure than he was confident of success.

There was another noticeable thing about the lawyer: He was so light-skinned and fair-haired that he appeared almost albino. His face was boyish rather than handsome, the whole effect made somewhat comical by a blond mustache, so fair and thick it reminded McGuire of yellow caterpillars he had seen as a child.

McGuire recalled that first meeting with distaste, a feeling that intensified as he read Cassidy's note.

I was here to see you at eight-thirty a.m., the note said. No one seemed to know where you were, and I have an urgent matter to discuss with you. Call me at extension 8162 the minute you arrive. By the way, most senior staff members begin their day here at eight.

By the way, how would you like to slide down a razor-blade banister? McGuire replied silently. He rolled the note into a ball, tossed it into the wastebasket, and dialed Cassidy's extension.

"I need to make use of your services," the young lawyer said stiffly, "on behalf of a client. Could we convene this morning?"

Convene? McGuire thought to himself. Who the hell says "convene" instead of "meet"? "Sure," he said. "What time to you want to, uh, convene?"

There was a short pause as though the other man were weighing McGuire's sarcasm. "I'll expect you here at eleven," he said.

Two hours later, after McGuire finished a pot of coffee and the morning paper, he was sitting across from Cassidy, whose every gesture seemed to be a measure of his self-importance. He pulled at his shirt cuffs until an equal length was exposed on each arm of his suit jacket, checked the knot of his tie, and displayed his teeth, before passing a small stack of paper across his desk to McGuire.

"Here is a summary of the case, prepared for your eyes only," Cassidy said. "After you've read it, I'll answer any questions you may have."

"Tell me about it," McGuire said, not moving his eyes from the lawyer's.

Cassidy blinked. "It's in the memo."

"I'll read the memo later. Tell me in your own words. Off the top of your head."

Cassidy made a strange movement, thrusting his chin forward and tilting his head at the same time. He breathed in, exhaled noisily, and began to speak. "Our client is a supplier of electronics parts. Their largest customer recently declared bankruptcy without any previous hint of trouble, while indebted to our client for almost three million dollars. Our client suspects criminal fraud, including the transfer of substantial sums of money out of the country. We would like to know a little more about the firm's actions, whether they appear to have engaged in criminal activity, that sort of thing." The lawyer made the same unusual motion with his head again and stared at McGuire.

"That's it?" McGuire said.

"Those are essentially the facts. You spent a few years on the fraud squad, I believe? Before becoming a homicide detective?"

McGuire grunted and picked up the stack of paper from Cassidy's desk. "It took you this much paper to tell me about a two-bit possible fraud case?"

Cassidy flashed a mocking grin. "I have given you a comprehensive appraisal," he said. "There is a good deal of work in that document."

McGuire stood up, still holding the papers. "At three hundred bucks an hour, right?" he said. "When do you want an opinion?"

"First, I'll require an estimate of your time," Cassidy said. Before McGuire could speak, he added, "And I expect daily summaries of your findings, plus a copy of a non-disclosure agreement . . ."

"A what?" McGuire said.

". . . signed by you and notarized by a partner of the firm . . ."

"Wait a minute, wait a minute . . ."

". . . as a condition of you accepting . . ."

"*Wait a goddamn minute!*" McGuire shouted.

Cassidy sat back, his well-manicured hands gripping the arms of the chair as though it were about to soar into flight.

"What's this non-disclosure crap?" McGuire said.

"It's my policy whenever I contract for services on behalf of clients." Cassidy repeated the motion, stretching his neck and tilting his head, and McGuire recognized it as a nervous gesture.

"If I say something'll be kept confidential, that's all you need."

"It's merely a formality." Cassidy was attempting to look angry, but his eyes, shifting from side to side, revealed more unease than outrage.

"Well, to hell with formality," McGuire said.

"Look, McGuire, if I have to talk to Pinnington . . ." Cassidy began.

McGuire tossed Cassidy's memo into the air and the sheets of paper fluttered down around the lawyer like oversized snowflakes. "When you're talking to him, be sure to say I threatened to roll your memo into a ball and make you eat the goddamn thing," McGuire said.

"You're insane," Cassidy said, rising from his chair. "You are certifiably crazy."

No, McGuire answered silently, turning to leave the office.

I've discovered that my best friend's wife is about to kill her husband. By sleeping with another man.

"You certainly put young Cassidy's shirt in a knot."

Richard Pinnington was leaning against McGuire's doorframe, grinning down at him. It was half an hour later, and McGuire had just placed another call to Wally Sleeman, leaving a message on the detective's voice mail system.

"I don't appreciate being asked to sign a non-disclosure agreement," McGuire said. He set aside the magazine he had been reading. "I consider it an insult."

"Barry considers it prudent." Pinnington's grin widened. "Do me a favor. Read the document he put together. Take the assignment. Get him off my back."

"Don't you run this show?"

Pinnington nodded. "I try to. Trouble is, once I lay down the rules, the young hotshots wait around for me to break them so they can climb on their morality horse. I try saying Damn it, do as I say, not as I do, but that doesn't work very well these days. So just take the assignment, let him think he's a hero, and we'll all go with the flow, okay?" He turned to leave.

"Dick," McGuire said.

Pinnington turned to stare at him.

"I'm not signing his non-disclosure form. I mean it."

Pinnington raised his eyebrows and shrugged. "So I'll tell him you signed a blanket agreement with the firm, covers everything."

"He'll ask you about it."

"Probably. And I'll tell him to haul his ass back to work." The smile resurfaced. "That's what you get to do when you run the show."

Within a half hour, a copy of Cassidy's long-winded and badly written memo arrived on McGuire's desk with Richard Pinnington's business card attached by a paper clip.

That night, two middle-aged men left a Thai restaurant on Kenmore Square, near Fenway Park. They were old friends, in town for an industrial marketing meeting hosted by an energy-supply firm. They had dined on lemongrass chicken and noodles while trying to outdo each other with stories of each employer's downsizing plans. One, the taller and older man, was from Columbus. The other, shorter but with a trim, athletic body, had arrived that afternoon from Richmond.

It was almost midnight when they stood squinting into the darkness outside the restaurant. One suggested they find a cab, but the other said it was a fine night, so why not walk back, get some exercise? They would be sitting on their asses inside the hotel for the next two days. All they had to do was find Boylston Street and follow it back to their hotel. The two men turned down a street flanking Fenway Park.

Ahead of them, a black youth stepped out of an alley on Ipswich Street. The taller man from Columbus was explaining the economic advantages of peak-shaving high electric rates with supplementary power. The shorter man from Columbus wasn't listening. He saw the dark pistol in the youth's hand. He stopped and held an arm in front of his friend, who saw the pistol as well.

"Your wallets," said Freeman Hayhurst. "Gimme your wallets."

"All right, okay," the taller man said. His wallet was inside his jacket. He withdrew it and handed it to Hayhurst.

The smaller man stood unmoving.

"Where's yours?" Hayhurst said.

The smaller man, from Richmond, remained motionless. He was memorizing Hayhurst's features, the tone of his voice, his size and age and weight. He would file it in his memory and play it back to the investigating officers. He would not let scum like this hopped-up black kid get away with terrorizing honest people walking the streets.

Hayhurst shot him twice, once in the neck, which opened a torrent of blood from a severed artery, and once in the chest.

The taller man stood frozen, unbelieving, while the body of the man from Richmond jerked in dying spasms at his feet. There had been no warning, no reason. This was a mistake, a joke. "Why?" he said, and Hayhurst shot him as well, three pulls of the trigger with the pistol barely an arm's length from the man's stomach.

CHAPTER 10

Sleeman was unavailable to McGuire the next morning. At lunch, Lorna glowed with excitement, like a child with a new doll, and he admitted that her joy added to her attractiveness. "You look good," he said. "No, you look great."

"You look good too," she said. "Maybe a little tense. Or nervous. Am I making you nervous?"

"It's not you. And it's not nerves. It's Cassidy."

She wrinkled her nose at the mention of his name and called him an arrogant snob.

McGuire agreed, but he knew it was more than Cassidy. He could handle bedbugs like Cassidy. He couldn't handle what he suspected, what he believed he *knew*, about Ronnie Schantz. And he couldn't eradicate the image of the woman who visited Orin Flanigan at noon hour, the woman whose eyes were those of a frightened animal when they met McGuire's at the elevator. He wanted to know what was behind the fright in those eyes.

"Don't let Cassidy get to you," Lorna said during lunch. "He's getting to you, isn't he? I can see it."

Damn it, I like this woman, McGuire admitted to himself. He liked the way Lorna gave him her total attention when he spoke. He liked the way she rested her hand on his when she did the talking. He liked the look of her, walking ahead of him as they left the restaurant, and the little-girl excitement that made her voice sound as though it were always teetering on the edge of laughter.

In his office, he placed another call to Sleeman, only to hear his voice mail again.

At three o'clock he called Lorna and told her he was going to Revere Beach.

"Have a nap," she said. "Rest up."

Ollie and Ronnie's house smelled of coffee and furniture wax. He found Ronnie in the living room, wearing a pink jogging suit, a bandanna knotted around her head. She looked up from polishing an oak end table. "I know I shouldn't bother, but I was getting worried about you," she said. Her voice was flat, distant, a little melancholy.

"That's funny." McGuire sank into an armchair. "I was getting worried about *you*."

"Me?" Ronnie returned to polishing the furniture. "Nothing to worry about where I'm concerned."

"What are you up to?" McGuire kept his voice low.

"I'm up to polishing the furniture."

"Is Ollie sleeping?"

She nodded. "He didn't have a very good night."

"Did you?"

This time she stopped and turned to face him. "What's on your mind?"

"Your painting class last night."

"What about it?"

"You didn't go."

"Of course I did."

"Without your painting kit."

She began to speak, thought better of it, and turned away, biting her bottom lip. Tears welled in her eyes.

"Who is he?" McGuire asked.

"None of your business."

"Does Ollie know?"

"Of course not." Her sadness changed to sudden rage. "And don't you tell him, damn it. Don't you dare say a word to him."

"Will you?"

"Will I what?"

"Tell him?"

"Mind your own damn business."

He watched her pour polish onto the wood with one hand and rub it savagely with the cloth in her other hand. Then he went upstairs to shower and change.

When he returned a half-hour later, she was in the same armchair McGuire had sat in, and she called his name as he passed the doorway to the living room. Her eyes were red-rimmed and wisps of hair had escaped from beneath her bandanna. He stood watching her until she rose from the chair and seized him, pulling him towards her. "Please, don't say anything to Ollie," she whispered. "I just need a few weeks of life away from here. It'll be over in a few weeks, okay? Okay?"

"It would kill him to know," McGuire said.

She breathed deeply once, then pulled away. "It's been killing me to stay here and nurse him for years," she said. "Nobody seems to think about that, do they?"

The next day, McGuire lost himself during the daytime hours in the details of Cassidy's assignment, and during the night in the delights of Lorna's body. He reveled in the abandonment of it, their shared stage of sexual desire in which there was no longer either an intention of procreation or a pretense of romance. There was only an affirmation of life and a defiance of the force pulling them down a slope they were descending at the same speed.

In the morning, he drove her to the office and watched her wave goodbye from the sidewalk. Then he drove to Revere Beach. When he peeked into Ollie's room, Ollie grinned at McGuire and winked. "Show me a picture of her at least, for Christ's sake," Ollie said. Ronnie bustled about, ignoring him, avoiding any kind of talk, any discussion. McGuire showered, changed, and returned downtown.

"Jesus, ain't you heard?"

McGuire smiled at the sound of Sleeman's voice through the telephone receiver. "Heard what?" McGuire said. His feet were on the desk. He was pulling at a thumbnail with his teeth.

"About Hayhurst."

"Who's that?"

"The piece of crap we let get away on the Common. The black kid with the gold tooth? He dropped two guys near Fenway the other night. Haven't you been watching the news, reading the paper? I must've been interviewed by every greaseball reporter in town yesterday. Double homicide on a couple tourists, dark street, blood in the gutter. The stuff that dreams are made of, right? Anyway, I'm the lead dick, or I am until we nail the little bastard, and then DeLisle will get his hair styled and take over."

McGuire dropped his feet from the desk and leaned his head on his hand. "Who'd he kill?"

"Two guys in town for a business conference. Salt of the earth, of course. You'd think they'd been fitted for angel wings. Both got kids, minivans, mortgages, and probably the flag tattooed on their chests. Christ, what a mess."

"This kid Hayhurst, he's out of control?"

"Totally. These guys were no threat to him. He just wanted to blast somebody."

"We could have had him. On the Common that day. We could have had both of them."

"Yeah, well." Sleeman said nothing. "Hell, ten years and twenty pounds ago, I would've caught him on Boylston. It's not all your fault."

Most of it is, McGuire thought to himself. "Any leads?"

"Tard, the other guy, he might roll over on him. We're danglin' five-to-ten in front of him, might settle for half that if he tells us where Hayhurst hangs out. Listen, I gotta get back, see what's come in. Anything you want, on that other stuff? Don't know if I can get it for you, not right away. Call me in a couple days, I'll see what I can do."

Lorna entered McGuire's office after lunch. She was wearing a ruffled poet's blouse and tight skirt, and she locked the door behind her and sat on the corner of his desk. McGuire set aside the report he was preparing for Barry Cassidy.

"Orin's not back today," she said. "He said he would just be gone a day or two."

"He didn't call in?"

"No. And that's not like him."

"Maybe his plane was late or delayed or whatever."

"Yeah, but it's still not like him." She moved closer to McGuire. "I'm seeing my mother tonight for dinner. Remember I told you?" she said.

McGuire said he remembered.

"You sure you don't want to come and meet her?"

McGuire said he was sure.

"Okay, why don't I give you a key and I could meet you back at my place."

"Not tonight," McGuire said. "I think I'll stay at the beach and catch up on the rest of my life."

"What's wrong?" She leaned to touch him. "Is Cassidy still getting to you?"

"No, not Cassidy. You hear about two tourists shot near Fenway the other night?"

"I saw something about it in the paper."

"I could've had the guy who did it." He told her about the confrontation on the Common two weeks earlier. "I lost my cool."

"Why blame yourself for what other people do? This kid, he's a louse."

McGuire nodded, told her she was right. And she was, he knew. But the knowledge of it, the guilt he felt for not living up to his own expectations, would hang over him for days. That was something else he knew as well.

He stopped at Zoot's on the way home for a slowly savored beer, telling himself he was waiting for the afternoon rush-hour traffic to dissipate.

It was almost seven-thirty when he entered the house in Revere Beach, and sensed she wasn't there. Ollie was sleeping, while the television set glowed mutely above his bed.

McGuire went into the kitchen, where he reheated and ate some leftovers, read the evening paper, and returned to Ollie's room around nine o'clock.

Ollie was awake but groggy. "New medicine Ronnie got me, makes my head feel like I'm a Saturday-night fool on Sunday morning." Ollie blinked back at McGuire, a sheepish grin on his face. "How long you been home?"

"Hour, hour and a half," McGuire said.

"You stayin' here tonight?"

McGuire nodded.

"Don't have to, you know." Ollie yawned. "Listen, Joseph, you got yourself a special woman, you go ahead, don't worry about me. I got Ronnie here, she's takin' care of me like she always has." He looked up at the television set, the program a rerun of an old detective series.

"Ronnie's at her painting class?"

"Yeah. She tells me she's workin' on something special. Won't say anything else. But I can tell she's thinkin' about it all the time." He yawned again. "Ain't she something? She's good, ain't she? You see those paintings she's done? Ain't she good?"

McGuire agreed she was good.

Ollie switched to the sports channel and together they watched a baseball game until Ollie fell asleep again. McGuire didn't want to watch the news. He didn't want a reminder of Freeman Hayhurst, or to see blood in the gutter.

Ronnie arrived home after midnight. McGuire was sitting in the living room, the lights extinguished, invisible in the corner chair until Ronnie flicked on the hall light and started at the sight of him.

"What are you doing in the dark all alone like that?" she said. She shrugged out of her coat, and McGuire noticed she was wearing a sweater and skirt combination, and a new gold chain around her neck.

"Waiting for you," he said.

"Never did before." She closed the hall door. With her back to him, she tucked the gold chain inside her sweater.

"You were never cheating on him before."

She turned to face McGuire, staring at him as though he were a stranger in her home. "Is he sleeping?" she asked. Her voice was calm, her face a mask.

"Yeah, he's sleeping." McGuire tilted his head. "You putting something in his medication?"

"It's a new formula."

"Phenobarbital? Something like that? Knocks you out, leaves you with a bit of a hangover after? They used to give it to my mother when she'd get too excited in the nursing home."

She walked into the room and sat across from McGuire. In the dim light from the hall she scanned the walls and furnishings, like an interior decorator critical of the client's taste and impatient to begin her work. "Why don't you just move in with your girlfriend?" she said. She avoided McGuire's eyes.

"I don't have a girlfriend," McGuire said. "Just somebody I sleep with now and then. Kind of like you."

"You could leave us alone to work this out, you know."

"Work it out? You and Ollie? How can you work it out when that poor bastard in there doesn't know there's anything to work out?"

"I'll do it. I'll look after things."

McGuire sat back in his chair. "You won't work it out. You'll just wait for it to *burn* out."

She brought her hand to her head. "It won't . . ." She closed her eyes.

"Won't what?" McGuire was torn between anger at this woman for what she was doing to his closest friend, and sympathy for her and her life. She had watched her only son die beneath the wheels of a bus. She had altered her life when her husband was brought back from a fishing trip unable to move any part of his body lower than his neck and right arm. She had rescued McGuire from his addiction to Demerol and codeine after his world collapsed around him in the Bahamas and Florida. How much could he make demands of her now? Did she owe McGuire honesty? Did she owe her husband fidelity? Why should she owe anyone anything?

McGuire rose from his chair and crossed the room. He knelt by her side to touch her hand with his own. "Hey, I can understand," he said softly. "Christ knows, I've fooled around enough in my day . . ."

She reacted as though he had set off an explosion within her. She gripped both arms of the chair and pulled herself up and away from him, a fury in her eyes. "What the hell are you talking about?" she said.

"I'm just saying . . ."

"How dare you compare what I'm going through with all your escapades, your whoring from here to the Bahamas. How dare you even mention them in the same breath!"

"The same thing drove us there, Ronnie."

"No, not the same thing. Not even close." She brushed by him to stand near the window, staring out at the night. "Do you know what people call me, what they've been calling me since he came back home strapped in his bed?"

McGuire watched her, waiting.

"They call me a heroine, a saint, all of that crap. They say it to my face and smile like I'm supposed to feel good about it. Well, nobody ever asked me if I wanted to be a saint. Nobody ever gave me a choice in the matter. *And I'm sick of it.*" She began to cry. "I'm sick of it. And what I want, what I needed most of all, was my *own* hero, not somebody who lies in bed like a baby all day, but somebody who can hold me. Somebody I don't *have* to be a saint with."

"Okay," McGuire said. "Okay, okay. But is there any room for, I don't know, *honesty* here?"

She wiped her eyes with the backs of her hands. "No, as a matter of fact, this isn't the time for honesty. Not right now. Not yet." She smoothed her skirt and stared down at her hands. "I'm sorry. I know you're doing this because you care for Ollie."

"So do you."

"That's what's killing me." She walked to him and kissed him on the cheek, and before he could react she swept by him and up the stairs, leaving him alone in the near darkness to wonder why, in spite of the many times he felt totally in control of a situation, in total mastery of every event, there were so many others in which he was helpless and confused, like a man on a raft with no land in sight.

The next morning in his office he was filling the coffeemaker when Lorna entered without knocking. She wore a plaid shirtwaist dress that made her look more suburban somehow, less like a downtown woman.

"How're you doing?" McGuire said.

"Not very good." She walked to the corner of his desk and began tracing circles on it with a forefinger.

"What's the matter?" The coffeemaker began to gurgle obediently.

"I missed you last night."

"I had something to do. And I wouldn't have been very good company anyway."

"Are you still thinking about that kid, and those two men he killed?"

McGuire nodded. "And other things."

"I thought you might call. I mean, we can talk about it, if it makes you feel better."

"Sorry. How about dinner tonight?"

Her face brightened, but there was something else, something holding her back. "I guess you haven't heard."

"Heard what?"

"About Orin. Nobody knows where he is." She walked to stand beside him and stare into the glass coffee pot. "He was supposed to come back by yesterday. His wife's frantic and everybody's going nuts upstairs . . ."

Behind her, McGuire's door opened. Richard Pinnington entered wearing a midnight-blue suit and a puzzled expression. "Lorna," he said. He flashed a smile that pulled the corners of his mouth apart.

She smiled at McGuire, then brushed past the other man, closing the door behind her.

"She tell you about Orin?" Pinnington said. His eyes swept McGuire's office as though taking inventory.

"Something about him missing." McGuire back sat in his chair.

"It's not like Orin," Pinnington said. "Not like him at all." He thrust his hands in his pockets and studied his shoes as he spoke. "Situation like this, even with a man like Orin, you get worried, concerned."

"It could be nothing," McGuire said. "A weekend fling with some woman . . ."

Pinnington looked at McGuire sharply. "What makes you say that?"

McGuire shrugged. He was thinking of the blond-haired woman. He hadn't seen her since Flanigan left.

"Orin's wife's frantic," Pinnington said. "He hasn't called since he left. Lorna doesn't know where he went. Just said it had something to do with a client. Whatever he's doing, he appears to be doing it on his own. There's nothing in his files, nothing on his calendar, that fits his work for the firm." He shot his eyes towards McGuire. "You were doing something for him, weren't you? Some project?"

McGuire opened a drawer of his desk, removed Flanigan's memo, and handed it to Pinnington.

"What did you learn?" Pinnington asked when he finished reading.

McGuire told him about the search for Myers and the trip to Annapolis.

"You gave him nothing in writing?"

"He didn't want anything in writing. Just where this guy was and what he was doing."

"I'll keep this."

McGuire nodded.

Pinnington paused at the door. "Lorna's a nice girl, isn't she?" Pinnington was of a generation that referred to any woman without either a husband or a university degree as a girl, regardless of her age.

McGuire agreed.

"Some firms, you know, have policies against romantic relationships developing among the staff . . ."

"You want me to stop seeing her?" McGuire said.

Pinnington smiled. "No, just thought I'd mention it." He waved Flanigan's memo. "Compared to this, it's a minor concern to me. Quite minor."

McGuire worked through the rest of the morning, calling contacts on the street and flipping through the statements, provided by Barry Cassidy, which described his client's suspicion of fraud. At noon, Lorna brought him a cheese Danish and a bottle of sparkling fruit juice. "Pasta again tonight?" she asked, and McGuire nodded. "Still no word from Orin," she said. "I'm so worried, Joe."

McGuire asked if the police had been called.

"Uh-huh. By his wife. But she doesn't think they're taking it seriously."

"They won't, for about a week," McGuire said. "Or until somebody comes up with something."

"Like what?"

McGuire shrugged. "Missing money. An abandoned car. A body."

"You can't be serious." Her eyes flooded with tears. "Nobody would want to hurt Orin!"

"Maybe Orin isn't hurt," McGuire said. "Maybe Orin's in Switzerland, making up a code name for his brand-new bank account."

"Not Orin. You don't know Orin. He told me . . ." She withdrew a tissue from the pocket of her dress and used it to dab at her eyes. "He told me one day that the biggest disappointment in his life, next to his daughter's murder, was that he couldn't make things right as often as he wanted. He said he became a lawyer because he thought lawyers could do that, make things right, and he said after thirty years he finally had to admit they don't do those things. Sometimes they even make them worse."

"Sounds as if he was ready to quit his profession."

"He gets so frustrated, watching bad things happen to innocent people. The day after he met you, he said maybe he should have become a police officer. Maybe he could have made more of a difference that way."

"If he thinks that," McGuire said, "he's a damn fool."

She paused at the door. "I have to get back upstairs. Mister Pinnington's coming over to check Orin's files, go over his accounts. I'll probably be stuck at my desk the rest of the day. Can I get a ride home?"

"Sure. We'll pick up a bottle of wine on the way."

By two o'clock, McGuire could find no evidence of criminal activity in Cassidy's case, as seen from a police officer's point of view. Bad management on the part of the client's customer, perhaps. Poor judgment in a few decisions. Maybe even sloppy book-keeping. But nothing that would persuade a prosecuting attorney to consider criminal charges.

He also realized he didn't have a complete set of files. A few were missing, and some names on documents and correspondence had been blacked out with heavy ink. When McGuire called Cassidy to inquire about the files, the lawyer assured him that the missing documents were irrelevant. When McGuire called again an hour later, asking about the blacked-out names, Cassidy told him it was a matter of client confidentiality and demanded to know when McGuire would have his report completed.

McGuire said "Probably tomorrow," and Cassidy snapped "Good!" and hung up. McGuire sat back in his chair, sweeping his anger at Cassidy from his mind and permitting himself to dwell on Ronnie's infidelity.

We are all, McGuire had read somewhere years earlier, responsible for our own happiness. Depend on yourself for your joy, your satisfaction, your ability to avoid the darker sides of your soul, those that emerge at four in the morning and occupy the empty side of your bed. That's what he believed it meant. How could he judge Ronnie for doing whatever it took to pursue her idea of happiness? How could he expect anyone to understand the things he had done in pursuit of the same thing?

He was pondering that idea when Richard Pinnington entered without knocking. Pinnington was holding Flanigan's memo to McGuire and a legal-sized file folder, and his smile was thin, nervous, and forced.

"Sorry to trouble you again." Pinnington closed the door behind him. "There's something about this memo Orin gave you."

"What's that?" McGuire leaned back in his chair, his arms folded.

"Orin wanted you to charge your time and expenses to this docket, right?" He held a sheet of paper for McGuire to inspect.

"Yeah, and I did. It came to about a thousand dollars."

Pinnington opened the file folder. McGuire noticed his receipts clipped to the inside. "One thousand and fourteen fifty-five," he said, peering over his glasses. "Plus four hundred dollars to Libby somebody."

"Skip tracer."

"Nearly a hundred dollars in incidental expenses?"

"Four bottles of good Scotch to a guy on Berkeley Street, did some digging for me. You want his name?"

"Definitely not."

"Didn't think so."

"And six hundred dollars of your time."

"Two and a half days. What's the problem?"

Pinnington closed the file folder and stared at it. "The problem is, Orin charged all of this to a docket that doesn't make sense. A client in Brookline. Wealthy family, five kids. A particularly messy divorce made more difficult due to all the assets involved. We're acting on behalf of the husband for shared custody rights, overseeing transfer of assets, setting up of trusts, all of that. The wife wants to move back to Canada, where some of the assets are held. Nothing too unusual, except that it's complex and we'll probably be involved for a year, maybe more . . ."

"And there's a chunk of money missing."

Pinnington shook his head. "No, not as far as we can tell. Everything's on the up-and-up, every penny accounted for. It's just that Orin gave you this docket for your services and expenses. But there is nothing in this case that even remotely concerns an individual named Myers. No reason for Orin to get you involved in this at all."

"Unless Orin was burying expenses."

Pinnington nodded.

"In a case so big and complicated that a couple of grand could sneak past in the billing and nobody would question it."

Pinnington stared back at McGuire. "Do you have any idea what's going on?"

McGuire shook his head. "You?"

Pinnington looked away, deciding whether to answer. "Orin's a bit of a softy, you know. Never learned to keep his emotions out of things somehow. It makes him a good lawyer in some ways, of course. He can be brilliant in the courtroom, wearing his client's heart on his sleeve, and sometimes even his own. But he has paid for it, emotionally."

"Anything I can do?"

Another tight, cool smile. "You could always find Orin, I guess."

"Talked to the police yet?"

"Orin's wife has, of course, but we have to, uh . . ."

"Keep this quiet in case your clients find out."

"To this point, there's nothing for them to discover. Nothing to be concerned about. But yes, we are waiting to evaluate the situation." Pinnington frowned, turned away, then looked back as though having made a difficult decision. "You know a woman named Susan Schaeffer?" he asked. "In her mid-thirties? Kind of blond hair?"

McGuire nodded. "Orin's friend. She comes up to visit him. I've seen her a couple of times."

"Lorna says she's been there every day at noon for three weeks or more, whenever Orin's not in court."

McGuire nodded again. "Well, there you are."

"Where are we?"

"Orin's gone middle-age crazy. Right now, they're probably naked in a hammock together down in . . ."

"Who?"

"Orin and the Schaeffer woman." Even as he spoke the words, McGuire admitted to himself he was envious, perhaps a little jealous.

Pinnington shook his head. "This Schaeffer person isn't with Orin. She was in here today. She sat outside Orin's office for an hour, crying," he said. "Kept asking about Orin, where he was, if we had heard anything. She didn't believe us when we said we knew nothing. Lorna finally had to ask her to leave."

"They're tracing his telephone calls," Lorna said when she got into McGuire's car after work that evening.

McGuire swung onto State Street and stared at the line of cars ahead of him, all enveloped in a light gray rain. Sometimes Boston was nothing more than a badly designed parking lot. Maybe McGuire didn't need a car at all. Maybe if he just moved downtown . . . He caught himself thinking of Ronnie again, wondering where she would be sleeping tonight, wondering how long it would take Ollie to discover and what he would do. What could he do? McGuire asked himself. Nothing except lie there and feel the pain.

The windshield wipers swept back and forth, and the heater made a sound that was something between a purr and a clatter. Lorna stared out her side window. An opening in the traffic appeared ahead of them, and McGuire lurched the car forward, swung towards the curb lane, and drove a precious fifty feet before encountering the next segment of the traffic morass.

"And his credit cards," Lorna said in a dull voice. She might have been reciting a mantra. "They're looking at his credit-card statements. Dick Pinnington says the police are coming by tomorrow. They're finally taking it seriously, him missing, I mean . . ."

"Well, middle-aged professional guy goes missing," McGuire started to explain, "and the first thing you think of . . ."

"There she is." Lorna gestured out the window.

McGuire followed her gaze to see Susan Schaeffer standing in the doorway of a clothing shop, out of the rain. She wore a shapeless fawn-colored raincoat, her hands thrust in the pockets, and she was scanning the windows of the office buildings and passing cars as though searching for a familiar face. Lorna lowered her side window.

"Ask her if she needs a ride," McGuire said.

"You need a ride?" Lorna called.

At the sight of Lorna, the other woman smiled. It was part joy at recognition of a familiar face, part nervousness, but something in McGuire responded to the light it generated and the sense, once again, that Susan Schaeffer was an immensely attractive woman whose beauty was muted by the weight of despair.

"You sure?" Lorna called out.

The woman mouthed "Thank you," then set out, her hands still in her pockets, her head down as though searching for crevices in the sidewalk that might swallow her from sight.

"I hear you had to ask her to leave today." McGuire moved the car ahead another few feet.

"She's a mess. I've never seen a woman such a mess." Lorna's left hand crept towards McGuire and rested on his thigh.

"What's the real story about her?"

"I really don't know. She first showed up five or six weeks ago. She had an appointment with Orin, a regular one. Then she started coming by every day that Orin was there. Usually, they would go out together for lunch. At first she was happy, a lot happier then now, that's for sure. You know, kind of a nervous happiness."

"Flanigan ever say anything about her?"

"Just introduced us. Said she was a friend."

"That's all?"

"A little more but . . . One day, he walked her down the corridor when she left, and when he came back he looked really sad. I said, 'Anything wrong, Mr. Flanigan?' And he looked at me in a kind of funny way and said, 'She's an innocent.'"

"She's *innocent*?"

"No, she's *an* innocent. That's how he put it. 'She's an innocent.'"

"I don't know what that means."

"Neither do I. But Orin likes her. I think she looks a little bit like his daughter. Did you see that picture of Orin's daughter on his side desk? Don't you think they look similar?"

"Now that you mention it," McGuire said, swinging the car into an open lane, "she does."

At Lorna's apartment she ordered Chinese food, and they ate from containers, watching the television news together in her cluttered living room. The hunt for Freeman Hayhurst rated only a passing mention; there was nothing new to report. McGuire declined a glass of wine and read the newspaper, while Lorna stretched out on the sofa to watch a game show. When he looked up half an hour later she was sleeping, her head resting against the arm of the sofa and her mouth slightly open, snoring gently with a sound that reminded McGuire of the heater fan in his car. He stared at her for several minutes, curious at his own reaction. No longer an object of lust and tenderness to him, she was simply another lonely middle-aged woman in his life.

"I'm a transfer stop," a woman once told McGuire. She had been shrugging into her coat, avoiding his eyes as she spoke, "and you're riding to the end of the line, right?" She said goodbye without looking back at him and, while he would think of her fondly whenever she invaded his memory, he didn't miss her. He missed so few of them.

He carried Lorna to her bed, where he lay beside her. She smiled, her eyes still closed, and snuggled against him, touching her lips to his cheek. He thought about undressing her, but closed his eyes instead. When he woke it was after three o'clock. Rising in the darkness and covering her with a quilt from a rocking chair in the corner, he let himself out of the apartment, closing the door behind him and listening for the lock to click into place.

The Chrysler started easily, and he began driving into the night. He relaxed in the glow of the dashboard lights, feeling the steady throb of the engine and the way the car wallowed slightly beneath him.

The city belonged to him and anyone else prowling the streets before dawn. A southern breeze made the leaves dance on the tree branches, many of them flaring into shades of yellow and red, the colors shining in his headlights, and some of the leaves released themselves in the wind's frenzy and sailed to the ground. He drove north out of the city and followed back roads through Everett and Malden and Melrose, the engine transferring all of its mechanical workings back to him in a muted clatter from beneath the hood. The transmission thumped periodically, friendly, like a cat that walks through a room and brushes your leg on the way.

He thought of Lorna and wondered why there wasn't something more there, during his times with her, to make him happy and content, so that his mind wouldn't wander to other women and other places. She was sensuous, she cared for him, and the hard carapace she wore as protection wasn't nearly as scaly as those of other women her age he had encountered, women whose hopes were almost abandoned, buried beneath the wreckage of so many bad relationships.

Many of these women had shown McGuire their marriage photographs, displaying a frozen moment from a previous generation, with the women wearing lace and silly tiny hats, and the men in cummerbunds and bow ties. Stiff-necked parents gathered around the wedding party, and at the sight of these photographs he always felt a terrible sadness waft over him. It was his awareness of all the pain and betrayals awaiting the smiling faces in the photographs, all those unseen beasts in the jungle, that disturbed him. We start out so trusting, he would remind himself, so confident there is goodness in the world, that we cannot believe what it is already planning to do to us.

He had no idea where the photographs from either of his two marriages could be found now. He believed his first wife destroyed them all in a fury of anger and despair when they separated. His second wife had taken their photographs with her, like a bounty, when she fled to Florida, and he hadn't thought about them, hadn't missed them, in years.

Comments about marriage from men like Wally Sleeman disturbed him, for although McGuire had dated many women in his years alone, he always did so with the expectation that the relationship could lead to something permanent. It was why he never visited singles bars, why in recent years he preferred being alone – and admittedly lonely – over sharing his time with someone whose presence embarrassed him, or someone he was using as a transfer stop.

Marriage remained, and always would remain for McGuire, the most natural and logical goal of a relationship. I enjoy being married, he assured himself once, and, like someone at his shoulder whispering the truth in his ear, he admitted, I'm just not very *good* at it.

He thought about it with as much honesty as he could gather, driving alone towards the dawn. He thought about himself and about women in his life and how he had failed, in so many small measures, everyone who loved him, and that was the root of his sadness now.

He speculated on the fate of Orin Flanigan. The obvious answers didn't work. He didn't believe Flanigan was having a fling with the mysterious Schaeffer woman, nor had he apparently embezzled client funds. His actions were totally at odds with everything the man had stood for all his life. Where was he? McGuire wondered. Chasing Myers across the ocean to South Carolina? McGuire didn't know. And I'm not being paid to know any more, he told himself. It's somebody else's job now, not mine.

He switched on the radio, tuning it to all-night talk shows hosted by gravel-voiced men who spoke calmly to near-hysterical callers who were concerned about space exploration, the power of the federal government, and the Red Sox infield.

He punched the Scan button on the radio over and over until he heard a voice that sang with a level of passion and pain unmatched for fifty years, and he lost himself in almost an hour of uninterrupted Billie Holiday, broadcast from some distant New England station. Her voice rose and fell with the strength of the station's signal, singing sad songs with titles like "There Is No Greater Love" and "You're My Thrill." As ancient and unfashionable as the music might be, the emotions it generated were as real and as fresh as the coffee he purchased from an all-night drive-in in Saugus.

At Swampscott the horizon began to bleed, and Billie Holiday's voice was replaced by a young announcer, whose words suggested he had been born at least twenty years after Billie Holiday died, chained to a hospital bed by narcotics officers. The man began to chatter about rising and shining and forgetting all the blues sung by, who was that again? Oh yes, Billie Holiday. Because it was time for the six o'clock news, followed by Jumpin' Jack Happy and the rest of the gang here at good old W-something-or-other. McGuire cursed, turned the radio off, and parked near King's Beach, closing his eyes and facing east, where the sun was beginning its silent explosion up from the sea.

CHAPTER 11

His bladder woke him an hour later. He stepped outside the car to relieve himself before driving south to Revere Beach, feeling clear-headed about some things, as confused as ever about others.

He arrived just after eight o'clock. Ronnie was seated at the kitchen table, a cup of black coffee in front of her. Her eyes were red-rimmed and she wore a frayed cotton robe. She looked up at him when he entered the room, and her mouth attempted an imitation of a smile.

"You okay?" McGuire said from the doorway.

She closed her eyes and nodded slowly. "I ended it," she said, looking away. "Last night."

"Tough?"

She nodded again.

"Need a hug?"

She shook her head. He thought about going to her anyway, but he knew she would resist him, that she would tell him this was something she had to deal with alone. "Sorry if I lectured," he said.

She brought her hands to her eyes. "You got a phone call," she said when McGuire turned to leave. "About an hour ago."

"Who?"

"Woman named Lorna. Wanted to know what happened to you. What'd you do, love 'em and leave 'em again?" This time her smile was more genuine.

"I'm gonna grab an hour's sleep," he said. "Ollie okay?"

"Ollie's fine," Ronnie said, staring back into her coffee cup. "Ollie's just fine. Don't worry about Ollie. Don't worry about good old Ollie."

He slept fully clothed, waking two hours later with his head filled with cotton. He showered, dressed, and came downstairs to find Ronnie cleaning the brushes from her paint kit, working with the intense concentration of someone attempting to save their own life.

"You know what we haven't had in a hell of a while?" he said.

"What?" Keeping her eyes on her work.

"Dinner together. You, me, Ollie, and the TV news. How about it, some night this week?"

"Sure." Stroking the back of her hand with a camel-hair brush, the motion imitating the application of color, or the caress of a lover.

He bent to kiss her forehead. "We'll talk about it tonight. I'll pick up some steaks, stuff like that."

Still stroking her hand with the brush, she spread her fingers wide and the soft hairs entered the spaces between them, one by one, over and over. McGuire watched the motions and sensed the barrier that locked him out and sealed her pain in. Then he left.

He spent the morning drafting his report to Cassidy, collecting all the data from the sources he employed – a forensic accountant who examined the balance sheets and profit-and-loss statements, a background search on the few people whose names Cassidy provided, a review of bankruptcy claims and civil-court actions. Everything came up clean. McGuire handed it to one of the stenographers. An hour later he climbed the stairs with his report in hand.

"You're absolutely certain of this? There is no apparent evidence of criminal intent?" Barry Cassidy held the half-dozen sheets of papers a few inches above the surface of his desk as though hefting their weight.

"You want a guarantee, forget it," McGuire said. "I don't give guarantees." He slouched in the chair opposite the younger lawyer. "Just opinions."

Cassidy's blue eyes narrowed slightly in his face, a face, McGuire noted again, that was boyish and pouting, would always be boyish and pouting, and a little snobbish. He probably went to one of those expensive prep schools in Vermont or New Hampshire, where they wear blazers and English haircuts, and their mothers send them cookies baked by a Filipino maid, and they talk half through their snobby goddamn turned-up noses. McGuire prided himself on his limited prejudices. The limits did not extend to privileged snobs barely half his age.

"I was not looking for a court document," Cassidy said. "I just need to know if it was complete."

"Well, it's as complete as I can make it. There are some things missing, and a lot of names blacked out. Letters, documents, invoices, other stuff I saw mentioned but weren't in the file you gave me."

"I gave you only what you needed." Cassidy watched him, his eyes unblinking. "I gave you *more* than you needed. Some confidential things, irrelevant to the matter, you didn't need so I . . ."

"Where'd you go to school?"

"I beg your pardon?" Cassidy looked annoyed.

"School. Where'd you go?" McGuire angled his head towards Cassidy's law degree hanging prominently behind his desk. "Before good old Yale. You a Yale man? You look like a Yale man."

Cassidy gave his familiar head jerk, chin up as though his tab collar was too tight – which it appeared to be, squeezing the flesh of his neck into a soft roll – then tilting his head to one side. "You mean my prep school? It was Rutland. In New Hampshire. Why do you ask?"

"You wear blazers there? Short pants?"

"Why is this of any importance?"

"Was your mother called Muffie?"

"My mother's name is of no concern to you."

McGuire exhaled slowly, sensing what he was doing, searching for an outlet for his anger, knowing he was bullying Cassidy. Hell, Cassidy wasn't responsible for the circumstances of his birth any more than McGuire could help being born to sullen working-class parents, a father who carried his abiding rage home every evening on his coveralls, and a mother who focused more attention on the whiteness of her bedsheets than on the happiness of her only child. He stood up. "There it is, the best I can do."

Cassidy smiled tightly. "I suppose we can ask for no more than that, can we?" As McGuire turned to leave, Cassidy added: "I would like all your notes on this matter."

"My what?"

"Your notes." Cassidy had turned to open his briefcase on the credenza behind his desk. "And any relevant documents.

Please seal them in an envelope with my name attached and call my secretary when you've done so. I'll send her to obtain them from you."

McGuire began to speak, then looked away. "Sure," he said. "I'll get right to it, Hopalong."

Cassidy lifted his head slowly, a pained expression on his face.

They called him that all through prep school, McGuire thought, as he turned to leave. Bet they made the little jerk miserable with a name like that.

He was at the copying machine when Lorna approached and said Hello as though she were ordering him to leave her alone.

McGuire looked up and grunted. Another sheet of his notes on Cassidy's investigation glided into the output tray.

A young lawyer walked by, a woman in a tweed suit, who smiled at Lorna as she passed. "Did you have a nice time last night?" Lorna asked McGuire, smiling back at the lawyer.

"Not bad," McGuire said. "Quiet evening. You?" The last sheet of notes slid from the machine.

"It was okay," Lorna said, glancing at the copies. "But I misplaced something."

"What was that?"

She stepped closer as though to use the machine. "You, you bastard," she said, barely moving her lips.

"Well, you found it now." McGuire carried both sets of the notes back to his office, listening to Lorna's heels clip-clopping after him.

"What the hell do you think I am?" she spat at him after closing the door behind her. "Some little bimbo, screwing her way through the office?"

McGuire sat in his chair, avoiding her eyes. "You're over-reacting."

"Over-reacting, hell." Her eyes grew wet, but the force of her anger trampled any other emotion she might have been feeling. "You just leave like that? You didn't even go home. You don't say goodbye, you don't go home, you walk out like I'm some kind of baggage you can leave anywhere."

"You want an apology?" McGuire looked back at her. Jesus, he had seen this movie before. He had been *in* this movie before.

"You're damn right I want an apology," she said.

"You got one." McGuire forced a smile. "I'm sorry."

Her expression relaxed. She folded her arms, looked away, then back at him. "Where'd you go?"

"For a drive. All night long. Wound up at Swampscott, watching the sun come up."

"Yeah?" She forced a smile. "I used to do that. Just before I got married. I had a car, a little Volkswagen, and I'd drive to some place near the ocean and sit there listening to the radio, thinking, wondering if I was doing the right thing, sometimes crying about nothing, just enjoying the loneliness. You do that a lot?"

"Sometimes."

She walked towards him. "Next time, take me with you?"

"Sure."

She rubbed her knee against his leg. "You wanta make up?"

He agreed to see her for dinner that evening, and later he was angry at his own weakness, angry at deceiving both Lorna and himself. But it was better than spending an entire evening at Zoot's, or returning to the charged atmosphere of Ollie and Ronnie's.

Ronnie's broken it off, he reminded himself. It's over. They need to be alone, the two of them, her and Ollie. If I stay with Lorna tonight, it will be good for everybody.

He sent the original copies of his notes to Cassidy, hid the second set in his files, and spent the rest of the day reading memos and reports directed to his attention, searching for any that might require his services, and feeling relieved at finding none.

Around three o'clock Lorna phoned him. "The police were just here," she whispered into the receiver. "Asking about Orin."

"What're they looking for?"

"Just what he did, where we thought he might be. Missing-persons stuff."

"They have any ideas?"

"Nothing. They said they're checking his credit cards, car rentals, airline records." She lowered her voice even further. "Joe, do you think he's dead?"

"Why ask me?"

"Wasn't this your line of work?"

"Not missing persons. By the time I got involved, they were dead beyond a doubt."

"You won't be annoyed if I'm not a hundred per cent tonight, will you? This is really upsetting."

McGuire assured her he wouldn't let it bother him, and promised to meet her at seven.

"I need time to get things ready," she said.

"Get what ready?"

"You'll see. I'm going to make something to cheer us up. Both of us."

Half an hour later he shrugged into his coat and walked out of his office, thinking of nursing a beer at Zoot's and eavesdropping on police gossip before going to Lorna's. He owed Lorna that much. Their expectations for this affair couldn't be different, McGuire knew. Somewhere in the back of their minds, they might have both started with hopes of a long-term attraction. Now, only Lorna believed in it. Or wanted to. Any port in a storm, McGuire thought. Any woman on a lonely night. Sometimes, he added, walking through the corridor towards the reception area, you can't be both honest and proud.

He would see Lorna tonight. He would make her laugh again. They would sleep in each other's arms.

In the office foyer he saw Susan Schaeffer wringing a handkerchief in her hands and staring at the receptionist. "You can't," the receptionist was saying. "I'm not authorized to permit you to go down there any more . . ."

Susan Schaeffer forced a smile. "It's all right," she said. "I'm sorry I bothered you."

McGuire stepped to the elevator, pushed the button, and stared at his shoes.

"Hello."

He turned to see Susan Schaeffer beside him, smiling in that strange, sad manner. He grunted and dipped his head. The elevator arrived, empty, and he stepped aside to permit her to enter.

"Where is Mr. Flanigan?" she said to him when the doors closed and the elevator began descending. Her eyes were brimming with tears.

"I have no idea." McGuire tried to maintain a cool, detached attitude.

"You were doing work for him. You went to find somebody."

"That's right."

"He's gone away. Did he tell you where he might be going?"

"I thought you might know."

"Me?" She stepped back as though she had been slapped, or was about to be.

"You two are more than good friends."

"Yes . . ."

"You're a client?"

"Not exactly."

"So maybe you do other kinds of business."

"I don't know what you mean."

The elevator stopped at the foyer and the doors opened, revealing a knot of people waiting to enter. Among them was Richard Pinnington, who started at the sight of McGuire and the woman, looking back and forth between them.

McGuire smiled at Pinnington. The lawyer watched McGuire leave, Susan Schaeffer trotting quickly behind him.

"Please tell me what you found out for Mr. Flanigan," she said when she caught up with McGuire at the door to State Street.

McGuire pushed his way outside. He remembered Thoreau's three rules for a happy life. Simplify, simplify, simplify. He was seeing Lorna tonight. He would make her laugh. She would make him feel good. Don't screw things up.

It was raining again, the drops falling gray and greasy to the pavement. He turned up the collar of his topcoat, scanned the sky, and jammed his hands in his pockets. Susan Schaeffer was next to him, waiting for an answer. "Strictly between me and him," he said. Too much rain to walk to Zoot's. He set out towards Quincy Market.

"It had something to do with me, didn't it?" She walked quickly beside him, trying to match his pace.

"Probably. Maybe."

"Have you talked to the police? About Mr. Flanigan?"

"Not yet." McGuire crossed State Street, hearing the woman behind him.

"If you will, are you going . . ."

McGuire stepped under an awning out of the rain, and turned to face her. He snapped his words at her, biting off the ends. "I don't know what kind of trouble you're in, but it's none of my business and there's no way I'm going to *make* it my business. If Orin's disappeared, leave it to the police, and whoever else wants to get involved, to find him. It's not my job, it's not *your* job, and if Orin broke a promise or stood you up, well, that's too bad and you probably didn't deserve it, but nobody ever does, do they?"

She stood staring at him, numb.

He threw her a smile, trying to soften his words. Then he hunched his shoulders against the rain again and set off down State Street. The hell with a beer, he told himself, he'd get an Irish coffee or two. There was a bar on Congress, near the market, with a decent jazz piano player from four o'clock on. Hear a little music, warm up with a couple of drinks, then go see what Lorna has for dinner . . .

He stopped at the corner and listened. There were no footsteps behind him.

He looked back.

She was standing beneath the awning, watching him. Even from that distance he could see the tears streaming down her cheeks, and the resignation and defeat in the slope of her shoulders.

McGuire walked back to her. "You got anywhere to go?" Water dripped from the edge of the awning onto his collar and down his back. He stepped further within the awning's shelter, and she backed away from him, hesitant, afraid.

She shook her head.

"I'm going to a place near the market for an Irish coffee. You want to join me?"

"Okay." She smiled and McGuire caught his breath. He had never seen a woman's beauty shine through so suddenly with a smile, as though a mask had been removed, or another woman had stepped into her soul. "We haven't . . ." she began. "I'm Susan."

"I know. My name's McGuire."

"I know."

"There's a little bar near the Bostonian."

"Okay."

They walked in silence through the rain, past Faneuil Hall and Quincy Market to Congress Street and the businessman's bar. Just inside the door the pianist, a slim, gray-haired man, was playing a slow twelve-bar blues, and he nodded at McGuire and Susan as they entered. McGuire paused at the bar long enough to order two Irish coffees, then led Susan towards a booth against an inside wall, away from the chill of the windows. He helped her out of her coat, admiring the lines of her figure in a dark sweater and wool skirt.

"This is nice," she said, glancing around after settling herself in the booth. "I've seen this place often, just passing by, but I've never come in."

"You live near here?"

"No." She angled her head towards Quincy Market. "I work over there. In a candle shop. Just in the mornings. I have afternoons to myself." She played with her fingers, looked up to see him watching her, smiled briefly, then folded her hands in her lap.

"Why are you so nervous?" McGuire asked.

She shrugged. "I guess because I haven't been with a man on a date since my divorce. This isn't a date, I know, but having a drink and so on . . ."

"When were you divorced?"

"Two . . ." She swallowed and began again. "Two years ago."

"Isn't it about time you began going out and meeting men?"

"I suppose so."

The Irish coffees arrived, and he watched as she sipped hers then set it down, wrapping both hands around the heavy glass to absorb its warmth. She looked up and saw him watching her, and she smiled again, still nervous. Her eyes were large in a face that could age from twenty to forty in the time it took for the lines on her brow to erase the brilliance of her smile. "It's good," she said. "I haven't had an Irish coffee in years. I'd almost forgotten how good they taste." She looked back at the pianist, who had slipped into a slow ballad, lush with thick chords. "That's pretty, the song he's playing."

McGuire listened for a moment, trying to hear the words in his mind. "I know it," he said. "Well, I *should* know it. It's an old song, the kind jazz musicians like. Hardly hear it any more. Hardly hear any old songs like that, except in places like this."

"It's lovely," she said, looking down at her drink. "My grandfather would have liked it. He loved old songs."

Her expression grew solemn and she was lost in her thoughts before looking up at McGuire and smiling with embarrassment. When she emerged from her reverie McGuire said, "What's your relationship with Orin Flanigan?"

"Friends. We're just friends."

"Some people think you're more than that."

"I know. But we're not." She bit her bottom lip. "Orin's doing something that he thinks needs to be done."

"What is it?"

"I can't tell you."

"Why not?"

"Because it's something he shouldn't be doing. I mean, it's not illegal, it's what Orin does, except he shouldn't be doing it."

"That doesn't make sense."

"I know."

"Did you know his daughter?"

She shook her head. "Funny you should ask that. Orin says I remind him of her. She's ten years younger than me, or she would have been. Do you know about her?"

McGuire nodded. "Have you and your husband really been divorced for two years?"

"Yes. Yes, we have. Honestly."

"And you haven't been out with anyone since?"

"No." She looked up at him with a pleading expression. "I'm sorry I can't tell you anything else, but there's more to this than you know."

She took another drink of the coffee, and McGuire watched the way she avoided his eyes until she smiled again. She rested her chin on her hand and stared in the direction of the piano. What was it Flanigan had called her? Innocent. No, *an* innocent. She appeared almost forty years old, an age when no one can claim innocence any more, but McGuire recognized that quality within her, along with something he couldn't immediately identify. Fear, perhaps. Vulnerability, certainly. And something he shouldn't detect in a woman like her.

"Want another?" he asked when she drained the glass.

"I'd love one but . . ." She looked up at the clock over the bar. "I have to be going . . ."

"It's barely five o'clock."

"I know, but I have to be home . . ."

"We'll go back to my car, I'll drive you . . ."

"No, please, it's all right." She was close to panic. "I'll take the subway . . ."

He reached to touch her hand. "Hey, it's not a problem." Beneath his fingers he felt the tension in her hand. "Just let me get to the men's room, then we'll go. It's the coffee. Can't hold as much as I used to." He rose from the booth. "Back in two minutes and we'll be off. Maybe buy an umbrella on the way. I can use one in this weather."

"Thank you." Her hands were trembling.

In the washroom, he remembered the title of the song the pianist had been playing. "Haunted Heart." Good. The brain cells weren't dying off as fast as he feared. He even recalled some of the words. Dreams are dust, something like that.

It was no more than three minutes later when he returned, rounding the corner from the washroom and seeing the empty booth with its two drained glasses. McGuire was standing looking down at them when the waiter approached and asked if there would be anything else. McGuire said Yeah, one more, and sat down, staring out at the rain and listening to the piano player.

CHAPTER 12

Lorna had prepared chicken Kiev, and rice pilaf with stir-fried snap peas. She served it with a French Chablis in cut-crystal stemware beneath the dimmed light of her chandelier. She wore a turquoise-colored silk blouse and fitted black skirt under a pink apron decorated with flowers and frills. She was playing a Barry Manilow CD on her portable stereo.

McGuire sat staring at his plate.

"What's wrong?" she asked.

McGuire shook his head.

"It's the music, isn't it?" She rose from the table and switched off the stereo.

"Thank you," McGuire said.

"If we're not gonna listen to music, will you talk to me?"

"Sure." McGuire cut into the chicken breast, releasing a small torrent of butter and parsley.

While McGuire ate, Lorna told him her daughter was arriving on the weekend, excited to meet this mysterious man who was making her mother so happy. She described an island she had read about in a travel magazine, just off the coast of

Puerto Rico, and speculated about visiting it for a week-long winter holiday with McGuire.

"Where are you?" she asked when McGuire only grunted in response.

"Right here." McGuire placed a piece of chicken in his mouth. It was good. So was the wine. Lorna was a good cook, a good lover, humorous, attractive. What the hell was wrong with this picture?

"No, you're not. Were you thinking about something at the office?"

"Yes."

"Maybe Orin?"

"Yes."

She leaned towards him and lowered her voice as though there were someone else in the room, listening. "He's dead, isn't he?"

"How would I know?"

"Your instincts. Admit it. Mine are telling me that. He's lying dead someplace, maybe murdered."

"You don't know . . ."

"They found his car at the airport. They're checking the airlines, trying to find out where he went."

McGuire sat back in his chair. "Who told you?"

"The police officers who were in today. I'm not supposed to say anything. Dick Pinnington told me not to tell anybody, so for God's sake . . ."

"What else did they say?"

She shrugged. "Not much. They took away a few files, his travel records, a list of his clients. Maybe one of them did it, one of his clients, or somebody on the other side. That's what they think, I can tell. Orin's work can get people upset, you know. Child custody and all. I've taken calls from parents who've lost custody cases to Orin's clients, blaming Orin because their children were taken from them. They get so angry, so full of rage."

"Anybody make a threat lately?"

"Nobody." She stared at her plate for a moment. Then: "You know what I think?"

"What?"

"I think that woman, Susan Schaeffer, I think she has something to do with it. With Orin going away."

"Why?"

"Because the last time Orin saw her, he was upset. I don't know, there may be nothing to it. But Dick Pinnington, apparently he left word that she's not to come in any more."

"What the hell's Pinnington know about this?"

"I don't know." She breathed deeply, as though working up the courage to speak. "You haven't seen her lately, have you?"

"Seen who?"

"That woman. Susan Schaeffer."

Without thinking, McGuire said "No". He began to correct himself, thought better of it, and speared the last piece of chicken Kiev with his fork. When he looked up, Lorna was glaring at him. "Something wrong?" he asked.

"Joe, you can do almost anything you want, but don't do one thing. Ever."

He chewed the morsel of chicken, staring at her, then swallowed. "What's that?"

"*Don't lie to me*!" Lorna tossed her dinner napkin on the table, fury in her eyes. "Sheila was at the reception desk today. She told me she saw both of you get on the elevator, you and Susan Schaeffer. You were talking . . ."

"That's right, we were . . ."

"What did you talk about?"

"Nothing special."

"Why did you say you'd never seen her?'

"I didn't think it meant that much to you, didn't think it was that big a deal . . ."

"Did you leave with her? Leave the building with her?"

"Yes." McGuire rested his elbows on the table, his hands clasped together. "We had a drink together and she . . ."

"*Why did you lie to me*?"

"Why are you so threatened by her?"

"I'm not . . ."

"Yes, you are . . ."

"Okay, maybe because I saw the way you looked at her. You didn't think I noticed, did you? She's younger than me and . . . The last two relationships I've had ended with me being hurt, goddamn it, and I . . . and because I know things about her."

"Like what?"

She stood up. "I need a drink."

McGuire rose from the table. "Maybe you'd better get me one too."

"Go to hell." She walked to the sideboard and withdrew a bottle of bourbon and a small glass tumbler.

McGuire watched her pour bourbon into the glass, her hand shaking. It's as good a time as ever, he told himself, and he turned and walked towards the front door.

"Where're you going?" Lorna called to him.

"Home."

"Why?" She walked towards him as he was sliding into his topcoat. "Hey, listen, I over-reacted, okay? I mean, I can't stand being lied to. Please don't go."

"I'm sorry," McGuire said.

"I told my daughter about you, my daughter Tracy." Her eyes were brimming, her face about to crumble. "She's coming home this weekend just to meet you . . ."

McGuire was at the door.

"Come on, come on," Lorna was pleading behind him. "Damn it, damn it, damn it . . ."

After he closed the door he heard the glass tumbler shatter against it on the inside.

"You know," Ollie Schantz had told McGuire several years ago, when they were partners, and Ollie's body was as strong and mobile as his mind, "any fool can start an affair." They were talking about a cop involved in a messy divorce from a shattered wife. "Any fool can start an affair," Ollie repeated, "but it takes a goddamn genius to end one."

"That woman called you again."

Ronnie was slumped in a living-room chair, the newspaper open on her lap. From Ollie's room he could hear the sound of a televised basketball game. McGuire removed his topcoat. "What woman?"

"The one who called you this morning. This time she was crying."

"Yeah." McGuire stood in the hall, watching her. "Well . . ."

She avoided his eyes.

"How're you doing?" he asked.

"I'm falling apart, is how I'm doing." Her voice was flat and dull, and McGuire visualized a desert scene in winter, gray and empty. "Like that woman on the telephone. Laura or something like that. You plan to call her?"

"No."

"Don't be a shit. At least call her. She sounds like she's a mess right now."

McGuire stepped into the room, closer to her, and lowered his voice. "How's your friend taking it? What you did last night. How's he handling it?"

Like a sluice that opens to relieve pent-up pressure, the tears began to flow and she turned her head away. "He doesn't understand," she said. "He just can't understand it. God, we're such adolescents when it comes to this, aren't we?"

"When it comes to what?"

She grasped his hand, squeezed it. "I used to call it either love or lust, and maybe that's all it is. But Jesus, Jesus, Jesus, at my age, I should be able to deal with it better."

He remained until she released his hand and blinked her tears away. "I'm all right," she said, wiping her eyes with the backs of her hands. "Go say hi to Ollie. Then call your woman friend. Some day soon, we can talk about all our wounds, you and me. All us casualties."

McGuire looked in on Ollie, who was snoring, his head to one side, his paralyzed body stretched unnaturally straight. McGuire closed the door, climbed the stairs to his room, and dialed Lorna's number.

She answered after one ring, and McGuire said, "It's me."

"I didn't think you had the guts." Her voice was hoarse and weak.

"To do what?"

"Call me."

"Look . . ."

"I welcome you into my house, into my life, into my family, into my *body*, and you lie to me, you walk out on me . . ."

"It wasn't working out."

"I thought you wanted something permanent, you told me you were looking for something permanent . . ."

"I don't know what the hell I'm looking for . . ."

"Well, whatever it is, you won't find it with that Schaeffer woman."

"What do you know about her?"

"A lot. A lot more than you know, believe me." Her voice dropped in tone and volume. "You two deserve each other," she said, and the line went dead.

He woke the next morning trying to piece together elements of dreams that lingered in his memory like commuters who had missed their train. After showering and dressing, he came downstairs just as Ronnie walked out of Ollie's room, carrying his empty breakfast tray, her head down. They passed in silence.

"You're finally awake," McGuire said, entering Ollie's room.

"Got tired a sleepin'." Ollie was looking out the window at his view of Massachusetts Bay. "How you doin'?"

"I'm okay . . ."

Ollie's eyes flicked towards McGuire. "C'mere," he whispered.

McGuire sat on the edge of the bed.

"Something's bothering Ronnie," Ollie said. "I don't know what. Maybe one of those woman things. Maybe something more." He lowered his voice even further. "She's even quit her paintin' class. And she's damn good at it too. Whattaya think? Why'd she do that?" Ollie turned his head in his slow, painful way to face McGuire. "You wanta talk to her? I think maybe she's lonely, what with you bouncin' on mattresses from here to Rhode Island every night."

"Ronnie's strong." McGuire stood up. "If she's got a problem, she'll figure out how to deal with it."

Ollie's good arm flopped towards McGuire, the fingers of his hand outstretched. "No, no, Joseph. Not this time. I've lived with that woman thirty years. I know when she's feeling pain, and that's what she's feeling right now. A lot of it. So help her, Joseph. Get her to talk, get her to laugh again, okay? Okay?"

McGuire nodded, reached for Ollie's hand, and let the other man squeeze his in return, Ollie holding McGuire in the grip of his hand and his eyes. "Talk to you later," McGuire said, and Ollie nodded.

He found Ronnie in the kitchen reading a newspaper, a cup of black coffee growing cold in front of her. McGuire sat and stared at her until she lowered the newspaper and looked back at him. "What?" she said.

"Ollie wants me to talk to you, see if I can cheer you up a little."

"So try." She raised the coffee to her lips, sipped it, made a face, and lowered it again.

"The guy loves you."

"You think I stopped loving him? You think I ever stopped?"

McGuire looked away, remembering. "When I was a kid, back in Worcester," he said, "there was a strange man who lived alone in a house across the street. I don't know what he did for a living, don't know if he was a pervert like some of the neighbors said, but he was definitely different. He would talk to me and the other kids like we were adults, and he would talk to our parents like they were kids. He'd see the parents dressed up in the evening, going out for a movie or something, and he'd call across the street to them. He'd say things like, 'Going out to play are we? Going to the playground maybe?

Swing from the monkey bars?' He'd drive the parents nuts."

"Fascinating." Ronnie folded her arms.

"One day he grabbed my shoulder as I walked past him on the sidewalk. I was maybe twelve years old, and he just stared at me at first, not saying anything. I wasn't afraid of him. None of us kids were. He wasn't threatening, just different. I asked him what he wanted. You know what he said to me? He said, 'You are allowed any thought. Every thought you have is a worthwhile thought. You are not responsible for what you think. You are only responsible for what you do.' Then he walked away."

Ronnie avoided his eyes.

"If he saw one of us kids not looking happy, if we were upset about something, he'd say 'Having your daily sadness, are you? Having a daily dose of sadness?' Our parents would tell us to stop moping around, but he'd treat it differently. He made it sound as though it were all right to be sad sometimes."

McGuire smiled at the memory.

"Once, when we were talking, he told me I should love not being what I really wanted to be, because then I would find out what I needed. It took me a long time to get my head around that one." McGuire became more animated, the memories of his strange neighbor fueling his thoughts. "Another time, I talked to him about space travel, because I was reading a lot of science fiction, Buck Rogers stuff. He listened for a time and then he said, 'Always travel to your inner nature. That's the only journey worth taking. Forget the space station.' I've remembered that. All those years. Sometimes, when I start thinking about some crazy idea that might make me happier than I am, I tell myself to forget the space station. When I start dreaming about things I should've done or somebody I should've been, I tell myself that I'm just trying to live on the space station. Helps me forget about it and start dealing with reality again."

"Oh, for Christ's sake, Joe." Ronnie glared up at him. "Dump your philosophy on somebody who wants it."

McGuire inhaled deeply and released it. "What he said is the kind of thing that stays with you over the years. When you're twelve, you don't know what the hell somebody like that is talking about, but you can't forget it, either. Then, thirty years later, it starts to make sense. Forget the space station."

She looked at McGuire. "So what happened to him, your crazy friend?"

"He hanged himself in his house. In the living room. One of the kids saw his body through the window, still twisting. The next week his house burned down. There was some talk that a couple of parents did it, just to destroy everything remaining of him. Because he was saying things to the kids that upset the parents."

Ronnie smiled and stood up. "That's the best you can do?" she said. She carried her coffee to the sink and poured it out.

"Probably."

"Didn't help him much, did it?" She was staring down at the drain.

"I thought about that," McGuire said, rising from the chair. "But I just figured that's where his journey took him. To a rope in the living room. It's everybody's daily sadness."

"Then leave me with mine," Ronnie said. "Just go away and leave me with mine."

McGuire thought about it in the long periods of wakefulness when it is always four a.m., in the mind, if not on the face of the clock. In the morning he rose early and dressed silently.

Downstairs he could hear Ollie snoring, and he stepped into the chill of the morning. He ate breakfast in a restaurant on Boylston Street, dawdling over the morning newspaper and taking a long walk through Back Bay streets, enjoying the solitude.

Then he returned to his car and drove to the market area. He parked in the elevated garage and walked towards Quincy Market. It was just after nine o'clock. A few end-of-season tourists snapped pictures of Faneuil Hall, while others sat on benches, sipping from paper cups of hot coffee.

He bought a black coffee at one of the market stalls and walked along the narrow corridor, exiting on the harbor side and returning within the glass-canopied atrium forming the north wall of the market building, where the souvenir shops were located. First he saw the sign, Quincy Candles, and then he saw her, standing behind the tiny sales counter, attaching price stickers to candles in fanciful shapes and garish colors. He watched how she brushed her hair from her eyes with the back of one hand, and how she paused to stare through the atrium glass at the walls of the South Market, across the open cobblestoned plaza. He noticed she wore no jewelry, not even earrings, and something about her expression, as she watched people walk by on the other side of the glass, had a familiarity about it that chilled him.

McGuire finished the coffee, crumpled the empty cup in his hand, and entered the store, where Susan Schaeffer was bent over her work.

She looked up at the sound of his footsteps. Her smile at the sight of him changed to something else. "Hello." Her hands fumbled for each other and finally clasped themselves together. "I'm sorry about leaving last night. I was enjoying myself, honestly."

"I didn't get a goodbye." McGuire picked up a wax candle molded in the shape of the Old State House. Did people really pay money for these things?

"It's difficult to explain . . ."

Two middle-aged women entered, clucking with approval at the souvenir candles. "Why don't you tell me later?" McGuire said, leaning on the counter and smiling at her. "We'll have that second Irish coffee we talked about."

She smiled. The smile altered her age, her cloak of sadness, and even her beauty, enhancing it, and he felt that sense of privilege and vulnerability that the attention of a beautiful woman could create in him.

"I hear the weather's turning warm later," he said. "Might be a good day for a walk along the Esplanade."

"Oh, I'd love that!" Her face grew animated. "I haven't been there for so long . . ."

"Excuse me, miss." It was one of the tourists, holding a wax candle shaped and painted to resemble Paul Revere astride his horse. "How much is this?"

"That's twelve dollars," Susan said to the woman.

"I'll meet you here," McGuire said.

"No, not here," she said. "At the Hatch shell. Around two. Is that all right?"

"Do you have anything cheaper?" one of the women tourists interrupted.

"Okay," McGuire said. "The Hatch shell." He nodded to the women as he passed. "It's a bargain," he said, and winked at her. He left the shop and turned to look at Susan, whose smile had grown wider, and he returned the smile, feeling he was doing something good, something right.

The receptionist almost leapt across her desk at the sight of McGuire when he entered the law offices a few moments later. "Mr. Pinnington is anxious to see you," she said. "In his office. I'll tell him you're here." McGuire glanced at the clock. It was well past ten a.m.

When McGuire reached Pinnington's office, Pinnington stood waiting for him, grim-faced and in shirtsleeves.

"What's up?" McGuire asked, but Pinnington said nothing until he closed the door behind him.

"You know they found Orin's car at the airport?"

Without being invited to sit, McGuire settled in one of the green leather wing chairs. Pinnington walked to his desk, rested a haunch on one corner, and stared at McGuire, his arms folded across his chest. "I heard," McGuire said.

Pinnington remained looking at McGuire for a moment. There was no challenge in his eyes, only patience, and when McGuire said nothing, Pinnington spoke again. "The police confirmed he caught a flight to Washington, with a return ticket for the next day. He rented a car at Hertz and gave his local address as the Willard Hotel."

"He wasn't registered there."

"He wasn't registered anywhere."

"And they haven't found the rental car."

"Wrong. They found it this morning." Pinnington looked down at his desk. "In the parking lot of a shopping mall near Weymouth."

"He flies to Washington, rents a car, then drives it back to Weymouth, practically home, and leaves it?"

"Difficult to believe, isn't it?"

"I wasn't serious. How long's the car been there?"

"Nobody knows. A couple of days, maybe."

"Fingerprints?"

"The police are checking."

"Do they know about Annapolis? About Flanigan sending me down there?"

Pinnington rose, walked behind his desk, and sat in his chair. "That's been the subject of a discussion this morning between myself and the senior partners."

"So they don't know."

Pinnington shook his head.

"You could be concealing evidence. Hell of a note, one of the biggest, most prestigious law firms in the state concealing evidence . . ."

"Of what?" Pinnington's tone was sharp. "Of a man who gives a false address on a car-rental contract? And who doesn't return the car where and when he promised? It could be the same scenario you proposed a couple of days ago. We could have a lawyer who has broken under the strain of his career or his marriage or any damn thing. How can we reveal confidential information for something so trivial? Don't lecture me on the law, McGuire."

"You're playing for time . . ."

"Don't lecture me on the law," Pinnington repeated, aiming a forefinger at McGuire as though it were a weapon.

McGuire rose from his chair. "There's no lecture," he said. "You're trying to work out the options. That's okay, I guess. But you and I both know that something serious is happening here. Maybe your facts don't say it, but my gut does."

Pinnington sat back in his chair, his tantrum over.

"I'm taking the rest of the day off," McGuire said. "You want me, try Zoot's. It's a bar on Boylston." He paused with his hand on the doorknob. "Lorna know about this? About Flanigan's car being found?"

Pinnington nodded. "She knows."

"How's she taking it?"

"Not well. We sent her home. She couldn't stop crying. She was upset even before she learned about Orin's car being found." Pinnington's eyes narrowed. "You wouldn't have anything to do with her state of mind, would you?"

"Probably." McGuire closed the door behind him.

"Believe it or not, McGuire," Sleeman said over the telephone, "I don't need another bottle of Scotch, thank you very much. What I need is this squirrel Hayhurst off the street, maybe off the planet."

McGuire was sitting at the bar in Zoot's, a Bloody Mary in front of him, the telephone plugged into an extension. "So I'll buy you lunch," he said. "The super cheeseburger. I remember hearing you say once that you'd give your right nut for one."

"Yeah, when I was on surveillance for twelve hours straight." He lowered his voice. "Jesus, I gotta get outta here sometime. Maybe I'll be at Zoot's around twelve, and maybe I'll let you buy me lunch and maybe I'll even have some scuttlebutt for you."

"Maybe you're a hell of a guy."

"Maybe I'll be selling shoes next week too, the word gets out and we don't nail Hayhurst."

"What was that?" McGuire leaned towards Sleeman, whose mouth was filled with almost half a cheeseburger. "I couldn't understand a damn thing." They were seated at the bar in Zoot's. The lunch-hour crowd buzzed and laughed behind them.

Sleeman held up one finger. With his other hand he replaced the remains of the largest, greasiest cheeseburger

McGuire had ever seen on the plate and seized a glass of milk. He drank half of it before speaking. "I said it's a coin toss. Whether your lawyer buddy dropped the car or somebody dropped him. That's what Shuttleworth's saying."

"Who's he?"

"New guy. Missing persons. He's okay. Anyway, he says the car was in a corner of the parking lot near a Burger King, keys behind the sun visor, your guy's overnight bag in the trunk, underwear, socks, clean shirt, shaving equipment. Not much."

"Prints?"

Sleeman shook his head. "Thing's cleaner'n the pope's nose."

"Who drops a car ten miles from his house and wipes his prints from it?"

"Not the guy who rented it. Why's he worry about prints? His name's on the contract."

"So it's somebody else who leaves the car, doesn't want ID." McGuire finished his coffee.

"Sure as hell. Thing is . . ." Sleeman removed about half of the remaining portion of the cheeseburger with another bite, and said something around his lunch that sounded to McGuire like "Suffers annooky."

"Goddamn it, will you stop talking with your mouth full?" McGuire said.

Sleeman nodded, swallowed once, wiped his mouth with a paper napkin, and leaned towards McGuire. "Listen, I got maybe fifteen minutes and then I'm due back on Berkeley Street, sittin' around waitin' for somebody to dump us something on Hayhurst. Jesus, I practically had to tell DeLisle I was goin' to my mother's funeral just to get away for half an hour."

"What'd you say just now?"

Sleeman was about to consume the remainder of the cheeseburger, thought better of it, and set it aside. “I said Shuttleworth’s a rookie.”

“You said that already.”

“So he’s still playin’ it as a missing. But you and I know, Joe, that a wiped-down car and an unopened suitcase after the guy does a vanishing act, that’s not a missing. That’s a dead. Right? Ten to one that’s a dead. Am I right, or not?”

CHAPTER 13

If the Public Garden is Boston's elegant outdoor living room, the Esplanade is the city's waterfront playground, a meandering grassland strip that separates the St. Charles River from the elegant brownstones of the Back Bay's most prestigious residential avenues. Near the eastern entrance of the Esplanade sits the Hatch bandshell, a massive wooden cornucopia. On summer evenings it fills with musicians ranging from hopeful folkies to symphony orchestras. As the Esplanade extends west towards Boston University, it grows less pretentious, and music lovers give way to touch-football enthusiasts, dog walkers, and romantics of all ages and pursuits.

It was almost two-thirty by the time McGuire found a parking space on Charles Street. True to the weather office's prediction, the day had grown soft and warm with the strange aura of melancholia and exhilaration that dominates a perfect New England autumn afternoon. The river shone blue, and the leaves on the maple and oak trees flashed gold and crimson against the sky.

She was sitting on a bench facing the river, her head back and her eyes closed, the sun flooding her hair as though it were lit from within. She wore a honey-colored leather jacket over her sweater; a pair of sunglasses were propped on her head, crowning her hair.

McGuire approached her, letting her hear his footsteps to avoid surprising her. She blinked up at him and smiled as he neared the bench.

"Been here long?" he asked.

"Only a few minutes," she said. "Isn't it beautiful here?" She crossed her legs and clasped one knee in her hands. "I just love it." Her dangling foot moved in a steady nervous rhythm.

McGuire sat beside her and they admired the view of Cambridge across the river. She assured him she had eaten lunch already, a sandwich at the candle shop.

"Have you heard anything?" she asked. "About Mr. Flanigan?"

"Yes."

"What is it? Please tell me."

"They found the car he rented in Washington. It was in a parking lot near Weymouth."

"Weymouth? What was he doing in Weymouth?"

"He wasn't there. Just his car."

She looked away. "I don't understand."

"Orin Flanigan caught a flight to Washington. He planned to stay overnight, but he rented a car instead. Which is pretty surprising."

"Is it? What's wrong with renting a car in Washington?"

"Well, you can bet he wasn't headed downtown. Nobody rents a car to drive into Washington. Of course, Washington's only an hour's drive from Annapolis."

She looked up and to her right, across the river.

"Ever been to Annapolis?" McGuire said.

"No."

"Do you think Orin Flanigan went there?"

"I don't know."

"Do you know any reason why he'd go to Annapolis?"

Instead of answering, she stared towards Cambridge.

"I went to Annapolis for Orin Flanigan," McGuire said.

"I know."

"He wanted me to find somebody for him. A man named Myers."

"Yes."

"He wouldn't tell me why, and he kept everything about it off the firm's books. Do you know why?"

"Because he was doing something he shouldn't."

"What was that?"

"I think he was trying to get a little bit of revenge for me. And he was trying to save a woman from going through what I went through several years ago, and please don't ask me to tell you what that was."

"Flanigan?" McGuire looked into the distance. "Orin Flanigan, big-city family-law lawyer, tries to play gumshoe? You're kidding me. What's really going on?"

He looked back at her. She was shaking her head, and her expression had hardened.

A wave of squeals and laughter exploded behind them. McGuire turned to see perhaps twenty young children racing towards the fenced-in playground, two women scurrying after them. The children began clambering over playground rides in the shapes of animals. They were laughing and shouting, some stumbling over their feet and others giggling at the joy, the euphoria, of being six years old and free in a playground on a warm autumn day.

McGuire turned from the children to look at Susan Schaeffer. At the arrival of the children, her expression had changed again. The hardness, the refusal to answer McGuire's questions, had dissolved into something else. Now she looked shattered, about to burst into tears. He reached for her, his hand gentle on her shoulder. "What's wrong?" he asked. "Just tell me what's wrong and maybe I can help."

"Will you take me somewhere this afternoon?"

"Maybe. Where?"

She turned to look across the river. "To Cambridge. Harvard Yard." She looked back at him. "Memorial Church in the New Yard. Do you know it?"

He said Yes, and they walked back to his car on Charles Street.

In the car, crossing Longfellow Bridge over the river, she looked down at her hands. "Are you looking into Orin's disappearance? Has the law firm asked you to do that?"

"No," McGuire said. "They haven't. If they did, I'd turn it down. I'd just get in the way of the police."

"So all those questions you were asking me, they were for your own interest?"

"That's all."

She stared ahead through the windshield. "Thank you."

To enter Harvard Yard on a perfect autumn afternoon is to touch the hem of privilege. Verdant and sun-dappled among oak trees that were massive and ancient when the Kennedys arrived as freshmen, the Yard is both foreign and familiar. Lecture halls, residences, and chapels, all idealized examples of

American Colonial architecture, echo the school's colors: crimson in their brickwork, and white in their carved wooden trim. Students and lecturers stride across lawns and along paths looking purposeful and relaxed, or recline on the grass, their backs against tree trunks, sweaters knotted around their waists or across their shoulders, books in their hands or on their laps, their hair long or their heads shaved, their clothes fashionably unfashionable, and for a short space of time in their lives they are as permanent as the buildings surrounding them.

A middle-aged man entering Harvard Yard on such a day grows conscious of his failings and deficiencies. Even now, the sight of the beauty and promise enjoyed by the privileged students nurtured McGuire's resentment and exposed his envy, feelings he had hidden for years. As he crossed the yard, McGuire managed to repress his anger towards those who shared this privilege, either as transient student or tenured professor. It had been years since he visited Harvard and, in spite of his envy for the students, he reminded himself that he loved the Boston area too much to ever move from it, that the weather and the traffic and the incessant political problems were a small price to pay for living in a place he knew he could never leave.

Susan Schaeffer spoke only once, to agree with McGuire that it was beautiful in the Yard, and they rounded University Hall towards Memorial Church, its white needle spire shining in the sun.

As they approached the building, McGuire heard organ music drifting towards them, something by Bach, he thought, or maybe Handel. Old music, anyway, rich and burnished by time.

The church dates back to 1931, a newcomer among the other structures in the Yard, but its architectural lines are directly descended from its oldest neighbors. Wide steps sweep up to the entrance. Inside, the pews march in puritanical lines forward to a surprisingly simple altar set close to the pews, as though defying the congregation to escape the wrath of the sermons.

There was another reason for the close proximity of altar and pews, and it was separated from the rest of the church by a filigreed screen: a massive Baroque organ, considered the best example of such an instrument in North America. The organ's great pipes soar upwards from a semi-circular console, all but the tops of the largest pipes hidden from view to those seated in the pews. Someone was playing the organ in sweeps of melody and curtains of chords.

Susan Schaeffer led the way into the church, the first time McGuire had seen her move with authority and poise. She paused at the end of one aisle and bowed, and McGuire halted behind her, drinking in the sight and the sound.

The church windows were open to the air, and the building was empty, save for the unseen organist at the console. The music, which had drifted lightly in the air outside the church, was now weighty and more authoritative. Bass notes seemed to begin in the very foundation of the building and rise upward through the floors and the pews, and higher notes drifted like ribbons among the open rafters. The organist was practicing; periodically he or she would stop at a phrase and repeat it several times before proceeding.

Susan Schaeffer sat in a pew midway up the aisle and closed her eyes. A slight smile played on her lips and the lines of her face faded. McGuire sat beside her, unsure of the purpose of their visit here. She had grown visibly relaxed and at peace. As had McGuire.

At one point the organist stumbled over an arpeggio, attempted to replay it, and stumbled again, and an explosive stage-whispered "Shit!" sounded back to the pews where McGuire and Susan were seated. Susan's shoulders hunched and shook with laughter.

They remained for perhaps ten minutes longer, then she rose and led him back down the aisle and out into the healing autumn air.

"What was that all about?" McGuire asked as they crossed Harvard Yard again. "Were you saying some kind of prayer in there or something?"

"No," she said. She knelt to pick up a large maple leaf, turned pumpkin-orange by the onset of autumn, and she stroked its texture with her fingers as she walked. "Sometimes I just want a place where I can feel safe for a few minutes. Any church will do, I guess. But that one's almost always open, and I used to visit it years ago, on my own. I just wanted to visit it again today." She bent with sudden laughter and reached a hand to his shoulder. "Wasn't that funny when the organist missed those notes? I mean, can you imagine if that happened in the middle of a service?"

"First time I saw you laugh," McGuire said. "I didn't think you could."

"I can laugh," she said. "I love to laugh. I look for ways to laugh all the time."

"You don't have to take me home."

They were crossing Harvard Street, wending their way through knots of students towards McGuire's car. She thanked McGuire again, and told him she could take a bus downtown. "That was a very sweet thing to do, bringing me here."

Instead of replying, McGuire guided her to the car. He paused before starting the engine. "Whatever you know about

Flanigan's disappearance, you should tell the police. You know that, don't you?"

"Yes, I know."

"Were you two having an affair?"

She smiled and closed her eyes. "No, we were not having an affair. That would have been impossible."

"Why?"

"Well, for one thing, Orin kept saying how I reminded him of his daughter. Do you know about his daughter?"

"Her husband murdered her."

"Orin and his wife never got over it. They'll never get over it. How could they? They blamed themselves for what happened, and Orin blamed the legal system, which he is a part of, for the fact that her husband received such a short sentence. Four years, I think."

"He told somebody you were an innocent."

She looked startled. "Innocent of what?"

"I don't know. Sounds to me like he was trying to settle a score on his own." McGuire started the car and eased out of the parking lot into traffic. "What's the connection between you, Orin, and this guy in Annapolis, Myers?"

"Please don't."

"Don't what?"

"Don't ask me these questions."

"Why not?"

"Because I like you. Because you've been nice to me." She looked out the window, avoiding his eyes.

"Is he your ex-husband, this Myers character?"

"No."

"Flanigan's specialty is child support. This Myers guy, is he running away from that?"

Another "no," and she closed her eyes.

McGuire drove in silence and turned onto Massachusetts Avenue. He was angry with her for not opening up to him.

She sensed his anger and rested her hand on his shoulder. "I'm sorry," she said.

"You say that a lot."

"I know. I have a lot to be sorry for."

"Like what?"

"Can I promise to tell you later?"

"Sure." They were approaching the Longfellow Bridge. Across the river, the downtown buildings shone in the late afternoon sun. "Tell me some other things about you."

"Like what?"

"Like why a woman like you hasn't had a date with a man for a couple of years."

She withdrew her hand. "You can drop me off at the market, if you like."

"You're not answering my question. And I'm not dropping you off at the market. I'm taking you home. No arguments this time. I'll just see you to your front door, all right?"

Almost in spite of herself, it seemed, she permitted a smile to shine through. "Now how is a girl going to argue with that tone of voice?"

"Where is it? Where do you live?"

"On Queensberry. Near the Fens."

"Not a bad neighborhood."

"No, it's not."

He drove up Boylston and onto Queensberry Street. On the way, she said, "I just realized that I don't know very much about you either."

"Not much to know."

"Tell me anyway."

"Well, I'm not a cop any more, and I'm not married any more either. I never voted for Reagan and I don't give a damn about what happens in Washington, Hollywood, or the music business."

She smiled at him. "You've told me what you aren't and what you haven't done. You haven't told me what you are and what you want to do."

"Hell," McGuire said, "I'm still trying to work that out."

When they reached Queensberry, she pointed to a brownstone several doors from the corner, and he pulled to the curb just beyond it. She touched his arm again. "Tell me if you think Orin's dead," she said. Her mood had grown somber again.

"If he isn't, he's doing a hell of a good job faking it," McGuire said.

She burst into tears and collapsed against his shoulder. He encircled her in his arm and recalled something Ronnie had said when he moved in with her and Ollie several months earlier. "You're a fixer," Ronnie told him. "You want to fix things between people. That's why you became a cop and that's why you couldn't stand *being* a cop. You couldn't stand it because there are too many things you can't fix when it comes to people. Ollie, he doesn't care when people are ruining each other's lives, he keeps his mind on the people who count to him, like you and me, but not the whole damn world. You're different. You want to *fix* it and you can't. And that's what makes you angry."

He had smiled at her words then, thinking there was maybe some truth to them, remembering how as a child he wanted to fix his parents' destructive marriage; wanted to make each love the other and so, perhaps, begin to love him too; wanted his father to stop drinking and his mother to stop despising her life.

Susan finished dabbing at her eyes with a tissue, and she leaned to kiss McGuire's cheek. "Thank you," she said. "You're not what Orin said at all."

"What did Orin say about me?"

She reached for the door and opened it. "Orin said you were tough as nails. But you're not at all, are you?"

"I'll come by, see you tomorrow," McGuire called to her as she closed the car door.

He pulled away from the curb and she stood watching him leave. Then she walked towards the brownstone. She climbed the steps and rang the brass bell, her head still down, waiting for someone to come to the door so she could enter.

McGuire arrived at Revere Beach just after six o'clock, glancing at the empty space in the driveway where Ronnie's car should have been.

When he entered the kitchen, he saw the note propped against a sugar bowl on the small table, his name written in her neat script on the envelope. He held it lightly in his hands for several seconds, as though it were about to burst into flames, then tossed it back on the table and walked to Ollie's room and the sound of the evening television news.

"Just in time for today's disasters," Ollie said, shifting his eyes from the screen to meet McGuire's. "So far, we got a drive-by shooting in Dorchester, a murder-suicide in Charlestown, and that kid who took you on, Hayhurst? They think he's the guy who pistol-whipped a couple of schoolteachers from Iowa." His face clouded. "You look like you've had your own fill of troubles. What's up?"

"Nothing special." He sat on the chair beside the bed. "Where's Ronnie?"

Ollie turned his eyes back to the television screen. "Gone back to her painting class. That's a good sign, ain't it? That she's feelin' better?" Ollie agreed with his own assessment. "Sure it is," he said.

If he asks, I'll tell him, McGuire told himself. If he doesn't ask, I'll keep my mouth shut. When Ollie didn't speak, McGuire said, "Ronnie give you dinner?"

"Oh sure, sure. She fed me. I'm okay." He turned his head to McGuire. "Listen, you want to go out for a while or something, you go ahead. I'm all right. There's a ball game on tonight, Sox and the Tigers."

"I don't think I'll be going out," McGuire said. He rose from the chair.

"You can, you know. I'm all fed and changed." Ollie's good hand tilted towards a plastic bowl of candies. "Ronnie left me some wine gums here. I'm all set."

McGuire was almost at the door when Ollie called his name. "You and Ronnie," he said when McGuire turned around, "you're worried about me, aren't you?"

"No more than usual," McGuire said.

"Well, you're worried about something. Both of you. I can tell. Listen, if it's me, forget it. Don't worry about me, okay? Ronnie's applied to get me one of those motorized wheelchairs, she tell you that? I said I'd never get my butt into one of those things, but I was watching a commercial about the Florida Keys. I never been there, the Keys. I thought, Damn, I'd like to sit under a palm tree for a week this winter and look at the ocean, watch the pelicans dive for fish, see the sun go down."

McGuire stood, waiting.

"So we talked about it, and Ronnie said it would do me a lot of good. I said maybe you'd come along with us, maybe you'd find a whole new herd of widows and divorcees to chase down there. What do you think of that?"

"I don't like Florida," McGuire said.

"Hell, this ain't Florida. It's the Keys. Different place altogether."

"Ronnie's right," McGuire said. "It'll do you a world of good."

He closed the door behind him and returned to the kitchen, where he eyed the envelope before picking it up again and opening it, making as little noise as possible. I would have told him, McGuire assured himself. If he'd asked, I would have laid it all out for him. He unfolded the small sheet of note paper.

> Joe,
> Ollie's been fed and he's comfortable. I'm not apologizing any more for what I did or where I'm going. I tried and I just couldn't do it (you know what I'm talking about). If you think I'm a selfish, unfaithful bitch, well that's just too bad. There's a possibility you could be reading this tomorrow morning, and if you are, why don't you go down the hall right now and change his diaper and see what I've been doing for years?
>
> I'm telling him tomorrow. Just to spare you the agony. If you're still acting so noble maybe you can do it for me. It's up to you.
>
> R.

McGuire crumpled the note into a ball and tossed across the room. Then he reached for the telephone directory, stared up at the ceiling while he recalled the name, and began flipping through the pages.

"Damn her," he whispered. "Goddamn her to hell."

There was a C. Simoni listed as the proprietor of Cedar Lane Gallery on Charles Street near Mt. Vernon. McGuire dialed first the number of the gallery and then the residence, counting nine rings each time before hanging up. After changing into a pair of worn jeans, low-cut Reeboks, a navy turtleneck sweater, and leather jacket, he left the house.

He found a parking spot on Chestnut Street and walked back to Charles. The evening had turned cool and damp, and couples on their way to dinner in one of the brass-and-wicker Beacon Hill bars walked with their arms locked together, huddling against the chill.

Cedar Lane Gallery was in a low storefront building, green, with a small gilt-painted sign on the door. Several paintings and prints were displayed in the window and hung in the one-room gallery itself. They were visible to McGuire through the glass, lit by small ceiling-mounted track lights, the only source of illumination inside the gallery. McGuire knocked on the front door several times, then stepped back to look up at the second floor, where a dim glow shone through curtained windows.

He examined the paintings on display. A few caught his eye because of their familiar style: semi-abstract watercolors executed with casual strokes and in subtle tones. He admired one of a harbor scene, another of an old farmhouse, a third of a seashore. Leaning against the window glass and shielding his eyes, he could read "C. Simoni" at the base of the watercolors, and, on the harbor scene, a price tag that said $3,000.

He walked across Charles Street, then east towards Cambridge and the Longfellow Bridge, which he had driven across with Susan just two hours earlier. He passed florists and antique shops and a small, dark bar crowded with couples, the buzz of their conversation spilling out through the doors towards him. He walked on, past a hardware store and another art gallery, to a sandwich shop almost as crowded as the bar, and he remembered that he hadn't eaten since his lunch with Sleeman. The sandwich shop had large plate-glass windows on either side of the entrance and he stood for a moment, thinking if he sat at a table near the window, he could watch the gallery across the street for Ronnie and her lover to arrive, if they weren't already upstairs in the near-darkness, ignoring telephone calls and knocks on the door.

He wasn't interested in seeing Ronnie. He wanted to see *him*, wanted to see the man who was threatening to destroy, whether he knew it or not, the only part of Ollie's life worth saving.

The door to the bar opened long enough for the chatter and laughter inside to spill into the street, and in the silence after it closed, McGuire heard a woman's voice, laughing.

He saw Ronnie with her arm locked in the arm of a man barely her own height. The man wore a denim jacket and jeans, and a patterned open-neck shirt beneath the jacket.

They stopped at the curb and the man withdrew a package of cigarettes from the pocket of his jacket, popped one into his mouth, and spoke around it to Ronnie, saying something that made her laugh again. Then he lit a match and cupped it in his hands, bending to light the cigarette. In the glow McGuire saw an aging but still-handsome face, the nose small and straight, set between two eyes that darted back to Ronnie's when the cigarette was lit. His hair was auburn, flecked with silver, a full head of hair that swept over his ears and down the back of his head. She spoke to him and he withdrew the cigarette. He placed it in her mouth and she inhaled, her head back and her eyes closed, while her lover watched her.

Carl Simoni spoke to her again, and when Ronnie erupted in a fit of coughing and laughing, Simoni's expression changed from delight to concern. He placed his hand behind her head, pulled her to him and patted her back. In that moment, his eyes met McGuire's without expression and McGuire watched Simoni comfort her.

Simoni kissed her on the cheek, and when her coughing subsided she began to laugh again, her back to McGuire. They kissed before Simoni guided her through the traffic across Charles Street. McGuire followed, several paces behind.

McGuire watched the man unlock the front door of the gallery and wait for Ronnie to enter before following her, slipping the night latch behind them. He watched Ronnie walk through the gallery towards a door on the far wall, and up the stairs, Simoni following her. He watched the lights glow suddenly bright through the windows of the second floor.

The lights would be extinguished soon, McGuire knew, and he walked away, not wanting to see it happen and know what it meant.

He walked to the end of Charles Street and up Cambridge to a bar, where he ordered pizza and a beer. Half an hour later he was sitting back in his car on Chestnut Street, tapping the steering wheel with his fingers, recalling the sound of Ronnie's laughter and the look of concern on her lover's face when she began to cough.

He had never seen Ronnie smoke before, and he had not heard her laugh like that, so easy and relaxed and genuine, in a very long time. He loved the idea that she could revel in such easy joy. He hated what she had to do to experience it. But now he understood.

Twenty minutes later he was back in the small white house in Revere Beach. Before he could slip out of his jacket, he heard Ollie's voice call his name.

"What's up?" McGuire asked when he entered Ollie's room.

"Little bit of excitement, put a fire under your buns," Ollie said, grinning up at him. "You know that guy, lawyer named Flanigan, down at that place where you're puttin' in time?"

"What about him?" McGuire asked, dreading the answer.

"He's in the river, under the Charlestown Bridge. That's where they found him this afternoon."

"How'd you hear?"

"Guy named Pinnington called, said you oughta know about it. Said he's going down to Berkeley Street, give the police whatever they need to know. That's how he put it. Said he'll do whatever it takes. Thought you should know, maybe join him there. I said I'd tell you if you showed up before the sun did."

CHAPTER 14

"What's your name again?" The night cop at the entrance to Boston Police Headquarters on Berkeley Street was still in his twenties, pink-cheeked and sullen-eyed. He ran his finger down a printed list.

"McGuire. Joe McGuire. I used to be in homicide here."

"That right?" The young cop didn't even look up. "Well, your name's not here, and if your name's not here, I can't let you up without permission."

"Then get permission," McGuire hissed.

The cop looked at him, his eyes like glass marbles. "Look, if you've got a problem, take it up with the citizen's commission . . ."

"You found a body in the river tonight," McGuire said. "I may know something about the circumstances, which makes me a citizen with information relating to a possible homicide. Now you get me in touch with the investigating team or I'll talk to somebody about putting your ass back directing traffic at the airport."

"Just who the hell do you think . . ." the cop began, until a voice behind McGuire said, "Joe?"

McGuire turned to face a middle-aged man in an oversized tweed topcoat, a wide grin beneath his salt-and-pepper mustache.

"Barton," McGuire said.

"Barnston." The man's smile wavered a little. "It's Barnston. Jerry Barnston."

"Yeah, right." McGuire shook the detective's hand. "Listen, I have to talk to whoever's working on the guy they fished out of the river an hour or so ago . . ."

"The lawyer," Barnston nodded. "I think it's Donovan's case. Come on up. Jeez, it's good to see you again."

Without looking back, McGuire raised a hand and twisted it around, over his shoulder, waving farewell to the duty cop, who said "Big deal" to McGuire's back and turned away, pulling at a thumbnail with his teeth.

Phil Donovan had been just another ambitious junior detective years earlier when McGuire and Ollie Schantz were the hottest homicide team on the force. Now he was a full lieutenant, adding another layer of arrogance to the personality of the thin, red-haired man who looked up from his desk as McGuire approached.

"What the hell is this?" Donovan sneered.

Across from him Richard Pinnington sat cross-legged, his open Burberry topcoat slung over his shoulders like a cape.

McGuire nodded at Pinnington and glared at Donovan. More than a year earlier, Donovan had shot Dan Scrignoli, a Boston cop gone bad, in front of McGuire's eyes. Scrignoli had been in the process of surrendering his weapon, withdrawing it from inside his jacket. Donovan claimed the action had been aggressive and threatening, and that he fired in self-defense. McGuire knew better. Scrignoli died later that day. Donovan received a public commendation for his heroic actions. McGuire and Donovan hadn't met since.

"I hear you're the guy to see about Orin Flanigan," McGuire said.

"McGuire," Donovan said, "I'm the guy you gotta talk to if you wanta take a leak in this place, okay?" The Irish detective was wearing a knit tie pulled away from the collar of his striped dress shirt, and his brown leather shoulder holster was unbuckled. A cheap black blazer hung over the back of a folding chair behind him.

McGuire seized the empty chair next to Pinnington, swung it around, and straddled it, resting his arms on the back. "How'd they find him?" he asked Pinnington.

"They found him dead, you dink." Donovan placed his feet onto the corner of his desk. "And smelly."

Pinnington's face turned crimson, and he avoided McGuire's and Donovan's eyes. "He was caught in some old reinforcing rod under the bridge. The body . . ." Pinnington brought his hand to his eyes and cleared his throat. "The body was mostly underwater. He could have been there several days."

"Made like a barge on the ol' Mississippi, just a-floatin' downstream." Donovan was watching McGuire, the grin frozen on his face.

"Suicide?" McGuire asked, although he didn't believe it.

"They don't . . ." Pinnington began.

"Sure, suicide." Donovan's voice had a serrated edge. "Guy parks his car in Weymouth, maybe hitchhikes twenty miles downtown, bops himself on the back of his head, and jumps in the river. Sure he does."

"Who identified him?" McGuire asked.

"I did," the lawyer said. "I couldn't ask his wife to do that." Pinnington stroked his forehead, his voice almost breaking. "It wasn't a pretty sight."

"Was there any identification on him?" McGuire said. "His wallet maybe?"

"Hey, McGuire." Donovan jabbed a finger in his direction. "Last I heard, your name wasn't back on the roster here, was it?"

"Was he carrying any ID?" McGuire said, speaking slowly.

"Yeah, he had ID," Donovan said. "What's that tell you, hotshot?"

McGuire shrugged.

Pinnington stood up. "Will you need anything else from me?" he said to Donovan.

The detective lifted a pad of lined yellow paper from his desk and looked at his notes. "Not right away. We'll be in, talk to you tomorrow."

Pinnington nodded. McGuire touched the lawyer's arm as he walked past. "Anything I can do?" he asked.

"No." Pinnington breathed deeply and seemed to rise in height. "I'm going to visit Nancy now. Orin's wife. This isn't going to be easy. You'll be in tomorrow morning?" McGuire nodded. "See me, first thing," Pinnington said.

"What else is there?" McGuire asked Donovan when Pinnington left.

"You can read about it in the papers." Donovan swung his feet off the desk and flipped his notepad to a fresh sheet. "So, what've you got to tell me?"

"How long had the body been in the water?"

"Hey." Donovan jabbed at the top of his desk as he spoke. "You wanta come in here like a concerned citizen and help with this investigation, you can do it. You wanta know anything else, you do like the rest of the city and wait your turn."

McGuire stood up. "Where's Eddie?"

"Probably home, pickin' his toes. What the hell do you want with Eddie Vance?"

"See you." McGuire turned and began walking away.

Donovan called McGuire's name. When McGuire kept walking, Donovan shouted again, and two detectives looked up from their computer terminals. "Hey, old man. You didn't find out shit in Annapolis, you know."

McGuire stopped and looked back at Donovan, who rose from his desk and approached McGuire, carrying his notepad with him.

"You went looking for some guy name Myers? Told Flanigan he was down there selling yachts? Well, that outfit never heard of him. Nobody's heard of him."

"A woman at the yacht brokerage . . ."

"Yeah, yeah, yeah. Broad named . . ." Donovan flipped a page on his notepad. "Diamond. Talked to her already. She never heard of the guy either. But she remembers you. Says you looked like just another cheap talker, come in acting like you want to lay a hundred grand on a yacht when you couldn't afford to buy a pair of oars, so she gave you the brush-off."

"You talked to people down there already?"

"Talked to Diamond and talked to her boss. Then we talked to the local dicks. They checked around, said Myers has dropped out of sight. He'd been spreadin' the word about sellin' yachts, maybe down in Miami or Lauderdale. Now we've got Florida checkin' up on him, runnin' their tracer program. He'll turn up soon. You've been out of the loop too long, you geezer. Everything's on computers now. We got rid of a lot of you dead-asses so we could get things done, you know what I'm sayin'?"

"When's the autopsy?"

"Why, you wanta go down, show Mel Doitch your crochet stitch or something?"

McGuire stared back at Donovan, who returned the look with a grin for a moment, then called across at two detectives who had been watching them over their computer terminals. "You guys heard of the famous Joseph P. McGuire? Hotshot homicide Louie? Well, here he is. Used to be a medicine man, poppin' pills in the combat zone. Now he plays skip tracer for a bunch of lawyers. Except he couldn't find his ass if the directions were printed on his hand."

Leave it, McGuire told himself. Just leave it. He turned to walk towards the elevator.

"'Course, you could tell us about that little piece you've been seen with lately," Donovan called to his back. "What's her name? Oh yeah. Schaeffer. Heard all about her."

"What?" McGuire turned to face Donovan. "What have you heard?"

"She and the victim used to play pinch-and-giggle in his office at noon."

"That's crap."

"Crap?" Donovan approached McGuire almost warily and his voice dropped in volume. "You think it's crap? How about this for crap, McGuire. Flanigan was the lawyer who acted for her ex-husband, to help seize her kids. He got custody of them for his client two, three years ago. Didn't Pinnington tell you that? How's that for a picture, McGuire? Lawyer helps a husband steal the kids and disappear, and the ex-wife starts cozying up to him, couple of years later. Course, the lawyer shouldn't have anything to do with an ex-adversary, should he? Except maybe he'll take a few quickie BJs in his office from some desperate broad who wants her kids back . . ."

McGuire's hand shot out and seized Donovan's neck, the same motion he had used when he bloodied Donovan's nose in the basement interrogation room more than a year earlier. At that time, Donovan had been so surprised when McGuire lunged at him that he had fallen backwards against the wall and it was McGuire's forehead, not his fist, that collided with Donovan's nose. Others in the room, including a perturbed Eddie Vance, had separated the two men before Donovan could react.

But this time the detective's hand went to his holster and withdrew his 9 mm Glock. He pressed the muzzle against McGuire's head. The two detectives leapt out of their chairs and ran towards Donovan and McGuire, one shouting, "What the hell!"

Donovan kept the gun pressed against McGuire's temple and said, "You think I wouldn't do it, asshole? You think I wouldn't?"

"What the hell's goin' on with you?" Ollie said

McGuire sat staring down at his feet. His hands were still shaking.

"Assault an armed cop with two juniors as witnesses?" Ollie Schantz was a teacher lecturing an errant student, a father trying to talk sense to a delinquent son. "Those juniors woulda said you looked armed as a Nazi platoon, it came down to an inquiry. They woulda nailed you as a nutcase, a *dead* nutcase, and Donovan would be golden, get a couple of weeks off to let his nerves settle, maybe he'd go to Hawaii or something, and he'd come back in harness and you'd still be worm food." He watched McGuire in silence for a moment, then said, "Why the hell'd you let a pus-hole like Donovan get to you?"

McGuire knew why. He just couldn't explain it to Ollie. He was having trouble explaining it to himself. It was almost eleven o'clock. "I'm going to bed," he said.

"Yeah, well now I've got somethin' to tell Ronnie when she gets home." Ollie turned back to the television. "You and Donovan making like a couple of drunken cowboys right there on Berkeley Street. Wait'll Ronnie hears about that."

McGuire said the words without thinking, as though they had been set in a trap, and Ollie had pulled the trip wire. "Ronnie's not coming home tonight." He watched Ollie's reaction from the door, surprised at his own words. I've been wanting to say them for a week, he thought.

"What the hell're you talking about?"

"She's not coming home tonight, Ollie. She told me in a note she left on the table. She'll be here in the morning and she's going to tell you where she's been all these other nights. And with whom."

McGuire watched Ollie swallow, watched his mouth work as though he were chewing around fish bones. "Get out of here," he said.

"Ollie, it's true . . ." McGuire began.

"*Get out of here!*" Ollie's voice was a rasp, a cry of rage muted by his inability to rise and strike out.

"You want to talk?"

"*I want you out of here! Out of my house! Get out!*"

McGuire walked slowly down the hall. He's known all along, he realized. In one small corner of his mind, the truth has been there all along, begging him to look at it, and he hasn't been able to see it until now.

He lay on the bed in his room, still dressed, watching his mind leap back and forth between the events of the day, from the probable murder of Orin Flanigan to the explicit infidelity of Ronnie Schantz.

Donovan said Flanigan had been struck on the head. Flanigan's car was left in a public place twenty miles from the river. And the body had been in the water for several days.

Then: Ollie knows about Ronnie. He's lying down there, unable to move, unable to hit the wall or even get drunk, for Christ's sake.

What the hell happened? McGuire asked himself. Something happened to send things out of control, and I don't know what it was, don't even know when it happened.

He recalled Susan Schaeffer in the Harvard Yard church that afternoon. He remembered the expression on her face as the waves of organ music washed over her and the trees moved in the breeze beyond the windows. He saw her there now, imagined himself with her, and the image relaxed him, soothed him. There was a sense of past tragedy about her that haunted McGuire, and he wanted to know, needed to know, the secret of her sadness. Everybody's daily sadness.

He glanced at the clock radio; it was over two hours since he left Ollie. Had he fallen asleep?

He rose from the bed, walked to the top of the stairs, and listened. He heard nothing. He walked downstairs and along the darkened hall. A sliver of light shone beneath Ollie's door. McGuire pushed it open to find Ollie staring at him.

"I thought I told you to get out," Ollie said in a voice like cardboard, flat and gray.

"You want me out, I'm out."

"How long've you known?"

"For sure? About a week."

"Who is it?"

"Her art teacher."

"Jesus Christ."

"How long've *you* known?"

"What the hell do you mean?"

"You had to be kidding yourself. You had to wonder about all those times she wasn't here when she said she'd be."

"I just . . ." Ollie moved his head, avoiding McGuire's eyes. "Ronnie's never had much time on her own. It's either been me chasing my ass around town with you, and she's back here hopin' I'm not wearin' a body bag the next time she sees me, or it's been me lyin' in this bed like a friggin' piece of dead meat, with her spending all her time keepin' me clean and fed. So when she got out and started her painting class, it made me feel good, made me feel not so guilty . . ."

"You hate her?"

"What kind of question is that? Goddamn right I hate her. I'd like to rip her head off. His too."

"And mine?"

"You got in my way and I could, maybe I would." He avoided McGuire's eyes again. "Maybe I would."

"You want something to help you sleep?"

"Yeah, a thirty-eight slug in my fuckin' head."

"What do you want me to do?" When Ollie refused to answer, McGuire stepped closer to the bed. "Ollie, you have to deal with it. She's going to make you deal with it. So what do you want me to do? You want me to be here when she gets home?"

Ollie closed his eyes. Cry, goddamn it, McGuire wanted to say, but no tears came. "Leave us alone when she gets here. Maybe later, maybe afterwards, we'll talk. You and me. And her, if she's still here, and she wants to."

"She didn't say she'd leave, Ollie."

Ollie whispered something, his eyes still closed.

"What?" McGuire asked, leaning even closer.

"I said she already has."

McGuire stood up. "You want the light off?" and when Ollie refused to answer, McGuire flicked the switch and climbed the stairs again.

A soft click wakened him, and he lay in the darkness, holding his breath until he heard the front door open and close gently. He glanced at the clock radio, where the numerals 5:47 glowed, and he listened to Ronnie's footsteps walking down the hall to Ollie's room and returning to the foyer, where the bottom step of the stairs creaked with her weight.

He opened the door just as she reached the stair landing.

"Hello," she said, as though she expected to greet him there.

"Is he sleeping?" McGuire asked. In the dim light he could see she was without makeup.

"Yes."

"I told him."

"Did you?" As though McGuire had told her what he had eaten for dinner the previous night.

"Are you surprised?"

"I'm surprised it took you so long. To tell him."

"Do you want me to stay? Be here when he wakes up?"

"No, I don't." She resumed walking, across the landing towards her bedroom. "This is between Ollie and me. It has always been between Ollie and me."

McGuire returned to bed, rose at seven, showered, and dressed in a sweater, slacks, and tweed jacket. Downstairs, about to leave, he paused at the front door, hearing the sounds

from Ollie's room. A soft voice speaking. Another voice crying.
He stepped outside, closing the door behind him.

Over eggs, toast, and coffee at a Boylston Street diner he read the *Globe*'s account of Orin Flanigan's death, describing him as a prominent local lawyer. The body had been discovered by two street people searching the riverbank for discarded soft-drink bottles. Police suspected foul play. Orin Flanigan was survived by his wife, Nancy. A daughter, Wendy, had predeceased him. Results of an autopsy would be revealed today. Funeral plans were pending.

There was nothing in the story about Flanigan's rented car being located so far from the body. McGuire thought about that, and about Flanigan's unopened luggage in the trunk. There was something important about it all, something he knew would elude Donovan. Donovan had elbowed and kissed his way to full lieutenant. The elbowing had pushed aside less-aggressive colleagues who were slow to seek credit for their achievements; the kissing had been directed towards Eddie Vance in the form of flattery and an inclination for performing the dirty work that Vance preferred to avoid. Donovan knew the politics of his job better than anyone McGuire had ever met. He was blind, however, to other aspects, like the ability to see beneath the surface of things. McGuire remembered Oscar Wilde's observation that, while many were lying in the gutter, some were looking at the stars. No matter where Donovan may be lying, McGuire suspected, he would never think of looking at the stars.

It was almost ten when he reached the law office. Secretaries and junior lawyers stood in small knots, many of the women with their eyes red-rimmed from crying, all of the men with stricken, ashen faces. When he called Richard Pinnington's office, the secretary informed him that Pinnington was in a meeting with the senior partners and had left instructions not to be disturbed for any reason.

McGuire made coffee, drank half a cup, tried to read some staff reports, finished none of them, and finally left his office to climb the stairs to the executive floor.

Someone was sorting papers at Lorna's desk, a middle-aged woman McGuire did not recognize. "Yes?" she said when McGuire paused in front of Lorna's desk.

"Who are you?" McGuire said.

"I'm filling in for Ms. Robbins," the woman said. "From a temp service."

"Lorna's not in?" McGuire said.

The woman pointed with a pencil towards Orin Flanigan's office. "I believe Ms. Robbins is in there," she said. "With some police officers. Detectives, actually."

"I'll wait," McGuire said, and he sat on one of the side chairs. The woman looked at him with disapproval for a moment, then shrugged her shoulders and resumed her work.

Within minutes, Lorna Robbins emerged, clutching a handkerchief. She was followed by Donovan, a younger, round-faced detective McGuire didn't recognize, and two uniformed officers carrying cardboard boxes stuffed with files. The younger detective held what appeared to be a black leather-bound address book in his hands.

At the sight of McGuire, Lorna veered towards the desk and stood staring at the telephone.

Donovan thrust his hands in his trouser pockets and looked back and forth between Lorna and McGuire. "Hey, Burnell, look at this," he said to his younger partner. "See, this is what happens to cops, they act like assholes too often. They lose half their pension, so they gotta take work as a hired hand for a bunch of ambulance chasers." He looked over at Burnell, who was watching McGuire with an expression that said the young detective was as indifferent to Donovan's taunts as McGuire appeared to be. "'Course, you get in a place like this, you get a few side benefits if you want 'em."

McGuire looked across at Lorna, who was stroking the telephone receiver with her fingertips.

The temporary secretary seated at Lorna's desk continued shuffling files, absorbing everything she heard.

"How are you doing?" McGuire asked Lorna.

"She's doing all right, and you're not to speak to her," Donovan said.

McGuire rose from the chair and took a step towards Lorna. Donovan moved between them.

"I want to see you, McGuire," he said. "At Berkeley Street. You want to bring a lawyer, bring one. But you'll need more than one of these corporate-law types."

"I'm not a suspect and you damn well know it," McGuire said.

"Not up to you to decide."

"You want to ask me questions, ask me now."

"When I'm ready." Donovan looked at his watch. "And I'll be ready about three this afternoon. So be there."

"The hell I will," McGuire said.

Donovan smiled, and McGuire was surprised not to see ice crystals on his teeth. "Oh, you'll be there. I'm bettin' you'll be there." He rested his hand lightly against Lorna's back. "You ready, Ms. Robbins?"

Lorna nodded and, still avoiding McGuire's eyes, permitted Donovan to guide her across the reception area, followed by the other detective and the two police officers, who struggled with their boxes of files.

Instead of returning to his office, McGuire took the elevator down to street level and walked up to the Common, where he found a cast-iron bench below the rise leading to the State House. He sat there for almost an hour, staring out towards the Frog Pond and the Public Garden beyond, aware that his subconsciousness was shaking out much of what it had accumulated in the past two days, separating it in a sievelike manner. But when he rose to return to the law office, nothing new was evident to him yet, and he told himself to give it time, give it all time.

The light on McGuire's telephone was flashing when he returned to his office, indicating a message on his voice mail.

"Come up and see me, soon as you can," Richard Pinnington's voice growled through the receiver. McGuire made a pot of coffee, drank a cup black while staring at the wall over his desk, and finally, twenty minutes after entering his office, climbed the elegant central staircase again, and walked down the carpeted hall to Pinnington's office.

Pinnington was in shirtsleeves, seated at his desk, with the harbor behind him shining in the September sun. Across from him, sitting upright in their chairs with pads of lined yellow paper on their laps, were Charles Pratt and Fred King, the firm's two senior partners. Pratt, a descendant of one of the firm's founders, who practiced corporate law, was a thin, gaunt man, who reminded McGuire of a stork. King was round-faced and boyish in appearance, and specialized in trademark registrations. McGuire wondered how someone could devote their entire career to judging the legality of something as inconsequential as a trademark, even if it meant earning an annual salary of a half-million dollars or more. King threw McGuire a tight smile. Pratt glanced at him, then down at a pad filled with neat handwriting.

"Been waiting for you," Pinnington said. "You know Charlie and Fred."

McGuire nodded at the two men. "Got the right man for the job," Fred King said, and the tight smile reappeared.

"Don't know if he'll take it," Charlie Pratt said in a scratchy voice. He had thin gray hair and bony hands, whose transparent skin revealed a network of blue veins.

"Close the door, will you?" Pinnington said.

McGuire closed the door, returned to the group, and seated himself in the remaining empty chair next to Pinnington's desk.

"You want a drink?" Pinnington asked. He gestured towards his sideboard, where crystal decanters with brass medallions saying Scotch, Rye, Cognac, and Vodka sat among matching crystal tumblers.

McGuire shook his head.

"Good man," Fred King said. "You're drinking alone, Dick."

Pinnington grunted, set aside a half-empty glass, and looked at his notepad like an actor taking a last reading of his lines before the curtain rises. "The police have seized some of Orin's files," he said.

McGuire was about to say he already knew, but held back.

"We might have sought an injunction, but that would have been misinterpreted," Pinnington went on. "Case like this, homicide, we can't be seen as obstructing justice. No matter what our motives are."

"They have any ideas?" McGuire asked. He knew, recalling Donovan's cockiness and instructions to McGuire, that they must.

"Apparently they do." Charlie Pratt's eyes didn't leave the notepad. "It may have something to do with the assignment Orin gave you last week."

"How much do they know about that?" McGuire said.

King began to speak, but Pinnington interrupted, raising his voice to talk over the other man. "They know you were doing legitimate investigation work on behalf of a very circumspect lawyer."

Pratt shifted in his chair. McGuire waited for Pinnington to continue.

Pinnington scratched the back of his head absently. "We have two concerns here. Our primary and over-riding goal is to get to the bottom of Orin's murder and see that whoever is responsible for it is tried, convicted, and punished."

"You hear anything more about Nancy?" King asked Pinnington.

"Only that she's under her doctor's care. She was . . . well, you can imagine the scene at the house last night." Pinnington bit his bottom lip and nodded, as though agreeing with his own assessment.

Pratt turned and looked directly at McGuire. "Our other concern is protection of the firm's name."

McGuire shifted in his chair. "How," he said slowly, looking at each of the three men in turn as he spoke, "could the reputation of this law firm be at risk in a murder investigation?"

"Key question," Pinnington said. "The answer is, there's no proof that it is. But there are some hints that it *could* be."

"Such as?"

Pratt, who had been looking McGuire up and down as though estimating his age and weight, cleared his throat, a signal that he wished to speak. "Orin Flanigan may have been having a liaison with someone he should not have been."

"If he was seeing somebody behind his wife's back, I don't think that's so scandalous, is it?" McGuire said. "I mean, this firm's got a good reputation, but nobody expects you all to be monks."

"It's more than that." Pratt looked down at his notepad.

Pinnington picked up the cue. "You're familiar with the Schaeffer woman?" he said.

McGuire nodded.

"Susan Schaeffer may have been an unofficial client of Orin Flanigan's," Pinnington said.

"What's unofficial mean?" McGuire said.

"It means he was performing services beyond his everyday duties for the firm," Pratt said. "There could be a fairly severe conflict-of-interest as well. In any case, he was doing work without payment."

"Without payment in coin of the realm," King smirked. "Ms. Schaeffer may have been paying him in other ways."

"I don't believe that for a minute." Pinnington sat forward in his chair and began shuffling through several sheets of paper.

"Neither do I," McGuire said.

"What makes you say that?" Pratt was looking at him, the older man's eyebrows lifted in speculation.

"Totally out of character for Orin," Pinnington said before McGuire could speak. "I'd stack Orin up against any lawyer in this town when it comes to ethics, personal or professional."

"Look." McGuire directed his words at Pratt. "If Orin Flanigan was doing unofficial favors for somebody, it may get him in trouble with you people, but it's hardly a criminal act. And if he's been having an affair with . . . with some woman, well, that puts him on the same team with half the people in town, no matter how much it might surprise you guys. So where's the danger to your reputation? Is it this conflict-of-interest thing? Is it something else, something bigger?"

The eyes of the other men locked for an instant. "The point is," King said, "we don't know."

"Or we're not sure," Pratt added.

"Well, what is it?" McGuire said. "You don't know? Or you're not sure?"

"You know that old rule about never asking a question in court that you don't already know the answer to?" Pinnington said. "We've got a lot of questions to which we don't know the answers. We don't *know* if Orin Flanigan was venturing into criminal areas, intentionally or not. Personally, I can't imagine it. But we just don't *know*. We don't *know* if there's an ethics concern here that the bar association may want to look into. We don't *know* if some messy private matter could become public because it's part of the murder investigation. If any of these things happen, we want to know how to deal with it *before* it becomes public. Not after."

"Damage control," McGuire said.

"Precisely." Pratt nodded like a teacher hearing the correct answer from a prize student.

"What's your opinion of the man heading the murder investigation?" Pinnington said.

"Donovan?" McGuire stared past Pinnington through the windows to the view beyond. Across the harbor, an aircraft rose from Logan Airport, the sun flashing for an instant from its wings. "He's a cattle stampede in a china shop."

"My sentiments exactly," Pinnington said. "I don't think subtlety is his strong suit. And that doesn't help our position."

"Look." Pratt swiveled to face McGuire again, and paused to let everyone know he was about to make a significant statement. "Right this minute, in the boardrooms of some of the biggest corporations in New England, senior management people are talking about Orin's murder. They know he was a senior partner, a major voice in this outfit's management. Now they're wondering what's going on over here. They already know, if they read the papers, that he disappeared while on some kind of business. They're sniffing scandal, whether it's there or not." He paused again, a little too theatrically, McGuire thought. "Those people are our clients. And they don't want their corporate legal counsel to have even a whiff of wrongdoing, understand?"

"We're talking about several million dollars in retainers and special fees here." Pinnington leaned back in his chair and looked over his fingertips at McGuire. "We have to know what to say and how to say it, if this becomes a debacle."

"Donovan and I are not exactly fraternity brothers." McGuire smiled at Pinnington. "As you could see last night. He won't co-operate with me any more than he has to."

"So you'll have to do it on your own," Pinnington said. "Privately."

"And discreetly," Pratt added.

Pinnington sat forward. "Use your judgment," he said. "You've got a sense of what this is all about. If you have to take off somewhere, you go. If you come across something you have to share with the police, of course you're obligated to do so."

"Just tell us first," King said. "Give us a running start."

"And keep Rosen informed," Pratt said.

McGuire's head turned to face Pratt. "Who?"

"Marv Rosen." Pinnington was watching McGuire carefully. "We retain him as the firm's criminal-law counsel. I thought I told you that."

McGuire looked down, shaking his head. "If there's anybody who dislikes me more than Phil Donovan, it's Rosen."

"We can't let that matter. Besides." Pinnington rose from his chair and looked out the window. "I just spoke to him a few minutes ago, told him to expect a call. He said he has great respect for you as a police officer."

McGuire snorted. "He charged me with assault and threatened to sue me and the city of Boston for a million dollars."

"That was strictly business on his part," Pinnington said, his back to the group. "Good lawyers don't harbor grudges. It gets in the way of their work."

McGuire was about to speak when the door behind him opened and all four men turned to look. It was Connie Woodson, Pinnington's secretary. She leaned through the partially opened door.

"I'm sorry," she said. "But there's a personal telephone call for you, Mr. McGuire, and it sounds terribly urgent."

Pinnington raised his eyebrows. "You want to take it here?"

McGuire rose from the chair and reached across Pinnington's desk for the telephone.

"It's line three," the secretary said before closing the door.

McGuire lifted the receiver, punched the flashing light, and barked his name into the receiver. He listened to a woman's voice delivered in a flat, bureaucratic tone. Then he thanked her, replaced the receiver, stood up, and looked out the window at the harbor view again. Another aircraft was rising into the air at Logan. McGuire felt fleeting envy for the passengers, whom he imagined were setting off for California or Bermuda.

"That was a matron," he said, his eyes on the jet. "At the jail. On Nashua Street." King sat erect in his chair. Pratt looked at Pinnington, who was watching McGuire intently.

"They have Susan Schaeffer in custody for questioning," McGuire said, surprised at the strength of his own voice. "She's being held as a possible suspect in Flanigan's murder." He was staring out the window where the aircraft was completing a turn, heading west now.

Bermuda, hell, McGuire thought. It's probably just going to Cleveland.

CHAPTER 15

McGuire was directed down a narrow hall lined with metal doors to a guard who ushered him into a room slightly larger than a closet. He sat at a counter staring through heavy glass into an identical cubicle in the next room. Just beyond the cubicle, two guards stood gossiping against a pillar. McGuire grew aware of others on either side of him, prisoners and visitors facing each other through armored glass, the voice of each audible to the other through telephone handsets.

One of the guards on the prisoners' side nudged the other, and both looked to their left, beyond McGuire's vision. He followed their gaze until a uniformed female guard appeared, leading Susan Schaeffer around the low wall forming the cubicle on the prisoner's side.

She was walking with her head and her eyes lowered. Her shoulders sagged, and when the matron guided her to the chair and she looked up for the first time to see McGuire sitting across from her beyond the glass, she began to cry. The matron watched her in disapproval for a moment, then withdrew to stand alongside the two male guards. From their glances and expressions, McGuire knew they were talking about her.

She breathed deeply, withdrew a crumpled tissue from a pocket of her smock, and dabbed at her eyes. Then she lifted the receiver to her ear and spoke into it. "Thank you," she said in a throaty whisper. "Thank you for coming. You're the only one I could think of to call."

"Have they charged you with anything?" McGuire asked.

"I don't know."

"What do you mean, you don't know? If you're not charged with anything, why are they holding you here?"

She answered with a shake of her head.

"Do you have a lawyer?" he asked.

"They're getting me one. They said they would."

"What happened?"

"They came to arrest me at the candle shop. A couple of hours ago. Two detectives."

"Who?" McGuire rarely felt sympathy for prisoners, because they all had a reason for being held within steel cages, at least temporarily. But his instincts told him this woman had no reason to be here, and her vulnerability appeared more intense than he expected.

"I don't remember their names," she said. "One has red hair, he's bitter and sarcastic . . ."

"Donovan."

"Yes." She rested her head on her hand. "Yes, that's him."

"What did they tell you? When they first picked you up, what did they say?"

"That I was being brought here to be questioned about Orin Flanigan's murder." She raised her eyes to McGuire's. "I didn't even know he was dead," she said. "Last night, when you dropped me off, I had a long hot bath and read a book and slept late this morning, so I didn't hear the news, didn't see a newspaper . . ."

"Why were they talking to you?" McGuire asked. Something was wrong. You don't jail a murder suspect on the basis of an hour's questioning, unless you want to confirm hard evidence before laying a charge.

"They didn't tell me. But they knew so much about Orin and me, about our . . . relationship."

"I'm going to ask some questions, find out what's going on. But you have to tell me now. Do you know anything about Flanigan's murder? Anything at all?"

Her eyes appeared to sag at the corners, and she shook her head.

"Okay, hang in there. Let me find out what's going on . . ."

She nodded, looking directly at him. "Please get me out of here," she said. "I can't stand it in here."

"I know," McGuire said. He looked across at the matron, who removed the receiver from Susan's hand. McGuire burst from the cubical and accosted the duty officer at the front desk. "Where the hell's Donovan?" he snapped.

"From homicide?" The officer shrugged his shoulders. "I guess he's up on Berkeley . . ."

McGuire spun on his heel, not responding to the officer's reminder that he hadn't signed out, that somebody'd get in trouble if McGuire's signature wasn't in the Signed Out column.

This time Stu Cauley was handling day security on Berkeley Street. When McGuire demanded to know if Donovan was upstairs, Cauley nodded, grinned, and said, "Tear a strip off his butt for me, will you?"

McGuire rode alone in the elevator, and grunted in acknowledgment at the few old and tired faces of detectives who recognized him when he stepped out on the Investigations floor. Across the room he saw Donovan sitting on a corner of his desk, a paper in his hand, speaking into the telephone. Donovan looked up at McGuire, then back at the paper in his hand. "Well, if you gotta, you gotta," he said. "But I'm keeping it in the file anyway, because there's something to this, I don't care what you say, or she says, or this dink standing across from me says." He grinned at McGuire, showing two crooked front teeth behind his thin lips. "McGuire, remember him? Or are you too young. Maybe you don't go back that far?" He tossed the sheet of paper aside, then slid from his desk and replaced the receiver. "Don Higgins says hello." Donovan sat in his chair and looked out the window. Higgins was a prosecuting attorney, a quiet, methodical man whom McGuire considered above corruption and profoundly boring.

"He's not going to press charges against Susan Schaeffer," McGuire said.

"He can't." Donovan shrugged. "We need more. We'll get it."

"What the hell are you doing, locking her up down there? You want to hold her for questioning, you can do it here, downstairs. You got her locked up with whores, with muggers. How the hell can you do that?"

"You don't know?" Donovan grinned at McGuire. "You really as dumb as you look, McGuire?"

McGuire breathed deeply. "What's going on?"

"What's going on is none of your business."

"If you haven't got anything to charge her with, let her go. She's dying in there."

"Another couple hours won't kill her."

"Donovan, you are such scum."

Donovan smiled as though hearing a compliment from an unlikely source. "What, we've been down to Nashua Street, have we? Checkin' out our little piece a cheese, seein' how she's handling gray bars and black dykes?"

"She had nothing to do with Flanigan's murder."

"Yeah? Well, a couple of people disagree with you, McGuire."

"Somebody gave you a blind tip and you dove right into it, didn't you?"

"A *good* tip, McGuire. And not blind. Somebody who knows what was goin' on between her and the victim, day after day. I knew you'd show up here. When I left that law office where you hang out these days, I knew you'd find out we picked up this Schaeffer woman, and I knew you'd come in, blowin' off steam as though you're still cock of the walk around here. I figured it would take you till three o'clock, but I don't mind if you're a little early . . ."

McGuire closed his eyes and looked away. "Lorna Robbins, right?" He remembered Lorna's embarrassed attitude that morning as Donovan and the officers removed files from Flanigan's office.

"Lorna Robbins knew Flanigan's comings and goings, knew about the relationship between him and Schaeffer, knew a hell of a lot more about Schaeffer than you do, McGuire. She's a credible source for an arrest on suspicion of first-degree murder."

"She tell you everything, Donovan? Did she?"

"Like what?" Donovan opened a desk drawer, removed a package of Dentyne, unwrapped two sticks, and popped them into his mouth.

"Like the fact that Lorna and I were dating each other up until a couple of nights ago?"

Donovan watched McGuire, chewing the gum with his mouth open. "Dating? What's that, something you do in high school? You were sleeping with her, the Robbins woman, right?"

"None of your goddamn business."

"Because you know, if you were and you dropped her for the Schaeffer broad, I mean, who could blame you?"

"Lorna Robbins sent you to Susan Schaeffer because she is hurt and jealous. If she said, if she even hinted, that Susan had anything to do with murdering Flanigan, she's doing it for revenge. That's her only motive, and you and Don Higgins know it. So let her out *now* or I'll see that you're slapped with a habeas corpus so goddamn fast . . ."

"We're talking like a lawyer now, are we?" Donovan spoke across the room to two detectives who had been eavesdropping on the conversation. "See what happens, you hang around lawyers too long? You forget you used to be a cop and you start talkin' like them."

"Just do it, Donovan." McGuire turned to leave.

"Hey," Donovan called to his back. "Hey, McGuire. You think you know everything about this case and that broad, down there on Nashua? Well, I can tell you right now, you don't know a damn thing, McGuire, and when you find out what's really goin' on, you're gonna look like the dummy you are."

"Now, please don't ask me to reveal any details." Don Higgins's carefully modulated voice buzzed in McGuire's ear. Beyond the telephone booth, the midday traffic on Boylston Street hummed past, and McGuire had to cover his other ear with his hand.

"I'm not asking for anything, Don." McGuire realized he was hungry, and he promised himself a steak at Zoot's later. "I just want to know. Beyond the things that Lorna Robbins said about Susan Schaeffer, was there any other evidence?"

"Only enough for questioning."

"It still must have taken a pretty strong statement to haul somebody in like that."

"There were claims of direct involvement, yes."

"Claims? That's it? Unsubstantiated stuff, gossip? Is that enough to be booked on suspicion of murder these days?"

"It came from a source close to the victim." Higgins sounded defensive. "His own private secretary. You have to assume some validity. And there were other considerations."

"Do you know there's a motive on Robbins's part? For saying what she said?"

"Phil Donovan called and told me that, a few minutes ago." McGuire heard Higgins exhale into the receiver. "Okay, repeat this and I'll deny it, but I have a feeling Donovan acted prematurely in making the arrest. Certainly, had we known this Robbins woman had reason to attack Miss Schaeffer . . . well, frankly we're all looking a little silly here."

"Don, I can't believe you agreed to book her without something more solid."

"It wasn't just the tip. It was the other thing too."

"What other thing?" McGuire heard a moment of dead air. "Is this is the other consideration you talked about? What other thing?"

"I can't go into that."

"Aw, come on, Don. Look, let's say I have a personal interest in this Schaeffer woman."

"All the more reason I shouldn't say anything."

"You're talking in riddles, Don. Come on, it's me, McGuire. You and I have traded secrets over the years . . ."

"Did you ever take this woman home?"

"Yeah, I took her home. Just last night. Nice little brownstone on Queensberry. What about it?"

"Then you know it's a halfway house."

McGuire closed his eyes. "No," he said. He had never lied to Don Higgins in his life, and he didn't feel like creating any sense of bravado, any false knowledge now. "No, I didn't know that."

"I'm surprised she didn't tell you." Higgins' voice softened. The two men, so contrasting in every aspect of their lives – social level, education, demeanor – had always retained something more than professional respect and something less than affection for each other. "She is on parole, so she is subject to arrest and confinement for twenty-four hours at any time on suspicion of possible felonious conduct in this state. You know that, McGuire. Anyway, Donovan's partner on this thing, he made inquiries today and confirmed her presence there every evening for the past several weeks. We could hold her overnight if we wanted, but I instructed Donovan to release her. By the way, I would appreciate it if you didn't identify me as the source of this information."

McGuire turned to watch the traffic pass. "Thanks, Don. I owe you."

"No, you don't," Higgins said.

McGuire stared at the traffic for several moments after Higgins hung up. Then he shook his head, flipped through the telephone book, dug in his pocket for a quarter, and made another call.

Half an hour later he was slouched against a scarred oak bench in a corridor of the old courthouse, his eyes closed. He should be with Ollie now, he told himself. He should be offering to do whatever he could, and trying to explain the things he couldn't do. He couldn't prevent Ronnie from leaving. And he couldn't condemn her now the way he might have a few days ago, not after seeing how her face glowed in the presence of her lover.

He had made so many errors, it seemed. An error in criticizing Ronnie, an error in believing he could save Ollie, now an error about Susan Schaeffer (although he knew nothing about its extent yet), and he recognized how little he knew about happiness in others, even as he sought it in himself.

"I have ten minutes."

McGuire looked up to see Marv Rosen standing in front of him. The lawyer's deep-set eyes were watching McGuire without expression. His blue suit hung perfectly on his slim frame. He held an oxblood leather attaché case in one hand, and a heavy gold bracelet dangled from that wrist. Behind Rosen, an aide stood waiting impatiently, a young man with an oversized mustache, holding thick files in front of him. The younger man reminded McGuire of a schoolboy currying favor by carrying a friend's textbooks.

McGuire rose from the bench, one knee popping audibly. "You got a place we can meet?" he said, and the lawyer nodded and turned to walk down the corridor, leading McGuire and his aide like a member of royalty with his entourage.

"I'd say we're an odd couple, you and me." Rosen pulled on the French cuffs of his starched white shirt, exposing gold cufflinks set with diamond chips. They were seated in a counselor's room, one of several small cubicles set among the courtrooms. Rosen flashed a tight smile across the battered oak desk at McGuire, who was wishing he were somewhere else. "But the law can be like politics at times. Strange bedfellows and all that."

"Pinnington suggested I make contact with you," McGuire said.

"I know. Dick's afraid of dealing with this kind of stuff directly. That's the problem with big corporate firms. Always so tight-assed about crime." Rosen's voice was almost warm towards his former adversary. "That's why I went into criminal law, you know. You get to work with real people, real problems. Corporate lawyers get uncomfortable around people like you and me."

McGuire looked across at Rosen, who, satisfied with the exposure of his cufflinks, sat with his hands clasped together in front of his face and stared over his knuckles. McGuire said nothing, knowing Rosen had more philosophy to dispense.

"You and I build our reputations, such as they are, by being associated with a certain class of people," Rosen was saying. "The same class of people cannot be *seen* with Dick Pinnington and the rest of them. Yet we're supposedly all in the same business."

McGuire figured he had let Rosen ramble long enough. "What do you know about a guy named Myers?"

"Myers?" Rosen looked up at the scarred and stained ceiling. "I'm not sure who you're referring to . . ."

"He was your client. You defended him on an embezzlement and tax-evasion charge . . ."

"Right, right." Rosen nodded. "I do remember Mr. Myers, yes. What about him?"

"He could be implicated in this."

"Really?" The lawyer looked concerned. "Pinnington didn't mention his name to me."

"You didn't get any files from Pinnington?"

"Look." Rosen spread his hands wide, as though about to reveal a basic fact of life to a small child. "I'm retained, just like you are, by Zimmerman, Wheatley. They need me, they use me. They don't need me, they don't call me. Either way, I cash my monthly retainer. The same as you, am I correct?"

McGuire nodded.

"Something else comes with the deal. You know what it is? It's the understanding that they don't tell us anything they think we don't need to know. That's good for both of us, McGuire."

"They didn't tell you about Myers."

"I just said that . . ."

"They didn't tell you that Flanigan assigned me to confirm his presence in Annapolis."

"Is that where he is?"

"Or in Florida. Myers doesn't owe you money, does he?"

"Trust me, McGuire. I may lose a case now and then, but I never lose money defending a client. No, Mr. Myers does not owe me any money."

"He seems to have a habit of skipping out on his debts."

"Not mine, he didn't."

"So how much do you know about Flanigan's murder?"

"Quite honestly, only what I read in the newspapers."

"Did you know Orin Flanigan?"

The lawyer studied his nails. "Of course I knew him. Orin was a good man. A good lawyer, a fine person."

"Do you think he'd ever be involved in anything criminal?"

"I never believe any of my clients can be involved in anything criminal, and a few of them surprise me by doing just that."

"But Orin Flanigan was never a client of yours."

"Of course not. And the idea of him doing anything beyond the pale is outrageous." Rosen permitted himself another quick smile and looked at his wristwatch. "What else do you have? I'm scheduled upstairs in a few minutes . . ."

"What about Susan Schaeffer?"

"Who?" The lawyer was already half out of his chair.

"Susan Schaeffer. Do you know her? Have you ever defended her?"

Rosen paused, blinked, checked his cuffs again. "I have never defended a client by that name . . ."

"But you know her, don't you? How?" McGuire was rising from his chair as well.

"Is this relevant to the question of Orin Flanigan's murder?" Rosen stood across from McGuire, his chin raised, his expression almost defiant.

"You're damn right it is. She's sitting down on Nashua Street right now on a cheap-shot suspicion charge. Of Flanigan's murder. Set up by a bunch of lies."

"Really?" Rosen eyebrows shot up his forehead.

"She could use a lawyer," McGuire said. "Somebody better than the legal-aid flunky they're probably assigning to her. You interested?"

"No." Rosen seized the handle of his briefcase. "Afraid not. Look, if any potential criminal activity arises that's directly connected to anyone over at Zimmerman. . . ."

"How do you know Susan Schaeffer?" McGuire demanded. The door to the corridor opened, and Rosen's aide stood waiting, a look of impatience on his face.

"Unless that's directly related to a question of criminal activity . . ."

"I just said it was, damn it!" McGuire thumped his fist on the table.

". . . I cannot discuss my knowledge of her or her activity, and if you persist in threatening violence, McGuire, I'll have you charged again, and this time you won't have the City of Boston to defend you!"

"Why won't you tell me? About Susan Schaeffer?"

"I just said, if I determine that it's relevant to my obligations to Dick Pinnington and his people, I may be prepared to discuss it . . ."

"You and I, we're supposed to be working together."

"As a matter of fact, we are. It would be a good thing if you tried to remember that." Rosen paused with his hand on the doorknob. His aide was already leading the way down the corridor. "Look, McGuire. When you're a police detective, you're expected to pursue every item of information, no matter how small it may appear, or how confidential. But you're not on that side any more. You're an operative. Your client isn't society any more. Your client is Dick Pinnington and *his* clients. You're no longer an instrument of the law, you're a cog. You go only where you're supposed to go and no further. You learn only what you're supposed to know and nothing else."

"I want to know everything."

"Of course you do. But get used to the idea that you probably won't. I'll tell Pinnington we met. He was concerned about that. And I'll tell him you agreed to contact me whenever you have any hard suspicions of criminal activity by a member of the firm. That's all."

McGuire made two telephone calls from a booth in the courthouse lobby. The first was answered by Ronnie Schantz, her voice expectant. "Yes?"

"It's Joe."

"Oh." She had been waiting for someone else to call.

"How are things going?"

"You want to guess?"

"I can come by if you'd like."

"No," she said. "Not yet."

"Tell me what's going on."

"I'm leaving. Today. I'm taking . . ." She stumbled, then regained her composure. "I'm taking my clothes, a few pictures, my jewelry."

"You're going to Charles Street."

"Yes. I'm going to Charles Street. I should have expected you'd know more than you let on."

"How's Ollie?"

"He's . . . I don't know. He's accepting it."

"Should I be there?"

"Not until I'm gone, okay? Like, after dinner tonight? Can you wait until then?"

McGuire said he would wait.

"I hired a nurse. We've been talking about it for a while, Ollie and me. The Benevolent Fund is sending her up this afternoon. I gave them a key . . ." Something caught in her throat, and she paused to swallow. "She'll be living here for the first couple of nights." Another pause to swallow a sob. Then: "Joe?"

"What?"

"Do you hate me? Do you think I'm selfish? Do you think I'm only thinking of myself and nobody else?"

"Yes, you're selfish," he said. "Yes, you're only thinking of yourself. No, I don't hate you. I wish you only happiness, Ronnie."

She was crying now. "Thank you. I promise to call, to see you, and maybe explain things . . ."

McGuire said, "Sure, you do that," and hung up.

"Where you at?" Stu Cauley's voice rasped in McGuire's ear, and McGuire read the number of the pay telephone to the duty cop. "Stay there, I'll get right back to you," Cauley said.

McGuire leaned against the side of the telephone booth, thinking of Ronnie and Ollie. He remembered the expression on Ronnie's face when Simoni passed his cigarette to her lips, and the sight of them walking away towards his studio and his bed. They were two middle-aged people playing young lovers, while McGuire watched like a man in a neighbor's garden at night, peering through lit windows, and while Ronnie's husband was lying in his bed, unable to strike the lover down and bellow to the skies, as he might have done a few years ago.

What now? McGuire asked himself. In a way, Ronnie was abandoning not only her husband, but McGuire as well.

The telephone rang and he lifted the receiver quickly, like a man shutting off an alarm.

"She's due out in fifteen minutes," the voice rasped, and McGuire told Stu Cauley there was a beer with Cauley's name on it waiting for him at Zoot's.

"Can't touch it," Cauley said. "Ulcer. Didn't you hear, Joe?"

McGuire said he hadn't heard.

"I'm heading out to pasture, end of next month," Cauley said. "Then maybe I'll come up to Revere Beach and trade lies with you and Ollie."

McGuire said it sounded like a good idea. Seeing Ollie at the end of next month would be a very good idea.

CHAPTER 16

She walked out of jail with her head down and her hands jammed in the pockets of her trench coat, a tan leather bag on her shoulder. McGuire rose from the low stone wall he had been sitting on and crossed the open area between them, the wind sweeping past to toy with her hair.

"Thank you," she said when he reached her. She wrapped her arms around him, and he held her while she shook, her body like a bird's within his embrace.

"My car's around the corner," he said. She dabbed at her eyes with a tissue from her pocket and nodded. "Have they dropped the charges?"

She nodded. "They had no reason to bring me here except that someone told them lies. About me and Orin Flanigan."

"I know."

"Who?"

"I'll explain later."

In the car she said, "Where will we go?"

"Where do you want to go?"

"Some place where we can be alone and talk. Where do you live?"

McGuire started the car. "We can't go there."

She watched him as he pulled away from the curb. "You're married after all," she said.

"Hell, no. I'm not married." He looked across at her. "I'm not married," he repeated, "but I can't go to my room, because there are some problems there."

"I'd invite you back to my room but . . ."

"You can't have visitors in a halfway house."

She turned her face away. "How long have you known?"

"Couple of hours. Maybe more than that. I could see it in you, the way you looked through windows, other things. People in jail, or just out of it, look that way. While you're on parole, they can hold you for twenty-four hours just on suspicion of a felony. They tell you that?"

She nodded.

"I know a place in Marblehead that serves a great steak and better fries." He was already swinging the car towards the bridge to Chelsea. "How's that sound?"

"I'm not hungry."

"You might be in an hour or so. If you're not, I'll buy you another Irish coffee and you can drink it while I show how to make twelve ounces of beef disappear."

She smiled at him. "You make it sound almost obscene."

"Do I?" He faked a frown. "I meant to make it sound erotic. Sometimes I get them mixed up."

She sat smiling at him, until her face clouded over and she turned to look out the window again.

McGuire followed the Salem Turnpike to Swampscott, and took Atlantic Avenue into Marblehead. At a stoplight, the

Chrysler hesitated when McGuire tried to pull away. Then the engine whined until the transmission engaged with the familiar thump. "Attaboy, Clunk," McGuire said.

"Who?" It was the first she had spoken since they had left Boston.

"The car's name," McGuire said. "It's what I call it. Makes a clunk every now and then."

"Tough homicide cop gives a name to his old car?" She was smiling again.

"Hey, I spend a lot of time in this heap. It talks to me, I talk to it. The restaurant's just ahead. See that old brick place on the corner?"

Once they were seated in the almost-empty dining room at a window table overlooking the old harbor, he ordered New York strip steaks for both of them. "This town, it's mostly Italian food. There's only one place between here and Rockport where you can get a decent steak, and this is it. How about a glass of wine with dinner?"

She shook her head. "Just a Coke will do," she said. She looked around, as though she had awoken in a strange room, unsure of how she had arrived there. "I can't believe what happened to me today. I'm taken from the store, I'm locked . . ." She stumbled, began again. "Locked up and accused of murder, and now I'm sitting down to a steak dinner with a view of Marblehead Bay."

"I've got a friend," McGuire said, meaning Ollie, "who says as long as life keeps surprising him, he'll stick around to see what's next."

"What's next?" She was looking directly at him, something she had avoided so far.

"Good steaks, great fries. Coffee."

"You know what I mean. This isn't exactly your classic first date between two grown-ups."

"I'm curious as hell about you. Nothing makes sense. You've got a felony record, you've done jail time, you had a married man crazy about you, and something you've done is connected to his murder." McGuire shrugged. "Can you blame an ex-cop for being curious?" When she didn't reply, he added: "I also think, Miss Schaeffer . . . or is it Mrs.?"

"I kept my married name."

"I also think you're one helluva good-looking woman, and I'm being that up-front with you because we're twenty miles from home and I'm buying you a good steak dinner, which means you won't slap my face or head for the door."

"I would never slap your face for saying that. And I'm not running away. I just have trouble trusting anybody. I also have trouble talking about what happened to me. It's over with, and I want to forget about it."

The waiter arrived with the wine McGuire had selected, and poured a glass for each of them. "I can find out, you know," McGuire said when the waiter departed. "But I'd rather you told me yourself."

"Sure." She turned the glass in her hand and looked out the window, towards the harbor. The sun was setting, and the water was bathed in the last light of day that always reminded McGuire of the ashes of roses. "Sure," she said again. "But I want you to know about me and how I grew up, what kind of person I am."

She told him she had been raised by her grandparents on a farm in Maine, while her mother recuperated from some mysterious illness that was never explained to her. "It was no illness," she said. "It was a constant series of miscarriages. My father wanted a son, he wanted one desperately. The doctor believed that my mother should stay in bed during her pregnancy, so I was sent off to live with my grandparents, who were lovely, gentle people." She had remained there when her mother died giving birth to a stillborn boy, and after her father lost his job and became an alcoholic. She had remained until she moved back to Concord to take a job with the telephone company. There, she began dating a man named Thomas Schaeffer, a telephone-systems specialist. "He was ambitious, he wanted to build something, his own company, become his own boss," she explained. "So we became engaged, but we held off marriage for a few years. After we were married, we delayed having children while Thomas – nobody ever called him Tom, for some reason – Thomas and two other men started their company."

Their steaks arrived, and Susan agreed with McGuire that they were very good, perfectly cooked and tender. They avoided discussing Susan's past while they ate, commenting instead of the dying light on the water, the seabirds circling above the pier, and the masts of the pleasure boats that rocked with the waves. When they finished, McGuire ordered coffee, and Susan slipped back into her story again.

"We bought a house in Newton and we had . . ." She looked down at her lap, and when McGuire reached to take her hand, she pulled it away and shook her head, saying she was all right, she really did want to talk about this. "I had a son we named James, but we always called him Jamie, and two years later we had a girl, Belinda. They were beautiful babies, beautiful children."

"Do you have pictures of them?"

She shook her head again.

"And you haven't seen them for two years?"

She nodded.

"Because you were in prison."

Another nod.

"Tell me what you did that sent you to prison."

"I'm trying to."

"No, you're not." McGuire set his coffee cup aside. "You've told me about your father, your mother, and your grandparents. That's not what sent you to jail."

"No, it didn't."

"What did you do?"

She looked up at him and a smile began to play at the corners of her mouth, an embarrassed reaction. "I stole over half a million dollars. From a bank."

"You robbed a bank?" McGuire's voice said he didn't believe it.

"Not exactly."

"What happened to the money?"

"I never touched it."

"I don't get it."

Susan looked around them. The restaurant had grown crowded since they arrived. The adjacent tables were filled with diners, all of them chatting, eating, enjoying the view of the harbor, or studying the menu. McGuire called the waiter over, asked for the check, and ten minutes later they were back in his car, driving through the gathering darkness along the shore road, south towards Boston, while Susan resumed her story.

"I loved the suburban life, all the corniness of it," she said. Their neighbors were families of similar age, with similar cars, similar interests, similar ambitions. They held neighborhood yard sales and neighborhood barbecues. The men played softball on Sunday afternoons in the park at the end of the street, and the women – those who didn't hold jobs to help pay for family expenses – played bridge and traded recipes and complaints about their husbands, how the men never seemed to understand their problems.

On their tenth anniversary, her husband bought her a new vacuum cleaner.

A few weeks later, she sat alone over a cup of coffee and realized she couldn't remember the last time her husband had called her by her name. She called him Thomas, but he never used her name. When she mentioned it to him that evening, he laughed, and over the next few days he would never speak in her presence without saying Susan, teasing her until she angrily told him to stop it.

The next time he called her by her name was the evening he returned from a ten-day management-training session in Chicago, and confessed that while there, he had had an affair with a woman from San Diego.

"It was impossible," she said. "Impossible in my mind. Thomas wasn't one of those people. I never believed he could be one of those people."

"What people?"

"People who would lie to me. People who would cheat and be unfair. When I was growing up, I thought everybody was like my grandmother and grandfather, honest and caring. Then I realized not everybody was like them, but that everybody should be. Eventually, I just divided people into two groups. People who were basically good and people who were basically bad. I thought my friends, my children, and especially my husband were basically good. It never occurred to me that he could be as deceitful as anybody else."

It never does, McGuire thought.

She cried over her husband's infidelity less than she expected to, but a numbness crept into her soul. He apologized, assuring her it had been just a fling and it was over, which may have been true, except that, not long after, she found a photograph of a slim woman with long flowing black hair in his briefcase one day while he was playing squash. The woman's head was tilted slightly, so she was looking up at the camera, one hand toying with her hair.

Susan fastened it to the refrigerator door with a Winnie the Pooh magnet, just above a crayon drawing of a cat, made by their daughter. Thomas was furious when he found it, accusing her of snooping and distrusting him, telling her the woman had given him the picture in Chicago. Susan did not believe it was a photo of that woman. She believed it was another woman, a new affair. Their argument continued in the bedroom, until the sound of their children crying outside their door ended the shouts and accusations.

"We did what every couple does in a situation like that," she said. They were enveloped in darkness now, passing Swampscott, where McGuire had sat alone, watching dawn arrive, a few days earlier. "We went to see a marriage counselor."

After six sessions, the counselor smiled and suggested, Yes, Thomas had stumbled, and Yes, perhaps he was not as romantic as Susan hoped, but a romantic ideal is like a perfect cloud in a summer sky, it is forever changing and evolving and all we can do is recall it as it used to be in all its perfection. On the way home in the car Susan told her husband she thought the sessions had been a crock.

"He kept saying he still loved me," she said, "and that he was sorry. Over and over, he kept saying it. I didn't believe him. I think I was too hurt and angry to believe him."

With her children in school, Susan decided to begin a new career. To brush up on her skills, she enrolled in afternoon classes at a business school, riding the MBTA downtown after lunch to sit in a classroom with other housewives and high-school dropouts, studying word processing and book-keeping. She enjoyed the freedom, the opportunity to practice new skills, and, within a week of beginning classes, she enjoyed the special attentions of the owner of the business school, who would frequently visit the classes to assist an instructor or simply to admire the female students.

After class late one afternoon he asked to speak to her, suggesting she catch a later train home that evening. He told her she was far too advanced for her classes. In fact, she was ready for a job right now, and he just happened to have a position open in the business-school office for a woman of her skills and her personality.

"He was very charming, very persuasive." Susan looked at McGuire as though begging him to believe her. "He said there would be some evening work, but I would be paid overtime for that, and there were a number of fringe benefits. He talked about me attending business-school training sessions in Miami and Dallas. He said he would send me there at his expense, that he needed someone to take over administration of the school. That first evening, he drove me home in his car, all the way back to Newton."

The man's name was Ross Myers, and he was so many things that her husband Thomas wasn't. He was exciting to be around, and attentive to her. He did romantic things that her husband had forgotten to do, or never learned – opening doors, paying her compliments, surprising her with flowers. He had an element of spontaneity about him, even a hint of danger in the things he said, the things he boasted about having done. Within a few weeks, she was staying downtown with him for dinner, making up stories to explain her absence. "I was amazed at how easily I could lie to Thomas and even to my children," she said. "I lied about where I was at night, and where I'd gotten the jewelry Ross bought for me. He kept surprising me with gifts, he kept telling me how beautiful I was . . ."

"And he was married."

"Of course he was married."

"And that didn't bother you?"

Instead of answering, she said: "I was married too, don't forget."

"Just a couple of people having a fling?"

"Yes," she said, and her voice carried a defiance that McGuire hadn't heard before. "No," she said, when he didn't reply. "I've thought about this for a long time, and I don't think it was just a fling. I'm not sure I loved Thomas, to tell you the truth. He was the father of my children, he was my source of security, and all of that, but . . . If Thomas hadn't hurt me the way he did, if we had just kept things the way they were, I suppose I would have been content. But he didn't, and when Ross started doing all the things he did for me, I found him exciting." She stared through the windshield as she spoke, her voice lower, as though she were speaking to herself. "Even when I found out what kind of person he was, the kind of person he *really* was, that was exciting too, I suppose."

"What'd this guy look like?" McGuire asked. "Myers. What did he look like?"

"He's a bit overweight, he was always worried about his weight. And his hair, he was afraid of losing his hair. He'd comb it just so, and never let me touch it. I touched it once when he was driving, just a gesture of affection, and he got angry with me, he told me never to touch his hair."

"Sounds like a total jerk."

She smiled, without humor. "You never heard of anyone falling for somebody who turns out to be a jerk? Or maybe just a terrible bitch? You never heard of somebody trying to convince themselves that perhaps they haven't made a terrible mistake after all?"

Susan discovered that Myers's business school wasn't bringing in as much money as Myers seemed to be spending. Instructors were constantly complaining about receiving only partial pay for their services. Myers had two partners, one a lawyer, another a restaurant operator. He would often meet his partners over dinner with Susan, and she would listen to him describe the success of the business in terms she knew were not true. He would boast about the potential earnings of the school before asking for money, an infusion of capital to expand the business.

One day, Myers handed her a first-class airline ticket to Miami, leaving the following week, and he said he would meet her there. When she told Thomas of the trip, she said she would be traveling alone to attend seminars. Thomas said he was proud of her success. He insisted on driving her to the airport and kissing her goodbye.

In Miami, Myers met her with a bouquet of flowers, and they drove in a rented convertible directly to Hialeah racetrack. She found it all new and glamorous, especially when they sat in the VIP clubhouse area, where other men greeted Myers as though he were an old friend. Drinks were sent to their table, there was much laughter and teasing, and appreciative looks at Susan.

Myers lost several thousand dollars that day, but he drove back to their room at the Fontainebleau as though he had won every race. He lost a similar amount the following day, but on the third day he won a few hundred dollars, and as they returned to the hotel from the racetrack he was elated. On the way he stopped at an upscale mall to buy her a new wardrobe, pulling skirts and sweaters from racks and telling her to try them on, nodding his approval or shaking his head in rejection as she emerged from the dressing rooms.

Back in the hotel she checked the price tags and realized he had spent much more on gifts for her than he had won at the racetrack.

The next day she told him she didn't want to accompany him to the racetrack. She had come all this way to Miami and had yet to walk on the beach. He left her in a dark mood to visit the racetrack alone, but he called the room each hour, and had the hotel page her as she sunned herself by the swimming pool, saying he was coming right back, an edge of anger in his voice she had never heard before.

In the room, he accused her of many things, all of them vile. Of inviting men to their room in his absence, of visiting other men in their rooms, of removing her bikini top on the beach. When she began to cry, he became remorseful, told her he was sorry, and offered her a drink. He left the room, returning with a bracelet from the jewelry shop in the hotel lobby. He made reservations at the best restaurant in Miami for just the two of them. They would have a romantic dinner followed by a drive along the oceanfront with the top down, he said, and maybe there would be a big, bright, full moon shining on the water for them.

Two days later they arrived back in Boston, where everything had changed.

Thomas ignored her when she arrived home in a cab, leaving her to struggle with her luggage alone. When she asked where the children were, he told her they were staying with his mother. She saw the fury in his eyes and the constant shaking of his hands, and she knew why.

"Ross's wife told him about us." She was looking through the windshield, as she spoke. The lights of Boston were ahead, a shining city in the darkness. "She called Thomas the day before we returned and told him everything. She had suspected me for quite a while, I suppose. When she had proof and knew I lived in Newton, she called every Schaeffer in town until she reached Thomas and told him."

"How did you feel?" McGuire asked.

"Guilty. And angry." She lifted her hand to touch her cheek. "What I had done was terrible. But Thomas had done it too. It wasn't revenge. I didn't set out to sleep with a man for revenge. I wasn't looking for revenge."

"But you found it."

"Yes." She lowered her head. "He cried. He hit his head against the wall until I begged him to stop. For the first time in our marriage he struck me. He slapped me and knocked me to the floor. He asked me if I wanted a divorce, and I said No, I just wanted things right, they hadn't *been* right for so long. He had been drinking all day, and he drank some more. He went out to the garage, and while he was there I called the children on the telephone to speak to them, I missed them so much. When I hung up, Thomas was standing in the hallway with a rifle in his hands, pointing it at me."

Her husband had purchased the gun that morning. He sighted along the barrel, mumbling to himself or to her, she never knew. She screamed and ducked below a table and he fired, shattering the window behind her. While he fumbled with the bolt action she ran to him, in part because he stood between her and the door. She hugged him and told him she was sorry, and he dropped the rifle and collapsed crying on the floor.

The police arrived, alerted by neighbors, and they arrested Thomas. Susan claimed that the gun had fired by accident, that he hadn't really meant to shoot her. He had been trying to frighten her, that was all. His lawyer claimed the trigger mechanism was faulty, and when he managed to have the charges reduced to attempted assault, Thomas was released on bail the following afternoon.

"Get out of there," Myers told her over the telephone. The children had been sent to Thomas's parents for safekeeping. Susan was alone in the house. "Just get the hell out. I'll find you an apartment downtown. We'll get you settled there and later on you can have the kids with you. But don't stay. He's liable to shoot you again when he gets home."

It made sense to her. Myers appeared concerned about her welfare, saying he was in the process of separating from his wife, but there were complications due to his business affairs. When she was settled downtown, he would join her. They would marry and she would never regret it. Some day, some time in the future, she would see that all of this pain and guilt had been worth it. But it was almost a year before Myers and his wife separated, and in that time she lived alone, except for visits from Myers. Meanwhile, her husband kept the children at home and sought temporary custody, claiming she had abandoned them. When she grew distraught over the charge, Myers told her not to worry, a good lawyer would straighten things out.

At the hearing, Thomas's lawyer, Orin Flanigan, submitted evidence that Susan had left the house without the children, who moved back with their father within days of her departure.

Flanigan was brilliant in his presentation, citing precedents and opinions over and over to prove his case. Susan's lawyer offered only a weak defense against the accusation, and there was no surprise when the judge awarded Thomas custody of the children. Susan could have the children two weekends each month and for two weeks in the summer. The judge would review the arrangement in a year. The divorce was granted. Myers promised that he would appeal the decision, that he would hire the best lawyer money could buy. She would get her children back. He would do it for her.

"I had nothing,' she said. "No husband, no home, no children. I had only Ross and his promises."

Susan was given $20,000 from the sale of the house. "Ross asked me to invest it in the business," she said. "He said it was a loan, and he would pay me back with interest."

"And you never saw a penny of it again."

"No."

McGuire thumped the steering wheel. "How could you be so stupid?" McGuire said. "How could you be so damn stupid?"

"You think I haven't asked myself that?"

"You screw up your marriage, you hurt your kids . . . I just can't understand how you could fall for this crap from a married man, a guy who sounds like he can't tell anything but a lie. You could have left him and started over again. Why can't women do that?"

"Men always say that, don't they?"

"Maybe men have got it right."

"And maybe it's none of your business." She spoke without looking at him. "Did you ever think about that?"

"Then why the hell are you telling me? Maybe it isn't any of my damn business. But you're the one doing the talking, aren't you?"

"I want you to know because I trust you, and that's very hard for me to do. I trusted Thomas, I trusted Ross, I trusted Orin, and now he's gone and I need to trust somebody, damn it." The tears were flowing. "I need to trust somebody."

McGuire recalled the afternoon in the church in Harvard Yard, when she reacted to the organist's curse with a sudden smile. He wanted to see that smile again.

"Do you want to hear more?" she asked him. She dabbed at her eyes with a tissue.

"Sure."

"Because this is the hardest part of all to talk about."

CHAPTER 17

A few months after she had moved into the downtown apartment, Myers suggested she might want to find another job. He gave many reasons. She was far too qualified for the work he was asking her to do. He was looking for ways to reduce overhead. She should gain wider experience.

He told her she had a wonderful mind for figures, and that her future lay in finance, probably banking or investment. One day he pulled her into his office from the hall and told her he had heard the Pinehurst Savings and Loan branch a block away was looking for someone in the securities department. When she protested she knew nothing about the business, he handed her a letter he had drafted, praising her ability as a student and identifying her as a top graduate of the Back Bay School of Business, specializing in financial management. He had already made an appointment for her to meet the manager that afternoon.

The S&L manager was impressed by Myers's recommendation, and Susan was hired immediately. To her surprise she enjoyed the work and the staff, and especially the customer contact. Soon many of the S&L's customers began asking for her, seeking her out because of her warmth, and her genuine concern about them. Many of the customers were older people, at or near retirement, searching for ways to maximize their investments.

A week later, Myers moved his business account there.

Soon after, Myers and his wife separated, and he and Susan moved to Marlborough Street in the most luxurious area of the Back Bay, a two-level condominium in an elegant brownstone. Myers took a new interest in Susan's children, and insisted on furnishing a guest room for them in the condominium. He took the children with him on weekend vacation trips, spur-of-the-moment long weekends in Florida or the Bahamas, where he bought them expensive gifts.

"You have to understand what I had given up for this man," Susan said. They were on Boylston Street now. "My home, my children, so much of my happiness, in a way. And he could be charming. He knew how to combine romanticism with a kind of danger, I guess. I had been a sheltered little girl, and then a sheltered wife. When it all blew up in my face, I didn't know what I wanted any more."

"So you let some tough guy fool you with his gentle side."

"It wasn't just that. I started feeling as if I had fewer choices to make. I would stay with Ross until I could decide where to go, what to do. That's what I kept telling myself."

He became more manic, wilder in his moods. He brought her breakfast in bed some mornings, and wouldn't be seen until the early hours of the following day. He began lying to her and she began lying to herself, accepting his apologies and believing his promises to marry her.

He would surprise her with gifts for her and the children, when they were with her. But as his apparent generosity increased, his dark side grew blacker. Once, in a fit of rage, he slapped her so hard she was knocked across the bed and collapsed in a heap on the floor, crying and holding her face, while he stood over her and berated her, calling her a cheap slut and a terrible mother, telling her that Thomas should have shot her after all, then lifting her in his arms and setting her on the bed, soothing her, bringing a cold cloth for her bruised face and assuring her that he loved her, he *needed* her, but there was just so much pressure in his life.

"He was controlling you," McGuire said. He was looking ahead, scanning the street as he always did.

"Totally. It was pathological. That's not my word. That's what the prison psychologist called it. I . . . What's wrong?"

McGuire had pulled to the curb and was staring through the windshield. Susan followed the line of his sight. There were few pedestrians. The air had grown cool and damp. The retail shops were closed and darkened. A man and woman were approaching, locked in conversation. Against the display wall of a men's-wear shop, next to a darkened service alley, a street beggar stood, wrapped in a blanket, smiling at the approaching couple.

"Is something wrong?" Susan said.

McGuire eased the car ahead, moving slowly, looking at the beggar as though willing the man to meet his gaze. He accelerated suddenly, swiveling his head from side to side. "Do you see a cop?" he said. They were moving down Boylston Street again. The traffic was light, and at the next corner McGuire swung right.

"Why do you want a policeman?" she said. "Tell me what's wrong."

"We need a cop," McGuire said. At the intersection he swung right again, down a deserted residential street. McGuire swore and the Chrysler accelerated again. "Keep your head down and hang on," he told Susan.

"What are you doing?" One hand gripped the door handle, and she reached the other for the dashboard to steady herself. "What's wrong?"

They were almost at the next intersection. "Tell me if you see a telephone booth. Or a cop." He turned right, heading back to Boylston again. "I might have to let you out at the corner."

"Don't let me out," she said. "I'm staying here. I want to see what it is that's turning you into a madman."

McGuire glanced over at her. In spite of himself, he grinned at her face, the resolve in her expression.

McGuire braked to a stop, looked along the sidewalk, and accelerated again. The Chrysler swung onto Boylston, the rear of the car fishtailing with the sharp turn and the car's speed. "Get under the dashboard," he said.

She did as he ordered, keeping her head just high enough to see what he was about to do. The street beggar was gone, leaving his blanket on the sidewalk like a shed skin. The man and woman who had been locked in heated conversation were nowhere to be seen.

McGuire swung the car into the darkened alley. He opened the door on his side of the car and shouted, his voice echoing between the brick walls, "Hayhurst!" and switched the headlights to high beams. In their sudden glare, a woman ran to huddle against the wall on the passenger side. A man stumbled towards her, away from the same street beggar who had been on the sidewalk in front of the menswear shop. The woman was frantic, panic-stricken. The man with whom she had been in such animated discussion two minutes earlier fell to his knees and began crawling towards her. The beggar stood with one hand raised to his eyes, protecting them from the glare of McGuire's headlights. In his other hand, he held a small black pistol.

"Stay down," McGuire shouted, and he accelerated the car, keeping it to the left, on the side of the alley where Hayhurst stood, and away from the two tourists.

Hayhurst shot once towards the oncoming car. He turned to run, extending his hand back and blindly shooting at the car a second time. Then, with McGuire approaching, he flattened himself against the wall, arms outstretched, to let it pass. McGuire pressed the driver's side door open until it connected with the brick wall and dragged against it in a shower of sparks. The car's speed was almost thirty miles an hour when the door collided with Hayhurst, who screamed loudly enough to be heard above the sound of the car's motor. The force of the impact drove the door back against McGuire's shoulder, and he winced before braking to a stop and looking over at Susan. "You all right?" he asked, and she nodded, her cheek pressed against the glove compartment.

He squeezed out between the battered door of the car and the brick wall and trotted back to Hayhurst, who was rolling from side to side on the concrete alley, spewing foul words and phrases. One side of his face was bloodied, and one leg was twisted at an unnatural angle. McGuire ignored him until he located the Beretta. He moved the gun further away from Hayhurst's reach with his foot and returned to kneel next to him. Hayhurst was grimacing as he spoke. In the light of the car's headlights, reflected from the walls of the alley, McGuire saw the gold incisor tooth. "You are one sorry badass," he said.

Behind him he heard the man who had been scrambling away from Hayhurst shouting for police at the top of his lungs, trotting towards Boylston Street. Across the alley, Susan was assisting the woman to her feet, looking from her to McGuire and back again, as though trying to connect the two images, or simply to convince herself that it was all real, that she really had made some sort of metaphysical leap from the quiet security of McGuire's car to a violent street episode.

"We could make a hell of a team."

McGuire handed Susan a coffee from the machine on the Criminal Investigations floor at Berkeley Street police headquarters.

She took it in both shaking hands. "No, thank you," she said. "I want to get out of here."

"We will. Soon."

She was looking around, studying the faces of everyone she saw. "I don't want to be here."

"If it matters, this kind of thing doesn't happen every day with me." McGuire sat next to her. "If I had seen a cop around, if I carried a cellphone. . . ."

"Buy a cellphone," she said.

"He might have killed them, you know." The man and wife, McGuire had learned, were from upstate New York. They had been arguing because the woman felt her husband was flirting with a waitress at the restaurant they had just left. Now they were seated, holding hands and leaning towards each other, at Wally Sleeman's desk, providing him with a statement. "Even if I'd called right away, he could have shot them both and been gone." An hour had passed since the Boston police arrived at the alley, brought by the husband's shouts and reports of gunfire. They found McGuire standing over the injured Hayhurst and watching his car's radiator leaking its contents onto the ground.

"What if that man, that Hayhurst character, had stayed in the middle of the alley, instead of trying to get out of your way?" she asked. "What would you have done then? Run him down with the car?"

"Sure."

"You're serious? You would have killed him."

McGuire looked away.

She stood up and walked to a window. When he followed her, she turned away, avoiding his eyes. "You don't have children, do you?"

"No."

"I could tell. Something happens when you have children. A woman I knew told me that. She thinks it only happens to women, and maybe she's right. She worked as a nurse in the trauma ward of a hospital for three years. She loved it. People would arrive with broken bones, gunshot wounds, limbs torn off, and she would be right in there, ignoring the blood and gore, and the screams. She said it was the biggest rush she ever had, working the night shift in the trauma ward. Then she took a year off to have a baby, and when she returned she couldn't do it any more. She was horrified by it all. She kept seeing these people as babies, like her own, I suppose, and she couldn't bear being in the same room with them." She turned to look at McGuire. "I hate what happened tonight, all the violence and intensity. Hate it. I want nothing more . . ." She caught her breath, and began again. "I want nothing more than to hug my babies, my children. That's what Orin Flanigan said he would help me do, if he could. Find my husband and my children. I was so horrified tonight, and I looked at you and realized that you loved it. You've been so sweet to me, nicer than anyone else besides Orin. And then I see that side of you."

"I did it for over twenty years," McGuire said. "It all came back, I guess."

She looked at him, saying nothing, then began scanning the faces of detectives and police officers as they passed.

"Joe." Wally Sleeman was walking towards him, carrying a clipboard and pen. "Need your statement now."

"What do you hear about Hayhurst?" McGuire said. "How's he doing?"

"Who cares?" Sleeman said. "Broken leg, cracked ribs, possible cracked pelvis. Cuts, abrasions, contusions. Listen, you could have backed over that son of a bitch a couple times and nobody would have complained. How the hell'd you spot him, anyway?"

"Just keep scanning the faces until something clicks. Who ever saw a street beggar with a gold tooth?"

"Never thought he'd be out in the open, working Boylston. We had everybody checking crack houses down along Atlantic Street, in that area. We were getting leads he was back on his home turf, and that's where Frank sent everybody. Nobody's checking street people. Face it, you got lucky." Sleeman was watching Susan. "I'm taking your date back to my desk for his statement, ma'am," Sleeman said to her. "Won't be five, ten minutes, then I'll need to talk to you, okay?"

Susan smiled and nodded.

"Nice," Sleeman said when they reached his desk. "Gettin' friendly with her?"

McGuire said he hoped to.

"More luck," Sleeman said. "The way I see it, McGuire, you're so lucky that the day it rains gold, you'll be carrying a fucking tuba."

CHAPTER 18

"You know you can't have your car back, even if that piece of crap could still run," Sleeman told McGuire. It was almost eleven o'clock. Sleeman was reviewing the statements McGuire and Susan had signed. "Not until we nail things down, couple of days maybe."

"If you can't put a new transmission in it, forget about giving it back," McGuire said.

"You want me to run you guys somewhere?" Sleeman looked at McGuire. "You going back to Revere Beach?"

"We'll take a cab," McGuire said.

"I gotta walk you out, this time of the night. I'll get you out the back way. We got all the media squirrels downstairs in front, waitin' for me to come down, do my dog-and-pony show. You guys want interviews? They've been yellin' for interviews."

McGuire shook his head, and Susan said "God, no."

Sleeman led them down the corridor towards the elevators, McGuire holding Susan's hand as they walked. "You know one of the best parts of this?" Sleeman said. "Frankie tight-ass took a couple days off to go down to the Cape for a break. He's the lead guy, the one who bragged that he'd bring Hayhurst in all by himself. He'll be banging his head against the wall when he hears about this. You make the collar and you're not even carrying a badge, and I get to make the announcement to the media squirrels." Sleeman laughed as though he had just heard an especially rude and funny story.

"Let's find a quiet place for coffee," McGuire said to Susan when they were outside.

"I can't talk now. How can I talk about me after what just happened?" Susan squeezed his hand. "I'm still shaking."

"You'll be shaking more later, when you have time to think about it. That's what happens."

They chose a rear booth in the first restaurant they encountered. Both ordered black coffee.

"Something else was bothering you back there on Berkeley Street," McGuire said. "You kept looking around as though you were expecting to see somebody you knew."

She nodded.

"Who? The cop who arrested you?"

"No. Somebody else."

McGuire waited. When she didn't speak, he reached across to touch her hand. "Maybe you're right. Maybe you should wait for some other time to finish your story."

She shook her head and managed a smile. "If I don't get through it tonight, I might never get the courage to tell you again." She looked at the clock at the front of the restaurant. "I have to be checked in by midnight. Tomorrow's my first day without bed check. I can start looking for a place to stay."

"I'll help you," McGuire said. He smiled tightly. "We'll fill up our day. You go looking for an apartment, and I'll start shopping for a car."

"Doesn't it bother you, what happened tonight?" she asked him. "You almost witness a murder, you get shot at, you nearly kill a man, and you act like . . . like some guy who's just finished his shift driving a bus or something."

"It'll bother me later," McGuire said. "When I'm alone and start thinking about it, yeah, I'll get the shakes a little, wonder if I could have handled things differently. Right now, I want to concentrate on you. I want to hear what happened between you and Ross Myers, and how Orin Flanigan got involved. You can finish telling me about it, or you can sit there wondering how close Hayhurst's bullet came to you. Believe me, thinking about that stuff does no good at all." He reached across to squeeze her hand again. "Tell me about you. I want to know."

She sipped her coffee and stared down into it as she spoke. "I had only been working at the S&L for a few weeks when Ross started pressuring me to do things, things I could never imagine myself doing."

It began with a $20,000 check, postdated two weeks later. Someone had given him the check as an investment in his company, Myers explained. He couldn't wait two weeks. He needed the money immediately, and he asked her to credit his account until the check could be cashed, telling her it would be covered anyway, so no one would be the wiser. She resisted that request and another, upset and disturbed that he could ask her.

A week later, he asked Susan to deposit a $30,000 check for him. Automatically, she told him she couldn't do it, but he laughed and threw her the check and told her to look at it. It was genuine, a cashier's check. He said there would be more like them and she could relax, everything was fine now, everything was genuine.

He broke through her resistance one Friday morning when he said another cashier's check would be coming for the same amount on Monday, but he needed two months' rent on the business-school office that day in order to extend the lease. A travel agency wanted the space, and if the money wasn't in the landlord's hands by noon, he would lose the lease and the business. All he needed was a weekend float. The money would be deposited on Monday, and everything would be fine. The business was turning around, perhaps they could sell the condo and buy a house up near Cape Ann, where she always wanted to live, where the children could visit.

She told him she didn't know how she would do it, but even as she said the words, she knew how, had known how for several weeks, and had played with the idea in her mind. Until then it had been only a fantasy, the kind of wild dream everyone has but few ever play out in reality.

Three months earlier, the S&L had installed a new computer system. A consultant had been hired to design and implement the system, and he remained to train the staff in its operation.

The system included a new method of handling securities that Susan found confusing at first. The young man training her was patient and considerate, and he told her he would set up a hidden file in the system that she could use to practice transactions. He had done this with other installations, he assured her, and the staff appreciated it. They could perform trial transactions and balances, generate monthly statements, and locate and correct their mistakes, without any data appearing on the bank records. The hidden file could never access actual accounts, so there was no potential for theft. But it could print hard copies of statements. It would be submerged within archive files, with a password only he and

Susan would know. When she was confident of the system, he would erase the file. No one would be the wiser. She would shine in the eyes of management.

It worked. During training sessions, she would make fictional deposits into the fictional account files, practicing the new procedures and routines. "You've got it," he said. "Next time I'm in, I'll erase the file and finish off the training program."

But he never returned. He called the following week, saying he was off to Dallas to repair a major systems failure. He would return in two weeks, three at the most, to erase the file. "Or I can give you the code and you can do it for me." She said she would do it for him, and he provided the erasure procedure. It would work only on the test file. Nothing else would be affected. She could erase it when she needed to.

The hidden file remained in place, and the morning that Ross Myers asked for the float, an elderly couple arrived to purchase a two-year term deposit of $40,000. She knew what she could do. She entered the amount in the training file and printed a receipt, telling them an official certificate would be mailed the following week. Then she deposited $30,000 of the couple's deposit into the business-school account and called Myers to tell him the checks could be passed.

"He almost jumped through the telephone at me," she said to McGuire. "Five minutes later he came into the branch with a dozen roses, handed them to me, and gave me a big kiss. One of the women came over and told me how lucky I was to have such a romantic boyfriend, and I remember how my stomach was tying itself into knots."

"And the check he promised to cover the thirty thousand never appeared."

"No."

"And you didn't stop there."

"No. I couldn't. I just couldn't."

When no money was deposited Monday morning she called Myers from the bank, frantic with worry. A woman answered the telephone at the business school, a voice she didn't recognize, and the woman told her Mr. Myers was busy, could he call her back? Yes, Susan said, yes, right away, it's urgent. When she gave her name, the woman asked if Myers would know what it was about.

There was no call. That evening she drank alone in the condominium until midnight, and then fell asleep. Myers arrived home after three in the morning with a gold ring for her and a host of excuses. When she asked about the check, he said it had been delayed a week, maybe more, but he would need more money, at least $10,000 more. In a panic she told him she would go to her manager and explain what happened, and Myers told her to go ahead. It was her they'd throw in jail, not him. Besides, he promised, he would cover the amount for sure and make it all up to her, and he would take her and the children to Florida for the weekend.

She hardly slept that night. Myers was right. There was no evidence of his involvement. If she admitted what happened, she would at least lose her job and the respect of the people she worked with, people she had grown close to. Except for her children, they were her only friends and family now. She worried as well about the elderly couple whose money she had diverted to Myers. She assumed the bank would return it, if she were to be found out. But she still felt guilty about deceiving them.

One step at a time, she told herself. She would find a way to cover their money from some other source. She would set a deadline for Myers to make up the money. She would get out of this mess somehow, and then she would get out of the relationship with Myers. She would not go to jail. She would not let her children see their mother as a criminal.

The next day, when she arrived at work, the branch manager called her into his office. She entered trembling, and at the sight of three men she had never seen before she almost collapsed with fright, until one of them smiled and stepped forward, his hand thrust out to shake hers. Another pulled out a plaque identifying her as Employee of the Month. Along with their congratulations they gave her a $100 gift certificate from Filene's.

The nightmare had begun.

She transferred $30,000 from a corporate account to cover the elderly couple's needs. But Myers needed more money, enough to free up some accounts receivable, he told her. Soon, he would be able to pay it all back. The next month she transferred another $30,000 to the business-school account, diverting funds meant for term deposits and issuing false certificates from the hidden training files. When enough cash became available from other depositors, she would issue real certificates, falsifying the date where necessary. Each morning she entered the S&L offices expecting to be confronted by bank officials or the police, and each day she told herself Myers would fulfill his promise to replace the money.

"I became numb," she said. "When you get so frightened, when you feel so beaten down, you become like a sleepwalker sometimes. That's how I started acting. Sometimes I just didn't care. Sometimes I almost wanted them to catch me, just to make it stop."

She was seeing less and less of him. He was spending more time in Florida, where he boasted of joining an exclusive club in Palm Beach and purchasing a condominium in Fort Lauderdale. He owned three racehorses, and shares in two others. He kept a car in Florida and leased another in Boston, telling her he was opening a second business school near Miami, and soon they would be living there year-round. He bought her jewelry, diamonds, watches, and fur coats, telling her they were purchased with gambling profits. He assigned the management of the Back Bay Business School to a woman with bleached hair and breasts that sat unnaturally high and firm on her chest, a woman who, the few times Susan met her, regarded her with something between amusement and contempt.

One day in early summer, when the children were due to stay with her for a week, Myers announced he wanted to take them to Florida for a few days. She was frightened and resisted, but the children begged her, they wanted to visit Disney World again as Uncle Ross promised. Myers was adamant, he had already made arrangements. She could fly down and join them for the weekend. He had always been gentle to the children, as he could be gentle and loving with her on occasion, and she finally relented.

The next day she called the condominium number, but there was no answer until the evening, when Ross answered and said everything was fine. He and the children had spent the day at the beach, and were having a wonderful time, and he would call her the following day. When he didn't, she rang several times, again with no answer, until he called her at work and told her, his voice changed and a hint of desperation in it, that he needed $50,000 and he needed it *now*, so she should have the money wired to Florida the following day.

She told him it was impossible. She was worried that someone could be overhearing their conversation. He became angry with her, cursed her, told her she had better start doing what she was told, that she would regret defying him. When he hung up she was shaking and crying, and she retreated to the washroom, where a teller came to tell her some man wanted to speak to her on the phone.

The man did not identify himself. He spoke softly, with a deep voice and a vaguely foreign accent. He told her to just do what Myers wanted and everything would be all right. When she protested, he said there would be a good chance, a *very* good chance, that her children would not be returning from Florida until it was done. She canceled the paperwork on several large term deposits that day, issued fake receipts from the training file, and transferred the money to Ross's account.

When he returned with the children two days later, he brought her gifts, but the children were changed somehow, a little distant to her, and she told herself she had to find a way to end this nightmare. She began to cut herself off from her children, because she was afraid Myers would use them again, and because she couldn't bear their innocence, their trust in her and love for her, when she knew what she was and what she was doing.

Myers's demands for money intensified. Once, when she told him she couldn't go on, he pulled her out of the S&L office and slapped her face until a passerby told him to stop. In the condominium he would beat her, leaving bruises on her arms and neck, and she would try to explain them away to concerned co-workers, saying she had been playing touch football with her son and had fallen several times, or that she had been hit with a tennis ball. He balanced the beatings with apologies and promises that he would soon be able to pay all the money back, promises that he had deals under way.

She attempted suicide, swallowing massive quantities of prescribed tranquilizers and waking alone the next day, terribly sick and even more severely depressed.

By the end of the summer, Myers was spending almost all of his time in Florida, and Susan was being treated for symptoms of extreme stress, mixing tranquilizers with alcohol, drinking and crying alone in the Marlborough townhouse, wanting someone to rescue her and desperately afraid of spending years in prison, as Myers had promised she would if she were caught.

She endured two surprise audits of the S&L, telling herself each time that this was when she would be caught. But she and the computer programmer had both done their jobs well, and she received another Employee of the Month award, cited for the constant flow of compliments sent her way by customers.

One evening at the townhouse, she received a telephone call from a woman whose voice she didn't recognize.

"She told me she knew who I was," Susan said to McGuire. "I was half-drunk, I was past caring who I was or who she was. She said she was Ross's former wife, his second wife, the one who had called Thomas. She said she knew what I was doing and that she wanted ten thousand dollars from me or she was going to the police."

"How did she know about it?" McGuire asked.

"She had been seeing Ross again. I learned about it later. I learned so much later. Anyway, I told her to do it, do whatever the hell she wanted, because I didn't care any more. You have to understand. I was cut off from my family, my friends, my children. I was constantly paralyzed with fear that I would be found out, and yet I was hoping I would be, if only to end this nightmare. If you have never been under the control of someone, maybe you can't understand. I was basically a little suburban housewife and mother who got herself involved with a psychopathic personality, somebody who knew how to push every button to encourage me, frighten me, intimidate me, manipulate me. Do you understand?"

McGuire said he was trying.

"You never will," she said. "Not totally." She smiled and set her empty coffee cup aside. "But I appreciate you trying."

At times, Myers would surprise her with expensive gifts and promise to restore the fun and excitement they used to have. At other times, he humiliated her by boasting of the women he was seeing in Florida.

She began asking herself how she had gotten to this place, how the good student, the daughter of a deeply religious father, the girl who never told a lie and never stole a thing in her life, had permitted herself to become so beaten and helpless. She had only wanted to be liked, the way her customers and her co-workers at the S&L appeared to like her without knowing the hidden truths.

She dreaded returning to the condominium each evening, dreaded the telephone calls from Florida demanding more money, dreaded finding him sitting in the shadows to frighten her when she entered, telling her he was flying back to Florida on an afternoon plane the next day and he needed another twenty, thirty, forty thousand dollars to take with him, sometimes cajoling her with gifts or flattery, other times threatening her and her children, or beating her.

She began stopping at a bar on lower Beacon Street after work, sipping a few drinks to build courage to continue home. Men would approach her and she would usually fend off their attempts at conversation and return the drinks they bought for her. But there were times when she was lonely and frightened.

"One day," she said, "I heard someone refer to a man I had seen in there before. They said he was a cop, a detective. I thought, perhaps if I could make friends with someone like that, a police officer who would understand what I was going through, he might be able to help me. I was so afraid of being caught, afraid of the shame. I couldn't stand the idea of prison, of being locked away. So I made a point of smiling at him, and he came over and sat beside me. We talked a little, and he said I looked like a woman who needed help."

McGuire's eyes locked onto hers. "When was this?"

"Three years ago last summer. He was nice to me, and he didn't ask questions, not at first. I liked him, I wanted to get him to like me. So I didn't tell him about Ross, not right away. We had to be careful, because he was married."

"What was his name?"

"Frank DeLisle."

McGuire sat back in the booth.

"It lasted less than a month," she said. DeLisle took her to New York one weekend. When she returned to the condominium Sunday evening, she found Myers in a drunken rage, demanding to know where she had been, and with whom. She refused to tell him. He told her he needed money the next morning, at least $30,000, and she said she couldn't do it any more. He beat her on the back and on the thighs, where the bruises wouldn't show, until she agreed to get the money for him. Then he became gentle and tender, as he always did when she agreed to his demands. He apologized for the beating, and told her what a wonderful woman she was, and how much he had missed her.

The next day she totaled the funds she had taken from depositors and transferred into the training file. She broke into tears when the amount came to over $700,000.

Myers called in the morning, asking if she had transferred the money yet, and she told him again that she couldn't do it any more. When he told her he was coming down to the S&L to *make* her do it, she called DeLisle and begged him to meet her at work as soon as possible. When he promised to be there within an hour, she alerted her manager that she was ill and might be going home early.

Myers arrived in a fury, hissing across the counter at her when she ignored him, trembling inside. Then DeLisle entered, flashed his badge, and stared at Myers with such hostility that he spun on his heel and left without a word.

"Frank wanted to know what was going on," Susan said. "I asked him to take me somewhere, alone. I had things to tell him."

In DeLisle's car she told him about the thefts. She gave him details on the training file, the threats Myers had made on her children, the beatings, and the manipulation. DeLisle listened in silence. He advised her not to go home that evening, suggesting she get a place to stay downtown. To her surprise, that was his only reaction. She wouldn't see him again until her trial, when he appeared as a prosecution witness, testifying against her, reading aloud from the notes he had made after she left his car.

She found a room in a tourist hotel, went to work the next morning, and was arrested for grand larceny by three detectives, who entered the S&L just before lunch.

They took her downtown for questioning. Bail was set at $500,000, a lawyer was assigned to handle her case, and she spent four months in jail awaiting trial.

"I kept reading about myself in the newspapers," she said to McGuire.

"I remember it," he said. "I remember hearing the story, and how nobody could believe that someone smart enough to fool the state banking authority could steal so much money and claim it wasn't for them. Just the newspaper reports, that's all I remember."

"When the police went to look for Ross, the condominium was cleaned out. The jewelry and the furs he bought me were gone, and most of the furniture had been sold. He got rid of everything he could in exchange for whatever money he could get his hands on. He destroyed all the photographs of me and my children, so everything vanished except my memories. Then he hired a lawyer and told them that a friend of his was in trouble, meaning me. This friend, he told the lawyer, might try to implicate him. He and the lawyer went to the police together. The lawyer. . . ."

"Marv Rosen," McGuire said. He shook his head. Frank DeLisle. Father Frank. DeLisle DeLovely, the good family man, the good cop who would not tolerate swearing in his presence, the guy everybody would go into the jungle with. Sleeping with Susan and then dumping her, dropping a tip when he discovered what she was up to, and then abandoning her. And Marv Rosen, defender of hopeless causes. No wonder he bragged that Myers hadn't stiffed him on any fees. Myers paid his legal fees with money Susan stole for him. Nobody stiffed Marv Rosen on fees, not ever.

"How did you know?" Susan asked. "About Rosen?"

"I've seen Myers's file. And I talked to Rosen yesterday."

"About me?"

"No. Only about Myers."

"Then you know what happened to Ross."

"Rosen gave the Internal Revenue an income-tax-evasion conviction, and the DA's office dropped the larceny charge."

"Because Ross's signature was not on any of the bank documents, it wasn't a strong case. He spent the money, but I was the one who took it." She was toying with her fingers. "They tried us separately. Frank DeLisle was a prosecution witness against me."

"Did your lawyer describe your relationship with DeLisle?"

She shook her head. "The prosecuting attorney said he would ask for a lighter sentence if it never came up. They wouldn't sacrifice a good police officer's career for such an indiscretion. That's what they called it. Instead of ten years, he would only ask for five. My lawyer said it was a good deal. They wanted to protect the reputation of a good cop, and they would take five years off my sentence to do it."

"Didn't anybody believe you?"

"Not really. I had a court-appointed lawyer, a young kid, really. They had my confession. I never told anyone that I was being beaten, I was too embarrassed. So the prosecution claimed I really *had* fallen or been hit with a tennis ball. Those are the excuses I had used. They said no one had beaten me. They said I had bought all these nice clothes and jewelry for myself, and that I had given money to Ross because I was afraid of losing him to other women. He testified against me, told them I had boasted about coming from a wealthy family in Connecticut, and that's where he believed the money had come from. My God he lied, he lied so much, he destroyed me there. My lawyer . . . he tried but he couldn't do very much. I had a good pre-sentence report and the judge agreed to the five years, just five years, that's all, my lawyer kept saying, telling me I'd probably be out in two but I kept thinking five years, five years, five years . . .

"After my trial, they brought me to the court as a prosecution witness against Ross," she said in a dull flat voice. "His lawyer, Mr. Rosen, tore me apart there on the stand, calling me all kinds of names, asking me what date I had done this, and why I had done that on another day, and of course I couldn't remember. In those last few months I had been like a robot. He showed pictures of me wearing fur coats and jewelry Ross had bought me. He said I had bought them with the money I stole, and asked where they were, and when I told him I didn't know, he said I had destroyed them because they were evidence that I was the criminal. I knew Ross had sold everything to pay Rosen's legal fees, but I had no proof. They had vanished. I couldn't afford to hire anyone to trace them."

"Myers got off easy," McGuire said.

She nodded. "Ross got one year in minimum security. He sent me a letter once, telling me he was spending his days playing ping-pong and basketball. I was in a federal prison . . ."

"Cedar Hill?" McGuire knew the place, a gray stone fortress on the edge of the Berkshires, with the oldest wing set aside for women prisoners.

"Yes." She swallowed. "This morning in jail, it all came back again, the humiliation, the loneliness, all of it. The prison psychiatrist kept telling me to adjust, but how could I ever adjust to that? While I was in Cedar Hill, I received a letter telling me my husband had obtained full custody of my children. At my trial, they didn't believe my testimony about Ross making me do those things, using my children the way he did. The lawyer who acted for my husband submitted the transcripts from my trial, and he used them to take my children from me."

"Orin Flanigan," McGuire said. Things were beginning to fit.

"Yes."

"And you couldn't locate your husband or children when you came out of jail, so you went to Orin Flanigan."

"He wouldn't talk to me at first. He said it was client privilege, a conflict of interest, and so on. But one day when I was pleading with him, nearly hysterical, his wife came in and saw me. It was after office hours, everyone else had gone home. I left, and I guess Orin's wife wanted to know what was going on. The next day Orin left a message at the halfway house, inviting me to come and meet with him. He told me I reminded his wife of their daughter, and we began to talk. He began to believe me. He searched court records, he talked to people, he sympathized with me . . ."

"Did he tell you where your husband and children were?"

She shook her head. "Orin said he was bound by law to reveal nothing about them without my husband's consent. All he said was that Thomas had moved west. He said he would try to find a way, a legal way, to put me in touch with them. But I think he was mostly angry at Ross Myers. He kept saying, 'These are the things that make the law such an ass at times,' meaning the way Ross was treated, compared with me." She looked up at McGuire. "I really think Orin loved me," she said. "Maybe like he loved his own daughter. He knew Ross had cheated the system, and he said it was unfair, that somebody should make him pay somehow. He wanted to see that Myers paid one way or the other, or to make sure that he didn't ruin the lives of other women. Then he told me about you. He said you were somebody who might be able to find Ross and do something, and maybe find Thomas and my children too."

"What did he mean, 'do something' about Myers? Do what?"

"I don't know. He told me that you had found Ross, that he was working as a yacht salesman in Annapolis, but he had gone sailing for a week or more. I said it had to be a joke."

"Why did it have to be a joke?"

"Because Ross could never stand being on a boat for more than five minutes, even sitting at the dock. He made friends with some high-rollers in Florida. We went to a party on a boat in Lauderdale one day, and we weren't even out of the harbor before Ross was sick to his stomach. He was *green*. He was so sick that the man who owned the boat turned back to shore and let us off. So Ross isn't a yacht salesman. He just isn't."

McGuire worked on that for a minute, remembering the aloof attitude of the woman at the yacht brokerage. "So why did Orin go?"

"Because he said he might have found a way to get back at Ross. Orin said he had seen his share of unfairness, he had even *done* his share of unfair things. He said he wished he was like you, somebody who could act on the spot. Somebody who could do things besides argue in court and shuffle papers." She smiled. "He would have loved to hear what you did tonight with that Hayhurst thug. He might dislike brutality, but I think he would secretly approve. Anyway, he said he was thinking of asking you to do what he was planning to do, except that it would mean revealing too many things about me. And he didn't want to."

"You told him Myers wasn't on that yacht."

She nodded.

"Where did he think Myers was? And how did Orin Flanigan expect to deal with him?"

"I don't think he expected to meet Ross. I think he knew something about Ross, about what he was doing in Annapolis or wherever he is, and he went down to stop it."

"Not by contacting the police. As far as I know, the cops knew nothing about Myers, and had no reason to pick him up. What was Flanigan like when you saw him last?"

"Determined. A little excited. He said, 'I'm going to blow the lid off Myers.' I asked him how, and he told me to just watch him." She looked at the clock again, and began to stand up. "I've got to be back there in fifteen minutes," she said. "Can we get a cab?"

Saying goodbye was awkward. When she left the cab, he watched her enter the halfway house, watched the door close, then told the cabbie to take him to Revere Beach.

CHAPTER 19

Ollie's house was dark when the cab pulled into the driveway. He paid the cabbie, unlocked the door, took three steps into the hall, and froze at a voice from the top of the stairs.

"Stay where you are or I'll shoot."

The hall light above his head was on, and he shielded his eyes from the glare.

"Who the hell are you?" the woman's voice said.

"I live here," McGuire answered, squinting up the stairs. "Who the hell are *you*?"

She was perhaps thirty-five or forty years old, tall and big-boned, with blond hair crew-cut on top, and long at the sides and back. She wore a Boston College sweatshirt over shapeless black slacks and high-cut basketball shoes, and she was holding an ugly black automatic. "Put your hands on top of your head."

McGuire raised his hands. "You got a license for that thing?"

"I'll tell you what I've got for it," the woman said. "I've got an NRA marksmanship award for hitting a target half your size at twice this distance. How's that make you feel?"

"Look," McGuire began, "Whoever you are . . ."

A buzzer sounded in the upstairs hallway. "Oh, for Christ's sake," the woman said.

"How you doing, Ollie?" McGuire called down the hall.

He could barely hear Ollie's response through the closed bedroom door. "What's going on?"

"What'd he say?" the woman asked.

"He wants to know what's going on," McGuire said. "Look, I really live here . . ."

"What's your name?"

"Hey lady, I *live* here," McGuire said.

The woman began descending the stairs, the gun aimed at McGuire, and he recognized it as a Hi-Standard .22. Loaded with Remington Fireball cartridges it would do almost as much damage as a .38. "My name is McGuire," he said. "You mind telling me yours?"

Something between a shout and a gargle echoed from the direction of Ollie's room.

"What do you know about somebody named McGuire?" the woman shouted down the hall, her eyes and the gun unwavering.

"He lives here, you stupid sack of tit," Ollie shouted. "Send him in here."

McGuire tried to suppress a laugh.

The woman breathed deeply and muttered something. "If you live here, where's your room?" she said.

"Up the stairs and on the right."

"What's in it?"

"One double bed, one dresser, a stereo system, and a bookcase."

"Any pictures?"

"Yeah. A poster of a town in France called Vence. It's over the bed. You starting to believe me now?"

She shook her head and lowered the gun. "I don't remember them saying anybody'd be coming in here tonight."

"You're Ollie's nurse," McGuire said, lowering his hands.

"First night." She lifted her chin and angled it towards Ollie's room. "He can be a real son of a bitch, you know that?"

"You coming in here or you gonna stand out there blabbin' all night?" Ollie shouted through the door.

"Mind if I see my buddy?" McGuire said.

"I'm sleeping in the other bedroom, his wife's," the nurse said. "My name's Liz Worthington."

"I suppose I should say it was nice meeting you," McGuire said. "But it wasn't."

"Nobody at the Benevolent told me they had a roomer," Liz Worthington said. "I saw the room upstairs and figured maybe it was their son's or something. Why the hell wouldn't they tell me that?"

"I'll be sure to ask them next time I see them," McGuire said.

The nurse began climbing the stairs. "I keep that door locked, the bedroom door," she said. "Just for your information."

"I'll sure as hell keep mine locked, too," McGuire said. She gave him a sharp look over her shoulder and continued climbing the stairs.

Ollie's bed was raised to a sitting position. "That broad upstairs? She had balls, she'd be storm-trooper material."

"How do you know she hasn't?" McGuire said, settling himself in a chair. "Balls, I mean. She pulled a gun on me, Ollie. And why didn't you tell her about me?"

"Thought I'd surprise you a little, that's all. Didn't know she'd cover your ass with that nasty little Hi-Standard, even if she *was* braggin' about her marksmanship scores," Ollie said. "If the damn thing'd gone off, at least you'd know it wasn't an accident. Jesus, Joseph, you're back on the hit parade. Been watchin' all the channels, tellin' how you turned that Hayhurst squirrel into roadkill. Didn't anybody interview you? They're sayin' you're like the Lone Ranger, doin' your good deed and then vanishing. They're after you like a belch after a beer. You really try to erase him against a brick wall? How's your car? They said, on channel eight, they said it took two slugs from the kid. And they said you were with some mysterious blonde woman. They love mysterious blondes, don't they? I mean, they're either famous or mysterious. This one's mysterious. So tell me about her."

"I'll explain later . . ."

"Explain it now. You think I'm going anywhere?"

McGuire looked away, then back at Ollie. "What'd you settle?" he asked. "You and Ronnie? I thought it would kill you, when you found out."

"It didn't kill me. Does it look like it killed me? Just wounded me in a different place. She packed some of her clothes, a bunch of other things she wanted. She'd already applied to the Benevolent for a nurse, did it last week. By the time they sent over Norman Schwarzkopf in drag, she was gone."

"How're you taking it?"

"The only way I *can* take it. By telling myself there's other stuff to hang onto." His voice softened. "So who the hell's Susan Schaeffer? And gimme the details on runnin' down that punk."

"Maybe I'd better make some coffee," McGuire said.

"Hey, it's that good?"

"So what are you going to do?"

It was an hour later. McGuire poured the remains of the coffee from the carafe into his cup.

"I don't know," McGuire said softly. The adrenaline was used up, and his body ached. He held his head in one hand, the empty cup of coffee in the other. "Donovan's running things like he's a chainsaw in a rose garden. Shit's flying everywhere, but not a hell of a lot's getting done."

"And you want to do something."

"Why would I want to do anything?"

"The same reason you want to breathe, McBoink. Go find Myers." Ollie's good hand reached for the bed control. With a muted hum the bed lowered him back to a horizontal position. "Check out Florida. Winter's coming, and horseballs like him can't wait to sit in the sun at Hialeah."

"And if I find him, what do I do next? Tell Donovan where he is?"

"Donovan probably already knows. He just doesn't have enough to work with."

"Wherever he is now, Myers killed Flanigan."

"Good luck doin' anything about it. Nobody's seen the guy. You didn't see him in Annapolis, nobody's seen him up here, there's no proof he was ever in the rented car. If they do find and arrest him, based on what they've got now, Myers'll hire his buddy Rosen again, and Marv'll bust a gut laughin' at a charge like that. Which you know will never come to court anyway."

"Why should I give a damn? I don't know Myers, and I never knew Flanigan much."

"Because he got away with hurtin' some woman who's got your eyes dropping like cue-balls into a corner pocket, that's why." Ollie closed his eyes. "Turn off the light. Maybe we'll all have breakfast together in the morning. You, me, and Door Number Three."

McGuire tripped the light switch and closed the door behind him.

As he walked along the hall towards the staircase he heard Ollie's voice again. "Find Myers."

CHAPTER 20

The man who identified himself as the owner of Bay Ridge Yachts spoke with a faded Georgia drawl. McGuire called him as soon as he arrived at Zimmerman, Wheatley and Pratt the next morning, grabbing breakfast on the way in, avoiding both Ollie and the nurse. The man told McGuire his name was Harrison Klees, "with a *K* and no *e* on the end."

Klees said no one named Myers worked for his company, nor had anyone named Myers ever worked for him. He was getting tired of answering these questions, and he really would like to get on with doing business and stay off the telephone. McGuire must be the third Boston cop to call him about this guy, whoever he was.

"Who asked?" McGuire sipped from his mug of coffee. Beyond his office door he heard the rustle of early-morning office activity – ringing phones, low conversation, and sudden brief volleys of laughter. "Who asked all the questions?"

"Well, someone from your department . . ." the man in Annapolis began.

"Who was it?" McGuire insisted. "Do you remember his name?"

"Irish. It was an Irish name."

"Lieutenant Donovan. He's been reassigned to another case. I'm on it now, and I need to hear your side."

"Well, like I told him when he called, and like I told the lawyer who was here, the one who was murdered, I don't know who y'all are talkin' about. I said I'd never heard of this Myers character before that lawyer showed up, and I don't want to hear any more about him. Heard too damn much 'bout him already."

"What about Mrs. Diamond? Anybody talk to her?"

"That lawyer did, and your man Donovan did, too. I told that Donovan fella about the lawyer coming here and asking for her. Christine wasn't in that day, the day the lawyer showed up. I remember that. Anyway, the lawyer showed me his card and said it was an urgent legal matter, so I let him call her from here."

"You didn't overhear the conversation?"

"Nope. They didn't talk long, and he was gone, the lawyer. Then I think the sheriff's office down here was trying to reach her, but I'm not sure if they did or not."

"Apparently she told somebody that Myers worked for you. She said he was delivering a yacht to the Carolinas."

"Yeah, well. You gotta understand that some funny people get attracted to these big boats. They come over here, and it's like somebody turns on a bullshit machine, they start acting like they just sold Rhode Island that morning, you know? She figured this guy for one of them. Plus, I remember a couple guys coming by here a week before that. They were looking for Myers too. Said they were told that Myers worked here, and they were the kind of fellas who found it hard to take no for an answer. Almost had to call the law myself to get rid of them. So she figured it was easier to say yeah, he works here, but he's gone for a week or so."

"She a good saleswoman for you?"

"Christine? She does all right. She's overcome a few problems, as you know . . ."

"Problems?" McGuire wrote *Diamond* on a sheet of paper and kept the pencil poised for more notes. "What kinds of problems?"

He could hear the other man exhale noisily in exasperation. "Don't y'all read your stuff up there? I mean, how many more times've I gotta *do* this?"

"I must have missed it. What kinds of problems does Mrs. Diamond have?"

"Well, losing her husband the way she did last year . . ."

"What happened to him?"

"He was in the New York–Bermuda yacht race, skippering his own craft, and they ran into a bit of a stomach-churner, and he got himself overboard. Only member of the crew not tethered. Terrible thing. Two kiddies and all."

"What did her husband do? For a living?"

"Bert Diamond was a damn fine dentist, orthodontics. And he had some investments around here, couple of strip malls up towards Glen Burnie . . ."

"So he left Mrs. Diamond comfortably off . . ." McGuire wrote a "$" under *Diamond*.

"I suppose . . ."

"What's to suppose?"

"Look, I don't go into detail with my employees, all right? I mean, their personal lives."

"Wait a minute." McGuire frowned and scribbled "?" after the dollar sign. "You're telling me Mrs. Diamond needed money?"

"I'm saying Mrs. Diamond had to pay off a lot of Bert's debts when he died, all those empty strip malls he had mortgaged to the hilt, hoping they'd turn to gold when the economy got going. They were worth practically nothing, and there was a whole lot of back taxes owin' on them, plus Bert had a lot of other payables. She was left with the house and not much more," Klees said. "But Bert looked after his kids. His kids are set up with a trust fund, but Christine, she had to go to work, and I offered her a job here."

"How old are the children?"

"About eight and nine. Two nice little boys. Listen, I've got a barrel-load of paperwork here needs doing . . ."

"Okay." McGuire tossed the pencil aside. "Thanks for your help."

"Am I gonna get any more calls like this?" Klees asked.

"There's always that possibility in a murder investigation."

"Just in case I do, maybe I can save myself some time, 'cause I'm getting tired of singing this same song, you know? What'd y'all say your name was again?"

"DeLisle," McGuire replied. "Detective Frank DeLisle."

"Favors?" Libby Waxman coughed into the telephone with a noise that sounded like a ton of gravel falling down a flight of stairs. "What the hell do you think this is, a United Appeal agency?"

"Come on, Libby." McGuire smiled at her reply. Some people got older and more crotchety, but funnier too. Libby was one of them. "I'm not saying it's a freebie, I'm just saying that one of them's a personal thing and I don't have a lot of money to play with. How about a two-fer?"

"This new stuff or old?"

"One's new, the other's more of the same."

"More of the same? That guy I told you about last time?"

"Yeah, Myers."

"Lawyer from that law firm you're with, somebody there got himself killed coupla days ago, right?"

"Yeah, I heard."

"Newspapers're sayin' he was last seen down Washington way, that right?"

"You're right on top of things, Libby."

"Which is not much more than a hooker's stroll from Annapolis. Where I told you Myers is."

"You're getting the picture."

"So whattaya need?"

"Just find out if Myers . . ."

"The guy I tracked for you."

"Just find out if he's been spreading fresh change around Pimlico, places like that. Or maybe if he's golden with the bookies."

"Won't take much. What else?"

"This one's easy for you. This one's the favor I need."

"I don't handle favors, McGuire." Libby's voice became clearer, and the edge grew honed. "You ever ask a bank to cash a friggin' favor?"

"I'm looking for a man named Thomas Schaeffer, used to live in Newton, moved out about two years ago. Guy works in telephones, telecommunication, stuff like that . . ."

"What'd he do?"

"He left town. With two kids."

"Why?"

"Does it matter?"

"It's a custody jump, right? Took off with the kids, wife wants them back?"

"Something like that."

"And the guy's straight? Doesn't gamble, doesn't do drugs? No record?"

"Except for a wife assault a few years ago, yeah."

"Where's the wife now?"

McGuire shifted the receiver to the other ear. "You need that stuff?"

"Wouldn't hurt."

"She's in town."

"Custody stuff like this ain't easy, McGuire. Nobody on the street knows anything. You got some other source, some clue?"

"Wait a minute, wait a minute." Someone at Zimmerman, Wheatley and Pratt must have Schaeffer's new address, McGuire suspected. If Schaeffer instructed Flanigan not to reveal his whereabouts, especially to Susan, would Flanigan refuse to provide it, caring about her the way he had? Was that part of the client-privilege guideline? Had Flanigan planned to provide Susan with her former husband and children's address? Or would he try to persuade her ex-husband to contact Susan himself?

"You still there McGuire?"

"Just a minute, Libby."

He remembered Cassidy, and the young lawyer's concern about maintaining secrecy on his client's case of suspected fraud. Something was off-balance with that guy, McGuire suspected. It was worth a shot – a long shot, but what the hell. He swiveled in his chair and yanked open a file drawer.

"Listen, there's one more thing," he said. "Something else to look into."

"What, you think I'm a wholesaler today? Three traces on one call?"

"This one's not a person," McGuire said, retrieving a file folder and opening it on his desk in front of him. "It's a company."

When the telephone rang ten minutes later, McGuire half expected it to be Libby with a detailed response to his request. Instead he heard Susan's voice.

"I'm down at the market," she said. "I lost my job."

"Because of yesterday? Being arrested?"

"Yes."

"Wasn't much of a job."

"No, but it's a condition of my parole that I either have a job or some sort of support."

McGuire told her they would meet for lunch, and he named a restaurant near the market.

"I miss you already," she said.

Next, McGuire called Berkeley Street to tell Wally Sleeman what he needed from him.

"What the hell're you up to now, McGuire?" Sleeman's voice had an amused edge to it.

"Just give me a rundown, verbal's fine," McGuire said. "And don't tell DeLisle."

"Why? Was it his case?"

"No, it wasn't his case. He was just a witness."

"You're not workin' with Rudy Zelinka, are you?" Zelinka was the Internal Affairs investigator, the gatekeeper of the

Boston Police Department's moral standards, although he was never described in such glowing terms by officers or detectives.

"No, it's strictly for me," McGuire assured Sleeman.

McGuire went for a walk around the block, returned to make another pot of coffee, and had almost finished scanning the newspaper when the telephone rang.

"You busy?" Richard Pinnington asked. The tone of his voice said it didn't matter.

On the way up the open stairway to Pinnington's office, McGuire passed Lorna descending to the fourteenth floor. He smiled at her but she turned away and continued downstairs.

Pinnington's door was open, and the lawyer beckoned McGuire inside from behind his desk. "Close the door, will you?" he said as McGuire approached. The lawyer was in his shirtsleeves, his embroidered tie loosened and pulled away from his unbuttoned collar.

McGuire swung the door shut and sat in one of the wing chairs, facing Pinnington's desk.

"Sometimes all you want to do is practice law and you get stuck with a pile of other people's crap," Pinnington said. He settled himself in his chair.

"Whose?" McGuire asked. This is not going to go well, he warned himself.

"Whose what?" Pinnington looked directly at him for the first time since McGuire entered his office.

"Whose crap are you having to deal with?"

"Jesus, it seems like everybody's. Orin's, his widow's, Barry Cassidy's . . ."

"Any of it mine?"

Pinnington stared at McGuire, as though thinking about it for the first time, which McGuire knew was a ruse. "As a matter of fact," Pinnington said. He looked down at his desk, then back at McGuire. "Cassidy's upset with you."

"So what? You said you could handle him. He got what he needed from me."

"Have you made any unauthorized copies of his documents?" Pinnington stared at McGuire, direct and unwavering, and McGuire felt like a hostile witness being cross-examined in a courtroom.

"Like what?"

"Client records, correspondence, whatever."

McGuire nodded. "Cassidy's client. The electronics outfit."

"So you did."

"Lorna told him, right?" She had been at the copying machine, watching McGuire.

"I don't know what Lorna might have told him," Pinnington was saying to the floor. "All I know is that Cassidy's accused you of unacceptable conduct, and I told him I doubted it very much. But it appears he was correct."

"I did it because he's hiding something."

"Such as?"

"I don't know. All I know is that he didn't give me all the files, and I've had this gut feel . . ."

"Gut feel?" Pinnington looked at McGuire as though he had heard something amusing. "McGuire, I'm talking facts, and you're defending yourself by saying you had a gut feel?"

"Instinct, Dick. Intuition. That's what you brought me in for, remember?"

"Yes, to use on behalf of our clients, damn it. Not against one of our own staff members, a guy in line for a partnership."

"Why didn't he give me all the information?"

"It's his prerogative not to." Pinnington rose from his chair and jammed his hands in his pockets. "Who are you to judge a lawyer's decision in these matters?"

"I'm sure he's hiding something . . ."

"Barry Cassidy has an exemplary record in everything he's done for this firm and our clients." The lawyer withdrew a fist and hit the desk. "He's a Yale graduate *cum laude*, he's married into one of the best families in New England, and I will not hear unsubstantiated rumors of unethical behavior. Not in this office, not from your mouth, not anywhere."

McGuire rose from his chair. "Sounds like we may have reached the end of our contract," he said.

"It's crossed my mind." Pinnington stared out the windows towards the airport.

McGuire turned to leave.

"You've been seen with that Schaeffer woman," Pinnington said. "The two of you, you were out playing vigilantes last night, I hear. I thought you were finished with all that cowboys-and-Indians stuff. I thought you were content to be associated with us and leave all the rough stuff to your friend Donovan and his cronies."

"It's tough to stop being a cop. Besides, I had a score to settle with that guy. He's a murderer. He would have killed more people if he hadn't been brought down."

"Brought down?" Pinnington swung his eyes to McGuire and grinned. "I hear you ran him over with your car." He turned to face McGuire. "Look, I still like you, and you've got your own gang of fans around here, too. Although I wouldn't count Lorna Robbins among them. I'm just asking you to kind of rein yourself in a little bit, okay? I saw Marv

Rosen last night. He says you're still acting like a cop instead of like a counselor. You know the difference, don't you?"

"Whatever it is," McGuire said, turning for the door, "it got Orin Flanigan killed."

His message light was flashing when he returned to his office. He punched his phone code and listened to Libby Waxman's washboard voice speak to him as though she were reading a shopping list.

"You there? You gonna pick this thing up or you want me to talk, give you what I got?" After a pause, she said, "Okay, this is what I got. First, your friend Myers, this one's easy, one phone call and I had what I needed two minutes after you hung up. Your buddy paid off a big-time gambling debt last week and it's a good thing, too, because the bookie he owed it to, the guy's got connections from here to Palermo, and Myers was only a couple a days from walkin' the streets without no feet on the ends of his legs. Whatever he tapped into looks like a gusher, because he's layin' down long green on short odds every day, but he doesn't show his mug around Pimlico any more, just does business with this bookie, phone calls and money drops. He's got the scratch but he doesn't have the smarts, which means he's the bookie's pension plan right now."

McGuire heard a wispy intake that he recognized as a deep drag on a cigarette, then a long, slow exhalation before Libby's drone began again.

"So that's that, and on the company you were askin' about, Amherst Electronics, it's owned by an outfit called TriTech Incorporated, which is what they call a shell. It spreads money around, but it hasn't been spreadin' it around with much luck lately, because three of its outfits've gone tits-up in the last two years. But there's this rumor, see, that has somethin' to do with one of the three families in this TriTech Company. This one lives in the Caymans where, like you already know, you can slide the odd boxcar-load of cash in and out, and there's no questions asked. Anyway, I got three names for this TriTech thing, so you might want to scribble 'em down. One's named Stoller, he's the guy lives in the Caymans, and he's got a rap sheet for fraud. Got a mouth looser'n panties on a bean pole. Found somebody on the street who knows him. Stoller used to be a fifty-buck-a-week punk in Southie. Now he's a million-a-year punk in the Caymans, frontin' other people and gettin' paid not to talk about it. But punks talk, McGuire, you know that, and Stoller's talked to some people he shouldn't, about some things he shouldn't. Guy still smells like cold piss and warm beer.

"He's got partners up here, and they don't smell of nothin' except old money and maybe Chanel. One a them's named van der Kramer and the other's De Coursey, that's a big *D*, small *e*, big *C* and *course*, with a *y* on the end, okay? They both got Beacon Hill addresses, the van der Kramers and De Courseys, when they're in town, which probably isn't a hell of a lot, because they also got places in Palm Beach and Kennebunkport and Squaw Valley, and for all I know on the moon, so there you are."

Another wispy inhalation and this time there was a longer pause before she spoke, her voice colored a little from the smoke that was escaping her lungs with the words.

"Now I gotta tell you, McGuire, don't hold out a lotta hope for this Schaeffer fella, the guy with the kids, 'cause he's been gone two years and all I know is he's west, Arizona or some place where the air's dry. You know that if there's nothin' on a record somewhere, or the guy isn't doin' deals here and there, that he's tough to find, and besides I can't do a hell of a lot with somebody dumb enough to go to Arizona to live, either in the suburbs or in the desert, but then what the hell's the difference in Arizona, right? Either way you're just cuttin' cactus, or whatever there is to do out there. So that's a blank, McGuire, but it's okay, I'm not chargin' you for that, and the Myers thing is free, because you already paid me and it was easy. Maybe you owe me a hundred on the Amherst deal, okay? So you keep your hair curly and your shoes shined, and you can come around and see me any time, okay?"

McGuire smiled as he replaced the receiver. He had written four names, Stoller, van der Kramer, De Coursey, and Schaeffer, on a sheet of paper, and he crossed the last name out.

He sat staring at the three remaining names while random thoughts formed in his head, ideas muscling their way to the front of his consciousness, until one of them dominated the view. Why not? he asked himself. He rose from his chair and walked through the office area and back up the stairs to the fifteenth floor, where he found the two secretaries for King and Pratt sitting at their desks. One of them, a red-haired woman in her forties, who wore her hair in a modified beehive style, looked up and smiled when he paused in front of her desk.

"Is there a file on our law staff somewhere that lists where they were educated, what kinds of awards they might have won, what their specialty is, that kind of thing?" McGuire asked her.

She looked across at the other secretary, a small woman with dark, badly permed hair, who was watching McGuire carefully. "Marie?" the secretary said. "Do you have a copy of that?"

Marie nodded, opened a drawer in her desk, and withdrew a file folder. "It's my only copy," she said, handing it to the red-haired woman.

"I just need a glance at it." McGuire walked to her desk and reached for the file, but she began to withdraw it. "Just a quick look," he said, and this time his hand shot out to seize it from her.

The dark-haired woman watched as he opened the file, which held perhaps two dozen typed pages. Then, throwing a look at the other secretary, she rose from her chair, walked to Fred King's office, knocked lightly, keeping her eyes on McGuire, and entered.

McGuire flipped through the sheets, each headed by the name of a Zimmerman, Wheatley and Pratt lawyer, listing senior partners first, then full partners, and finally staff lawyers, all in alphabetical order. He located Barry Cassidy's sheet just as Fred King's door opened. The lawyer stood buttoning his jacket. The secretary named Marie stood behind him, her arms folded. "Bit of research, Joe?" King said.

"Public records," McGuire said. "Nothing I couldn't find in a lawyer's *Who's Who*." He began reading:

> *CASSIDY, BARRY JEROME MONTROSE, B.A., LL.B.; b. Boston, MA, 28 Oct. 1967, s. William S. (M.D.) and Helen (Montrose); educ. Rutland, Boston College (B.A. 1988), Yale (LL.B. 1991) . . .*

King's voice was closer now. "Dick Pinnington and I had a talk a few minutes ago," King said. "There's nothing for you to be doing here, is there?"

McGuire took a step away from the lawyer and continued reading.

Admitted to the bar 1993, attended state conference on corporate litigation 1996, member Massachusetts Law Society 1997, recording secretary Greater Boston Republican Lawyers' Advisory Group 1998 . . .

"McGuire, I don't believe you are to have access to documentation of any kind without Dick Pinnington's permission." King was walking towards him in measured strides. He whispered something to Marie, who nodded and reached for her telephone.

The woman with copper-colored hair sat watching the scene, a hand to her mouth.

Member Mass. General Hospital Volunteer Citizens' Organization 1998, Chairperson corporate law review subcommittee of Yale Law School Alumni Association 1998–99, contributor "Data Analysis Impact on Corporate Law" Yale Law School Review *March–April 1999 . . .*

"Give me the file." King was approaching McGuire, his hand outstretched, and with his next glance McGuire discovered what he had been looking for, or at least had hoped to find, and there it was.

Committee member Prospect Hill Community Recreational Council. Married to Kirsten Maureen, daughter of Michael and Maureen De Coursey, Boston, MA. . . .

McGuire closed the file and tossed it at King. Several sheets of paper spilled from it onto the floor. "All yours, Fred," he said. "You might want to read the part about Cassidy. You know that fair-haired twit down the hall? If he doesn't find his name listed as a partner here next month, he might find his ass in jail."

He trotted downstairs and called Sleeman again, who told him what he needed to know. "I know the name," he said, meaning the name on the court document he had accessed. "Didn't know she had anything to do with Father Frank."

"Maybe she didn't," McGuire said. "Maybe he was just bragging about it."

"Sure as hell didn't brag about it to the judge."

After McGuire hung up, he savored both a final cup of coffee and a vaguely reassuring feeling of victory before returning upstairs. He walked past Pinnington's secretary and through the partially open door to find Pinnington behind his desk, making notes on lined sheets of paper in a three-ring binder. Pratt stood nearby, speaking softly into Pinnington's telephone. Fred King was slouched in one of the wing chairs.

"We're cutting you a check," Pinnington said after glancing up. He appeared to be expecting McGuire. "For your three months of service. We'll want you to sign a release . . ."

"Make it certified," McGuire said.

"Make what certified?" Pinnington looked up from his notes. King's smile metamorphosed into a smirk.

"The check. I want it certified." McGuire looked across at King and returned the cold smile.

"You think Zimmerman, Wheatley would bounce a check for a lousy fifteen thousand dollars?" King said.

"Probably not," McGuire nodded. "But I want to cash it today for a chunk of money. It'll be easier if it's certified."

"You're a goddamn pain," Pinnington muttered, not lifting his head.

"Pain, hell," McGuire said. "Up to now I've been a mild itch."

Pinnington looked at McGuire again, his eyebrows arched, and McGuire waited until Pratt finished speaking on the telephone and replaced the receiver. "There's some information in Orin Flanigan's files I want," McGuire said.

King snorted. Pratt looked from McGuire to Pinnington and back again.

"Well, forget it," Pinnington said. "First, Orin's files are possible evidence in his murder investigation, and second, I wouldn't let you read our telephone directory right now . . ."

"He grabbed the personnel file right out of Marie's hand," King said from the corner.

"You want the check certified, come back in an hour," Pinnington said.

"I want an address from Orin's file." McGuire stood with his hands in his pockets, looking at each of the men in turn. "It has nothing to do with Flanigan's murder."

"I said forget it," Pinnington said.

"Whose address?" Pratt asked. His voice was soft, his manner wary.

"Thomas Schaeffer," McGuire said. "Flanigan acted for him in a child-custody case about two years ago."

"Schaeffer?" Pinnington frowned at McGuire. "Let me guess. He's Susan Schaeffer's former husband."

McGuire nodded.

"You're nuts," King said. "That's a breach of confidentiality, especially if the client gave specific instructions not to reveal his whereabouts. No lawyer in town would agree to that. Why don't you just clear your desk out . . ."

"I'm trading something for it," McGuire said.

"Like what?" It was Pratt. He rested one buttock on Pinnington's desk.

"The fact that your boy Barry Cassidy not only has a serious conflict of interest with a client . . ."

"Cassidy?" It was King, his mouth open and his eyes swinging from Pinnington to McGuire and back again.

"You've really got it in for him, haven't you?" Pinnington said.

"What else?" Pratt said.

"He may have been involved in concealing criminal activity . . ." McGuire began.

"What *is* this crap?" King said, still smiling.

"Why don't you just get the hell out of here?" Pinnington slammed the binder closed.

"Wait a minute, wait a minute." It was Pratt. His arms were folded across his chest and he leaned towards McGuire but spoke to King. "Close the door," he said. Then to McGuire: "What are you talking about?"

McGuire waited for King to return and stand beside Pinnington. "Cassidy is married to a woman, Kirsten, I believe her name is," he said. "Her maiden name is De Coursey. He gave me documents to examine on a company called Amherst Electronics, a customer of one of your clients, Saugus Incorporated . . ."

"Ray Finkle's company," Pratt said to Pinnington.

"Amherst is owned by TriTech, a holding company headed by a guy named Stoller, who lives in the Caymans." McGuire paused to look at each of the three men in turn, and when they made no comment, he went on. "TriTech is supported by two silent investors, Boston families. There's no record of either one on any documents Cassidy gave me. But of course, neither is TriTech. That wouldn't have been so hard to find anyway. Finding the families was the hard part. One's named . . ."

McGuire removed the crumbled sheet of notepaper from his pocket and glanced at it. "van der Kramer." He looked up again and smiled. "The other's De Coursey."

There was a pause while each of the others absorbed McGuire's news.

King was the first to act. "Doesn't mean a thing," he said, waving his hand in McGuire's direction.

"Sure," McGuire said. "Look it up. There are a dozen De Courseys in the telephone book. I mean, what can the odds be, right?"

"Where'd you discover this?" Pratt said.

Pinnington lowered himself into his chair.

"TriTech is the name Cassidy blacked out on all the documents," McGuire said. "I didn't know TriTech owned Amherst, or that they were headquartered in the Caymans, either. I didn't get that information from Cassidy. As a matter of fact, he did everything he could to keep me from knowing about it. Which is why he also was worried that I might make copies of the stuff he gave me."

"A bit of *prima facie*," Pratt said.

"Three of TriTech's investments have gone broke in the last two years, just like Amherst did." McGuire looked at each man as he spoke. "Amherst was bought a couple of years ago. All its assets were liquidated and it didn't pay any suppliers for the last six months. I'm not an accountant, but it sure as hell looked to me as though ten million dollars disappeared from Amherst after it was bought." His eyes hung on Pinnington. "I'll bet everything I own against your ass that it's somewhere in the Caymans, along with ten or twenty million from the other two companies. These guys are running scams and your man Cassidy's making sure their tracks are covered."

Pinnington's face was a pale mask.

Only Pratt spoke. "What are you going to do?" he asked.

"Here's what I'm *not* going to do." McGuire placed his palms on Pinnington's desk and leaned forward, looking into Pinnington's eyes. "I'm not going to let anybody, especially Thomas Schaeffer, know where I obtained his address. If I had a week and a thousand dollars to spare, somebody I know might locate him anyway. But I don't want to waste the money or the time. The second thing I'm not going to do is, I'm not going to pass copies of my notes along to the Law Society, or to a buddy on the Fraud squad, or to one of the hairball reporters at *Eyewitness News*, who keep wanting to interview me about last night. I'm not going to tell anybody that, when Amherst Electronics folded, it left a two-million-dollar debt after paying a five-million-dollar dividend to its partner in the Caymans, who just happens to be in bed with a family connected with your heir apparent, Barry Cassidy, B.A., LL.D., Yale alumni, good Republican, future general partner, and all-round dickhead. And who, instead of blowing a whistle or bowing gracefully out of the picture, appears to have used me to confirm that everybody's nose was clean." McGuire took a long, slow breath. "That's what I'm not going to do," he said. "What I'm going to do now is go to lunch, come back in an hour, clean out my office, pick up my check, and look inside it for Thomas Schaeffer's address, which I am told is somewhere in Arizona."

Susan was waiting for him in a booth, the *Globe* open in front of her, a half-filled cup of black coffee sitting to one side. McGuire bent to kiss her on the cheek.

"You're big news," she said. The front page of the newspaper showed McGuire's car being towed from the alley, along with a mug shot of Hayhurst and an old police-file photo of McGuire.

He shrugged out of his sports jacket, tossed it on the seat, and sat across from her. "What are the terms of your parole? Can you leave the state?"

"If I have permission, and if I report back when they tell me to."

"Permission from whom?"

"The police."

"You might be going to Arizona this weekend."

"Why?"

"To find your ex-husband. To see your kids."

When she finished crying, he squeezed her hand, ordered soup and salad for her, a beer and sandwich for himself.

"You'll come with me, I assume."

"I hope," McGuire said. "I never assume."

When they finished eating, he left her to use the pay telephone and call Frank DeLisle.

Facing Pinnington and the other lawyers had been almost a joy, a retribution of sorts. Dealing with DeLisle, he knew, would not be so easy.

DeLisle was waiting for him in the marble foyer on Berkeley Street, the detective tossing peanuts into his mouth from a crumpled paper sack, making small talk with uniformed officers and staff people as they passed.

"What's up?" he said when McGuire led him towards an empty corner.

"You owe somebody a favor," McGuire said.

DeLisle tilted his head back and emptied the remaining peanuts into his mouth. He chewed on them while squeezing the empty bag into a tight paper ball. "I owe half of Dorchester

Street favors," he said. He waved and smiled at a woman staff member walking towards an elevator.

"This one doesn't live in Dorchester," McGuire said. "She lived for two years in Cedar Hill."

DeLisle looked at McGuire, then down at the crumpled paper in his hand. "Susan Schaeffer. I heard you were seeing her." He looked up at McGuire. "How's she doing?"

"What the hell do you care?"

DeLisle looked around for a place to dispose of the paper. "I discovered evidence of grand larceny, so I did what I'm supposed to do."

"You ever thought about acting as a defense witness for her?"

"I was prosecution, for Christ's sake."

"Yeah, and you were married, too."

"What the hell's that supposed to mean?"

"Bit of a problem up there on the stand, right, Frank? Maybe being asked just how you got to know her so well, then going home to the wife, who starts asking questions about those nights you spent on some case, those nights when you were in a bar or somewhere else? Did you ever tell her, your wife, that you went to New York one weekend on an investigation? Is that what you told her?"

"I don't need lectures from you, McGuire."

"You could have saved her, Frank."

DeLisle discovered something interesting about the toes of his shoes.

"You could have crossed over before sentencing," McGuire said. "You could have made a difference of two, three years in the sentence, which would have kept her out of Cedar Hill. Maybe you could have got her probation by testifying about the pressure she was under, what Myers was doing. I think it's called being a friend of the court."

"Now you're talking like a lawyer."

"You owe her, you bastard."

"I owe her what?"

"She needs approval to leave the state for a few days. Terms of her parole. You vouch for her, talk to Higgins and his friends, fill out the form, she can go and not worry about getting shafted by the parole board. Can you do that?"

"Why should I?"

"Because if you do, maybe I'll forget your wife's name and telephone number. Carol Ann, right? Isn't that your wife's name?"

DeLisle tilted his head at McGuire. "You plan on taking her someplace, the Schaeffer woman?"

"Arizona."

"What's in Arizona?"

"The Grand fucking Canyon."

Upstairs, McGuire waited while DeLisle obtained a travel approval, took it from the detective without a word, and bounded up another flight of stairs to the next floor, where he found Donovan and Burnell bent over a computer terminal. The red-haired detective looked up briefly as McGuire approached from across the open office area.

"You found Myers yet?" McGuire said when he reached Donovan's desk.

"Who?" Donovan's eyes returned to the computer screen. Burnell looked up and nodded at McGuire.

"Myers. The guy who killed Orin Flanigan."

Donovan glanced over at McGuire and grinned. "Thank the man, Carl. Looks like he's solved another case for us, and he's not even drawing salary any more."

"Have you talked to him yet?" McGuire said. "Myers?"

"Don't know where he is," Donovan said. "He moved out of his apartment couple of months ago, said he was going to Florida. Florida doesn't know about him, but they're still looking. How's that?"

"And you talked to the yacht broker and Christine Diamond."

"Both say they don't know about Myers. They signed sworn statements, so what can I tell you?" Donovan turned back to the computer and began striking keys.

"You check Flanigan's telephone records?"

"None of your damn business."

"Anybody see Flanigan in Annapolis?"

"Nobody we can find. Told the car-rental agency that he was staying in Washington."

"You got the autopsy report?"

"Whose?" Donovan popped a stick of gum into his mouth.

"Flanigan's. You got Doitch's report on him?"

"It's here," Donovan said. "Why? You want to look at it? Some nice pictures in there, if you like looking at bald dead lawyers."

"Let me see it."

"What's this, you're givin' the city a freebie?"

"How'd he die?"

"He drowned, which is what happens if your lungs suck more water than air, right?"

"Doitch measure the water in Flanigan's lungs?"

"To the c.c.," Donovan said.

"How much was there?"

"Look it up in the goddamn file," Donovan said to the other detective. "Get him out of our hair."

Burnell turned to a file drawer and pulled it open, while Donovan tapped at the computer keyboard. "Here it is," Burnell said to McGuire.

"Don't show him the whole thing," Donovan said. "Just tell him how many gallons Doitch found in Flanigan so he'll believe he wasn't cut up with a machete."

Burnell flipped through the file to the autopsy report. "Point six three liters," he said. He looked up at McGuire. "That's how much water was in the lungs."

"What kind?" McGuire said.

"What?" Donovan stared at McGuire as though he were about to break into laughter. "What *kind*? What, you expect maybe *soda* water?"

"Salt or fresh water?" McGuire said to Burnell.

"The guy was found in the Charles River, remember?" Donovan sneered. "At least a mile from the bay . . ."

"And he was last seen in Annapolis," McGuire said. "Which is surrounded by salt water." He looked at Burnell.

"Brackish," Burnell said.

"Which means salt and fresh," Donovan said. "Which tells you nothing, if the tide was in that night."

"The tide wouldn't come that far up the river," McGuire said.

"You sure about that?" Burnell said.

"Check it out. And call me here, would you?" McGuire withdrew a pen from his jacket, and scribbled Ollie's telephone number on a slip of paper from a wastebasket.

"Do as he says, Carl," Donovan said. He turned back to the terminal. "I mean, this is the great Joseph P. McGuire, right? Hero of the Boston Police Department. Uses his car to run down hoods. Tracer of lost persons, saver of lost souls." A grin appeared on Donovan's face, lit from the soft glow of the terminal. "Screwer of women jailbirds."

Don't, McGuire thought. For once, he heeded his own advice.

A white envelope was on McGuire's desk, his name written on the front with a black felt pen, when he returned to his office. His file drawers were empty, and the coffeemaker was set in a brown cardboard box on the floor.

Inside the envelope was a certified check for $15,000, and a note on Pratt's personal letterhead that said "See me."

Pratt's secretary told McGuire to go right in, and he entered the lawyer's office, which was furnished in Early American antiques. "Please close the door," the birdlike man said. When McGuire did, Pratt gestured towards an oak Windsor chair fitted with a Colonial-print cushion, and McGuire settled himself into it.

"You might as well know that your departure from the firm isn't being greeted with unanimous . . ." – Pratt pursed his lips and stared down at his desk, searching for the word – "euphoria."

"It seemed unanimous in Pinnington's office," McGuire said. "Where's the address?"

"Right here." Pratt handed a folded sheet of paper to McGuire. "I have your word as a gentleman that you will never reveal the source of this information."

"You have it." McGuire opened the paper and glanced at the address and telephone number. Green Valley, Arizona. "I would have found him sooner or later. I preferred sooner."

"I often have this notion," Pratt was saying, "this radical idea, that when a firm gets beyond a certain size, I don't know, maybe fifty, sixty people, and I don't mean just law firms, I mean companies of any kind. After they get to be a certain size, they should think of hiring a full-time disturber." He looked at McGuire. "You know what I mean?"

"Somebody who raises hell," McGuire said, placing the paper in an inside jacket pocket.

"I'm thinking of someone whose function is to ask 'Why are we doing it this way?' 'What's really going on over here?' 'What if we tried this or that?' He would be exasperating, of course. Or she, I suppose." Pratt paused as though pondering the idea. "The whole idea is that they couldn't be fired for asking embarrassing questions."

"And you think I'd be good for the job."

"I think you'd be perfect. And I wouldn't abandon any ideas of continuing your association with our firm. Good lawyers have an ability to separate their emotions from their interests, you know. Most of us, anyway."

"Maybe Orin Flanigan didn't."

"I've often felt that. I've often believed that same thing." When Pratt extended his hand, McGuire shook it.

"By the way," Pratt said as McGuire turned to leave, "Cassidy and Dick Pinnington are huddled together discussing Barry's future with the firm."

"Does he have one?" McGuire asked, his hand on the doorknob. "Cassidy?"

Pratt smiled and shook his head.

CHAPTER 21

Susan was standing at the window of the halfway house, holding a valise, watching for him. A gray-haired woman waited at the door while Susan came to the taxi cab and McGuire handed her DeLisle's letter. She returned to the residence and gave it to the matron, who read it, nodded approval, and shook Susan's hand, before passing her a small valise that had been resting on the floor nearby.

"I can't believe it," Susan said when she was in the cab. McGuire looked past her to the halfway house, where someone was standing with the curtains slightly parted, watching McGuire and Susan drive away.

He stopped the cab twice, once at his bank to deposit most of the law firm's check and take the rest in cash, and again at a travel agency, where he purchased two return airline tickets to Tucson via Chicago while the cab driver stared at the fare meter. Then they continued north to Revere Beach with Susan beside him.

He hadn't felt this good in years.

The noise assaulted his ears from the second floor, a metallic wail above a staccato beat that reminded McGuire of a wobbly steel wheel, kaching-ching-bang, kaching-ching-bang, over and over.

"What the hell is that?" he said. He was holding the door open for Susan to enter. The buzzer sounded from Ollie's room. "Wait here," he said to Susan, and he climbed the stairs two at a time until he was at the door leading into Ronnie and Ollie's former bedroom, now occupied by Liz Worthington. When he rapped loudly on the door, the volume of the music dropped.

"Who is it?" a woman's voice called from inside.

"It's me. I live here, remember?" McGuire said. "So put the gun down." He pushed open the door to find the nurse standing in her bare feet, wearing black leotards and a pale blue tunic. The gun was in her hand, and she placed it on the dresser while McGuire watched. On the dresser sat a massive portable stereo, and the scratchy beat of the music spilling from the unit sounded to McGuire as though an autistic animal were trapped within, trying to claw its way to freedom through the speakers.

"What do you want?" Liz Worthington said.

"I want you to put a bullet through that son of a bitch," McGuire said. He pointed at the portable stereo.

"That's my music," she said. "It's a statement of angst and alienation." She smoothed the front of her tunic. "It's also fun to dance to."

"You dance to that shit?"

"I dance to keep me fit and make me happy."

"You turn every one of those CDs into beer coasters and I'll be so goddamn happy I'll dance across Massachusetts Bay!"

"It's not just music, you know. It's artistic expression."

"Well, you got the first part right. And how'd you like to see me express myself artistically with a fire ax?"

She rested her hand on the gun. "If you enter my room without my permission and armed with a weapon, I'll shoot you, and that's a promise."

McGuire muttered to himself and returned to the top of the stairs to see Susan looking up at him, her eyes wide and her expression distraught. "Is everything all right?" she asked as he descended the stairs.

"Just normal insanity," he said. He took her arm and guided her down the hall to Ollie's room.

"You're like the cavalry riding over the hill just when the bad guys're ready to burn the virgins." Ollie's bed was propped to a sitting position and his moon face was red and creased. "I couldn't take it any more. The more I pressed this damn buzzer, the more she turned up that crap until she couldn't hear me . . . and who the hell is this angel?"

McGuire introduced Susan, who grasped Ollie's good hand as it flopped across the bedsheets towards her.

"Joe, you gotta do something about that woman upstairs," Ollie said.

"Like what?"

"You gotta kill her, Joe."

"I can't kill her, Ollie . . ."

"Yes, you can. It'll be justifiable. Tell you what, you do her and I'll confess to it . . ."

McGuire turned to look at Susan. "He's joking," McGuire said.

"No, I'm not." Ollie's eyes swung to Susan's. "I'm serious. I've got a forty-year-old butch nurse who says my biggest problem isn't that I can't walk, it's that my life's dull, with no inspiration."

"So maybe the music'll inspire you."

Ollie turned his head to mumble at the wall.

"What's that?" McGuire said.

"I said it's inspiring me to explore her ass with a loaded shotgun." He flashed a smile at Susan. "Sorry."

"We're going to Arizona," McGuire said.

"You wanta take Dizzy Miss Lizzy with you in a trunk?" Ollie asked.

"She looking after you? Really?"

"Yeah, yeah. She does what's needed to be done. She's pretty good at that, I gotta admit. She knows the ERA of the Sox pitching staff, and what a naked reverse is."

"A naked what?" Susan asked.

"Football talk," McGuire said. "Ollie, we'll be gone two or three days. We're going to find Susan's kids. You'll be stuck with her, the nurse."

"Go, go," Ollie said.

McGuire and Susan left the room to find Liz Worthington in the kitchen. "In case you're wondering, I only cook for him," the nurse said.

"Try to keep it that way," McGuire said.

He led Susan upstairs, carrying her valise. In his room he closed the door and stroked her hair and inhaled the aroma of her.

They left early in the morning, the cab weaving through the light Saturday traffic to the airport. McGuire wore his brown tweed jacket over a blue Oxford-cloth shirt, khaki trousers, and Timberland deck shoes. Susan chose a deep-blue polished cotton skirt, pale blue jersey top, and beige suede jacket, her hair pulled back and held by tortoiseshell combs. During the flight to Chicago, and while they waited at O'Hare to begin the second leg to Tucson, she swung back and forth between excitement and anxiety.

In Tucson he rented a car, and with the help of the rental agency's map he found Highway 19 heading south towards Nogales, the highway weaving among low brown hills studded with saguaro cactus. The sky shone like a blue crystal and the air was dry, warm, and benevolent. Within half an hour they encountered Green Valley, an affluent development stretching away on both sides of the highway, extending outward from a low-rise shopping mall that seemed to be its epicenter. McGuire pulled into the mall, found a pay telephone, withdrew the notepaper Pratt had provided, dropped a quarter in the telephone slot, winked across at Susan, who remained in the car, and dialed the number.

"Hello?" A woman's voice. McGuire asked if Tom Schaeffer was in. "No, but I expect him back in an hour." She asked who was calling; McGuire said it was a friend, and he would call back.

A waitress in a nearby coffee shop gave him directions to Schaeffer's house, and when McGuire returned to the car he said, "You sure you can handle this?"

"I have to," she said. "I've been dreaming about this for two years. I have to."

They drove west among tidy houses with red-tiled roofs and manicured lawns. Late-model minivans were parked in most driveways, and the tops of swimming-pool slides projected above backyard fences. Dark-skinned men with thin mustaches, wearing khaki shirts and trousers, washed cars and trimmed lawns in front of some homes, and dark-skinned women with black hair that shone like coal swept the front walks or shook dust from rugs and blankets.

Schaeffer lived in a cul-de-sac among a half-dozen other homes, and almost as soon as McGuire turned the corner, Susan leaned forward in the seat and her hand flew to her mouth.

Ahead of them, in the shade of a low tree on the lawn of the house, which faced down the short street, were two children. A boy wearing blue jeans and a San Jose Sharks T-shirt, lying on his back, tossed a baseball into the air and caught it, over and over. A girl stood talking to him, a small Navajo blanket gathered around her shoulders like a cape, her expression somber. She raised one hand from beneath the cape to brush a lock of hair the color of bleached straw from her eyes and looked up as McGuire's car approached.

"It's them," Susan whispered.

McGuire pulled the car into the driveway while the children watched, the boy sitting up. "What do I do?" Susan said, and McGuire told her to go to them.

She walked from the car and around the front of the vehicle. The girl, whose age McGuire guessed as eight, stared open-mouthed as she approached. The boy, perhaps two years older, rose to his feet and leaned against the tree as though ready to dart behind it for protection.

McGuire opened his door and stepped out onto the driveway.

"Belinda." Susan dropped to one knee, her arms outstretched. "It's me," she said to the girl. "It's Mummy."

The girl dropped the blanket and ran to Susan's open arms, and they cried together while the boy and McGuire watched. Then both swung their eyes towards the front door of the house where a dark-haired woman wearing thick glasses, a yellow dress, and a shocked expression stood on the threshold, staring at Susan and the girl.

"Jamie?" Susan said, stretching one hand in the boy's direction. "Jamie? Please come and hug Mummy."

The boy hung back, his eyes on the woman in the doorway. At the sight of the woman Susan stood, one hand pressed against the back of the little girl's head. "I'm Susan," she said to the woman. "I'm their mother."

The woman nodded and tried with little success to smile. "I know," she said. "I know."

The woman invited McGuire and Susan inside. Susan carried Belinda, who wore a blue two-piece bathing suit beneath the blanket. The boy tagged along, looking as uncomfortable as McGuire.

Inside, the house was furnished in Santa Fe style. The whitewashed walls were hung with oversized abstract paintings, the sofas and chairs were overstuffed and covered in Navajo blankets, and the wooden furniture was either dark and heavy or constructed of bleached saguaro wood, painted in pastel greens and blues. The ceilings were high, the layout open, and McGuire was struck by the awareness that a good deal of money was needed to create a mood the Hopis and Navajos and Mexican tribes had refined through centuries of poverty.

The woman introduced herself as Sylvia, Thomas's wife. She watched Susan indirectly, swinging her eyes away when Susan glanced in her direction. She explained that Thomas had gone to the hardware store for gardening supplies, and should be back any minute. "May I offer you something to drink?" she asked. Her posture was stiff and unnatural, like someone awaiting punishment. Susan, settled on a sofa with

Belinda on her lap, declined. The boy stood near her, his expression solemn. When Susan reached for his hand, he remained as rigid as a rake handle.

McGuire said he'd love a beer, and Sylvia nodded and walked like a zombie through a wide archway towards the kitchen area.

"Tell me what you've been doing," Susan said to the children, who looked at each other and weighed their responses.

McGuire strolled away to a location from which he could see through the archway into the kitchen. Sylvia was standing at the sink, her hands forming tight fists and resting on the counter, her shoulders hunched, her eyes squeezed shut.

Outside, a car door slammed. McGuire looked to see a slim, bearded man emerge from a Lexus SUV and glance at McGuire's rental car in the driveway. The man's forehead was high, above aviator-style sunglasses, and his graying hair was close-cut; he wore a long-sleeved denim shirt and loose cotton trousers, and he walked to the side of the house, where Sylvia opened the door to greet him. As McGuire watched, the woman spoke in a low voice, then clung to him, while Thomas Schaeffer stared over her shoulder at McGuire from behind his sunglasses.

"He's here," McGuire said to Susan.

Schaeffer entered the house and walked across the tile floor, his eyes flashing briefly at McGuire. "Belinda, Jamie," he said. "Go into the kitchen and help Sylvia, will you?"

"Go ahead," Susan said, and she kissed her daughter's cheek.

The adults watched the children leave. "How are you?" Schaeffer asked Susan, who said she was fine and introduced McGuire. Schaeffer kept his eyes on Susan. "How long have you been out?"

"A few weeks." Susan moved closer to McGuire and reached for his hand. "Nearly three months. Your beard looks good, Thomas. It suits you."

"How did you find us?" Schaeffer asked.

"Ways and means," McGuire said.

"Joe used to be a policeman," Susan said. "A detective."

"You can't take them back, you know," Schaeffer said to Susan. "I won't let you."

"I know." Susan released McGuire's hand and toyed with her own as she spoke. "I know."

"Sylvia's getting something to drink," Schaeffer said. "She's a little surprised. And upset." One hand stroked his beard as he spoke.

"She seems very nice," Susan said. "When were you married?"

"A year ago last month." Schaeffer slid his hands into his pockets. "You look good," he said to his former wife. "Really good."

Susan thanked him and reached for McGuire's hand again. "Joe's been helpful. Things have not been good. Orin Flanigan was murdered last week, did you hear?"

Schaeffer nodded. "Boston Police called here. They asked a few questions. I couldn't help them, of course." He looked at McGuire with a curious expression. "Excuse me," he said. "I'd better go help Sylvia."

When he was gone, Susan pressed herself against McGuire and wrapped her arms around him.

McGuire asked how she was holding up. "I'm all right," she said. "But Sylvia seems nervous, doesn't she?"

"She has good reason to be," McGuire said, and when Susan looked up at him, McGuire said, "Her husband's still nuts about you."

They sat on a patio shaded by the wide overhang of the house. A light breeze danced with the hanging plants, and the afternoon sun heated the red hills till they were almost incandescent. The conversation was awkward, the pauses lengthy and strained. Sylvia dropped first a glass and then a tray before she retreated to the house, where McGuire saw her watching them through the window.

Thomas Schaeffer described his job as a development executive with a Tucson communications firm and speculated on the impact of digital transmission, a topic McGuire found desperately boring. Belinda sat on her mother's knee. Jamie remained aloof on the pool diving board, swinging his legs and looking stricken, glancing sidelong at his parents and this stranger, avoiding their eyes.

"How long are you staying?" Schaeffer asked McGuire.

"Until tomorrow," McGuire said.

Schaeffer nodded, as though in approval. "I'm not sure what my legal rights are," Schaeffer said.

"About what?"

"About, I don't know . . . restricting access to the kids, visiting rights . . ."

"Thomas," Susan said, and both men turned to look at her. "I'm their mother. I want them to grow up happy and I want them to understand me. I want them to know what I did and why I did it. But I would never try to come between you and them."

Schaeffer looked away, west to the low scrubby hills.

"That's a Lexus you're driving?" McGuire said, standing up.

"Yeah." Schaeffer was pulling at his beard again.

"You mind showing it to me?" McGuire said. "I'm thinking of buying one. Some street punk beat up my old Chrysler."

The two men walked around the side of the house, and McGuire paused at the Lexus, one hand on its hood.

"You don't want to talk about my car," Schaeffer said.

"No, but I'd like you to cut Susan a little slack," McGuire said. "It's not your kids you're worried about, is it? It's your marriage."

"Sylvia's falling apart in there." Schaeffer tilted his head towards the house. "She's been afraid of this happening since before we were married. Susan showing up, I mean."

"What did you do, brag to her about your glamorous and notorious ex-wife?"

"I guess." Schaeffer smiled, embarrassed. "I guess I did."

"She thinks she can't compete with Susan. She thinks you'll fall all over her."

"Sylvia's a good woman," Schaeffer said. He shrugged, unsure of how to continue. "She's a good woman," he repeated, agreeing with himself, and McGuire felt a wave of sympathy for these people, a man unable to sever emotional ties with the mother of his children, a woman whose husband could say nothing more flattering about her than that she was "good."

"You happy here?" McGuire asked.

"Hell, yes." Schaeffer swept his arm to encompass the desert landscape. "Who wouldn't be?"

"Susan meant it when she said she wants happiness for her children." McGuire walked along the side of the car, tracing its lines with his fingertips. "And you know it." He stopped and looked back at Schaeffer. "Something wrong with Jamie?"

"He's kind of my favorite. And he's the oldest. Maybe he remembers things I told him about his mother."

"Yeah, well." McGuire shielded his eyes and stared through the window glass at the interior of the Lexus. Leather upholstery, CD player. Hell, he'd never be able to afford one of these. "You still feel that way? About Susan?"

Schaeffer shook his head. "You're a bright guy. You can figure out how I feel about her."

"Yeah." So can your wife, McGuire thought, walking to the rear of the car. "Well, you know, maybe you could tell your son that. Because he looks like he's having a hell of a time dealing with this woman who's his mother, the one he hasn't seen for a few years. She doesn't have a wart on her nose or ride a broom, maybe like he expected."

"You have kids?"

"No. Just a long memory." He continued walking around the car, the other man a few steps behind.

"When I go back into the house, it's Sylvia's emotions I'll have to deal with. What can I say that'll calm her down? Tell her Susan won't come around any more? That she should get over her idea that Susan's some kind of competition?"

"Nice car." McGuire was walking back towards the pool area again. "Nice house, nice location. Good family. Sounds like you've got a great career. You're not really dumb enough to throw it all away by making a play for your ex-wife, are you?" He smiled at Schaeffer. "Maybe that's what you tell her. That's what I'd say."

McGuire and Susan declined a half-hearted invitation to a barbecue dinner, but they accepted Schaeffer's offer to return the next day, and his invitation to take them for a drive through the desert and show McGuire how his Lexus performed. Belinda cried when they left, but Jamie hung back, and when his mother pleaded with him to come and kiss her goodbye, he turned on his heel and returned to the pool.

They found a motel outside Tucson and registered for the evening. In bed, Susan sobbed against his shoulder, then brightened again and spoke of her children, how healthy they looked, how well they seemed to be doing in school. Around dusk, McGuire walked across the highway to a restaurant, returning with fried chicken, and they sat in bed, watching local news stories, wiping the grease from their fingers on towels from the bathroom.

Belinda ran laughing across the lawn to greet her mother when Susan and McGuire arrived the next morning. Jamie walked to her, smiling and embarrassed.

In the car, with Schaeffer driving, McGuire sat up front and listened to the other man rhyme off the vehicle's various features and specifications, while Susan and the children chatted behind them. Sylvia had begged off, saying she had so much to do that day.

They stopped for ice cream, Susan and the children lining up at the take-out counter while the men remained in the car.

"You had a talk with your son," McGuire said.

"Yeah, I did." Schaeffer was watching his former wife as she bent to speak to Belinda. "Sylvia too." He turned to McGuire. "Sometimes," he said, "it's harder to give up your enemies than it is to give up your friends."

McGuire thought it was probably the most profound observation Schaeffer had made in many years.

"Can we go see the babies?" Belinda asked. Her lips were smeared in strawberry ice cream. When Susan asked What babies? the young girl said, "The Indian babies, painted on the wall."

"It's called the Chapel of the Sky," Schaeffer said. "Because the artist decided not to rebuild the roof that had fallen in."

They drove north to an adobe building among groves of saguaro cactus. Behind the chapel rose terra-cotta hills scattered with mesquite and other ragged foliage. Belinda ran ahead, leading her mother into the chapel, which was no larger than a suburban bedroom. Schaeffer stood at the entrance, watching Susan and the children. To the south and below, the city of Tucson stretched like the embodiment of all that could go wrong among a landscape that was harsh and beautiful and true: tall rotating signs announced the location of gas stations and fast-food outlets, and the sounds of diesel trucks down-shifting through the city disturbed the sense of peace that otherwise blanketed the chapel. McGuire sat on an out-cropping of rock, closed his eyes, and absorbed the sun's warmth.

"You really a detective?"

McGuire opened his eyes to see Jamie seated next to him. The boy was round-faced and blue-eyed, and a cowlick of his sand-colored hair stood at attention, crowning his head.

"Used to be," McGuire said.

The boy pondered the news. "Sylvia's afraid of you."

"Why?"

Jamie shrugged. "Do you like it here? In Arizona?"

"Yes. I like it a lot."

"So do I." The boy scooped a handful of dust from the ground and sifted it through his fingers. "Do you think my mom's pretty?"

"Your mother is very pretty," McGuire said. "She's more than that."

Jamie rubbed the dirt from his hands. "Sylvia says, if my mom stays, she'll leave."

"How do you know that?"

"I heard my dad and her talking last night. They thought we were asleep."

"What do you think of Sylvia?"

"She's okay."

"We're not staying."

Jamie shrugged. "If my mom needs me, like you said she does, and she goes back to Boston . . ." He left the words hanging in the air.

"You can't figure out how somebody can need you and still be two thousand miles away," McGuire said, and the boy nodded. "She doesn't need you in the next room or in the next house as much as she needs you here." McGuire thumped his chest. "She needs to know you're there, because that's where people you love are. Can you understand that?"

Jamie nodded. "I think so."

They sat in silence for a minute until McGuire said, "So, you ever thought of becoming a cop?"

Schaeffer gave them a tour of Tucson over the rest of the morning, stopping for lunch at a fast-food drive-in, and touring Old Tucson, where actors portraying cowboys engaged in street shootouts.

"You ever shoot anybody?" Jamie asked McGuire a few moments after seeing a re-enacted gun battle. The two were standing next to a corral fence watching horses.

"Yes," McGuire said.

"Was it like that?"

"It's never like that. It's maybe the worst thing in the world." McGuire's tone of voice and his expression, suddenly distant, silenced the boy. All the way back to Green Valley, McGuire felt Jamie's eyes on him.

At Schaeffer's home, Sylvia greeted them wearing a red satin halter top, balloon pants, and more makeup than the day before. She made another half-hearted invitation to McGuire and Susan to stay for drinks. They declined, and in the driveway Belinda and Susan hugged goodbyes. The girl pecked McGuire on the cheek, then ran sobbing into the house, pursued by Sylvia. McGuire shook hands with Jamie and asked if the boy knew much about the Apaches that had once lived in this area of Arizona. When Jamie said Yes, McGuire promised to come back and learn as much as the boy wanted to tell him. He shook hands with Schaeffer and gave him Ollie's telephone number in Revere Beach. Then he put his arm around Susan's shoulder, and guided her back to the rental car, her face wet with tears.

They were booked on an early evening flight through Chicago. "We could have stayed a little longer," he said, but she shook her head and gripped his hand, staring out the window at the passing desert scene.

"It's beautiful, isn't it?" she said. "Aren't they lucky to live here?"

McGuire turned off the highway to a side road before the airport, and followed a narrow dirt track leading up into the low hills south of the city. At a sharp turn on the crest of a ridge, the road provided a panoramic view of the desert area to the east of Tucson, and he pulled to the side and switched off the engine.

"I find it harder than ever," she said, "to believe that I did what I did."

"You want to get out and walk around?" McGuire asked, and she shook her head. Then she leaned against him, there in the car, her cheek pressed against his chest. "When I was able to read the Boston papers," she said, "when I'd get them at Cedar Hill, they were usually a week or so old, and I would read the obituary columns, looking for his name."

"Whose?"

"Ross's. I'd look for Myers in the death notices. I couldn't believe he would still be alive. I thought he would be killed in jail or on the street when he got out, but he wasn't. Or maybe he was. Maybe he's not down in Annapolis after all. Maybe he's dead. Did you ever think of that?"

"Who would kill him?"

"Lots of people wanted to. The men who invested in the business school. Two of them lost everything. Everything. Ross spent it on . . . I don't know . . . gambling, for sure. He spent it on the horses he owned and the clubs he belonged to, the cars. The women. I'm sure he spent much of it on women. The wife of one man who put money into his business, a lawyer, she divorced him over it. The lawyer had given Ross everything he owned, even mortgaged his house, when Ross said he could double his money for him. He was such a controller. You have no idea. He controlled me, he controlled his partners . . . Nobody could believe that anyone was able to lie so often, so convincingly. Honestly, he was a sociopath. And the bookies . . ."

"You don't tell lies to big-city bookies," McGuire said. "Not for long."

"Ross could tell lies to anybody and get away with it."

Below them the desert was a carpet and a panorama, an unreal vista of shapes and colors and shadows. She snuggled closer to him and stretched her arm across him, resting her hand on McGuire's hip.

"He would tell the most outrageous lies," she said, "and people would believe him. Eventually he thought I'd believe anything he told me, just because I wanted to believe it. That's what a controller does, isn't it? He figures out what you want to believe, and he tells you the lies you want to hear. He told me once . . ." She laughed without any humor and began again. "He told me that I only imagined what I actually saw, that I didn't really see what I *knew* I had seen."

"What was that?" McGuire was watching an aircraft on its final approach to the airport, gliding down, down, its landing gear lowered.

"I was coming home one evening, and I saw his car parked in the driveway of the condominium. I saw something moving inside, and I didn't know what it was, or who it was. I thought it might be Ross, in trouble or something, so I went to the window and looked in." She sat up and looked through the windshield at the descending aircraft. "He was in the car, on the front seat. Doing it, right there in our driveway, with some woman friend of his. I mean, there he was with his pants down and her legs . . ."

McGuire, remembering a similar scene, made a fist and pounded the steering wheel. "For Christ's sake," he said, and started the engine. "Damn, damn, damn."

Susan was frightened at his sudden outburst. "Why do you get angry when I talk about Ross?"

"I'm not angry with you," McGuire said. He swung the car around on the narrow road. "I'm pissed at myself for not making a connection." He removed a hand from the steering wheel to squeeze hers in reassurance.

"Where are we going?" she asked.

"To the airport. To make a telephone call and change my flight."

"Why?"

"Because I think I want to go back to Annapolis. Right away. Soon as I can."

"You *think*?" she said.

McGuire covered one ear with his hand and pressed the receiver against his other ear, trying to catch every word of

Ollie's scratchy voice over the din of the airline terminal.

"Brunell, Burnell, something like that," Ollie was saying through the speakerphone by his bed in Revere Beach. "Sounded like some young pecker anyway."

"He's okay," McGuire said. "What'd he say?"

"He said Doitch told him he'd probably have gotten around to it anyway, but with his workload and under the circumstances and all, place the body was found, backlog, no suspect . . ."

"Well, is it or isn't it?" McGuire almost shouted into the telephone.

"There's no way that all the water in the lawyer's lungs came from the river. No way at all. Some entered, but it was mostly salt water. The guy didn't drown in the Charles. He drowned in an ocean somewhere and was dumped in the goddamn river."

"Okay, okay." McGuire was feeling the familiar excitement.

"How you doin'?"

"Listen, if Burnell calls back, tell him to check the car they found in Weymouth . . ."

"They got a match," Ollie interrupted. "On fibers on the body, probably in the trunk. I thought about it already and asked Burnell. How many times I gotta tell you, I'm only paralyzed from the neck down? You goin' back down there?"

"If I can change my flight from Chicago, yeah."

"How about Susan? She comin' back on her own?"

"If she agrees."

"Give her a kiss for me. Then send her up here, and I'll tell her some tales, straighten her out about you, make sure she knows what she's getting into."

"What about your nurse?"

"Susan'll be an antidote."

McGuire promised to call when he had news, and hung up. He turned to kiss Susan on the cheek. "That's from Ollie," he said. He scanned the terminal, looking for the airline counter. Then he stopped, turned to her again, and pulled her to him, pressing his mouth against hers and stroking the back of her head with his hands, weaving his fingers through her hair, never seeing the stares and smiles of passersby. When he finished he looked at her eyes, which were smiling back at him, and said: "And that's from me."

He explained it to her on the flight to Chicago, telling her that all he wanted to do was fit the pieces together and place the puzzle in the lap of the police. "You go on to Boston, stay at the halfway house. I'll rent a car in Washington and drive to Annapolis."

"Can't it wait?" she said. "Can't you take a flight tomorrow?"

"If I have to, I will. But if I do, I won't sleep all night. Besides, he must be getting spooked, ready to move on."

"Can't you just give everything he knew to the police, and let them take it from there?"

"Donovan's liable to blow things. He'll resent having to use raw information from me. Besides, this one I want to see through for myself, because I was so damned blind to it until now."

She rested her head against him, the Arizona desert far below them, while McGuire admitted to himself there was another reason to wrap things up on his own, a reason that connected him with Orin Flanigan: because he wanted to see Myers pay. He wanted to be there to see the man turn pale.

CHAPTER 22

The flight to Washington left half an hour after McGuire and Susan arrived at O'Hare, the last one of the day. At the check-in counter, McGuire promised to call her the next morning from wherever he was staying. He pressed more than enough money into her hand for the cab ride to the halfway house, kissed her, seized his bag, and trotted towards the gate. He turned once to wave at her, before handing his ticket to the flight attendant. For the first time in his life, he questioned the energy driving him, the intensity that exploded whenever he grew this close to a resolution, to a settling of accounts.

McGuire's obsession with Myers had built from the moment Susan described her life with him: the beatings, the lies, the deceptions, the arrogance. From his days as a rookie Boston cop, McGuire considered domestic violence among the most abhorrent aspect of his work. He had seen more than his share of battered wives and battered children, had encountered more than enough spineless men who would bow and scrape in the presence of other men whose respect they craved, and later terrorize those whom they should have loved, who expected their love and instead harvested only their contempt and brutality. They were men who manipulated people around them, their tactics coolly plotted, clear of conscience. They were con artists and sociopaths, popular with those with whom they wanted to ingratiate themselves, ruthless with those who provided only the means and the trust.

He had never encountered one with the apparent malice of Ross Myers. He pictured Myers lavishing gifts on women, spending money to impress his friends at the hundred-dollar betting windows in Florida, while Susan cowered in Boston, shaken by every demand for more money and unable to stop the flow, to halt the descent.

It was past ten o'clock when he landed at Washington, where he rented a car and set off for Annapolis. The traffic was light, and just after eleven he pulled the sedan onto State House Circle and down Maryland Avenue to the Academy Bar and Grill. He stepped aside as three young men left the restaurant, one wearing a St. John's College sweatshirt, the others fastening their jackets against the night chill.

Inside, he was washed with warm air and the aromas of fried onions and beer. He walked through the restaurant area and past the bar, where perhaps half the stools were occupied. A gaunt bartender with unruly hair and bad teeth glanced up and nodded at McGuire.

"Who's your Bud distributor?" McGuire asked him.

"Our what?"

"Who owns the beer distributorship? Who ships your Bud to you?"

The man shrugged. "Rollie Wade. It's his company. He doesn't deliver it."

"Who delivers it?"

"Depends. Some days it's a guy named Banting. Usually it's Dan Daniels. You know either of them?"

McGuire shook his head and walked away, choosing a table near the far wall, where the bartender watched him with a mix of curiosity and suspicion.

Two waitresses were on duty, one bleached-blonde and heavyset, the other younger with a long, dark ponytail that swung with every step. When the younger one stopped at McGuire's table, he ordered a beer. When she returned to set the glass on his table, he smiled up at her. "There's another waitress who works here," he said. "About thirty, thirty-five. Brown hair, not as long as yours. I'd like to see her."

"Eileen," the young woman said. "She's in tomorrow. That'll be two-fifty."

McGuire handed her a five, told her to keep it.

"She's got a boyfriend, you know." The waitress tucked the money in an apron pocket. "At least, she did last time I heard. A jealous one, too."

"I know," McGuire said. "They still living together?"

She shrugged. "I don't think so. Not any more."

"He still drive the Mercedes?"

"It's a Cadillac. You having anything to eat?"

McGuire said No. He took two sips of the beer, tapped his fingers on the table, and left.

Half an hour later he was registered in a motel room outside the town, tossing and turning in bed, willing himself towards a sleep that refused to arrive for hours.

"I couldn't sleep." Susan's voice was shaking but strong through the telephone wire. "All night long, I couldn't sleep."

McGuire sat up in bed, staring at dappled morning sunlight on the painted concrete-block wall of the motel room. "I didn't do so well myself," he said.

"Did you see him?"

McGuire said No. But he expected to. He gave her Ollie's telephone number and address. "Take a cab up there," he said. "I'll call when I've got something. While you're waiting, get Ollie to tell you stories about us. They'll have you in stitches. Some of them might even be true."

After hanging up, he dialed Boston again and counted nine rings before a woman's angry, scratchy voice answered. "McGuire, you doorknob," the woman spat through the phone after he identified himself. "The cats and I aren't even out of bed yet."

"Calm down, Libby. I need a favor."

"I don't do favors when I'm awake," Libby Waxman almost shouted. "The hell makes you think I'll do one for somebody who gets me out of a sound sleep?"

"Just for me, Libby."

"What?"

"I need a name."

"Whose?"

"The bookie in Baltimore, told you about Myers."

"Are you nuts?"

"He's a bookie, Libby. If he's a bookie, he's got other customers besides Myers, so they gotta know his name too. That's all I'm asking. Just give me his name."

"What? You wanta place a bet?"

"You got it. What's the guy's name?"

"Lou. Lou Wachtman." She spelled the last name for him.

"You're such a sweetheart," McGuire said. "I almost wish I was there in bed between you and the cats. Thanks."

"Wait a minute," Libby said. "You wanta make a bet, don't you want his number?"

McGuire said No, he had all he needed.

He was too excited to eat, too driven even to have coffee. After showering and dressing, he checked out of the motel and drove through a brilliant autumn morning across the Severn River bridge into Annapolis, parking in front of the Academy Bar and Grill.

This time he didn't try opening the front door, but walked around the corner and down the service alley to the rear of the building. The rear door was unlocked, and he edged his way past trays of hamburger rolls and cartons of beer bottles into the bar area. From the dining room next door he heard the jangle of silverware being shuffled.

She was bent over one of the larger tables. Her hair was gathered on top of her head in Gibson-girl style, and the stained sweatshirt she wore was shapeless and frayed.

"Eileen," McGuire said.

She turned to glance at him, her left hand clutching several stainless-steel dinner forks. "You the guy from the bakery?" she said, and looked back at her work, placing silverware on the round tables. "You still owe us four dozen rolls, Jenny tell you that?"

"I'm not from the bakery," McGuire said. He stepped into the room, scanning the booths to make certain they were alone.

"Where you from?" She didn't look up.

"Boston."

"You just visiting? 'Cause if you are, we don't open until eleven."

"I know." McGuire seated himself at one of the tables between her and the door. "I've been here before."

She continued setting the forks in their correct location, but McGuire had seen her shoulders freeze for a moment, and now her actions were slower, more deliberate, as she tried to contain her emotion. She walked to a service counter in the corner and dropped the remaining forks into a tray with a loud clatter. She looked directly at him, then closed her eyes. "You're the guy," she said, recognizing McGuire, remembering.

"Where is he?"

"I don't know." She was wiping her hands on a towel.

"Yes, you do."

"No, I don't."

"You know how to reach him, I'll bet."

"I haven't seen him in . . ." She shrugged. "Nearly a week."

"You pick him up in Weymouth?"

"Where?"

"Near Boston. Did you pick him up there one night in a shopping-mall parking lot? About a week ago?"

She dropped the towel on the serving counter and began to wipe her hands on her jeans. "Is he in trouble?"

"Oh yes. Ross Myers is in very big trouble."

"With the same people?" She looked across at him. "Are you with them?"

"You mean the people from Baltimore?" McGuire said.

She nodded and bit her lip. "You're not going to hurt me, are you?" she pleaded. Her eyes were filling with tears. "I've got three kids, for God's sake . . ."

"Tell me where he is."

"*I don't know!*" She leaned over the counter, refusing to look at him.

McGuire walked to her. When he placed a hand lightly on her back, she cringed. "I'm not going to hurt you," he said. "Just tell me how to find him."

She shook her head, unable to speak.

"Somebody's threatened you before?"

She nodded her head.

"Both of you?"

Another nod.

"Look." He moved his hand from her back to her upper arm, and she turned to look at him, a woman on the cusp between the final bright years of her youth and early middle age. She seemed to have grown ten years older since McGuire entered the room. "Get a message to him. Through somebody who knows how to reach him."

"Jake knows," she said. "He knows how to find him."

"Who's Jake?"

"The night bartender."

"Thin guy, bad teeth?"

She nodded again, not looking at him.

"Okay, you get hold of Jake and tell him to pass a message to Myers. Tell him it's got something to do with Lou Wachtman, his bookie, who doesn't even know about it yet, so there's no sense Myers calling and asking him. Tell Myers I've got a way to settle things with Wachtman and get Myers out from under the money he owes. I'll be out in the open, where he can see me. Just tell him to get his ass and his Cadillac over here this afternoon between two and three and meet me . . ." McGuire looked around, recalling the layout of the town. "Up near the State House. In the park on that hill surrounding the State House. I'll be alone, and he'll be able to check if he wants. Okay? You tell him that?"

She nodded again.

"Did Myers tell you how he got to Weymouth?"

"He was delivering a car there. For a friend."

"Sure he was," McGuire said. "Sure he was."

It was mid-morning when he drove through town and across the bridge to Bay Ridge Yachts, where a heavyset man in a pink polo shirt and elastic-waist slacks stood near the entrance, staring up at the hull of a trailered yacht with a critical eye. Across the breast of his shirt, McGuire read *Bay Ridge Yachts*, embroidered in aqua thread.

McGuire pulled his car near the man, who was making notes on a clipboard, and lowered his window. "Mrs. Diamond in today?" he asked.

"Who?"

"Christine Diamond. She back at work yet?"

"Haven't seen her." The voice was familiar, the words had the soft edges of a well-worn Georgian drawl.

"You Harrison Klees?"

"That's me." Klees underlined something he had written on the clipboard paper. "What can I do for you?"

"Nothing," McGuire smiled, and as Klees watched he swung the car back towards the street where he had seen a telephone booth. He found a B. Diamond in the directory, remembered that her husband's name was Bert, deposited a quarter, and dialed the number.

After three rings a woman's voice answered.

"Mrs. Diamond?" McGuire said.

"Yes?" Was there a hint of a tremor there? McGuire thought he heard one.

"I was just talking to Mr. Klees down here at the office, and he said I should perhaps see you about . . ." He looked up at several sailboats sitting on cradles nearby. On the hull of one he read *Nonsuch 26*. "A Nonsuch twenty-six I'm kind of interested in."

"We don't have a Nonsuch for sale that I was aware of," she said. "We had one last month, but I believe it was sold . . ."

"Oh, is that right?" McGuire looked down at the open telephone directory, memorizing the address. "Son of a gun. Well, I'm sorry to have bothered you. Thanks a lot."

He walked back to the car, repeating the address from the telephone directory over and over in his mind.

An attendant at a gas station directed McGuire to North Point, a slim finger of land extending into the bay beyond the town. The road followed the crest of the point, with views of Chesapeake Bay on either side. The houses on North Point Road were large and elaborate, set at the end of long lanes, many with decorative stone gates at the entrance. The lots were large, and the rear yards were enclosed by high fences and shrubbery for privacy.

He found 3327, a large white Cape Cod with extensions on either side and twin brick chimneys. Behind it, McGuire could see a garden area extending to the shore. As he drove through the open gates and closer to the house, he noted a boathouse and an oversized dock on the shore. The lane led all the way to the dock. He saw a small sailing dinghy bobbing in the water.

He parked the car behind a gray Volvo in the driveway and walked to the heavy black door with its massive brass hardware: Colonial handle, letter slot, kick-plate, and a door knocker shaped like a schooner. He clattered the knocker against the door three times and waited, hearing only the wind and the faint crashing of waves against the dock and onto the shoreline.

The woman who opened the door had the same face as the one McGuire had met in Bay Ridge Yachts a week earlier, but in other ways she was not the same person. She wore no makeup, and her eyes were puffy, as though McGuire had wakened her. A man's white shirt hung over her thin shoulders and almost halfway down the black tights she wore with black ballet slippers. "Yes?" she said. She looked past McGuire to see if he were alone, or to look for a car on the road perhaps.

"Hello, Mrs. Diamond," McGuire said.

"Do I know you?" One hand rose self-consciously to the top of the shirt, pulling it closed near her neck.

"Well, we've met." McGuire heard a television set in the background, an all-news channel reporting the tragedies of the day. "I came looking for Ross Myers, and you told me he was sailing to South Carolina, remember?"

He sensed her reaction, and shot his foot forward to prevent the door from closing. She screamed, "Get away from me!" and tried to close the door against him.

"Take it easy," McGuire said.

"I've got a gun!" She was forcing her weight against the door, a losing battle.

"Well, I haven't," McGuire said. "I just want to talk to you."

She released the door and ran for the stairs, stumbling and falling halfway up, then rising again, scurrying in panic to an upper hall. McGuire heard one dresser drawer open and close, then another. He stepped into the foyer and closed the door behind him. To his left, above an enormous brick fireplace, hung a large oil painting of a sailboat crashing through blue-green waves in what appeared to be a typhoon, except the mood was not of danger but of romance and heroism. McGuire wondered again about people who worshipped toys of wood and canvas and brass, toys that cost more than the average home, toys whose only function was to amuse, to divert, to relieve boredom.

He heard quick, short footsteps approaching down the upstairs hall, and even before he turned to look, he raised his hands in surrender.

Christine Diamond stood at the top of the stairs, her quick spastic breathing and her nervousness making the gun in her hands jump as though pulled by strings. Doggone, McGuire thought to himself, when did every woman in the United States of America get herself a weapon?

"I told you I'm not armed," McGuire said.

"Get out of my house." The gun wandered in one direction, then the other, and McGuire decided the safest location for him was exactly where he was, because it seemed to be the only place where the gun wasn't pointing.

"I just came to tell you something."

"I'll call the police."

"That's fine, but you'll have to put the gun down to do it, so I'll just keep talking."

"I don't want to hear . . ." she began. Her head went back, her eyes closed for a moment, and she took a deep breath.

McGuire lowered his hands and placed them in his pockets.

When she opened her eyes and saw him standing there, she relaxed a little, and leaned against the stair railing. "Please go," she said.

"I want to see Myers."

"I don't know where he is."

"When did you see him last?"

"Three days ago."

"Can you call him? Can you reach him by telephone?"

Her face crumbled and her shoulders sagged. McGuire took a step to climb the stairs, but she stiffened and raised the gun in his direction again. "Go away," she said through her tears.

"What has he done?" McGuire asked.

She shook her head.

"Did a lawyer named Flanigan call you?" McGuire asked. "Did he come to see you? Did Flanigan warn you about anything? About not trusting Myers?"

"I don't know what you're talking about," she said between sobs.

"Flanigan's dead. They found his body in the Charles River, a mile from the ocean. His lungs contained salt water. Myers drove his car to Weymouth and left it there. Do you understand what I'm saying?"

"No," she said. Then: "Yes."

"Don't trust him," McGuire said. "Whatever you do. Don't believe anything Myers tells you, okay? Especially if it has anything to do with money." McGuire turned for the door, then looked back. "If you can reach him, or get a message to him somehow, tell him to meet me at the State House, in the little park that surrounds it. I'll be there this afternoon, from two o'clock on."

The tears flowed freely, and her chest heaved with sobs.

"I'd like to help you," McGuire said, his voice softening. "If you want me to stay or something. . . ."

"No," she said. "Please go."

"You thought I was from Baltimore, right?" McGuire said. "He's had people come here from Baltimore, threatening you, maybe? Threatening your kids too?"

"Please go away," she said. She sank to the floor, the gun in her hand. "Please just go away."

McGuire opened the door and stepped into the freshening air. The breeze chilled him, and he realized he had been perspiring. His hands were shaking and, as he walked to the car, he told himself they were shaking not from fright but from anger, from a helpless rage he needed to defuse.

He drove back into Annapolis and parked the car in the town square abutting the harbor. From a telephone booth near a seafood stall, he placed a collect call to Revere Beach, and heard Ollie's raspy voice accept the charges through his speakerphone.

"The hell you up to?" Ollie asked.

"Planting some seeds." He asked if Susan were there.

"Sittin' here listenin' to me tell lies about you," Ollie said. "'Course some of them ain't lies. I'm lettin' her guess which ones."

"Hi, Joe." Susan's voice sounded hollow and distant. "Are you all right?"

McGuire assured her he was fine, and she made him promise to look after himself. Then he told Ollie and Susan about the waitress Eileen, about the bartender and the beer distributor, about Christine Diamond, and about using the Baltimore bookie's name as bait to draw Myers.

"You want a couple ideas?" Ollie asked.

McGuire said Sure.

"One, if anybody's been puttin' pressure on those women, I'm bettin' it's Myers himself. He's gettin' somebody to do it for him, squeeze whatever he can. You know the drill, Joseph. Bookies and the muscle behind them, they don't mess with girlfriends and kids. Not their style. They go after the bettor, get *him* to mess with the girlfriends and kids. Am I right? Susan, am I right about that?"

"I think so," he heard Susan say in a small voice.

"What else?" McGuire said.

"Susan and I've been talkin', see." Ollie paused, waiting for a reaction from McGuire. "I figure, from what she's told me about the guy, he thinks he's invincible. He pisses away over a half million . . ." Ollie's voice sounded weaker, as though he had turned his head. "Sorry there, sweetheart," McGuire heard him say to Susan. "Still got this thing about swearin' in front of a good-lookin' woman. Anyway, he gets to burn the money, and somebody else takes the fall for it. You catch him doin' elbow push-ups on one woman, and he slides you off to another one, who he calls when you leave and gets to cover his ass for him."

"He's cocky."

"In a manner of speakin', yeah. Thinks you're a bit of junk on the sidewalk he's gotta step around on the way to his Caddy, and he'll brush you off like dandruff."

"So what's it mean?"

"Means you got the son of a bitch right where you want him."

"He killed Flanigan."

"'Course he did. Flanigan wouldn't go down to threaten Myers, even if he could find him any easier than you did. He went down to cut off Myers's supply of cash, warn off whatever woman the creep was usin' like he used Susan and some others. He figured this Diamond woman was the new patsy, and he was going to let her know what Myers is all about, tell her not to give him a penny."

"I could have done that myself. Or he could have put the local cops onto him."

"Not a chance. You didn't know what was up, and Flanigan wasn't ready to tell you, because it would have meant tellin' all the stuff Susan put up with. He was protectin' her, he promised not to let anybody else know about it. Susan told me that. And how'd he know what Myers was doin' with this Diamond woman? Here's a bet, Joseph. I'll bet that Flanigan did a little diggin' on his own, through business directories and stuff, and found out where the Diamond woman lived . . . what's that?"

Susan had said something to Ollie. Now she spoke louder, so McGuire could hear. "Who is this Diamond woman?"

"Flanigan never mentioned her name?" McGuire said.

"He just said he knew what Ross was up to now," she said. "He never mentioned a woman's name." Susan lowered her voice. "I think he felt it was better if I didn't know too much."

"Maybe Flanigan found out she was a widow, which would start bells ringin' and lights goin' on," Ollie said. "Flanigan shows up, ready to keep Myers away from his latest meal ticket, which is the widow Diamond. Maybe Flanigan wanted to play like you do, and come back with proof that he was scammin' somebody."

"He wanted to see Ross in jail," Susan said. "He told me that. 'He should be locked up for what he did to you,' Orin said."

"If Flanigan's going to cut off Myers's supply of cash to pay Myers's bookies, then either Myers gets rid of Flanigan or he's liable to find his kneecaps in a different place from the rest of him, right?" Ollie said. "For a guy like Myers, it was an easy choice. All he's got to do is get Flanigan alone somewhere, bop him on the head, and hold him under water."

"He puts Flanigan in the trunk of the car, drives to Boston, dumps him in the Charles, and gets picked up in Weymouth by the waitress." McGuire was thinking of the dock at the rear of Christine Diamond's house, and the salt water of Chesapeake Bay.

"Joe, be careful." It was Susan's voice, closer to the speaker phone.

"I'm meeting him out in the open," McGuire said. "On the grounds of the State House. He won't do anything there."

"If he shows up," Ollie said.

"Even if he doesn't, I've got enough pieces to put the story together. I know where he got the name he gave me, calling himself Rollie Wade. That's who I asked for when I came back that night, and the bar owner said he's a good guy. Myers read the name off the beer distributor's receipt, standing right in front of me. He's doing something with Christine Diamond. She's frightened out of her mind. And I know he's around here, not down in Florida where Donovan's looking. Although it sounds like he's getting ready to move on. Whether he shows or not, I'm coming home tonight. I'll turn everything over to Donovan and hope he'll have sense to follow up on it. If he interviews the waitress, she'll put Myers in Weymouth. That may be enough."

"You still haven't said whether he'll show," Ollie said.

"I'm betting he'll come by to see what the offer's about. He's got nothing to fear from me. If he convinces himself there's no trap, and he thinks I've got something that can help him, he might show. Maybe he'll feed me something. Maybe not."

"You just want to look the guy in the eye, is what you want to do," Ollie said. "You're not as upset about poor Flanigan as you are about the scumbag makin' you look like a dummy, sendin' you off to his lay of the day, who brushes you off."

"Maybe," McGuire said. Then: "You sure you're okay?"

"Hell, yes. I got a Marine sergeant to change my diaper and a good-lookin' woman to laugh at my jokes. What the hell else does a man like me need?"

CHAPTER 23

McGuire spent the balance of the morning wandering through the old town, among the restored Colonial houses and window-shopping in stores on Maryland Avenue. He returned to the harbor area at noon, ate oyster stew and sourdough bread at a dockside restaurant, retrieved his rental car, and drove back to State House Circle.

The Maryland State House sits on a hillock well back from the harbor, the proud old building perched like a red brick monument, surrounded by winding paths and small gardens extending down to the road, perhaps fifty feet below. Streets radiate out from State House Circle, leading to the harbor area, to the Naval Academy, and to upper-class residential areas.

McGuire circled the State House several times, following the paths, his hands in his pockets but his eyes alert. From one side of the hillock he could look down Maryland Avenue towards the Academy Bar, and he watched the building from afar for several minutes before returning to the highest point of the hillock. He chose a bench with a clear view to both sides and down the slope to the street.

He watched students from nearby St. John's College wander past in their grungy attire, and naval cadets parade by in crisp whites with close-cropped hair like peach fuzz.

At two-thirty he stiffened at the sight of a maroon De Ville cruising slowly along State House Circle. It disappeared towards Maryland Avenue, and when the Cadillac didn't immediately return, McGuire swung his attention to a blonde woman who walked past, looking too carefully at McGuire. He sent her, McGuire told himself. She's checking me out.

Ten minutes later the De Ville was back, cruising from the direction of Maryland Avenue. It pulled to the curb in a no-stopping zone on State House Circle below McGuire.

After a moment or two, the driver's door opened and a clean-shaven man emerged, his fairish hair little more than a coating of fuzz on his scalp. He wore a black-and-white-checked jacket and black trousers over a white shirt open at the neck, the collar outside his jacket. McGuire felt his pulse quicken and spiders explore the back of his neck.

Ross Myers closed the car door and looked around before circling the front of the car and smiling through the windshield at someone in the passenger seat. He looked up at McGuire and the smile grew broader as he began to ascend the path, his head constantly in motion, surveying everything and everyone around him.

Ten feet from McGuire, Myers stopped and slipped a hand into his jacket. McGuire swung his weight forward onto his feet, prepared to move if Myers were armed. Myers withdrew not a weapon, but a gold cigarette case. Still gazing everywhere but at McGuire, he removed a cigarette from the case and placed it in his mouth, dropped the case back into his jacket, slid his hand to an inside pocket, and pulled out a gold Dunhill lighter. He brought the lighter to the cigarette, inhaled deeply, threw his head back, and exhaled. Then his eyes met McGuire's.

"What, you love this crummy town?" he said. "Can't stay away?'

"You got it," McGuire said.

"What's this crap about Wachtman?" Myers's eyes were moving again, here and there. When they settled for a moment on the Cadillac parked below them at the curb, McGuire followed their gaze to see the blonde woman smiling up at the two men from inside the car, her lemon-colored hair falling in waves to her shoulders. The woman waved and Myers returned her greeting with a gesture of his hand. "You working for Wachtman now?" he said over his shoulder.

"What're you afraid of?" McGuire asked.

Myers looked back at McGuire. "Afraid? Are you kidding me? Tell you one thing, I'm sure as hell not afraid of *you*. I asked around after you left. I remembered you from Boston. Big hero up there, weren't you? Got your name in the papers, solving murders, playing the big shot. Then, when they kicked you off the force, you started popping pills, right? I got all the goods on you." He brought the hand holding the cigarette to his mouth, speaking past it, and McGuire noticed a ruby ring on one pinkie finger.

"You're afraid, Myers," McGuire said. "You came here because you thought there might be a chance of getting out from under the debt with your bookie, right? You saw me from the street, sent your newest woman friend up to check things out. You came damn close to having your kneecaps removed by your bookie's hired muscle. Is that why you're letting your hair grow back, shaved your little beard off?" McGuire sat against the bench, his arms extended along its top. "I'd say you're getting ready to get the hell out of town."

Myers looked amused. "You gamble?"

"Never."

"'Course you don't. I can tell. Yeah, I had a little bad luck. But you ride that stuff out, every gambler knows that. You get a bad horse one day, you get a good one the next. That's what it's all about."

"Christine Diamond a good horse?"

Myers looked away, tapping ash from the cigarette. "Yeah, Chrissie's a good one. She sure fooled your ass, didn't she? I went back, you know. Me and Eileen, after I called Chrissie from the bar and told her that you were some flunky out to borrow money from me. She said she'd blow you off, and then Eileen and I went back and finished what you interrupted, right there on the cloakroom floor. How's that make you feel, jerk-off?"

"The blonde in your car, down there. Is she a good horse?"

"Go to hell." Myers took a final drag on the cigarette and flicked the butt into the bushes.

"And Susan Schaeffer," McGuire said, rising from the bench. "She a good horse?"

"Susan?" Myers examined the fingernails of one hand, sunlight catching small diamonds flanking the ruby of his pinkie ring. "How do you know Susan?"

"I knew Flanigan, too."

"Never heard of him." The response was too sudden. Myers dropped his hand and raised his head, finding something fascinating in the trees above and behind McGuire.

"Sure you have. You arrived to see if I could really help you settle with Wachtman. But you came up here to find out how much I know about Orin Flanigan's murder."

"I came for another look at a loser, that's all."

"Did Orin tell you about me? Before you killed him? Orin was here to get some revenge for Susan, maybe get enough on you to put your ass in jail. Maybe to do a favor for Christine Diamond too."

"You seen her? Susan, you seen her around?"

"Yeah," McGuire said.

"She must've just got out, right? How's she look?"

McGuire took a step towards the other man. "She was just another good horse to you, right?"

"Naw." Myers looked almost vulnerable. "She was okay."

"You son of a bitch," McGuire said. "You better get a faster car than that piece of chrome down there on the street. And some track shoes and whatever else you need to run with, Myers. Because I'll stay on your ass until it's in jail, or until I take a hot iron and brand you right across the forehead with a big *A* for asshole."

"That's why you're here?" Myers looked at McGuire with new interest. "Because you got the hots for Susan?" He waved a hand in the air as though intent on catching a fly. "You got the wrong idea about women. You think a woman can do what I do?" Myers thrust his hands in his trouser pockets and leaned against a tree trunk, his stomach spilling over the edge of the waistband. "How many pimps did you bust as a cop? How many of them had two, three, more women peddling their asses on the street for them? I was never a pimp, never had to be. I just had women who wanted to do things to make me happy. If they want to believe all the stuff I lay on them, whose fault is that, huh? Whose fault is that?"

He pushed himself from the tree as though to walk away, then stopped and looked back at McGuire.

"You used to take dope, right? Prescription pills? Am I right?"

Behind Myers, at the foot of the hill, a gray Volvo pulled to a stop behind the Cadillac.

"You think dope's an addiction?" Myers took a step towards McGuire, an index finger pointing like a weapon at McGuire. "You know what the biggest addiction of all is? I'll tell you. It's money. It's being rich." He rubbed his index finger and thumb together. "It's having money, all the money you ever need. It's going to a casino and dropping more money in one night than jerks like you make in a year, sometimes *making* more money than you make in a year, and not giving a damn about it, either way."

McGuire saw the door of the gray Volvo open. A dark-haired woman stepped out wearing a buff-colored trench coat and sunglasses.

"You get a taste of it, and you never want to go back." Myers was unaware of the arrival of the Volvo behind and below him. "You get on a plane, and once you turn left instead of right, once you go first class, up front with the champagne, maybe sitting with a good-looking broad wearing mink and diamonds, there's no way you fly economy, you know what I'm saying here?"

The woman in the trench coat looked up at McGuire and Myers, then walked past the Cadillac, glancing into the window as she passed.

"And you know something else, McGuire? Some of us, not you, you loser, but some of us, that's how we get to live. That's the *only* way we live, because there's no way none of us is ready to break our asses paying off a mortgage or driving some rusted piece of crap the rest of our lives, watching our wives gettin' older and uglier. No way."

McGuire's eyes shifted away from the base of the path, where the woman in the trench coat was approaching, and back to Myers. "I can prove you were in Weymouth, driving Flanigan's car, a couple of days before his body was found. Not even Marv Rosen will save your ass from this one."

"Bullshit."

"The waitress at the bar told me. She picked you up and drove you back here, and she'll testify against you."

"The hell she will. Broad's in love with me."

"She'll do it, Myers. Or face a charge of accessory in a first-degree murder."

"You're not even a cop any more. What do you care anyway?"

"I told you. The same reason Flanigan came here. Because of Susan. Because of what you did to her."

"You schmuck." Myers permitted himself a short laugh, and began to turn away, his eyes on McGuire. "You dumb schmuck."

McGuire saw the reaction of Myers at the sight of the woman in the trench coat, her head up, her hands in her pockets, her attractive face creased with anger and moist with tears.

"One of your horses?" McGuire said. Christine Diamond had stopped a few feet below Myers, blocking his route back to the car. "Is this one of your good horses, Myers?"

The anger faded from Christine's face. Her shoulders sagged and her chest began to heave with sobs so heavy that her words were fluid, hardly intelligible. "How could you?" she said to Myers.

"Hey, come on . . ." Myers began.

"It's gone." The woman's voice rose to a shriek. "It's gone, all of it. Everything Bert left for my babies, it's all *gone*!"

"It's not gone," Myers said, but he was looking past her at the blonde woman who had stepped out of the Cadillac and stood watching from the base of the rise. "I gave you the papers, the certificates . . ."

"*They're forgeries*! Every one of them . . ."

"Who told you that?" Myers was looking for another path, one that would permit him to escape the woman's fury. He glanced behind him at McGuire, who had positioned himself to block his retreat in that direction. "Look, I got places to go," Myers said. He turned back towards Christine Diamond.

"With that woman down there in your car? How much do you plan to get out of *her*?" She was trembling now, her sobs buried within her anger and rage.

McGuire moved to a location where he could read and memorize the license number of the Cadillac. Behind him, he heard Myers speak in a low voice, then Christine Diamond shout again, an explosion of rage and anger: "Don't you have any heart at all? Don't you?"

"What the hell are you doing?"

McGuire turned to see Christine Diamond holding the same small black automatic she had pointed at him back at her house. She was aiming it at Myers's stomach and crying. The gun wavered from side to side as sentences tumbled from her mouth in fragments: "Everything's gone . . . you lied and lied and lied . . . How could you?" and she fired.

Myers stepped back and watched the red stain on his white shirt grow and expand. He looked back at McGuire, an expression of fear on his face that transformed into something else, and McGuire pictured a small boy who had just been spanked.

Myers turned to flee, one hand at his stomach, the other flailing ahead of him as though pulling him forward and out of danger. From the bottom of the hill McGuire heard a wail, high and piercing, and he wondered for a moment as he scrambled back along the path how an ambulance could have arrived so quickly, until he recognized the sound not as a siren but as a woman's voice, screaming in fear from beside the Cadillac.

Christine Diamond fired again. The bullet exploded on the ground near the bench where McGuire had waited for Myers. Its impact forced Myers to scramble to his right, away from it, and as he did, he stumbled forward onto his stomach.

Another shot struck Myers in the back and a second scream, lower in pitch and even heavier in anguish, escaped from Myers's throat as McGuire reached Christine Diamond. He seized her wrist in his hand and pointed the gun at the ground, while her finger squeezed the trigger over and over until the little automatic was empty. She stared at McGuire, seeing him for the first time. "I don't care," she said. "I don't care what happens to me now. Do you see?"

McGuire nodded and assured her that he saw.

Twenty feet away, Myers writhed on the ground, his body twisting like an impaled snake's, and his voice a guttural cry of agony.

On the street below the hillock, as traffic stopped and pedestrians ran in all directions, some towards the shooting scene, others away from it in fear, the blonde woman shrieked and pounded the roof of the Cadillac, over and over.

The police first interviewed McGuire at the scene, where they discovered him seated on the bench, cradling Christine Diamond in his arms. Later, back in the state police office, they asked him all the usual questions.

When he finished answering their questions, he called Revere Beach and described the scene to Ollie and Susan, who begged him to return quickly, and he promised he would. When he hung up, two state officers announced that Myers had died on the operating-room table, and that Christine Diamond was being charged with first-degree murder.

"It won't stick," McGuire said. "A first-degree won't stick." They asked him to let them do their business, so McGuire nodded. "How much did he get away with? From her?"

"The woman says over four hundred thousand dollars," one of the troopers said. "If you believe it." He removed his trooper hat, revealing hair trimmed within a few millimeters of his skull. McGuire guessed the trooper's age at twenty-two, twenty-three max.

"You don't?" McGuire said.

"Her husband left it for her kids," the trooper responded. "In trust. She couldn't legally lay a hand on it." He shrugged. "Hell, any damn fool can figure it out."

"Obviously I'm not any damn fool," McGuire said. "So explain it to me."

The other trooper, older than the first but still yet to reach thirty years of age, spoke in a voice that said he was annoyed, either with McGuire's obtuseness or his persistence. "The husband died last year. By the time the estate was settled and the bills paid off, all she had left was the house. So she had to go to work selling boats to support herself. Meanwhile, each of her kids got two hundred thousand dollars in trust that she could invest but she couldn't touch, she was just a co-executor along with a lawyer. It's pretty clear what happened. She teams up with this guy Myers, he gets some phony stock certificates printed, she tells the lawyer Myers is on the level, and they both get their hands on the money."

"That's what you think?" McGuire said. "That she was in on it? To get her hands on the money in the trust fund for her children?"

"She's the one who took the documents to the lawyer," the first trooper said, "as security for the loan. They were supposed to be worth six hundred thousand. She talked the lawyer into holding them and releasing the money."

"She didn't know they were phony," McGuire said.

The older trooper snorted. "That's what *she's* saying."

"You really think a woman, bright as she is, would fall for a story from a guy like that?" the younger trooper said. He bent from the waist towards McGuire, as though he didn't want McGuire to miss a word. "You think she would trust him with that much money, all the cash she's got in the world, that her husband left for the kids, without wanting to get her hands on some of it herself? You think a woman would do that and not know that he's pissing it away on new cars and bookies and gifts for her and probably other women?"

McGuire lowered his face into his hands. My God, he thought to himself. They're not only making them younger every day, they're making them more stupid, too.

"Maybe she was just jealous," one of the troopers was saying. "We're looking into that. The victim, he was engaged to that woman who was waiting for him at the car."

"The blonde woman," McGuire said without looking up.

"They were leaving for the Bahamas tomorrow. Apparently he has some investments there. They were going to run a yacht charter or something."

"You a betting man?" McGuire looked up and smiled at the trooper.

"No sir, I'm not."

"Too bad," McGuire said. "Because I'll bet my ass against every dollar you can raise between here and Nassau that Myers has no investment money anywhere. There's a better chance that he would launch a yacht charter in Las Vegas than in the Bahamas. A month from now that blonde woman, whoever she is, would find herself by the side of the road with nothing to her name but her underwear, if that." He stood up. "Now, can I get the hell out of here? I'd like to get back to Boston, where cops are cynical about things, and have a right to be."

CHAPTER 24

McGuire and Susan were making chili the next afternoon when Burnell called from Berkeley Street. "Thought you should know," the young detective told McGuire, "that we just heard from Annapolis police. Myers had been staying at Christine Diamond's house, and he was there the day Flanigan arrived. Mrs. Diamond had taken the children to Baltimore that day, with a school excursion."

"Myers must have said something to get Flanigan over there when the lawyer phoned."

"Maybe said she couldn't come to the telephone. If Myers didn't use his real name, Flanigan wouldn't have known who he was going to meet. Anyway, it sounds as though Myers gave Flanigan directions to the house. Flanigan shows up, maybe Myers gives him the same story he gave you, finds out why he's there, realizes the game is up, and gets Flanigan down to the dock or the boathouse."

"Hits Flanigan on the back of the head and holds him under the water."

"You can drive right down to the dock there, apparently," Burnell said. "To launch boats. He could have driven Flanigan's rented car down there, put the body in the trunk, and headed north. The Diamond woman, she remembers that Myers wasn't there when she got back from Baltimore late in the day. The waitress at that bar you visited? She says Myers called, asked her to drive his car north and pick him up."

The next day, McGuire went shopping. From a downtown used-car dealer he chose a ten-year-old sedan with good tires, a better stereo system, and an interior that smelled like pine trees.

On the way back to Revere Beach, he thought about taking Susan away for a few days. To Cape Cod, perhaps. Or in the opposite direction. A night in Cape Ann, then on to Maine. They could find a bed-and-breakfast in one of those coastal towns where the September air is so crisp in the morning you can see your breath, and warm afternoons that send you in search of an ice-cream parlor and maybe a beach to walk on.

"What do you think?" he asked Susan. They were sitting on the back porch of Ollie's house, drinking coffee.

"It sounds terrific," Susan said. Then: "I don't know though . . ."

"If it sounds so good, why do you say you don't know?"

She set her coffee cup down and looked away. "I think I'd like to go back to the halfway house for a while," she said. "They're holding my room until the end of the month."

"You don't like sleeping with me?"

She reached a hand to him. "I love sleeping with you."

"Then what's the problem?"

She stroked her forehead, as though she felt pain there. "Thomas called while you were out."

"Thomas?" Then McGuire remembered. "Your ex-husband."

She nodded. "The children, Jamie and Belinda, they . . . well, they keep asking about me. When I'm coming back. Belinda hasn't stopped crying since we left. Thomas said he and Sylvia had a talk. She's a good woman, you can see that. She agreed that the children should see more of me."

"We can go back for visits."

"I'm thinking of more than that." She breathed deeply, as though inhaling courage. "I checked with the supervisor at the halfway house. She said if I can obtain clearance from the court, I can move out of state."

McGuire understood. "To Arizona."

"Yes. I loved it there. We could go together."

"Arizona?" McGuire tried to imagine himself moving there, and couldn't. "Isn't it easier to stay here, and visit?"

"I need a job. I need a means of support." She bit her lip. "I need to see my children more than two or three times a year."

McGuire shook his head. "I couldn't move to Arizona. I couldn't imagine living there. No ocean, no snow. No police buddies."

"I'm going, Joe. I loved it there."

"I know. I can tell."

"I would prefer that you came with me."

McGuire shook his head. "How about I visit now and then?"

"I wish you would. I hope you will."

McGuire drove Susan back to the halfway house that evening. She had called Thomas that afternoon.

"It will take a couple of weeks for me to get the papers in order," she said. "Thomas says the children are so excited they can hardly sit still. He says there are lots of jobs there. I can get an apartment in Tucson. Can we still go to the Cape together before I leave? Will you promise to come and see me in Arizona when I'm settled? You know how terrible it gets here in November, it's so cold and damp. Wouldn't you like to get away for a few days then? You might even get to like it there." When he smiled and shook his head, she pulled him towards her. "I'm sorry. I'm so sorry."

He arrived back at Revere Beach after ten o'clock to find Ronnie's car in the driveway. Inside, she was seated at the kitchen table, looking through a box of old photographs. From the upstairs bedroom, McGuire heard the repetitive thumping of Liz Worthington's portable stereo.

"Look at this picture of Ollie," Ronnie said. She held a photograph for him to see. It was as though she had never left, as though McGuire had just returned from a walk around the block. "You took this, didn't you? It was Ollie's birthday, and you and Dave Sadowsky and Bernie what's-his-name . . ."

"Lipson."

"Bernie Lipson. A nice man. You took Ollie to that bar on Newbury for his birthday . . ."

"What are you doing here?" McGuire pulled up a chair and sat down.

"I came back to check up on my husband."

"You moved out."

"I know." She gathered the photographs together, like a deck of cards. "You don't have to tell me that." She looked up at the ceiling. "God, can't somebody tell that woman to turn that music off? She's terrible, Joe. She's not feeding Ollie right, she's not taking care of him . . ."

"Not the way you did. Ollie's all right. How are you doing?"

"Fine." She looked at him and smiled. "Terrible. I'm fine and I'm terrible, okay?"

"Okay."

"I thought you had a live-in girlfriend. Ollie told me about her. Where is she?"

"On her way to Arizona." McGuire told her about Susan's plan to move closer to her children.

"You can visit her," Ronnie said. "You two can work something out. A lot of people do."

"So I hear," McGuire said.

Don Higgins fast-tracked Susan's request for a waiver of her travel restrictions. Within a week she was free to leave Massachusetts. She would register with the parole office in Arizona and keep the office in Massachusetts informed of her address there.

"I can leave any time," she said. "Maybe after we go away for a week, up north somewhere."

"Go now," McGuire said. "Go as soon as you can."

"I thought you would say that," she said. "I knew you would say that."

The day after McGuire drove Susan to the airport and stood watching her walk through the gate to the aircraft, and stood long enough to see the jet take off and turn west before driving to Zoot's, where he sat alone for an hour and drank only soda water, Ronnie arrived home again. She was there when McGuire arrived.

"I can't make it work," she said when he walked through the door. She was at the kitchen table.

"With Carl?" McGuire said.

"Without Ollie. So we've been talking, Ollie and me." She had been back for visits each day for a week, spending her time in Ollie's room, banishing the nurse while she was there. "We have an arrangement." She smiled with more irony than pleasure. "I'm moving back. We'll have a nurse to spell me a couple of days a week."

"And you'll keep seeing Carl."

She nodded. "Now and then. Believe it or not, I think it will be harder on Carl than on me."

"I believe it. What will you tell Ollie when you're not here?"

"Nothing. We have a deal. Don't ask. Don't tell."

"I've heard about deals like that."

"That nurse, Liz, she's leaving today."

"Darn. Just when I'm starting to like Eminem."

"So we're back where we were a month ago, you and me and Ollie."

"Almost," McGuire said.

She rose from her chair. "I bought some of those pastries you like," she said. "Those little pecan tarts full of butter and sugar. And there's fresh coffee made. Ollie was asking when you'd get home. The baseball playoffs are on television." She looked at her watch. "They just started. Why don't you go in and watch them with him? Take some tarts and coffee with you."

He walked to her and hugged her. "You know what Ollie used to call you, down on Berkeley Street?" He stood back and looked at her, his hands on her shoulders. "You know what he'd say after bragging about something you did for him, or something you'd said to him?"

"What?"

"He'd say you were a good broad."

"Wonderful. I'm a good broad."

"It's his highest compliment to a woman."

"I know. Isn't it disgusting?" She held his face in her hands. "Isn't that a terrible thing for a lady like me to put up with?"

Then she walked to the cupboard and took down a coffee mug and a small plate.

A minute later, McGuire was walking down the hall to Ollie's room, a coffee in one hand, a plate of fattening pastries in the other. "That you Joseph?" Ollie called through the partially opened door.

"Nobody else," McGuire said.

"Get your butt in here. Sox are up by two. Who do you like?"

"Anybody at all," McGuire said. He nudged the door open with his foot and looked back down the hall at Ronnie. "Anybody at all."